Incorrigible lover of a happy-[...]
Jessica Gilmore is lucky enc[...]
of London's best-known theat[...]
daughter, one fluffy dog and two dog-loathing cats,
she can usually be found with her nose in a book.
Jessica writes emotional romance with a hint of
humour, a splash of sunshine, delicious food—and
equally delicious heroes!

Michelle Douglas has been writing for Mills & Boon
since 2007 and believes she has the best job in the
world. She lives in a leafy suburb of Newcastle, on
Australia's east coast, with her own romantic hero, a
house full of dust and books, and an eclectic collection
of sixties and seventies vinyl. She loves to hear
from readers and can be contacted via her website:
michelle-douglas.com.

FAKE DATE ON THE ORIENT EXPRESS

JESSICA GILMORE

TEMPTED BY HER BEST FRIEND BILLIONAIRE

MICHELLE DOUGLAS

MILLS & BOON

First published in Great Britain 2025
by Mills & Boon, an imprint of HarperCollins*Publishers* Ltd,
1 London Bridge Street, London, SE1 9GF

www.harpercollins.co.uk

HarperCollins*Publishers*, Macken House, 39/40 Mayor Street Upper,
Dublin 1, D01 C9W8, Ireland

Fake Date on the Orient Express © 2025 Jessica Gilmore

Tempted by Her Best Friend Billionaire © 2025 Michelle Douglas

ISBN: 978-0-263-39682-9

07/25

This book contains FSC™ certified paper
and other controlled sources to ensure responsible forest management.

For more information visit www.harpercollins.co.uk/green.

Printed and Bound in the UK using 100% Renewable Electricity
at CPI Group (UK) Ltd, Croydon, CR0 4YY

FAKE DATE ON THE ORIENT EXPRESS

JESSICA GILMORE

MILLS & BOON

For Rufus,
who has been the very best of good boys this year.

CHAPTER ONE

TALLULAH JENKINS—TALLY TO her nearest and dearest—burst through the narrow door, put out a trembling hand to steady herself against the swaying of the train and announced dramatically, '*Zut alors!* Ze meestress. She is dead!'

The assorted group sitting around the long oval table looked up almost as one, their expressions a mix of surprise, unsuppressed excitement and, in a conspicuous couple of cases, disinterest. Their crystal glasses were half empty, their porcelain plates scraped clean. A wine waiter hovered in the background; another stood frozen in the act of clearing the plates.

'Dead?' A broad middle-aged man sprang to his feet. 'But how?'

'Stabbed!' Tally burst into loud sobs. 'Weeth 'er diamond letter opener!'

'Stabbed?' the man repeated, looking around to make sure everyone at the table had taken in this vital information. 'Come, *mademoiselle*, sit down and tell us all you know. We are stuck on this train until tomorrow and the telephones are cut off. If we don't apprehend this desperate villain now, he or she may get away scot-free—or we could all be murdered in our beds!'

The eight other people sitting at the table responded in different ways to this alarming news. One man, eyes already glittering with drink, merely motioned for his glass to be refilled, one pretty young woman continued to tap away at her anachronistic phone. A heavyset man just a few years older than Tally looked her up and down, his eyes lingering on her legs in a way that made her want to pull down her short black skirt as far as possible and wish her stockings weren't quite as sheer. Surely no real French maid would have worn an outfit that barely hit mid-thigh in the nineteen-twenties?

The rest of the group, however, entered into the spirit of the occasion and joined Hank, a Pinkerton's PI from Chicago—aka Neil, her employer—in cross-examining Tally who, between sobs, gasped out a tale of poison-pen letters, diamond thefts, secret liaisons and a conveniently dead much older husband who had left her murdered mistress a fortune, weaving in seven red herrings and one real clue. The key, Neil said, was to make the mystery difficult enough for them to have a real sense of achievement at solving the murder but simple enough to ensure they *did* solve it, especially when, like tonight, the murder took place against a backdrop of cordon bleu cooking and plenty of free and very expensive wine and unlimited spirits.

Finally, her interrogation over, Tally tottered to the door of the dining car, silk handkerchief to her eyes, uneasily aware that the heavyset man was tracking her every move. Intoxicated and entitled guests were always a risk at a gig like this, even in a venue as rarified as the Orient Express. She paused and turned, to take her scripted last dramatic look in the room, ready to deliver her final clue, only to meet the gaze of the man who sat at the head of the table. Impeccably dressed in a tuxedo Tally could tell was the real thing, tailored and made to measure, he had taken little part in the scene she had just starred in, but neither was he concentrating on drinking or leering. Instead, he was watching the other participants keenly. This must be Lucas West, the man rich enough to fund this entire extravaganza.

Tally held his gaze for a second too long, almost dropping character, feeling curiously more exposed under his assessing look than she did under the increasingly overly appreciative glances from his guest. Recollecting herself, she announced that she had found poison in Madame's belongings and, with a tremulous, appealing look at one of the more sober men—no need to encourage any of the others—that she was scared she wouldn't survive the night. Then out she tottered, shedding Cécile the second the dining car door closed behind her. She had, she reckoned, forty minutes to retire Cécile for now and change into Miss Wydenham, lady's companion and suspect number two, so she hastened through the two carriages of guest suites to the third carriage where she, Neil, Carmen and Freddie were being luxuriously accommodated alongside a couple of the guests.

Her compartment was unlike anything she had ever stayed in before. Opulent, cleverly designed, with all mod cons packaged in authentic vintage style. The comfortable sofa converted into a double bed and she had her own small breakfast table and dining chair. The wardrobe was just big enough to hold her several costumes, the tiny but utterly luxurious bathroom more than adequate for a change of hair and make-up. In fact, she had endured much smaller changing rooms and sleeping quarters when working in repertory theatre.

None of the troupe had expected to be staying in the luxurious en-suite accommodation, all more than happy with the historic twin cabins with shared bathrooms offered at a relatively lower price, but Lucas West had booked the dining car and three sleeping cars for exclusive use, which had meant a very welcome upgrade. Tally meant to enjoy every moment of it. Tomorrow night she would be sleeping in a five-star hotel in Venice before an evening flight home the following day, and then be handsomely paid for two days' work. It was a nice gig. But she thought as she stared at her make-up-free face in the mirror, it wasn't the gig she wanted.

She was thirty and still taking bit parts and commercial ventures like this, still aspiring to a career. In fact, she shouldn't be here right now. She should be in Croatia, on the set of what promised to be the next big fantasy franchise. She had been so close, down to the final two and she had absolutely killed it in the final auditions, she knew she had, but she had still lost out, to a girl nine years younger. It wasn't her first disappointment, not by a long way, but it felt like the most ominous. The role had felt like Tally's last chance. Now what? She wasn't sure she had many years of pulling off a French maid left. Then she would be the dowager, the long-suffering wife, the dowdy spinster.

But there was no time to dwell on that now. Briskly, she washed her face and redid her make-up, replacing the red mouth and long black lashes which characterised Cécile with a more demure look, putting on Miss Wydenham's tweed skirt and twinset, picking up a small bag which held a string of garnets and a pistol and with a sigh of relief pushed her squeezed feet into a rather nice pair of heeled brogues. She quickly brushed out her hair and re-pinned it, more severely than Cécile's, this time with no little perky cap. Her character brief was tidy, nondescript but with a hidden intelligence and a concealed beauty. Whatever that meant.

Tally took one last look at her script, making sure she had the clues right and her story straight, and left her suite. Just walking along the carriage was an adventure, with the beautiful wooden doors on one side opening into the suites, windows on the other showcasing the moving view as they travelled across France. The whole train was like a magical playhouse. If she had been a passenger she would have never tired of exploring, but these guests were evidently used to luxury on a grand scale, or not confident enough to show their excitement.

Another entrance, another scene, a few more dropped clues and several more red herrings, doing her best to convey a woman determined to present a demure front but unable to conceal occasional flashes of hidden fire, until her flustered exit after strategically dropping her bag and feigning shock at the spilled contents. Tally took a deep breath. One more scene and then she was free for the evening to enjoy her small but perfectly formed compartment.

It was a short but intensive trip. The train had left Paris in the late afternoon when, after everyone had settled into their compartments, the seeds of the mystery had been sown by Carmen playing the mysterious rich widow over cocktails and dinner. The murder had been timed for after dinner, with the rest of the evening taken up with various interviews and interrogations until a light late supper was served. The guests would then be free to go over the clues—or carry on drinking—before they too retired. Tomorrow the sleuthing would resume after breakfast with more interviews, more clues and an attempted murder or two before the afternoon summing up and solving of the case, leaving time for afternoon tea before the train reached Venice in the early evening. Tally just hoped the guests chose their culprit correctly, she didn't want her wrong character to be summoned to face justice. The downside of playing multiple parts.

Okay, time for Lucia, the murdered woman's niece, ward and probable heiress. She shimmied into the flapper dress which she had loved at the costume fitting but was now wishing was a little less tight and a little less short. Even in her frumpy-with-hints-of-sassy secretary's garb she'd found the man who had been overly interested in her maid's persona had made her feel uncomfortable. What he was going to think when he saw her in this little—very little—black dress she didn't want to imagine, especially if he kept drinking at the rate he had so far. Tally had been raised in a pub, she was more than comfortable taking care of herself, but this was a small, enclosed place, she was working and he was the guest of someone who was paying a lot, a really big lot, more than Tally could fathom, for his entertainment. Which meant a carefully aimed knee really had to be the very last resort.

She managed to avoid any eye contact with the drunker guests when she sashayed in, cigarette holder in one hand, rope of pearls in the other, to breathlessly deny any relationship with the murdered woman's latest lover, allowing herself to be tripped up by the detective's questioning. Instead, she concentrated on a woman of her own age who was obviously taking the whole murder mystery brief seriously, from her gorgeous beaded dress and hairband to a notebook full of observations. At one point Tally moved and found herself making eye contact with Lucas West again, her pulse speeding up as she met cool blue eyes. Rich and handsome, that was an unfairly devastating combination. She couldn't help allowing Lucia to flirt a little, batting her eyes in his direction, enjoying his reluctant almost smile back, surprisingly disappointed when with a muttered excuse he slipped away, hand already drawing his phone out of his pocket.

But throughout the scene she was aware that the leering man was even more fixated on her than before, his eyes running over her as if he could see through the sequins and fringes and tight support garment which had been the only way this dress had gone over her hips. The dress designer had clearly not got the loose fit flapper dress memo. She was really glad when she could deliver the last line and make her overly dramatic exit.

Ouch. As soon as she was alone Tally leaned against the wall and rubbed her heels. The high heeled, crystal buckled shoes were very cute but once again half a size too small. She considered kicking them off but wanted to get back to her room and enjoy a much-deserved long shower and room service as soon as possible so instead she pushed off the wall and hobbled along the corridor, opening the door to the next car, pausing as she heard the dining car door open and close and footsteps tap behind her. Damn, back into character again, Lucia would never allow shoes to beat her. She straightened and took a painful step when a voice slurred, 'Hey, wait.'

Tally's heart sped up. She'd been followed and now she was going to have to find a firm but diplomatic way to tell Mr Wandering Eyes to keep his hands and eyes to himself. Or maybe she could get to her compartment before he caught up—but there were two connecting doors and another full carriage to go before she was safe and he was gaining on her fast she could tell, even though she didn't dare to look around. Didn't want to indicate she could hear him.

'Hey, you with the legs, wait up.'

You with the legs.

With lines like that, it was no wonder the man was chasing actresses down corridors. Tally stepped into the next carriage, letting the door swing shut behind her and trying to quicken her pace. Why hadn't she taken her shoes off? But if she had stopped to do that, he might have cornered her in the previous corridor and she would have felt more vulnerable with a bare foot.

Although she was feeling pretty darn vulnerable now.

At that moment a door to her left opened and Tally saw a tall broad figure standing there. Acting on an instinct she couldn't explain, she swerved in and threw her arms around the man's neck.

'Play along,' she murmured against his neck, surprised that she was able to notice even at a time of high stress that her hopeful saviour smelt really good, expensive yet tasteful and somehow sexy.

Not now, Tally.

'I've missed you,' she said, loudly enough for the man still lumbering up the corridor to hear.

There was an excruciating pause. Was she about to be summarily evicted from the room? Sacked? Cost Neil his lucrative luxury train murder mystery contract? Or would the man misinterpret what was going on here? That wouldn't be difficult with the skimpy dress and the embrace and all.

'I... I've missed you too?' Thank goodness. This guy clearly hadn't trained at drama school with many hours of improv, but she would take what she could get.

At that moment the drunken man stopped, his large body filling the narrow doorway. 'Here you are... Oh!' Tally couldn't bear to look round but she could imagine the knowing look on his face and cringed. 'I get it. Three's a crowd. You're a lucky man, West. I noticed her as soon as we boarded. Nice work.'

West? Oh, *fiddlesticks*. Of all the rooms on all the train, she had had to choose the one belonging to the client. How unprofessional was that?

Then, to her relief, her pursuer was gone. Tally knew she needed to let go, step back and apologise to Lucas West, but to her surprise her legs felt boneless. The only thing keeping her upright was the solid torso she leaned against and the arms that were somewhat gingerly holding her up.

'Sit down.' Lucas West's voice was low, a little gravelly and reassuring, as she was lowered onto a sofa. Tally noticed somewhat dimly that the suite was bigger and even more luxurious than hers. There was a separate sitting space, a permanent bed at the other end, already made up. A round table sat next to the window with a couple of glasses and a decanter set on a tray, more drinks and glasses in shelves behind it. Like her room, the walls were glossy walnut inlaid with gold, the green velvet décor both soothing and extravagant. 'You need a drink.' A whisky was shoved into her hand and her fingers automatically closed round it. 'You are in no state to work tonight. I'll let your boss know.'

'No, no, don't do that. The show must go on and I've dealt with men much more tenacious than him. Besides, my scenes are done for the night. I'm sorry, I'm not usually so easily spooked. I'm not sure what came over me.'

'No, I can only apologise for the behaviour of someone whose presence here I am responsible for. Please believe me when I say that Mr Johnson will be sorry for his behaviour at some point very soon.'

'I'm sure it would have been fine.' What was she doing, excusing his associate's behaviour? 'Like I say, I don't usually panic. He just seems to have had a lot to drink…' She trailed off.

The man's lips thinned. 'Which is no excuse. Are you sure you're okay?'

'Absolutely fine. Honestly. I'm done for the night and am planning to enjoy my very lovely room and the very attentive room service before going over tomorrow's scenes. Hopefully, your…' friends? colleagues? associates? She wasn't entirely sure what this very extravagant private corporate event actually was. '…the rest of your party are busy solving the clues in there. There are some keen sleuths determined to work it out.'

'I'm glad.' But he didn't look glad. He looked thoughtful and more than a little annoyed. Not with her, Tally was pretty sure. But she knew that the drunken man would have cause to regret his behaviour. A shiver of something primal shivered through her. She wasn't the kind of woman who looked for a protector, but she had to admit it was rather nice for once to feel taken care of.

'Anyway, thank you again.' She put down her undrunk whisky and stood up. 'I'll let you get back to your guests. Happy detecting. Cécile, Miss Wydenham and Lucia will see you tomorrow.'

He didn't smile, just nodded, clearly still lost in thought, but she felt a frisson shiver through her as she slipped out of the still open door and limped down the corridor to her own carriage.

'Don't get too used to playing the damsel in distress, Jenkins,' she told herself firmly. Like all parts it was fun for a moment, but not reality. After tomorrow she would never see her rescuer again.

Lucas West watched the actress make her exit, her fresh floral scent lingering in the air. He should thank her; he'd had his doubts about Hunter Johnson from the start but couldn't put his finger on why. Good to know his gut was to be trusted. For a moment there his temper hadn't been. He would have quite liked to pin the lecherous weasel up against a wall. Not that the girl—woman—needed him to. It had been a masterly played diversion, although one that could easily have backfired.

Right, time to return to the group before Johnson spread his story and endangered the actress's reputation for nothing more than a moment's gossip. Maybe he should have a quick word with the murder mystery director, make it clear the actress wasn't at fault. He turned on his heel, only for his phone to ring again. He checked the caller ID before answering. 'Felix?'

His tension dissipated at his brother's amused tone. 'How's it going, Poirot?'

'You were right. This is a fascinating psychological experiment, apart from anything else.'

When his brother had suggested they take the family majority shareholders of Vineyard, the iconic preppy clothing company they were trying to buy, on a murder mystery jaunt on one of the world's most iconic trains, Lucas had deduced his brother was out of his mind. It was obscenely expensive and insanely decadent. But Felix had argued that there was nothing like the combination of alcohol, competitiveness and out of this world experience to show how someone really ticked. And he was right. Which was why Felix was usually the people person. It was unfortunate that a nasty dose of flu had meant he hadn't been able to come too, leaving Lucas to schmooze alone.

He might not be his brother but, hopefully, the goodwill generated by the trip alongside the above market price he was offering for their shares meant at least two guests would sell to them—and then WGO would be the Vineyard majority shareholder and which of the current board remained would be solely up to him.

Speaking of which. 'Johnson will be straight out,' he said curtly.

'Not surprising. His dossier is quite something.'

'There's something about Brianna Wu. She definitely has the right combination of people skills and intellect we need. I could see her as CEO. The rest need more analysis, so I'd better head back. I'll report further when we get into Venice tomorrow evening, but let's have those offers ready to go as soon as we are done here. I'll call tomorrow.'

'Look forward to it. Are you heading straight home tomorrow?'

'I'm spending a couple of days in Venice to carry on negotiating and then I've got some time booked in with Roberto; it made sense seeing as he's in Tuscany at the moment.'

'Work or play?'

'I've told him it's work, but, in reality, it's neither.' Lucas sighed. 'I'm a little worried about him, to be honest. I'm glad he's left England; the damp spring didn't do his chest any good at all.'

Roberto Leonardi was Lucas and Felix's late father's godfather, Lucas's mentor and his business partner during the last fifteen years as Lucas had transformed the small old-fashioned clothing manufacturer and retail chain his father had bequeathed him into a major fashion, design and retail powerhouse. Losing their father while still in their teens had been a shock for both boys, but Roberto had stepped in unobtrusively and sensitively, personally as well as corporately. Lucas owed him a debt that could never be repaid.

'Be careful.' He could hear the laughter in Felix's voice. 'I have it on good authority that the *bella* Isabella has joined him in Tuscany and you know what that means…' His brother whistled a few notes that were just about recognisable as the wedding march.

'No care needed. She's safely engaged to that *conte*. Thank goodness.'

Roberto had never accepted that Lucas owed him. After all, as an investor, WGO's success had benefit-ted him as well. But Roberto had always hoped that his oldest friend's grandson and his beloved granddaughter Isabella would make a match of it, bring the two families together, and Isabella had made it clear on several occasions that she was not at all averse to the idea. As a result, the announcement of her engagement six months ago had come as a huge relief. Lucas might feel indebted to Roberto and love the man almost as a father but that did not mean he wanted to be shackled to a spoilt heiress whose only interests were shopping and influencing.

'Oh…' Felix barely suppressed the glee in his voice. 'Haven't you heard? The engagement is off, which means *la bella* Isabella is back on the market. Summer in Tuscany, what could be more romantic?'

'Dammit.' Now that was awkward. Roberto hadn't looked at all well the last time Lucas had seen him, which meant it was going to be difficult to wriggle out of well-meaning suggestions that Lucas entertain his granddaughter while the older man took it easy.

It wasn't that Lucas wasn't capable of standing up for himself, he just didn't want to distress his well-meaning mentor more than he had to. It would be different if he was in a relationship, but he wasn't even casually dating at the moment. He'd grown up with a never present father who had neglected the family business and his family to enjoy an eventful love life; there was no way Lucas was repeating the same mistakes. His personal life could wait until WGO felt unassailable and he could afford to split his time between work and pleasure.

He said goodbye to a far too cheerful if still croaky Felix, then pocketed his phone and made his way back to the restaurant car, where he continued to watch and listen to the heated conversations as clues were analysed and witness statements scrutinised.

The evening continued, a mixture of drinking and sleuthing finishing with an excellent late-night supper which brought the night to a conclusion. Lucas lingered to say goodnight to his guests, glad when he could return to the solitude of his suite. Unlike the majority of his guests, he had barely drunk anything throughout the evening and so, after loosening his bow tie and shrugging his jacket off, he settled down with his laptop to get through some of his outstanding emails.

But it was hard to concentrate. Not because he was tired, he was used to long hours and late nights, but because he kept remembering the feel of a tall, gently curved body pressed up to his, felt the whisper of breath against his ear as the actress exhorted him to play along, saw the bravado in long-lashed brown eyes as she made out the incident was no big deal, even though he had felt her heart hammering against his.

Lucas raked his hand through his hair. 'Idiot,' he muttered.

It had been too long since his last relationship had come to a sticky end. Madeleine had not just known but sung along to his score, too busy herself at first to be interested in anything other than being asked and asking for an occasional plus-one, the odd dinner date and the occasional shared night. But after a few months she had become more demanding, unhappy when he had declined an invitation, started to suggest spending days and even weekends together. Lucas had liked her, been attracted to her, but hadn't been interested in anything more serious, and although he wasn't deluded enough to think he had broken her heart, he knew he had bruised her pride. Hurting her had never been his intention. He was angry with himself for missing the signs and allowing things to progress so far, and so he'd decided to take a dating hiatus, asking old friends to accompany him when he absolutely needed a plus-one.

Single life usually wasn't a problem, he was too busy to even notice most of the time, so why was he so unsettled tonight? It was probably the thought of Isabella free and single and Roberto playing hopeful matchmaker with no *conte* as shield.

It was a shame he had no shield of his own. Unless… no. Ludicrous.

But Lucas couldn't help opening the printed brochure detailing the trip's itinerary, his eyes drawn immediately to the cast information, a little paragraph detailing the history of the company and then four profiles, complete with pictures. There she was. Tally Jenkins. Dark eyes, a mass of wavy chestnut-brown hair, an amused expression smiling out. Quick-thinking, convincing, able to play multiple parts…

She would make an excellent shield. Not that there was any way he could ask her. And even if he did, it was unlikely she would agree. But as Lucas finally settled down to sleep in the surprisingly spacious bed, he couldn't help dwelling on how the answer to his immediate problem might be right here. If only it wasn't such a ridiculous idea.

CHAPTER TWO

TALLY ENJOYED AN excellent sleep in her comfortable bed, followed by an equally excellent breakfast, served on the small table by a smiling young man in a smart uniform that looked, like everything else, as if it came from the nineteen-twenties. She watched the mountainous views flash past through the window as she tucked into perfectly poached eggs on ambrosial toast, berries and whipped yogurt and then a selection of pastries she didn't exactly need but definitely wanted, before readying herself for the first scene of the day.

The day passed quickly. She managed to ignore the knowing looks from the man who had frightened her yesterday and did her best not to react to Lucas West, no longer dressed in black tie but a devastating linen suit that set his honed body off to perfection. Everyone looked better in nineteen-twenties costumes, she decided, the tailoring and cut flattering everyone.

She managed not to think about the events of the night before whilst in character and it wasn't until the clues had been solved, a denouement enacted and bows taken that she had the opportunity to consider possible consequences. She had been horribly unprofessional last night. This might not be a usual gig for her, but she was asked to work with Neil enough to make it a semi regular and lucrative income. She'd hate to lose out because of a simple mistake like launching herself at the client. She needed to apologise to Lucas for gatecrashing like that.

But how? When? She couldn't exactly approach him in front of any of the guests but he was never alone and Venice was rapidly approaching. The guests would be met on arrival by private cars and whisked away to a luxury resort for a night or two. Not that the actors could complain, they were also being treated to a night in the famous city, although their return the following evening would be on the kind of budget airline she doubted Lucas West and his guests even knew existed.

Now they were nearing Venice the guests and actors, including Tally, changed back into normal clothes, and they all gathered back in the dining car for final thanks. It was odd seeing the guests as herself, no longer in vintage dress but her smartest pink linen trousers and a white blouse with the kind of puffed sleeves that would have gladdened Anne Shirley's heart. She was aware the whole time of Lucas West, the watchfully quiet centre of a talkative group, and every now and then she felt his eyes rest on her, a thoughtful expression on his face making her shift uncomfortably.

Tally found herself in conversation with the youngest female guest, who had modelled a little and was hoping to break into acting, and although she looked for a moment to try and get Lucas West alone, there was no opportunity. By the time the train came into the station and their luggage had been loaded into the taxi he had disappeared, and her chance had disappeared with him. She gnawed her lip, thinking furiously. Should she say something to

Neil herself? But Lucas West hadn't seemed angry, not with her anyway. Maybe she was worrying over nothing.

Her indecision was soon forgotten as the water taxi sped them up the Grand Canal to their hotel. It was Tally's first time in the famous city and she was soon overcome by the sights, sounds and smells. It was exactly like she had dreamed it would be only more vibrant, much busier. She was soon snapping away, sending a quick selfie to her mother and stepdad with a Wish you were here. Her mother responded with a photo of the beer delivery for that day waiting to be unpacked and a laughing crying emoji.

The small troupe were staying in an upmarket chain. It didn't take long to check in and shower before meeting for a meal but although Tally was desperate to explore by the time they had eaten it was past ten and so she decided to get up early and make the most of the next day before her late flight. She excused herself right after dinner and went straight to bed, setting her alarm for a wincingly early hour.

Sure enough, she was up and out by seven, after donning a hat and a pair of sunglasses along with the trousers and top she'd worn the evening before. She'd kept her make-up down to sunscreen and mascara along with a bright red lipstick. Her mother wasn't one for dishing out loads of advice but one thing she always did say was there was nothing like a dash of lipstick, as armour, to finish off an outfit or to cheer you up and Tally had soon realised it was true. Whether her mother's wisdom came from her long dead acting career or from being a pub landlady for the last twenty-five years Tally wasn't sure, but it was good advice. She quickly messaged the murder mystery chat to say she was off to explore and slipped away. She liked the rest of the actors, and was grateful for the job, but they weren't the people she would choose to spend time with on her first visit to Venice.

Her steps took her first to St Mark's Square. It was, just like the water taxi up the Grand Canal, almost achingly familiar, with the palace dominating one end and restaurants with tables set up amongst the rows of pillars already hosting some early breakfasters. Tally hadn't eaten so, preparing herself for what she knew would be an exorbitant bill, took a seat and ordered coffee and toasted brioche with eggs and sat back and people watched.

The square was mostly empty when she sat down, but over the next hour started to get busier and busier. She knew this was nothing, that the famous tourist destination would soon be crammed—the travel guide she had read had suggested getting there very early or in the evening after the cruise ships and day trippers had left. Glad that she had managed to enjoy it whilst quiet she paid the bill, managing not to wince at the price, and slipped away down a side street.

It was surprising how easy it was to return to solitude; she was just a couple of streets—or canals—away from the tourist areas and she almost had the historic city to herself. Lost in a daydream of colour and beauty, Tally wandered narrow paths alongside narrow canals, making friends with cats and exploring shops selling everything from high end jewellery to expensive stationery to the ubiquitous masks. The actress in her was enthralled by the masks and she was sorely tempted by a simple carnival one which only covered the eyes.

It was delicately decorated with black and gold swirls and fastened with a black velvet ribbon. She held it up to her face and stared at herself in the mirror, charmed by how instantly it transformed her, made her mysterious. But the price tag was far more than she could justify and reluctantly she went to return it.

'You should buy it.' The voice, low and gravelly and assured, quivered through her and Tally turned quickly, the mask still in her hands. 'It suits you.'

Lucas West was dressed in the immaculate grey linen suit he'd worn yesterday despite the heat of the day which saw most other tourists in jeans and T-shirts, but somehow he looked cool, unruffled. His dark, almost black hair was ruthlessly combed back, but one strand had rebelliously slipped over his forehead, softening the hard angles of his face, the darkness of his hair a stunning contrast to his blue eyes.

'Mr West!'

Of all the mask shops in Venice he had to walk into hers. But that was good, wasn't it? She had wanted a chance to apologise.

'Lucas, please.'

'Lucas.'

Ugh, now why did she sound so breathless? Yes, he was undeniably gorgeous—and why should she deny it? It was an objective statement, just like saying Venice was gorgeous, or the mask was gorgeous, but neither of those made her knees suddenly weaken and the breath leave her chest.

She looked at the mask. 'I love it, but I don't need it.'

Damn it, now she sounded wistful.

'And you only buy what you need?'

'I try to. Good for the planet and the bank balance.'
Plus, when one had moved back into one's childhood
bedroom over a pub after a bad breakup, space for belongings was at a premium.

Lucas studied her, frowning. 'You should have it,'
he said. 'Let me buy it for you. As a thank you gift for
your work yesterday.'

'You already paid us and put us up in a hotel here,'
she protested. 'I think most people would consider a
night on the Orient Express and a night in Venice more
than enough of a thank you.'

The corner of his mouth twitched but he didn't reply,
just held out his hand for the mask. Tally shifted, unsure. It was difficult to argue with someone who didn't
reply. Her only real options were to agree or to put the
mask down and walk out of the shop. The latter might
be a more principled stance but felt rude.

'Please,' he said, low and coaxing, and Tally couldn't
help but laugh, although half in exasperation.

'It's not necessary, but if you insist,' she said, handing him the mask and reminding herself that he was so
rich he had just hired out part of the most famous train
in the world. 'But I must buy you a drink to say thank
you. There's something I had hoped to talk to you about
anyway and didn't get the opportunity before. Bumping
into you like this is serendipitous.'

'Serendipitous,' he echoed. 'Funny, that was exactly
the word I was looking for.'

Lucas hadn't set out to find the actress—Tally. He'd still
been mulling over his crazy idea when they disembarked
and when she had disappeared it had felt like the answer

to his unspoken question. But bumping into her felt like fate. And her offer of a drink even more so.

They left the small shop in silence, Tally clutching her paper bag, but she gave a rapturous sigh as they stepped out into the small alley.

'It's rare to visit somewhere that's exactly how you hoped it would be but even more so, don't you think?' she said.

'First time in Venice?' Lucas asked.

'First time in Italy, to my shame. I wish I had more time here, not that I'm complaining,' she added hurriedly. 'I am very grateful for the hotel and the opportunity to explore. How about here?'

Here was a small café restaurant next to the mask shop. Like so many cafés in Venice it had a small, windowless interior, dominated by a large, curved bar, the majority of the tables and chairs set up outside.

'Fine, what would you like?'

'I'm paying, remember. What would *you* like?'

Lucas sat down somewhat cautiously on a rickety chair. The street was narrow, quiet, the view mostly the walls of the street with a glimpse of canal at the end, but Tally seemed delighted with her choice.

'I much prefer somewhere off the tourist trail, the kind of place locals use, don't you?'

Did he? Lucas travelled a lot but usually he was entertaining and the restaurant was picked by his PA, or he would grab a quick bite alone, often in the hotel or somewhere nearby. But she was right. The coffee smelt delicious and the location was as peaceful as Venice in late June got.

Tally thanked the waiter as he set down the coffees

and took a sip of hers, before biting her lip. 'So, like I said, I'm glad I ran into you, and not just because you were absurdly generous and bought me a mask.' Her eyes were hidden by her sunglasses, her straw hat low on her forehead, but her cheeks were pink and her voice more than a little self-conscious. 'I wanted to apologise.'

That was unexpected. Lucas sat back. 'Apologise? Why?'

'It was really unprofessional of me to deal with that situation the other night the way I did. I put you in an awkward position. I'm very grateful you didn't report me to Neil, but I just wanted you to know that I don't usually go around embracing clients. I should have...'

He held up a hand to cut her off. 'No, I'm sorry. Sorry that a guest of mine put you into that situation. I hope it goes without saying that there will be consequences, but you absolutely do not owe me an apology or need to second-guess any decision you made.'

'That's... Thank you.'

Lucas took another sip of his really excellent coffee and assessed her discreetly. Her mass of hair was pulled back into a ponytail underneath the hat, but what he could see was a chestnut-brown, streaked through with natural-looking blonde and coppery highlights, glossy and shiny. She had an expressive face, with high cheek-bones and a dimple at the side of her full mouth. Her linen trousers and white top looked fresh and classy, the red lipstick adding a touch of style. She clearly had manners, was quick on the uptake, knew how to play a part...

'Do you have another mystery booked after this?'

She shook her head. 'Not for me. I'm not a regular member of the company but I fill in when needed. Pritti, who usually plays the roles I did, was at a family wedding this week so Neil asked me to cover.' She laughed. 'It wasn't a hardship. I've done it before, and when he told me that in addition to the fee I'd get a night on the famous Orient Express and a night in Venice I wasn't exactly going to say no!'

'Must be interesting, being an actress.'

'At times, but it's an insecure world. I actually spend more time behind the bar of my mum's pub than I do on stage or screen, but when it works out it's glorious.'

'And what's next?'

'Auditions, I guess.' Her mouth twisted and she paused for a moment. 'Actually, I don't have anything lined up so bar work it is, I suppose. At least I'm lucky to have that.'

Which meant she was free for the next few weeks.

'Tally is an unusual name. Is it a stage name?'

'All mine, short for Tallulah. My mother's first professional role was in *Bugsy Malone* and I was named in homage to that. I always thought it could be worse. She could have played…oh, I don't know… Goneril or Titania, and then where would I be?'

'Tallulah.' It suited her. 'It's unusual enough to mean you didn't need a stage name, I suppose.'

'Yep. Small mercies.'

She had finished her coffee and sat back, looking around the street as if it was the most beautiful of surroundings and not a nondescript alley in an unfashionable part of Venice. 'I'm glad we got a chance to clear the air. And thanks again for the mask, but this city won't explore itself and I need to be back at the hotel to grab my things and leave for the airport for five. What are your plans?'

'Does head back to the hotel and tackle my emails before a business meeting with some of yesterday's guests sound really dull?'

She laughed. 'I mean, it's an option. Not as much fun as trying every water taxi to see where I end up and wandering around hidden corners, but each to their own.'

She was an off-the-beaten-track kind of tourist. It figured.

'Tallulah Jenkins, would you have dinner with me tonight?'

The words were out before he could stop them. Throughout this chance meeting Lucas had been telling himself that his idea was a mad one, but the more time he spent with her, the more it seemed plausible. She needed a job; he needed a way to keep Roberto happy. It could work.

'Dinner?' Thanks to the sunglasses, he couldn't tell if she was excited or horrified by the suggestion, her voice gave nothing away.

'No expectations. Not a date.' Ouch, that was awkward. It was a good thing Felix wasn't here to hear this mangled attempt at whatever this was.

'Not a date, got it.' Was she laughing at him? Understandable if so, that had been the opposite of smooth.

'Not that you are not dateable, but I'm not looking for anything like that right now.' What *was* he doing? Some negotiator. 'Just dinner, a chance for you to explore some more of this city.'

'Obviously, that would be lovely.' She didn't sound wholly convinced but he couldn't blame her for that. 'Thank you for asking, but I'm flying back this evening.'

'To bar work? I mean, do you have to rush back? I could ask my PA to change your flight and extend your stay.'

'I couldn't ask you to do that.'

'You're not,' he pointed out. 'I'm asking you. And I know it seems a little unorthodox, and I don't blame you for being wary, but there's possibly something… I just need to think about it. But I understand if you want to get back.' In fact, it might be easier all round, especially now he had made such a hash of asking her.

'I…' She was clearly undecided but then seemed to come to a decision. 'No, actually another day here would be lovely. Thank you.'

'Great, let me have your number and I'll send you some details about this evening and my PA will take care of the rest. Thank you, Tally.'

There, no decisions, no irreversible offers made, but the possibility was still there. This evening could be a sort of unofficial audition, a trial to see how at ease in each other's company they could be, if he would want to spend a week in her company—and vice versa.

Who knew, if it worked out then maybe it could be a longer-term arrangement, for the rest of the year? He had a few weddings and business events to attend and his female friends were nearly all coupled up and too busy to attend anything but the most unusual or luxurious events with him. He wasn't a superstitious man but Lucas couldn't help but think that fate had sent him Tallulah Jenkins for a reason and he would be an idiot not to take advantage of that.

CHAPTER THREE

TALLY CONTINUED TO explore but it was hard to throw her-self into sightseeing when her mind was going over and over the conversation she had just had, and the bizarre outcome of it. Had she really agreed to stay in Venice for an extra night in order to have dinner with a handsome and rich man which was explicitly not a date but for some unspecified reason? Like what? What would Lucas West want with a sometime actress stroke barmaid? Would she feel more excited if it *was* a date? She was out of prac-tice, it was true, too bruised for too long to throw herself back into the bearpit that was modern dating.

At that moment a message popped up on her phone from Candace at WGO, confirming that her hotel stay had been extended and that she just needed to message with her preferred flight home and it would be con-firmed for her. Wow, life really was different for the rich. Tally quickly messaged Neil to let him know she was planning to stay on for another day or so and then set about exploring some more, determined to stop won-dering what the evening had in store and to make the most of this unexpected opportunity. Maybe, if her re-turn flight was an open one, she wouldn't need to return to London immediately. She quite fancied heading out to the islands, exploring further afield. She wouldn't be able to afford her hotel, of course, but there must be a hostel somewhere for the more budget minded traveller.

Lunch was toasted ciabatta stuffed with cheese and vegetables, more ambrosial coffee and then a mid-afternoon gelato to keep her going. It had been far too long since she had last had a holiday. Not since, well, not since Max, and that had been a rainy week in the Lake District which had been more mud than sunshine. Tally waited for the usual sweep of pain and loss to hit her, but for the first time in eleven months she didn't physically recoil at the thought of her ex, she just felt sad. Sad that it had ended so brutally, sad that she hadn't seen it coming.

No, she was *not* thinking about Max right now. She took her gelato along a hidden canal, the houses on either side crammed together, rising above her three or four storeys high, peeling and faded and shuttered and full of hidden mysteries. She walked to the end and stood looking out to sea at the afternoon sun dancing off the swell of the waves. What a magical, impossible place this city was. And here she was, free to explore and enjoy it. No ties, no responsibilities, no reason to rush back. Maybe she had been looking at this all wrong. Instead of bemoaning her broken relationship, her move back above the pub, the loss of Max, she should turn it all around. She was free. No responsibilities. No rent. No one would bat an eye if she said she was going to head off to the Lakes, to Verona, to Florence after this. She could. Maybe she even would.

Maybe.

Her phone lit up with a message, another from Candace, confirming arrangements for that evening. She was to meet Lucas at eight, at a vaporetto stop close to her hotel. Dress code: smart.

That might be a slight issue. She had three costumes in her borrowed case but she didn't think an overly short and tight flapper dress met the brief, although it was smarter than the maid's outfit. Her own bag only contained a T-shirt to sleep in, the crumpled dress she had worn to board the train and a pair of shorts, a T-shirt and a hoodie. Why hadn't she inherited her mother's pack rat genes? Charlene Jenkins never went anywhere without an outfit for every conceivable and inconceivable occasion. She would absolutely have packed something suitable for a smart dinner with a handsome millionaire just in case.

Tally had limited time and an equally limited budget but found a couple of high street chains in the busier part of the city and, blessing the early summer sales, managed to pick up a silky green slip dress and a pair of jewelled sandals with a matching bag, spending the rest of her budget on a beautiful bronze throw from one of the many market stalls. A shower, a hair wash and a wrestling match with the hotel hairdryer later and she had to admit she looked quite nice. The heat and humidity demanded she indulge her waves rather than tame them so, with a liberal use of sea salt spray, she coaxed them into some order before spending some time on her make-up, elongating her eyes and lashes before adding her usual dash of red lipstick.

She took a step back and surveyed herself cautiously. Not bad. The green of the dress and the bronze wrap enhanced her brown eyes and she was optimistic that the sandals weren't going to pinch. Thank goodness she had had a pedicure before coming away. She would do.

She carried that confidence with her as she left her hotel and made her way through the evening crowds to the vaporetto stop, adding her sunglasses as protection against the still bright setting sun. A good costume wasn't essential for the confidence to inhabit a character, that was one of the first things Tally had learned at drama school, but it helped. What you needed was a core belief in who you were portraying, a deep-seated knowledge.

Tally Jenkins might not have expected to be heading out for dinner in Venice that night rather than being crammed into a too small seat on her budget flight home but she wasn't going to show it. She looked good and she knew it, an old hand at turning cheap outfits into couture with just a state of mind, and so she was poised and outwardly confident as she waited for Lucas, two butterfly clips holding her hair back from her face, wrap folded on her arm. But she still jumped when he spoke, too lost in the view to hear him approach.

'You look beautiful.'

Tally half turned, a little breathless, annoyed at being caught out. 'Thank you, so do you.' Another linen suit, this one a light blue, his shirt impossibly white, hair slicked back apart from that one rebellious lock, sunglasses that definitely cost more than her whole outfit. 'I mean…' so much for poised and in control '…you look good too.'

Ugh. Nice going, Tally.

To her relief, his mouth twitched with suppressed amusement. 'I'll gladly take either. Ah, here's our ride. Ready?'

'Absolutely.'

The boat he handed her into wasn't one of the public

taxis. Instead, it was a private launch with polished and comfortably upholstered wooden seats, the pilot clad in a smart uniform. Two glasses and a bottle of champagne chilled in an ice bucket and a deep-sided bowl held crisps. Tally's stomach gurgled. That ice cream seemed a long time ago.

Also, how cool was this. Cool and maybe just a little OTT for something that apparently wasn't a date and carried no expectations. Obviously, Lucas was richer than Croesus, or so she assumed after the last few days, but even multi-millionaires could have ulterior motives. She glanced over as he expertly slit the foil on the champagne cork, popping it silently and efficiently as if he had popped a thousand champagne bottles before. Which he almost definitely had.

Champagne. A private boat. It might not be a date but was Lucas West trying to *seduce* her? Tally watched him pour the champagne, her eyes lingering on strong, corded wrists, moving up to fixate on the vee of his throat, tanned against the white of his shirt, and her pulse began to speed up, insistent and almost pleasurably painful. Would that be a bad thing? It had been far too long since she'd had sex and Lucas was undeniably attractive. Sexy even.

It wasn't that Tally hadn't had offers since Max had finished their relationship, or unceremoniously dumped her, depending on who she was talking to, but as she preferred to steer clear of actors and the rest of her would-be suitors were regulars at her mother's pub—although, to be fair, not all were twice her age; Leroy was at least three times—she hadn't taken any of them up. As for the apps, they were a depressing tragi-comedy of ghosting, lies and misrepresentation. If that was the best that was out there then Tally had reconciled herself to being alone. Maybe one day she could do one of those marrying herself ceremonies.

But if Lucas West *was* interested in her, even as a one-off, one-night thing, then maybe she could hold off on buying the dress. Tally Jenkins still had it, whatever *it* was.

Lucas handed her the glass of champagne and she took it with a smile. The pilot of the boat waited before Lucas sat down before setting off, so smoothly her champagne barely moved in the glass.

'Cheers.' She held her glass up to Lucas. 'And thank you for this treat.'

'You're welcome. Thank you for being so accommodating.' Lucas held his glass up to her then sat back, brow furrowed as if deep in thought.

Tally reassessed the situation. He wasn't *acting* like a seducer. He wasn't leaning in close, arm around the back of her seat, smiling into her eyes. If this wasn't a seduction, maybe it was a kidnapping. She had no idea where they were going after all. But then he wasn't acting like a kidnapper either. Not that she had any idea what a kidnapper acted like, outside of an episode of a police drama she'd had a two-minute bit part in the preview as the victim whose kidnap and murder the alcoholic disgraced ex-policewoman heroine had to solve.

'It's easy to be accommodating when you're being spoilt rotten. This whole gig has been extra special. It's going to be hard to return to the usual cycle of trying to get through to my agent and submitting videos after this.' She laughed. 'Not that I'm complaining, I chose this life after all.'

'Did you always want to be an actress? Or should I say actor?' Lucas asked.

'Either works. And no. Anything but.'

'That makes sense.' Oh, he looked even more handsome when he almost smiled.

'I know. I knew better, you see; my mother was an actress and she did her best to put me off.'

'Was she in anything I would have seen?'

'Not unless you were a soap addict in the mid-nineties?'

'Well, I was about five so not so much.'

'In that case, no, I doubt it. She had some bit parts as a child actor, then *Bugsy Malone* in the West End before getting her big break in her teens as the daughter of a new family on the street in *River Close*. For a while it looked like she was going to have a really big career. She won awards, was on the front of magazines, in the headlines, but by the time she was twenty-one it all started to fall apart. The role ended in true soap melodramatic style with a shootout, a hostage situation and a tragic death on the eve of her wedding, then she had me and finding work as a single mother proved harder than she'd hoped.'

It was always a relief when people hadn't heard of her mother. It meant they had no idea who her father was and she preferred it that way. It was so awkward when people remembered that old scandal. She could see them scanning her face for a resemblance to him, hungry for any nugget of gossip about his life. Not that she had any nuggets to drop. It was hard to have the inside information when you were so far on the outside you were practically in the Arctic Circle.

'And yet here you are. Despite your mother's warnings.'

'I must be a glutton for punishment. I went to university to study History but ended up spending all my time in the drama club. Then I auditioned for drama school, assuming I wouldn't get in and knowing if I did I couldn't afford it, but they gave me a scholarship. I got an agent on graduating and thought I had made it. That fate had big things in store for me. But eight years later here I am. Barmaid, occasional murder mystery participant, bit player on several early evening dramas, star of three commercials, repertory theatre veteran and survivor of one almost in the West End musical that closed in under a week. I promise myself every six months that I'm ready to walk away and yet somehow never do. How about you? Did you always want to be...?'

To be what? Young, hot and rich? Smooth arranger of hotels and flights—at least through his PA? Tally realised she had no idea what Lucas actually did.

'A businessman?'

Oh, that was lame. Really, really lame.

Lucas half shrugged. 'The business was founded by my great-great-grandfather. Like you, it's a family legacy, I suppose.'

Clearly a much more successful legacy than Tally's.

'To family legacies,' she said, holding her glass to his again. 'And how they get us in the end.'

'To family legacies,' he echoed. His expression was hidden behind his sunglasses, but for one moment Tally could have sworn that Lucas looked almost wistful.

* * *

Now they were here, Lucas wasn't sure how to broach his idea or even if he should. Objectively speaking, the whole thing was absurd. Besides, she probably had a boyfriend, something he should have checked before embarking on this madness. It wasn't like him to be so disorganised. Usually, a plan fell into place almost as soon as he thought about it, each step laid out like a path ready to be followed. This whole idea, on the other hand, was a chaotic and potentially embarrassing mess. But here they were, approaching the private island on which could be found Venice's most exclusive restaurant.

On a summer's night like this, most of the tables were set up al fresco, lit up by candles, discreet low lights and fairy lights twisted through trellises and trees. Tables were set at discreet distances, perfect for romance and assignations—or to ask an awkward question. Lucas glanced over at Tally, who was gazing on the scene with obvious delight. The setting sun cast a golden glow over her, eyes wide and full mouth parted as she exclaimed how gorgeous it all looked, and Lucas realised again what a beautiful woman she was. Which was good. Beauty was a costume of its own and it would be helpful for the role he had in mind.

The next few minutes were taken up with the usual business of greetings, being seated, menus handed over, specials relayed in appropriately respectful tones, water ordered. He'd barely touched the complimentary champagne from the boat, which now stood chilling in a bucket by the side of the table, the service so seamless he barely noticed it arrive.

He established that Tally ate fish not meat.

'I know,' she said laughingly. 'I'm a hypocrite but it works for me.'

She opted for vegetables prepared *de misto* to start, followed by the *risotto al nero*, an iconic Venetian dish in Venice which, the waiter assured her, was unsurpassed here.

Lucas ordered the same, food the furthest thing from his mind, then sat back and surveyed his companion. Unlike most of the women here, her dress was almost definitely not real silk, the stones glittering in her ears were not real diamonds, her sandals hadn't been handmade for her, but she wore the ensemble with such confidence she outshone them all. Her hair was loose, held back by pretty clips, the waves falling down her back, and her expression gave nothing away.

'So,' she said as the waiter finally moved away, choices noted, champagne poured. 'This is really lovely but I can't help wondering what it's all for. What do you want from me, Lucas West?'

Direct and to the point. He liked it. 'Does it have to be for anything?'

'Oh, yes.' She nodded solemnly. 'You barely know me, I'm not one of the guests you were trying to impress. We already did the apology dance and you bought me a mask so it's not about what happened a couple of nights ago.'

'A mask hardly makes up for the fact that you were intimidated whilst working for me.'

Lucas's tone was harsher than he had intended but he was still filled with rage when he remembered the slight quiver in her body as she had pressed herself against him, the shadow of fear in her eyes. He didn't usually believe that violence solved anything, but he bitterly regretted not aiming one perfect punch at Johnson's smug, repellent face. Knowing he'd get his revenge in the boardroom went some way to consoling him, but not far enough.

'And if this is a romantic evening…' She paused and looked around at a setting made for romance—or discretion—and bit her lip. 'It's all very beautiful but you don't need to pull out quite so many stops to impress me. Not that I'm not impressed, it's hard not to be.'

'I'm not trying to romance you,' Lucas said, although part of him wished it was that simple, a few days' dalliance with a beautiful woman in a beautiful city. He'd been single for far too long. Maybe it was time to forget how things had turned out with Madeleine and find another equally busy, equally as uninterested in long-term relationships woman who was after something mutually beneficial. 'I would like to employ you.'

Her brown eyes widened. 'Employ me? You…what… need a resident actress on-site? Or a resident barmaid? I *can* multitask.'

'No, but I do need a plus-one for the next week, and possibly, if it works out, over the next few months.' His mouth twisted as he thought of the several corporate events he had to attend and the couple of weddings cluttering up his diary.

'A plus-one?' Her brow furrowed and then she broke into a wide incredulous grin. 'Get out! You want me to be what…your fake girlfriend? How very nineties romcom of you. I love it!'

Lucas wasn't sure if the romcom reference was a good thing or not. 'Obviously, you would be paid for your part, and I would give you an allowance to ensure that you had all you need to play the part.'

Tally leaned forward, eyes sparkling. 'Depends what part you need. If I am Tally Jenkins, jobbing actress who you met on the Orient Express, then I have all I need, but if I am Tallulah Jenkins, society woman of mystery, then that could be very expensive indeed. Let me get this straight. You are asking me to pretend to be your plus-one...'

'Actually, I want you to pretend to be my new girl-friend,' he corrected her, and her smile widened.

'Girlfriend for the next week, possibly longer, and you are prepared to pay me and outfit me to do so. Why?'

It was a fair question. 'You are the right age, quick-thinking...' Should he say beautiful when this was a business arrangement? 'You know how to dress for myr-iad parts,' he said instead. 'You are an actress so used to pretending, and you said yourself you have nothing lined up. All I am doing is offering you a job.'

'Not one I can put on my CV,' she murmured. 'Well, that's all very clear, thank you. But I didn't mean why *me*. I get that for all the reasons you just said. But what I don't get is why *you*. Either you're a very convincing conman or you're on the serious side of rich. You're easy enough on the eye, don't seem to have any terrifying personality quirks, your hygiene seems okay, you can plan a seriously impressive evening out—surely you can get any woman you want without needing to draw up a contract?'

'Probably,' he admitted, and she laughed. 'But I need someone who isn't looking for hearts and flowers and a happy-ever-after, who won't be offended when I'm too

busy to message or call, who doesn't need all my attention and is quite happy if they are left alone while I talk
to clients or prospective partners. That kind of plus-one
takes more finding than I have time for.'

Tally was leaning forward, pointed chin propped on
one slender hand, regarding him with fascination. 'I can
see that. Is that your usual type?'

'Usually, yes.'

'I see that you're not going to find the perfect woman
immediately, but I still am surprised you need to employ
one. You strike me as a pretty organised kind of guy.
Surely you would have been aware you would need a
plus-one before now?'

'The summer's events have been looming,' he admitted. 'But I received a piece of news yesterday that ex-
pedited matters. Tally, before I go any further, let me
know if this sounds like an outrageous proposal and you
have no intention of saying yes, and if so, we can put
this aside, enjoy what promises to be an excellent dinner and return to Venice with no hard feelings.'

He sat back, champagne glass in hand, outwardly cool
but, to his surprise, Lucas realised he wanted her to say
yes. That he was enjoying her company. That he liked
the way she questioned him, the amusement in her eyes.
The fact he was attracted to her was beside the point.
He didn't need attraction for the role he wanted her to
play. In fact it complicated things.

'I haven't decided yet,' she said after a while. 'It's
definitely not a yes, but it's not a no either.'

'That sounds fair.'

The waiter came over at that moment to refill their
glasses and to bring them a plate of freshly baked bread

with a saucer of delicious-smelling olive oil and a trio of tapenades.

He waited until Tally had enthusiastically helped herself to the bread and spooned a little of each tapenade and the olive oil onto the side of the plate before tackling her very pertinent question.

Why now?

'Have you ever heard the saying that it takes one generation to build a fortune, one to cement it and one to squander it?'

'It's not a saying often used in the pub, but yes.'

'Well, in our family it took one generation to move from the mill floor to mill owner, another two to grow the business to something established and lucrative and one to set about a managed decline. My father should never have been a businessman. He was happiest in London, at his friends' country estates or Mustique villas, throwing and attending parties, conducting a long string of love affairs. As for the business, it was at best unmanaged decline, at worst asset-stripping. When he died, he left behind a tangled personal life, a lot of debts and a business whose value seemed to be in what was left of its reputation and the property it was housed in. I was eighteen, Felix, my brother, fourteen.'

'Wow. I know a little what it's like to have an unsatisfactory parent. I'm sorry.'

He nodded in acknowledgement. 'Roberto was my father's godfather, my grandfather's best friend. We had been supplying his business with wool and other materials for years. And he said if I wanted to turn things around he would help me. He offered me a kind of apprenticeship so instead of university I headed to Milan, spending two years in every part of his business from shop floor to stockroom whilst studying remotely.

'Thanks to him, WGO is no longer known for catalogues in the back of Sunday supplements selling clothes that were old-fashioned fifty years ago but for in-demand high fashion. Our suits are worn by stylish successful men around the world and our women's fashion is expanding exponentially. Our wholesale business supplies brands all over the world. We turned around the retail business, keeping the bricks and mortar and finally expanding into online despite a difficult time for retail, acquiring brands, companies and manufacturers as we grow. The company hasn't just turned around, it's bigger, better and healthier than it ever has been and changing and growing all the time. That was the point of this trip. My guests are the last family shareholders in a US preppy clothing company I want to buy.

'But what I need you to understand is that Roberto gave me the tools I needed, the self-belief, and the capital when no bank would touch a failing business headed up by an eighteen-year-old novice and he was by my side the first few years. I owe him everything.'

He stopped. Lucas wasn't sure when he had last said so much in one go. But Tally didn't look bored, she looked fascinated.

'And I guess Roberto is the reason you're in desperate need of a plus-one.'

Lucas nodded. 'Not so much Roberto, but his Achilles heel. His granddaughter. Isabella.'

CHAPTER FOUR

TALLY HAD NEVER been anywhere like this. A restaurant on a private island in the middle of the Venetian lagoon, brought here by private boat with champagne laid on. It was the kind of life she imagined living if she ever made it, the kind of life her father wouldn't even blink at. And she could carry on living this kind of life for another week, for the rest of the summer if she said yes to Lucas West's surprising proposition.

She didn't know if she was disappointed or relieved that this wasn't a seduction attempt. It would be easier to say no but thank you if he wasn't quite so devastating. If he wasn't looking at her out of eyes a dark blue like the dusk lit sea, if she hadn't had the feeling that he had just revealed far more than he had intended, far more than the mere words he had said.

She knew what it was like to have a father figure instead of your own actual father. The need to keep proving yourself, to show your love and gratitude, the awareness that love might not be conditional but felt that way.

'So, let me guess.' She kept her tone deliberately light as the waiter set a plate filled with a delicately arranged feast of fresh vegetables so lightly battered and fried it was as if they had been plucked fresh from the earth in front of her and merely waved in front of a flame. 'Roberto thinks that a marriage between his best friend's grandson and his own beloved granddaughter would be the very thing to allow an old man to die happy but, much as you love him, for whatever reason that's a step too far?' She took a bite of a courgette and closed her eyes as she savoured the taste. 'What have they done to these? How can a vegetable taste like this?'

'They are good, aren't they?' Lucas looked much more at ease now he had told her why they were here. 'And yes. Apparently, he and my grandfather used to say we were destined for each other when we were babies and now he would like nothing better than that prophecy to come true.'

'And why is it such a problem? If you married her you wouldn't have to go around begging out-of-work actresses to pretend to be in love with you.'

'I don't want to marry *anyone* just yet. All my energies go into work, I don't have the emotional bandwidth for a wife and family now. And even if I did, well, Isabella has been raised in a very privileged way. She's never had to work a day in her life. Our values...' He shook his head. 'She's very beautiful but that's it. I don't need or want a trophy wife.'

'And how does she feel about you?'

'I don't know,' he said, looking uncomfortable now. 'She's very flirtatious, it's hard to know how serious she is, but Roberto takes her at face value. It's all very awkward. He's not well and I'm worried about him, which is why I'm going straight to his villa in Tuscany after I finish here tomorrow. But I just found out that not only is Isabella's latest engagement over but she will be staying there this week. I don't want her teasing to get his hopes up, not while he's unwell. He looked very frail last time I saw him…'

Some of Tally's amusement at the absurd situation she had found herself in ebbed away. This wasn't the slightly farcical, possibly sordid scenario his proposition had first conjured up but a man trying to do the right thing, although in a rather clumsy way.

It was almost a shame that the whole idea was obviously impossible. She rather liked the idea of Roberto and was intrigued by the glamorous Isabella. Not to mention a week's stay in a Tuscan villa. But of course she couldn't say yes. It wasn't acting; it was deception.

Wasn't it?

'And there's no one else you could ask? No occasional date, no one whose DMs you've been sliding into, no amenable ex who can help you out?'

'Like I said, the business needs my full attention.'

'Ah, the elusive work-life balance. It's nice to see it in action.'

'So, what do you think?'

What she should think was this was the most absurd idea she had ever heard. But on the other hand, she had just played the most stereotypical parody of a French maid because she had lost out on the opportunity of a lifetime. What was waiting for her back in London apart from her childhood attic bedroom, shifts behind the bar, long anxious hours waiting to hear from her agent and crushing disappointment? She speared an asparagus and looked over at Lucas.

'It depends,' she said. 'Partly on how you think this

will work and whatever the going rate is for a fake girl-friend these days and partly on how I feel about it. Can we drop it for now while I mull it over?'

'Of course.'

The rest of the meal was as delicious as the starters had promised, Lucas a sometimes amusing, if serious bordering on occasionally brooding companion but as the sky darkened, the stars replaced the sun and the lighting became more intimate, Tally was aware of a low feeling in her stomach, her chest, one that was almost disappointment. What had she expected this evening to be? Certainly not a job offer. For a moment there she had thought she might be enjoying a fairy tale moment, something not quite real, that wouldn't translate into the real world where their lives were so very different but a lovely memory, something to help restore her tattered self-esteem, to bury any vestiges of longing for Max and the life he had shattered.

But who was she kidding? Rich, successful business-men didn't fall for jobbing actresses, not in the real world. Of *course* he was offering her a job. The attraction she had felt in the cabin, that shiver of awareness, the surprising pleasure she had felt at seeing him this morning were one-sided and that was to be expected. He wanted her professional skills only. It made complete sense and she was silly to take it so personally.

It was just... Her world was one of artifice, of characters played and discarded, of smiles and quips and occasional authority when she was behind the bar. When did she get a chance to be herself? Tallulah May Jenkins? She would have quite liked it to be Tallulah sitting here in this idyllic location with this gorgeous successful man on an actual date, not Tally, about to haggle over the terms of a contract.

If she accepted it, that was. And although it was just a job Lucas West was offering her, nothing more sordid, it still felt wrong. Lovely as a week in Tuscany and any number of unspecified black-tie events sounded, she was going to have to say no. And as she made the decision, she knew he sensed it, some of the intimacy replaced by his usual formality. He was ever the courteous host but she could tell that he too was playing a part. That he often did. That maybe he was so used to it he had no idea where the mask ended and the real-life Lucas began.

It was intriguing, but none of her business. So best not to dwell on what was going on under that courteous expression—or wonder about what seemed to be a well-honed body under the expensive clothes. Best not to feel like she scored a point every time he reluctantly almost smiled or feel like she had scored a goal when he even more reluctantly laughed. It wasn't her job to get to know him. And whatever her answer, tonight was work.

Tally toyed with the remains of her risotto. It was amazing, as was the glass of red wine that accompanied it, but she couldn't appreciate either of them properly, aware that Lucas was awaiting her answer.

'I...' she began, just as he started to speak.

'Thank you...'

She stopped, a little relieved by the delay. 'You first.'

'No, I interrupted you. What were you going to say?'

'Just that I have had a lovely time tonight. Thank you so much for asking me and for making it possible with the flights and the room. I am really grateful...' She paused, searching for the right words.

But he was way ahead of her. 'But you're not comfortable accepting my proposal?'

'No.' Tally was grateful to Lucas for making it so easy. 'I understand your reasons, but…' she started, distracted by the sound of her phone. Who on earth was calling her? Even her grandmother preferred messaging, usually with a series of emojis that were harder to decipher than the most complicated cryptic crossword. 'I'm sorry, it's probably spam. Let me send it to voicemail.' She lifted her phone out of her bag and hesitated when she saw her friend Layla's name flashing on the screen. 'Hang on.'

She pressed accept. 'Layla? Is everything okay?' She smiled apologetically at Lucas, who nodded and turned his attention to the pudding menu the waiter had placed in front of them.

'Tal, I'm sorry, I know you're away with work. Is this a good time?'

Not a butt dial then. 'It's fine, I have a minute. What's going on?'

'It's the wedding.'

Tally froze. Layla wouldn't be calling unless it was a crisis. Her oldest friend was marrying her childhood sweetheart in just a few weeks' time and, as maid of honour, Tally had been involved in what felt like every detail, from helping Phinn plan the perfect proposal to researching honeymoon destinations. There had been Say Yes to the Dress moments, a hen night in Brighton, more hours than she could count sitting in Layla's sitting room making table decorations and place cards and helping reorganise the table plan for the thirtieth time. There was still an old-fashioned night-before-the-wedding hen night in the pub to enjoy—but not too much, as Layla wanted everyone tucked up by ten—and bridesmaid duties on the day itself. The whole event had been a welcome distraction from her still lingering heartsoreness over her own breakup and crushing disappointment workwise. She was almost as invested in the wedding as the bride and groom. She wasn't sure she could cope with a crisis.

'The wedding?'

'I swear I had no idea,' Layla continued.

'Idea about what? Layla, the wedding *is* still on, isn't it?' Increasingly lurid thoughts were passing through her mind. Phinn was the mildest man possible, a primary school teacher who liked nothing better than a gruelling walk through icy winds to some barren peak followed by a pint in a pub and a game of Scrabble, a startling contrast to life-and-soul city girl Layla, but somehow they worked. Had Phinn been cheating? Had Layla? She'd know, wouldn't she?

'Of course the wedding is still on, idiot. But annoyingly with the addition of your ex. I had no idea Phinn had actually invited him until I got a text today asking for a plus-one. Cheeky sod. Oh, I'm so cross with Phinn. He knew we got you in the breakup. Obviously.'

But it wasn't that simple, was it? For four years they had been a foursome. Tally and Max, Layla and Phinn, meals out, weekends away, long evenings in her mother's pub. They'd all been roped into Charlene's Christmas pantomimes more than once and gone along to cheer her successful Shakespeare and a Pint summer initiative. If Tally and Max hadn't broken up then he would have been an integral part of this wedding, probably an usher. It wasn't fair to expect Phinn not to invite him. Or not to allow him a plus-one.

And Tally would have to smile and be gracious and not weep into her wine or flirt outrageously with someone else or beg Max to take her back because it was Phinn and Layla's day—but, oh, God, it was going to be hard. She hadn't even seen him in months and now she was going to have to watch him dance with someone else, kiss someone else. Love someone else.

'Is it too late to turn my bridesmaid's dress into something really showstopping?' She tried to sound amused rather than devastated. 'I know technically it's your day but, under the circumstances, it seems the only option.'

'We'll take it up to mid-thigh and down to your navel if you forgive me.'

'Sounds great.' She looked over at Lucas, his gaze fixed on his phone. Summer events, he had said. Plus-one at weddings and business events. Surely that would go both ways? She wouldn't need a fabulous dress and a game face if she had someone like Lucas West on her arm. Checkmate, Max. Tally rapidly recalled the last incarnation of the seating plan she had seen. There was space. 'But what would be even more helpful is if I can have a plus-one too. I'll pay, of course.'

'Don't be ridiculous. I'm sure we can manage another chicken somehow. But a plus-one? *Who?*'

Layla's surprise wasn't unexpected but it was a little depressing. Surely Tally's prospects weren't *that* bad?

'I'll fill you in later. Tell Phinn I forgive him but if he ever hurts you…'

'You'll end him, I know.'

'As long as he knows. Thanks for the heads-up. I have to go. Love you.'

She finished the call, sat back and picked up her wine glass, needing Dutch courage. Was she actually going to do this?

'I accept,' she said. 'But not for money, not as a job, but as a reciprocal agreement. I have a wedding of my own I need to attend in a few weeks and my ex will be there with a plus-one.'

Understanding filled Lucas's gaze. 'I see.'

'Yes, well,' she said uncomfortably. 'It was almost a year ago and I should have moved on by now. I *have* moved on.' Kind of. 'But I am petty enough to want to show him that. So, here's what I propose. I will spend this week in Tuscany with you and in return you will come to Layla's wedding with me. No wages, we are doing each other a favour. If things go well and we both want to carry on then we discuss the rest of the summer after the wedding.'

Lucas's eyes narrowed assessingly as he thought her proposal through. 'Agreed.'

'If any other events come up between Tuscany and the wedding then I am happy to accompany you, but I'll need some notice. I'll have some shifts to do at the pub, hopefully some auditions.' Speaking of which, she needed to let her mother know she wouldn't be home for a week.

'Agreed,' he said again. 'But one caveat. I will supply you with a wardrobe for this week and for any other event you accompany me to.'

'There's no need for that,' she protested, although she knew her protest was unconvincing as she mentally assessed the smarter parts of her wardrobe and found them sadly wanting.

'There's every need,' he said grimly. 'Roberto is supposed to be resting but he may have organised parties, dinners out, opera trips. You need to be convincing as my girlfriend and that means looking the part. I'll get Candace to send you a list of possible occasions and dress codes and transfer you the funds you'll need. I have a few meetings tomorrow so you can have the day to shop. I'll meet you around three-thirty. It's a four-hour journey to Tuscany, so be prepared.'

'New wardrobe. Fed and watered. Got it.' She felt a little dizzy—it was all happening so fast.

'Good.' He paused, looking a little uncomfortable. 'And Tally, thank you.'

'No need to thank me. You are doing me just as big a favour. It's a reciprocal agreement.'

'A reciprocal agreement,' he echoed. 'Right.'

Tally took another sip of her wine. It wasn't hard to decipher the doubt in his tone. Lucas West was clearly someone who was used to paying for what he needed. His PA booked his restaurants, he would send his shirts out to be ironed, why not purchase a plus-one too? She'd shifted the whole arrangement. Made them equals. It would be fun seeing how he managed that.

Tally was waiting as arranged by the vaporetto stop. Punctuality was a good sign, Lucas thought as the boat's deckhand carried her bags onto the boat he had arranged to take them to the outskirts of the city where roads replaced canals and a car awaited. His gaze fell on the luggage piled up beside her. He'd directed that a prepaid credit card be delivered to the hotel that morning and, judging by the number of cases, Tally had made good use of it.

'I don't normally travel with so much stuff,' she said breathlessly as she climbed onto the small boat. 'That big case is actually my costumes—luckily, Neil doesn't need them back just yet. Those two bags are new. I bought a ridiculous amount for one week but you did say to be prepared for every eventuality and I took you at your word. Only this small one is actually mine.' She must have seen his gaze linger on the two new bags and added a little defensively, 'I've already sent all the receipts to your PA. It's harder work than you know shopping for a whole new wardrobe in just a few hours. I thought it would be like a movie montage, with me swirling around in huge skirts and looking cute in hats while assistants applauded but instead it was like a really messy supermarket sweep.'

'I'm sure whatever you got will be fine.' He took in her current outfit, a pink striped jumpsuit with a matching pink headband holding back her mass of wavy hair. 'Is that new?'

'It is. It kind of gave me fifties Riviera vibes. Too much?'

Lucas's mouth was unexpectedly dry. 'No,' he managed after an excruciatingly long moment. 'Not too much. You look…nice.' What she looked like was strawberry ice-cream, sweet and enticing with a hint of spice. The jumpsuit showed off her long legs to perfection, nipping in at her waist then flaring out with delicious ruffles across her chest. 'It's fine.'

To his relief, his phone lit up once they were underway and he spent the short ride to the car park in conversation with his lawyers, switching to hands-free once they were out of the city and he had the measure of the car he'd hired. Tally merely gave him an amused glance when one call immediately replaced the other, busying herself on her phone or looking out of the window but, despite himself, Lucas was always aware of her, of the swish of her hair, her floral scent, every shift and small sound.

The time passed quickly, the powerful car eating up the miles, the calls occupying his mind as they drove south, and it wasn't until they entered the green hilly countryside of Tuscany that his phone finally stopped ringing.

Tally shifted to look at him. 'Okay,' she said. 'Time to concentrate on the mission. We need to establish our story arc.'

'Our *what*?'

'Our meet-cute, our history. What should we already know about each other? What stage are we at?'

Lucas blinked. This was already more complicated than he had envisioned. But then he hadn't really thought about what would happen after she had said yes, hadn't thought she *would* say yes or even that he would ask her at all. And this was why he didn't do impulsive.

'I thought we would tell the truth,' he said slowly. 'We met on the Orient Express and...'

What came next? They were attracted to each other? He couldn't deny that he *was* attracted to Tally but that was a complication he had no intention of adding to what was already a stressful situation.

'I invited you along,' he finished, aware it wasn't the most compelling story. 'Keep it as simple as we can.'

'Hmm…' Tally tapped her fingers on her knee as she considered. 'It would do if you were simply inviting me to a party, but not for a week away. It's a bit much to ask someone you've known for two days to someone else's house and, more importantly, it's not going to be the deterrent you need.'

'Okay then, what do you suggest?'

'Where do you live?'

'London.'

'Whereabouts in London?' she said patiently.

'Chelsea. My father had a house there and I use that,' he added, aware that she was right, she needed some personal details. 'My mother still lives in the family's Yorkshire estate when she's in the UK. I spend some time there but mostly I'm in London or here in Italy or travelling.'

'You don't sound like a Yorkshireman. Okay, Chelsea is perfect.'

'Is it?'

'Absolutely. My stepfather's pub is off the King's Road. You might even have been in it. In fact, for this story you *have* been in it. Let me think…' The tapping intensified but for once Lucas didn't mind the distracting noise. 'Right, you came in for a pint a few months ago—is that something you would do?'

'Maybe. Occasionally.'

'All we need is occasional.' She tapped some more, her eyes fixed unseeingly on the horizon. 'I was behind the bar; it was a quiet night and we flirted a bit.'

If Lucas had been wearing a tie he would have loosened it. He tried to imagine himself walking into a pub and casually flirting with a pretty barmaid. With *this* pretty barmaid. 'Right,' he managed.

'After that we saw each other a few times around, the way you do when you're aware of someone and they seem to be everywhere. You know?'

Just like bumping into Tally in that mask shop. Had that really been just yesterday morning?

'Then we ended up having a drink together. But I was still raw over Max and you were busy and things kind of tailed off…'

'That sounds a bit weak,' he objected. 'How about I was called away on a secret mission or you got amnesia?'

She laughed. 'Unexpectedly vivid imagination. I like it, but as your friends are unlikely to believe the secret mission and mine know I didn't have amnesia let's go with you being really busy and then I had a big audition I needed to concentrate on and so we didn't break up exactly, we weren't really together, but it came to an end. However, we've both been thinking about reaching out and so yay, what a fabulous coincidence to bump into each other on the train and here we are.'

Lucas thought about it, testing her story as if it were a new product, idea, brand, stretching and examining, looking for holes and weaknesses. It wasn't the most dramatic origin story but it had the ring of truth and that was probably more important than high drama or romance. 'Agreed.'

'So, what did we talk about on those walks and almost dates? Let me see. Tally Jenkins, sometime actress, more time barmaid, you know that. I grew up over the pub with my mum and stepdad, Steve. They got married when I was five and Steve is my dad to all intents and purposes.'

'Do you ever see your real father?'

'No. I've never seen him, never heard from him. Child maintenance was paid monthly until the month I left school and then stopped. It couldn't be clearer that he wants nothing to do with me.' She said the words almost airily, with the ease of long practice, but Lucas couldn't help thinking that she said them as if by saying it they were true. He got that. He was president of the club for growing up with disappointing self-interested fathers after all. 'Okay, my best friend is Layla, who is a teacher, and marrying Phinn, another teacher. You are coming to their wedding with me. I was with Max for four years. I think that's everything vital.'

'Why did you break up?'

'Different values, the usual.' She bit her lip. 'When I met Max he was in a band, the day job in finance was just to pay the bills, but at some point that changed. The band became first a hobby and was then replaced by cycling and the job became a career and he was ready for a mortgage, settling down, kids. A girlfriend with an uncertain income who is sometimes around all the time or might be away for a week or weeks or even months doesn't fit with that lifestyle. In the end he said it was the job or him.'

'And you chose the job?'

She looked away. 'I said I didn't do ultimatums. So, I am back living above the pub, auditioning and doing my best to prove him wrong in every way and succeeding badly.'

'Which is why you need a plus-one?'

'Exactly. Okay, what will I need to know about you to pass the still fairly new girlfriend test? Name? Star sign? Favourite pet?'

'You know my name.'

'You don't have a middle name?'

'I don't think that's relevant.'

Lucas concentrated on the road ahead but was aware of Tally twisting around in her seat to stare at him, a grin lighting up her face.

'You *do* have a middle name! And one you hate at that. Hmm, let me see. Cedric? St John? Lancelot?'

'I sincerely hope you are never the mother of sons.'

'I'm just guessing, not suggesting them for our future imaginary offspring. Come on,' she coaxed. 'How bad can it be?'

'It's not *bad*,' he said a little stiffly. 'It's just embarrassing.'

'Come on, Lucas, isn't this exactly the kind of thing you'd confide on a springtime walk in the park?'

'No, it's the kind of thing that makes me want to change my name by deed poll. Okay—' as she started to speak again '—it's Jupiter. Okay?'

Tally didn't answer and when he glanced over, he saw her gazing at him in fascination. *'No,'* she half whispered at last. 'Really? As in king of the gods. Wow. That's a lot to live up to.'

'You can see why I don't advertise the fact.'

'It could have been worse,' she said after a while. 'It could have been Mars. Or Hades, although Pluto is the Roman variant, isn't it? Not that Pluto is any better.'

'My mother was a classicist. She wanted Jupiter to

be my first name but my father for once did the sensible thing and said no. They compromised on a middle name.'

'You have a brother, don't you?'

'Yes, Felix.'

'Please tell me he's been saddled with Hercules or Apollo.'

Despite himself, Lucas couldn't help a half smile. 'Neptune.'

'Wow. Any sisters, a lucky Proserpina or Venus? Although you could get away with a Diana or Minerva quite easily, I suppose.'

'No sisters. Just two sons with slightly out-there middle names even by *The Times* birth column standards. Otherwise, we had a pretty normal certain class of English upbringing. Home between Yorkshire and London, prep school at seven then Eton. A bored and angry mother who drank too much, spent too much, had too many affairs and a spendthrift, negligent father whose claim to fame was being on the front page of the tabloids kissing the inner thigh of a cabinet minister's wife. That,' he added grimly, 'was a fun day at school. No pets as we were never in one place long enough. My birthday is October, whatever that means star sign wise. I left school at eighteen as you know and took over the business when my father died, mother alive but lives in the Bahamas and occasionally plays lady of the manor in Yorkshire. We're not close. I *am* close to Felix. No significant relationships; I have been concentrating on work and that seems to be an issue after a few months for most women, hence the need for you.'

He didn't have to look at Tally to know she would be

open-mouthed and wide-eyed. He wasn't sure what had led him to say all that, especially the part about his father. It was no secret, google Peter West and it was still the most significant part of his Wiki bio, but it wasn't information he usually freely volunteered. Nor did he usually show his bitterness and anger quite so clearly.

'Okay,' Tally said after a while. 'I think you know most of the pertinent things about me. Single mum, pub, stepdad, reluctant and yet still going actress, recent heartbreak. I grew up with a selection of pub cats, most beloved was the very originally named Tabby, who lived to eighteen and was still coaxing titbits until the day she died. Never had a dog, always wanted one.'

'Me too,' he volunteered, surprised at himself. He'd long forgotten that old yearning for a dog.

'There you go, the thing we have in common.'

'Star sign, Aquarius...' Of course she knew that. 'No siblings. The only thing you don't know that you should is about my father. He's kind of...oh!' As he turned off the road into the gates leading into Roberto's villa and vineyard, 'Is this it? Oh, my goodness, I wasn't expecting this! This gig gets better by the day!'

CHAPTER FIVE

TALLY HADN'T KNOWN what to expect from her residence for the next week; Tuscan villa as a concept was somewhat outside her experience, but whatever she had imagined, it certainly wasn't as grand and yet welcoming as the vista that greeted them. Arched, elegantly designed iron gates ushered them into a sweeping drive, rows of vines all around, stretching out as far as the eye could see, undulating green hills in the background. The drive had been long and now it was late evening, the sun was low on the horizon, casting a warm golden glow over the idyllic scene.

In the distance she could see a pink building and as they got closer exclaimed in delight as she took in balustraded balconies, a sweet little turret on one corner, an entire tower complete with narrow windows perfect for shooting arrows out of on the other side. Formal gardens were laid out in front of the villa arranged across shallow terraces, while orange, lemon and olive trees clustered together in an orchard on the far side.

'Wow...' she breathed again, her vocabulary deserting her. 'This is really something. How old is it?'

'Part of the villa dates back hundreds of years. Roberto's family has made wine here for generations on his mother's side. His father's family are from Milan.'

'Hence the business connection, I suppose. I like clothes well enough—' she couldn't help smoothing down the linen jumpsuit as she spoke, feeling slightly guilty as she remembered just how much of a spree she had gone on, panicking at all the unknowns that lay before her as she bought enough clothes for a month not a week '—but overall, I am team wine, especially if it's produced somewhere as beautiful as this.'

'You and Roberto both. He spent most of his life in Milan, expanded the family business diligently, but his heart was always here. He has passed the clothing side onto his son, but nothing would prise him away from his vines. Not even doctor's orders.'

A momentary cloud passed over Lucas's face. It was hard to get a reading on her make-believe boyfriend most of the time, but one thing Tally did know: he really did love Roberto. She liked that about him, the way he so willingly attributed his success to the mentorship of another. He might be proud but he wasn't prideful.

He pulled the car into a small car park towards the back of the house, a dusty square surrounded by low buildings that looked as if they had once been stables. 'Okay, ready?'

Tally took a deep breath. 'Almost. There's one thing we haven't established.'

His brow creased. 'What's that? I have family, pets and exes memorised. Do I need your favourite colour as well?'

'It varies depending on mood. Today it's pink, as you

can see. But no, nothing so simple. What we need to do is establish how we are when we are together.'

Establishing trust when playing lovers or a love scene was usually a slow process, built up layer by layer. A light touch, eye contact, a slow dance to intimacy, usually directed by someone else. But there was no time for any of that. In a couple of minutes' time Tally was going to have to convince two strangers that she and Lucas were reunited lovers, still in the honeymoon stage, so attached they couldn't bear to be parted now they had found each other once again.

More importantly, Lucas was going to have to do the same, only his role was much harder. These people knew him, could read him, were aware of his business first, love last approach to life. They were bound to be sceptical, unsure of Tally, and their current body language wouldn't fool anyone, especially not someone who knew Lucas intimately.

'We need to act like we're in love,' she clarified.

'Right.' His expression, as usual, gave nothing away but she thought she saw a flicker of alarm in his eyes. 'Well, we've got our stories straight so…'

'So that's part one, but it's no good *telling* people we're mad about each other, we have to *show* them. We have to be consistent, believable with every look and tone and movement.' She unbuckled her seatbelt and turned to face him. 'Look at me.'

Slowly, Lucas shifted until he was mirroring her, his shoulders as set as his actually rather marvellous mouth.

'Look at me again,' she said, her voice low, intent. One casting director had described that particular tone as like molten honey. 'Look at me as if I'm the only person you want to see, as if everyone else and everything else is merely a distraction, as if you're just waiting until you can get me alone and...'

Her mouth dried up, her imagination not failing her but instead supplying her with a dizzying array of images detailing exactly what Lucas might do to her and she to him when alone. She could feel her breath hitch, her neck and chest flush, heat pool low in her stomach before spreading out and down, an ache sweet and painful between her legs. She allowed her gaze to linger on the hard lines of his mouth, tracing every millimetre of his lips, to dip down, past his stubbled chin to the exposed vee of his throat then back up, up, up until she met his gaze, his eyes darkened to a fierce navy like a storm-tossed sea. He no longer seemed guarded but nor was he vulnerable. Instead, he was looking at her as if he could see through her, right to the heart of her, as if the pink and white jumpsuit didn't exist. The ache intensified and her lips parted, her body swaying towards his, her hand reaching up as if by its own volition to touch his cheek.

'Lucas,' she breathed, only to jump back, the spell shattered, as a hand rapped on the window. He drew back, his gaze still fixed on hers, a pulse beating in his cheek.

'Lesson learned,' she said shakily, trying to recover her equilibrium. 'Good job. Just try to channel that every now and then and we should be fine.'

It had happened before, she told herself as she fumbled with the door handle, this crossing of lines from faking to feeling. It happened all the time. That was why sets and rehearsal rooms were rife with flings and affairs. Acting wasn't pretending, it was being, and if she was to do her job well, she had to let herself fall into the illusion. It was just a good thing Lucas was an apt pupil.

But as she slid out of the car and found herself enthusiastically greeted by a clearly unwell Roberto, who refused the stick his assistant tried to give him and could only be dissuaded from taking her bag by Lucas taking his arm and walking him firmly back to the house, she couldn't help wondering just how much acting she had been doing in the end. She had to be careful. She was here to do a job, paid or not. It wasn't real, no matter how swept up in the moment she had been.

The late evening sun was real though, the air, sweet and fragrant with herbs and citrus and summer flowers was real, the gorgeous old villa was real, cool and shady inside, with high ceilings and tiled floors. Lucas had disappeared with Roberto—so much for proving to everyone that they couldn't keep their hands off each other.

But, on the other hand, even without knowing Roberto she could see his skin was sallow, his hands shaky, that there was an air of frailty around him, one he seemed to want to deny. She could also see how worried Lucas was, saw the care with which he escorted the older man. It was a good sign, showed she hadn't been misled by him, that there was a good heart under the remote manner and tailored suits.

Elena, Roberto's assistant, still carrying the rejected stick, suggested that she might want time to freshen up before dinner and, after four hours in the car, Tally agreed. She was led through the large welcoming entrance hall, down a wide tiled corridor and up a winding staircase to a pretty sitting room, its half-shuttered windows overlooking the vineyard. A second staircase in the corner led up to a semi-circular bedroom with two doors on one side. Tally took in the curved walls on one side, set with three charmingly leaded windows, each with a cosy window seat set beneath them, and realised with delight that her room was in the turret she had admired from the car. The whole was painted white with the wooden floor polished to a warm golden glow. The room was large, a huge bed dominating the middle, two inviting-looking chairs either side of a low table against the opposite wall. A huge olive rug lay on the floor, the same colour picked up in the blinds, cushions and bed-linen, abstract nature inspired prints on the walls.

'Oh, this is gorgeous,' she exclaimed.

'Your bathroom is through here,' Elena explained, opening one of the doors in the wall bisecting the room. 'Can I bring you anything? Wine, coffee?'

Both sounded amazing but Tally wasn't even used to room service in hotels—she counted it an upgrade if there was a coffee machine instead of plastic sachets—so she shook her head diffidently. 'Oh, no, but thank you.'

'Drinks are being served on the terrace; dinner will be in about thirty minutes. Can you find your way back downstairs?'

Two staircases, a corridor, another staircase. Maybe.

'I'm sure I'll be fine,' she said, not sure at all. 'Thank you again.'

'Prego.'

Elena nodded and headed back down the stairs, leaving Tally to continue looking around. They had headed straight here but somehow her cases had preceded her and had been set next to the bathroom door. The bathroom contained an inviting-looking standalone tub alongside a rainfall shower so big it was practically a wet room with two sinks lined up under the mirror. Another door led to the loo, discreetly hidden away in its own little room with another sink. The double doors next to the bathroom led, not into a walk-in closet as she had imagined, but into an entire dressing area with open built-in wardrobes and a dressing table.

'Wow...' she murmured again, grabbing her phone and taking a picture to send to Layla. 'I don't want to ever leave. Look at this.'

Tally grabbed her cases and dragged them into the dressing room, quickly hanging up a few dresses and tops she thought might crease, leaving the rest to be dealt with later. She unpacked her make-up bag and wash bag, leaving the first on the dressing table, carrying the second through to the bathroom, where she washed her hands and face, before quickly reapplying some concealer, mascara and lipstick and combing her hair.

She would have to do. Anything more and she would be late for dinner.

Cautiously, Tally made her way down the winding staircase to the sitting room below. It was all part of the same suite, she realised, decorated in the same olive and crisp white tones, with two comfortable sofas, a bookcase filled with books in Italian and English and a thick rug softening the stone floor. At one end she spied a small kitchenette containing a kettle and toaster. Thank goodness she would be able to fend for herself after all. No awkward summoning of staff for a cup of tea. Whatever the rest of the week would bring, she had been housed very well. First the Orient Express, then her very comfortable if slightly anonymous hotel room and now all this spacious splendour. The two rooms together were bigger than her and Max's flat, let alone her bedroom above the pub.

Speaking of Max. She had to soft launch Lucas in a believable way. Max might have blocked her but most of his friends hadn't. She checked the time and then quickly took a selfie, leaning against a window, the setting sun behind her. She posted it, adding a few hashtags—*#nofilter #tuscany #vineyard #unexpected-break*—and captioned the whole *Begin Again*, selecting the Taylor Swift song of the same name to accompany it.

Ha. Max had never liked her to wear high heels either, she thought as the lyrics ran through her mind, but at over six foot she doubted Lucas would have similar hangups. Most people exchanged their bridesmaid's shoes for something more comfortable for the evening part of a wedding but Tally vowed that she was going to exchange hers for the most vertiginous heels she owned.

Picture posted, she slipped her phone back into her pocket and set about trying to retrace her steps. Forget Rapunzel, this felt like Hansel and Gretel. If only she had thought to sprinkle some breadcrumbs on her hurried journey to her room.

Lucas checked his watch. 'Maybe I should go check on Tally…' he began when, right on cue, she rushed onto the terrace, breathless with apology.

'I'm not late, am I?' she asked anxiously. 'I assured the nice lady who showed me to my room that I would easily find my way back but I got hopelessly lost. You have a lovely home,' she added. 'I know this now because I have explored every inch.'

Roberto laughed and took Tally's hands in his. 'I am glad you approve. Now, what can I get you? Prosecco? A Pinot Grigio grown here on the estate, or something a little richer?'

'Prosecco would be lovely, but only if there is one open. Do you make that here as well?'

'I don't grow the Glera grapes needed, but it is local and organic.' Roberto handed her a glass. 'And how do you like your room?'

'Oh, it's amazing. I feel like a princess in there, real Rapunzel vibes, thank you.'

As he watched Tally charm Roberto, Lucas felt his worries unfurl. He had made a good choice. She was seemingly totally natural and at ease.

'Isabella is out with friends but she should join us after dinner,' Roberto said as he led them towards a table in the corner of the terrace. 'So tonight, we dine al fresco, just an informal dinner amongst friends.'

Dinner was delicious, a simple but perfectly dressed salad before a small serving of rich and delicious pasta *arrabiata*, followed by chicken for Lucas and Roberto and fish for Tally. They ate slowly, Roberto and Tally discovering a mutual love of books and theatre and, to Lucas's relief, the conversation flowed naturally without much input from him.

He didn't mean to be so silent, to leave Tally to do the heavy lifting, but as the two chatted easily, recommending books and plays and films, he realised how much of his life, his conversation, his thoughts revolved around work. The books on his bedside table were about business, or histories of commerce and clothing, he listened to business podcasts when running or working out, rarely watched television and theatre was something he did to entertain or be entertained, along with the races and watching rugby and other forms of corporate hospitality. When had he last read for pleasure? When had he last done *anything* purely for pleasure?

His gaze fell on Tally, glowing in the candles and fairy lights as she gesticulated, so full of life and vibrancy it almost hurt, and his cheek tingled where she had touched it earlier, his whole body heating at the memory of her intense stare, the way she had leaned in, the scent of her. That was work for both of them, but there had been a painful pleasure there too.

The plates had been removed and a platter of fruit and cheese brought out to groans from Tally, who was proclaiming that this was one of the best meals she had ever eaten to protests from Roberto that it was nothing and he would remedy the simplicity this week, when a figure entered dramatically from the house, framed in the light spilling from the hallway. Tally might be an actress but Isabella instinctively knew how to stage a scene to her advantage. Roberto's granddaughter wore an off-the-shoulder tight-fitting black dress that hugged her slender curves, her hair sleek, framing her heart-shaped face. Large dark eyes regarded Lucas reproachfully.

'But Lucas, no one told me you were coming,' she said in Italian, ignoring Tally completely.

'Now, Isabella, I am sure I mentioned it yesterday. And English please, our other guest does not speak Italian,' Roberto remonstrated. 'Tally, this is Isabella, my granddaughter. Bella, meet Tally, Lucas's friend.'

Tally stood and held her hand out. 'So lovely to meet you. What a beautiful home you and your grandfather have here.'

Isabella's eyes flickered between Tally and Lucas before she took Tally's hand, like a queen bestowing a great favour on a lowly subject, and Lucas saw Tally's mouth twitch with amusement.

'Thank you. I spend most of my time in Rome or Paris, but it is nice to be in the country sometimes.' She dropped Tally's hand and into a seat in one languid movement. 'So, how long have you known each other? Luca, I thought you were too busy for *friends*.' She imbued the last word with meaning.

Lucas was more than grateful for Tally's foresight and professional skills as she expertly took Roberto and Isabella through the tale she had concocted with just the right amount of smiles across to Lucas, appeals to him to concur and one outstretched hand, which he took and squeezed, her skin silk under his touch.

Roberto listened with a benevolent smile, Isabella with narrow-eyed precision, questioning Tally closely, getting sulkier and sulkier as the story developed. Lucas knew that it wasn't, and had never been, that Isabella wanted him particularly. He had no title, he was rich, true, but everyone she knew was rich. No, it was more that Isabella was used to being worshipped by all who knew her and it irritated her that Lucas had never shown any inclination to join her court.

'You did brilliantly,' he said low-voiced as they stood after dinner, enjoying the warm evening air. Isabella had flounced off, clearly put out at not being the centre of attention, while Roberto was talking to the housekeeper as the table was cleared.

It wouldn't do for Lucas, living so closely and intimately with staff. The villa had three full-time members of staff, plus Roberto's longstanding assistant who accompanied him everywhere. His own assistant had never been to his flat, and he could see no reason why she would. His cleaning was done by an agency, he catered for himself or ate out. Even the Yorkshire estate, large as it was, had live-out cleaners and grounds people rather than live-in. But there was something comforting about seeing familiar faces, being greeted warmly, having the same room every time he came here. The villa was home in a way neither of his family houses were.

A thought belatedly occurred to him. 'Where are you staying?' he asked. Tally had said something about feeling like a princess and Lucas had a sinking feeling he knew exactly what that meant. And of course it did. This was the twenty-first century. It would be seen as odd not to put a couple, however short their relationship, into the same room.

'The turret, can you believe it? It's just incredible, the views and so beautiful. And of *course* you have seen it.' One of the things he liked about Tally was how quick she was on the uptake. 'It's *your* room, isn't it? That makes sense. I can't believe we didn't discuss the whole sleeping arrangement part.'

'The sofas in the turret sitting room are very comfortable,' he said hurriedly.

'I'll take them. I can't turn you out of your bed. I'll just say your snoring drove me away.'

Her smile was low and intimate and stirred something deep inside him. It was hard not to imagine her in his bed, a mass of chestnut hair spread over the pillow, the sheet revealing more than it concealed, that particular wicked smile curving her full lips and... *Good God*, he needed a cold shower. And how was he supposed to get any sleep with that image in his head?

'No, you're my guest. I'll take the sofa,' he said brusquely. 'Can you find your own way there? I want to make sure Roberto gets to his room okay.'

Tally glanced over at their host. 'He's been on really good form all evening, but he does look tired now. I hope I didn't overdo it.'

'No, no, I think he's had a lovely evening, the two of you had so much to talk about...' He hesitated, not sure whether the lively conversation had been part of her persona. That, in some way, would feel worse than pretending they were together. To let Roberto feel he had found a kindred spirit but all along it was fake, but to his relief she nodded in agreement.

'He's such a theatre buff. Some of the things he has seen are, like, totally legendary. I'm in awe.'

'In awe of what?'

He hadn't heard Roberto walk up behind them and he turned, glad the conversation was so innocuous. This double life was exhausting. He didn't mind a certain subterfuge in business, it was par for the course, but his personal life had always been straightforward. After untangling the mess of his father's affairs and dealing with the fallout of his mother's emotional messes, the last thing Lucas had ever wanted was a complicated love life of his own, real or fictional.

'Your life,' Tally said with a warm smile. 'You should write a book; I don't suppose you kept a diary? The things and people you have seen, I'd read it.'

'Sadly not, and even if I did, I am not sure it would be much use. Probably a detailed account of what I ate, a briefer account of my day at work and, as a footnote, *I saw Laurence Olivier as Mark Antony. Not bad.*'

They all laughed but Lucas eyed Roberto with some concern. He was sallow rather than his usual olive, his eyes tired. Losing his father had been one thing, losing Roberto would be quite another.

'Let me walk you to your room,' he said, taking Roberto's arm.

'No, no, I can't allow you to neglect your lovely companion.'

'Not at all,' Tally said, dropping a kiss on Roberto's cheek as if she had known him for ever. 'It means I can get to the bathroom first, he's a terrible shower-hogger.' She winked at them and walked away, leaving both men looking after her appreciatively.

'I like her, Lucas.' As one they turned and walked slowly back into the villa, the older man leaning on the younger man's arm. 'She is fun, which you need, always so serious, but intelligent too, witty. I know I made no secret of my hopes for you and my Bella, the dreams of a foolish old man, but Bella needs an attentive man and you need a woman who will stop you brooding and working too hard. I like this Tally. I like her for you.'

'It's early days,' Lucas said, a little uncomfortable. One evening in and his plan was going better than he had expected but he didn't want Roberto to get too invested in Tally, not when she would be gone at the end of the summer, if not before. And if Roberto had already realised that Isabella and Lucas were not right for each other, had he needed to bring Tally along at all? By trying to do the right thing, had he just made everything far more complicated?

It was only one week. How invested could Roberto really get? But as his mind replayed the memory of Tally leaning towards him in the car, his cheek heating where she had touched him, he realised that maybe it wasn't Roberto he needed to worry about. If he wasn't careful, Lucas might be in danger too.

CHAPTER SIX

TALLY WOKE UP feeling as if she hadn't slept at all. It wasn't the fault of the bed, which was comfortable to a fault. The sun had risen early but the blinds did a good job of keeping the room cool and dark, and although they had eaten late, she had trained her digestion to manage that, used to post theatre meals and late suppers after evening pub shifts.

But her sleep had been fitful, her dreams vivid, full of trains and fear and intense blue eyes, dreams of weddings and standing in front of Max in a gold foil eighties-style bridesmaid's dress, while Isabella pouted on his arm and Lucas ignored her on the other side of the room. But worse had been the moments when she'd lain there awake, reliving the moment Lucas slipped out of the bathroom. Her light was off and she had pretended, for both their sakes, to be asleep. It felt a lot less awkward. But she had still been aware every moment he was in there, had heard the sound of the shower and had to work very hard not to imagine him under it. Had to work even harder not to relive the moment he left the bathroom, towel around a narrow waist, dark hair slicked back. She had been right, there was a very fine body under those suits, lean and muscled in all the right places, strong and capable...

Maybe this was a good thing. She was supposed to be attracted to him after all. Actually *being* attracted could only enhance her performance. And she hadn't fancied anyone since Max. This buzzing in her skin, heaviness in her belly, was a sign she was ready to get back out there.

She just needed to get through the next few weeks maintaining professional boundaries whilst playing the exact opposite. No big deal.

She hadn't heard Lucas get up, nor heard him come upstairs to use the bathroom, but when she got downstairs, showered and ready for the day in crisp red linen shorts paired with a sleeveless buttoned-up white shirt decorated with a red and blue nautical pattern, a red scarf taming her unruly waves and her sunglasses in her hand, she could see that he was long up and gone, the sheets from the sofa tidied away as if they had never been, his suitcases neatly to one side. One thing she needed to do was make it look a little more like they were cohabiting. But not until after coffee.

Breakfast was set up on the terrace where they had eaten last night. Lucas was already there, tapping away intently on his laptop, a slight frown pinching his forehead. Tally realised that she could probably count on one hand the number of times she had seen him smile, which was a shame, he was quite devastating when he did. Although he wasn't exactly unattractive now, shirt sleeves rolled up to show those really very capable-looking wrists, his nice tanned forearms, his equally capable fingers typing precisely, easily, not too fast and not too slow, and really, Tally, what on *earth* was she doing getting turned on by a man typing?

That was it, the final straw. Her libido was back and as soon as she had shown off her very handsome successful new beau to Max, she was going out and finding the perfect post-relationship relationship. Nothing too serious, something frivolous, a treat. Although it was a shame in some ways to squander the opportunity she had right here. Lucas wasn't frivolous, he was usually serious, but he was *definitely* a treat. He looked up and she half jumped, sure he could read her very inappropriate mind.

'Are you going to stand there and stare or are you going to join me?'

The table was set with a cheerful red cloth and held a basket of fresh-looking bread, a dish of olive oil, a selection of cheeses and hams, honeys and jams as well as delicious plates of fruit and a bowl of yogurt.

'I didn't want to disturb you, you looked so busy. Are you ever not working?' she added as she pulled a chair out and collapsed into it.

'Not really. Coffee?' She nodded and he poured some steaming coffee from a jug and passed it to her, followed by a milk jug. 'There's a lot to do.'

'But you must have other people who can take on some of the load. What about your brother?'

'Felix is a people person. He's invaluable for schmoozing, PR, that kind of thing. Really, it should have been him on the Orient Express not me, but he had been ill, which was why I stepped in.'

'Lucky for me,' she murmured, not really intending to be overheard, but he nodded.

'Lucky for both of us.'

'Although—' she lowered her voice although she couldn't see anyone within hearing distance '—Isabella certainly wasn't pleased to see me, I didn't get any hands-off-my-man vibes. I reckon you're safe from that direction at least.'

'Isabella was never the real issue, I knew I could handle her, it was more about not upsetting Roberto, but from something he said last night, I get the impression he knows that his dreams for Isabella and me are just that, that we wouldn't really suit. I think I have you to thank for that. He liked you a lot.'

'Me?' Tally felt absurdly touched. She had really enjoyed her conversation with their host the night before, it was nice to know the feeling was mutual. 'I doubt it. It was one evening, he barely knows me.'

'Ah, but he has always claimed to have good instincts.'

'Why, Mr West, are you complimenting me?'

His expression didn't change but his eyes were warm, and Tally grabbed her coffee, flustered.

Lucas returned his attention to his laptop while Tally concentrated on the excellent coffee and contemplated the array of food, quickly scrolling through her emails and messages as she did so. There was nothing in her email folder apart from offers for clothes she couldn't afford, restaurants she used to go to with Max and holidays she could only dream about. Nothing from her agent. She was used to the pang of disappointment, had lived with it for eight years, but it never seemed to lessen somehow. Indeed, since losing out on her last role it seemed worse somehow, as if her last chance had slipped by without her noticing it.

The group chats on the other side were predictably busy. She had messages in the hen night chat, the bridesmaids' chat, the one set up with her drama school friends, the never dull pub regulars' stream of nonsense, but she scrolled through them quickly, simply replying with a heart or other appropriate emoji.

Her mother had taken her decision to stay in Italy for a week with a surprising lack of questions, but Tally suspected Charlene was sick of her daughter moping around the flat and that she and Steve were glad of a few days' privacy. For people who had been married for twenty-five years, they could be horribly prone to PDAs. In fact, now she came to think of it, far more so than she and Max had ever been, even in the privacy of their own home.

Her reverie was broken by Roberto, who walked out apologising for his lateness and hoping they had all they needed. Even Lucas pushed his laptop away long enough to assure Roberto that they were fine and the last thing he needed to do was worry.

'I was hoping to show you this beautiful region,' Roberto told Tally as he slowly lowered himself into a seat, Elena hovering behind him, clearly wanting to help but aware he would wave her off, irritated. 'But I find I am a little fatigued today.'

Lucas was instantly alert. 'You stayed up too late last night,' he scolded. 'Is having us here too much? We can go and stay elsewhere…'

'Not at all.' Roberto laid a hand on his arm. 'I am very glad you are here and that I get to spend time with

Tally, but today I listen to my doctor and rest.' He pulled a face that made it clear how little he liked that idea. 'But you two must go out and explore.'

Tally didn't need to be a mind-reader to decipher Lucas's expression. 'Lucas has work to do, but I can entertain myself very well. I'm sure there are lovely walks around here.'

'You can borrow my car,' Lucas said, clearly relieved, but Tally shook her head.

'I don't drive. Born and bred Londoner. There's a bus every five minutes. But I'm very self-sufficient, promise. I'll be fine.' A vineyard, beautiful scenery, a tempting-looking pool. She was sure she would manage.

'Absolutely not,' Roberto said. 'Lucas can take a day off every now and then. Maybe even two. Visit Siena, Lucca, San Gimignano. Go on a wine-tasting tour or two, I can arrange that for you, and then when I have more energy we will go to Florence and I will take you to my favourite restaurant. What do you think?'

'It all sounds *amazing*,' Tally said, trying not to sound too eager and put Lucas on the spot. 'But honestly, I was an unexpected last-minute guest and no one needs to put themselves out for me.'

Her arguments were fruitless. Roberto had it all planned out and unless they wanted to upset an elderly man, they had no choice but to agree.

'I meant it, you really don't have to worry about me,' she said to Lucas as they walked back to their turret. 'Just drop me off somewhere and you can come back here while I explore. I don't mind.'

'And upset Roberto? Impossible. Besides, he was right. Maybe I *can* take a day off.'

Tally stopped and whirled around to face him. 'You can what? Do you want to say that again for the camera?' She pulled out her phone and held it teasingly up as if recording, laughing at his exasperated expression.

'It's not that big a deal, I do take time off occasionally,' he said, but she could have sworn his mouth was twitching with a rare smile.

'Well, I'm honoured one of these rare times is with me. Okay, let me get a few things together. I'll meet you back down here.'

She skipped off to her room trying to quell the excitement in her stomach. It was just a day sightseeing, not a declaration. But Tally couldn't help feeling that workaholic Lucas willingly choosing to spend time with her over work was a very good sign indeed.

Tally's *few things* included a bag with a change of shoes, a cardigan and scarf, two different types of suntan lotion, water bottles, a hat and some snacks as well as a battery pack and a book. Lucas had changed into shorts and a short-sleeved shirt and was ready long before she was but, to his surprise, he wasn't irritated by her absent-minded packing and her several rememberings of *just one more thing* before they were finally on their way.

Nor did he mind the loss of a day as much as he'd thought he would. How could he when the sun shone, the landscape was idyllic and his companion clearly ready to enjoy the experience? Besides, he didn't need to lose the whole day. There would be plenty of places he could work while Tally went sightseeing.

'I've always wanted to visit Italy,' she confided as he drove round sweeping curves, the hills and vineyards unfolding in front of them. 'I can't believe I'm here at last.'

'All of Italy or any particular part?'

'All of it from Sicily to the Dolomites. I think it's always felt like the ultimate in sophistication, you know, all those Regency youths on their grand tours and Edwardians in Florence.'

'Why didn't you visit before?'

'That's a very good question. We didn't really do holidays when I was young. We were too poor before Mum married Steve and then afterwards there was the pub. He didn't like leaving it, especially in school holidays because they were the busiest times. Now I can usually take over so they can get away, but back then we were lucky to get a weekend in Margate and that was before the hipsters moved in. Layla and I went on a couple of holidays, but that was more *"lads, lads, lads"*, you know? Cheap, and as cheerful as too many shots could make it and devoid of any culture whatsoever.' She laughed. 'Fun, though.'

'And what about with your ex? Max, isn't it?' He could feel his jaw tighten just saying his name.

Tally bit her lip. 'Max is very outdoorsy. His idea of a perfect holiday is carrying all your clothes on your back and walking from one remote spot to another or taking a very small boat onto a very large body of water or dangling off a cliff face on a rope, those kinds of things. And he had a lot more money than me, so he tended to go away with his friends.'

'You never holidayed together?' Lucas wasn't sure why he sounded so horrified. After all, he'd never been the romantic holiday type himself.

'Oh, we did, but not the kind of exploring culture with added sunshine holidays I wanted, more short breaks or holidays where he could do his thing. A house by the sea with friends, a hotel in the Lake District, that sort of thing. It was nice, but very much on his terms. Plus...' She shifted, and when he glanced over at her, he could see that she was gazing out of the window, her oversized sunglasses shielding her expression.

'Plus what?'

'Oh, it was just another battle in the war of our relationship. That I couldn't just take time off like anyone else, but might get work with short notice, or when I did get a job, a play for instance, then I was all in for however long it was. We couldn't plan anything, and he got tired of the disparity of income as well. Said I was holding him back.'

'He sounds like a prince.'

'I thought he was, once. Anyway, what about you? You actually *lived* in Italy, you lucky thing.'

'In Milan from eighteen to twenty.'

'Formative years. Have you travelled much?'

'All over. The US of course, Australia, a lot of Europe, China, Vietnam and Thailand, India.'

'Oh, my goodness, I feel very parochial now. Were you backpacking? What was your favourite country and why?'

It was his turn to shift uncomfortably. 'The thing is, they were all business.'

'*All* business?'

'Capital cities and business hotels and trips to factories and headquarters, fancy restaurants and boardrooms.'

'No sightseeing?'

'There wasn't really time.'

'How sad.' She said the words as if she really meant them, as if she was sorry for him. This unemployed actress who had hardly ever set foot outside her own country's capital city was sorry for *him*.

'Sightseeing always felt too frivolous, you know? There was always so much to do.' Why was he trying to explain and who was he trying to convince? Himself or her?

'So, no *"lads, lads, lads"* trips to Magaluf? No romantic strolls by the Seine with someone special?'

'By the time I was twenty my friends had stopped inviting me along on holiday. Our lives were so different. They were at university, barely responsible for themselves, but I was responsible for hundreds of jobs.' His voice trailed off. He hadn't meant to set himself so far from his peers, to lose touch with people he had known all of his life, but the chasm between their lives had been too great. He too serious, they too immature. Nothing in common any more apart from a shared education and the memories of his last carefree months and years before he had been catapulted into an adulthood some were only just now achieving.

'Okay, well, that's it. I am a barely travelled ignoramus and you are a well-travelled ignoramus so today I vote we sightsee like the tourists we don't know how to be. Deal?'

Lucas's hands tightened on the wheel as he thought about his never shrinking inbox, the decisions that had to be made, the disputes to solve, budgets to approve, marketing plans to interrogate, a merger to complete.

The Vineyard takeover was at a delicate stage, four shareholders had agreed to consider selling but none had yet signed, despite promises in Venice. He had thought today might consist of dropping Tally off in various towns while he took himself off to the nicest hotels to work until she needed a lift to the next destination. That he might join her for lunch, maybe a walk at the most.

That was what he *should* do. But it wasn't what he *wanted* to do. He wanted to explore small towns and hidden alleyways and medieval churches and see them through Tally's eyes, eat lunch in a cobbled square and watch the world go by. If she could find beauty and romance in an unremarkable Venetian backstreet, what would she see in Siena?

'Okay.' The words were out before he could stop them. 'We sightsee.'

It wasn't the first time Lucas had been to Siena, or Lucca or San Gimignano, but his earlier visits had been for specific purposes, for a meal with Roberto, or to collect him from a meeting or party. He had never before taken the time to really see the charming old towns, take in the stunning backdrops, beautiful architecture and preserved historic charm of these Tuscan jewels he'd previously taken for granted. But there was no taking for granted with Tally, who saw an adventure in every alleyway, a perfect view at every stopping point, a story in every shuttered house.

'How did Shakespeare conjure up these kinds of scenes when he had never travelled here?' she asked as she gazed at the fan-shaped central Sienese square. 'I know this isn't Verona, but you can just see the Montagues and Capulets stalking around on these cobbles, swords at the ready, eyeing each other and waiting for the other to break, can't you? Juliet behind shutters in a walled garden like that one over there.' She whirled around, clearly seeing the scene play out before her.

'I bet you are a brilliant Juliet.' He could envision her, impassioned and yearning, hair streaming down as she stood on a balcony, and what on *earth* was wrong with him? He had never been given to such flights of fancy before.

'I was always too tall for Juliet. I was usually the nurse, sometimes Lady Capulet. But it didn't stop me dreaming, learning the part in the hope I might get a sudden change of role. She speaks some of the most beautiful poetry ever written, don't you think?'

'I don't know.' Once again, he felt at a loss, uncultured.

'*"My bounty is as boundless as the sea, my love as deep; the more I give to thee, the more I have, for both are infinite."* You know,' she said a little wistfully, 'sometimes I quite make my mind up to give it up, find my plan B. Not because I'm thirty or because my idiot of an ex wanted me to, but because I've had enough of the rejection and the uncertainty and the constant desire to be doing rather than trying to do. Choose a plan B while I'm young enough to have a choice, to be able to progress in some sort of career. But then I stand somewhere like this and speak words that are five hundred years old and I know there is nothing else I'd rather do.'

'Does your mum miss it?'

'Not the very brief flash of fame, no, although I think the early part of it was fun. But to her the pub is the stage where each of us play our part, sometimes scripted. She puts on a pantomime every Christmas, and a Shakespeare festival every May—you might have heard of it? Shakespeare and a Pint? It's pretty popular. And of course she's queen of the karaoke machine. She told me that she'd made a conscious choice, that she chose me and stability and Steve and that she regrets nothing, but you should see the way she comes alive, even in the backroom of a Chelsea pub on a makeshift stage, so I don't know if she's saying what she wishes was true rather than how she really feels.'

'You said you never see your father?'

'I've never met him and as far as I know he's never met me or shown any desire to see me. He has a very different life, made his own conscious choice. I could be angry or sad or have unresolved daddy issues and who knows, maybe I do, but my choice is to move forward with my life and to remember it's his loss. Steve has been the constant presence in my life. He adores my mother, he loves me, he's still housing me at my advanced age. I can't ask for more than that.'

'There's a lot to be said for constancy.'

'It's a bit of an unsung virtue, isn't it? Sounds a little unfashionable in a hectic twenty-four-seven social-media-obsessed world full of reality TV shows, but I agree. There's a lot to be said for it. Now, if I could just have a constant career, I would be happy.' She laughed but the wistfulness he had noted was still lurking in her eyes.

'Come on,' he said, not sure why but knowing he wanted to see her smile. 'I don't know about you but I'm hungry and Roberto has recommended an excellent restaurant somewhere near here.'

Lucas had no idea how it happened but that day set

a pattern for the next few days. He rose early, worked through his outstanding emails and sent a message to Candace to rearrange his diary. Then, after breakfast, he and Tally set out on a sightseeing journey that took them into Florence for a hot crowded morning of sightseeing before Roberto joined them for a long lunch, for shady walks through leafy woods and several visits to vineyards, all with the beautiful Tuscan hills as a backdrop. Lucas didn't know when he had last been so relaxed. So entertained. So attracted. Tally was a ray of sunshine, usually vibrantly dressed, her mass of chestnut curls tumbling around her shoulders or held back with a colourful scarf, taking in every sight with an enthusiasm that was as welcome as it was novel.

The evenings were usually spent back at the villa for long dinners with Roberto, who was beginning to look a little better if still frail. They saw very little of Isabella, who apparently was enjoying a budding romance with a film director who had a villa close by. She arrived back late one evening, dark eyes bright with news.

'Sam is having a party this weekend for the cast of his new film and we are all invited.'

'Sam?' Tally asked.

'Sam Abraham.' Her tone clearly meant *Keep up*, but one of the many things Lucas was increasingly beginning to like about Tally was how little notice she took of Isabella's snubs.

'*That's* who you are seeing?' Tally's eyes widened. '*The* Sam Abraham? But he's a legendary director. I've seen his *Romeo and Juliet* more times than I can count, *The Draft* is seen as the ultimate Vietnam movie when everyone thought there was nothing else to say, and as for his adaptation of *Tess*…' Her voice tailed off and she sat, wine untouched, gazing reverently into the distance, occasionally murmuring phrases that might or might not have been names of films.

'You'll have to excuse me,' Roberto said. 'Once I would have been the last to leave but I think I have enjoyed my last Hollywood party.'

'If I had been invited by Laurence Olivier and Vivien Leigh to dinner, I would have no regrets either.' Tally smiled at him. 'But how exciting! Sam Abraham! He's a genius, and he always has the most interesting casts.'

'But surely you attend things like this all the time,' Isabella said, clearly surprised by Tally's excitement. 'You are an actress, after all.'

'If you mean have I been to the first night celebration and wrap party after a three-month tour of *The Importance of Being Earnest* or some other classic through small towns and theatres across the UK more times than I can remember? Then yes. But have I been to the Tuscan villa of one of Hollywood's most respected directors? Then no. But of course, we will stay here with you, Roberto, if you can't go. Maybe next time I get such an opportunity I'll be cast, not the guest of a neighbour.'

She laughed, but Lucas could see the yearning in her eyes. Of *course* she wanted to go. It would be like him turning down the opportunity to meet an investor or a brand he wanted to align with. She'd said she wasn't ready to give up on her dream and here was an opportunity to meet some really influential people.

Personally, Lucas could think of nothing worse. But this wasn't about what he wanted. 'I'm sure Roberto will enjoy an evening to himself for once.'

His friend looked up with an understanding nod. 'Of course, there's a book I would like to finish. You young ones go and come back with all the gossip before I tell you about all the film stars I met in my youth and you will have no choice but to indulge an old man.'

'No indulging necessary.' Tally met Lucas's gaze and he knew that she was aware that he had agreed to go for her. 'We love your stories. And thank you, Isabella. I'd love to go.'

What was happening? Not only had he willingly spent days sightseeing rather than working but now he was agreeing to go to the kind of event he would usually avoid. Of course, it was important to Tally, a potential boost to her career, and he owed her thanks for the way she cajoled and indulged Roberto. But it wasn't just for that reason; if Lucas was being honest with himself, he liked to see Tally smile. To be the cause of that smile. And he had no intention of thinking about why.

CHAPTER SEVEN

THIS WASN'T TALLY'S first industry party. Okay, the couple she had attended she had been a waitress, hoping for a fairy tale moment where she caught the eye of someone powerful, was beckoned over and had her life transformed. And, to be fair, it had kind of happened, not the life transformation part but the beckoned over bit, not because they wanted to offer her a screen test but because they wanted another canapé.

But this was different. This time she was going as a guest and on the arm of someone who was a success in his own right. Tally hadn't realised, back on the Orient Express, just how much of a success. Hadn't realised that Lucas West headed up WGO, once West Gentleman's Outfitters, fifteen years ago, as he had said, the kind of brand found in the back pages of a Sunday supplement, but now the first choice for fashion-forward people with money to spend.

Lucas had mentioned that his father had left WGO on its knees and he had stepped in but Roberto had filled in the gaps, clearly bursting with pride for Lucas's achievements. It was Roberto who'd told her how Lucas was responsible for turning the brand around, expanding it. That WGO still wove much of the wool used for its signature suits in factories founded two centuries before. That Lucas had bought up other brands and other factories around the world to own a portfolio she could barely comprehend. That his designers and higher end brands had outfitted several films and plays, that stylists dressed award nominees in his clothes, that their invitation to the party tonight was as much down to Lucas's presence in Tuscany as it was to Isabella's ongoing flirtation.

It should have made her nervous, but instead it gave her a surprising strength. She didn't have to wow anyone, have a pitch ready, she could just be herself. Or at least the version of herself currently posing as the girlfriend of a successful and handsome man.

Tally had been grateful that she had given in to Lucas's insistence that she purchase outfits for all occasions including formal ones, otherwise she would have had to resort to the flapper dress she had worn on the train. Instead, she sashayed down the stairs in a red silk halter neck dress. The long skirt swished satisfyingly around her calves but her back was completely bare. She'd pulled her hair up into a messy bun, tendrils falling around her face, and matched her lipstick to the dress, emphasising her eyes with smudged kohl and lashings of mascara. Long delicate gold earrings, a cluster of bangles and a pair of high heeled sandals completed the outfit and the look in Lucas's eyes told her that whatever it was she had wanted to achieve, she had managed it.

'You look…' He stopped.

'Presentable, I hope. Tall?' That was what Max would have said the second he clocked her shoes.

'I was going to say beautiful,' he said softly, and the connection Tally was always aware of tugged deeper, harder, electricity zinging through her as she took his arm. Sometimes she could have sworn he felt it too. There was something about his hooded unsmiling gaze, an intensity that took her breath away. She was conscious of a satisfaction in how he sometimes forgot himself and relaxed with her—the pleasure she took in making him smile, in seeing that blue gaze warm with approval. But he had never acted on that warmth and although she routinely took his hand, touched his shoulder, slid an arm around him when they were with Roberto, she maintained a physical distance at all other times. Their budding friendship was complicated enough without adding sex into the equation. He might not even *want* to sleep with her and the last thing they needed was that particular awkwardness.

Although she was pretty sure that he was attracted to her in turn. But whatever held him back was his business.

Roberto had arranged for a driver to take them to the party and so, after promising to return with many stories and tales and to enjoy herself, Tally slid into the back seat, Lucas joining her. Isabella was already there, no doubt cementing her role as hostess.

'Do you regret asking me to stay?' she asked as the car pulled away and headed down the drive. 'I'm not saying that you were imagining things, but it looks to me like Isabella is quite capable of sorting her own love life out without any help from her grandfather.'

'Oh, she's more than capable, and Roberto knows that. He just worries. His health, as you see, is not good and if we were both single he wouldn't be able to help playing matchmaker. Just look at the way he keeps organising days out for *us*. Yes, with hindsight, it was an unnecessary precaution but—' his voice lowered, as if he were speaking to himself '—but no. I don't regret it.'

'Not even after four nights of sleeping on the sofa?' she teased. 'I'm more than willing to take my turn, you know.'

At that moment the car turned in at a pair of gates even more ornate than Roberto's. Their destination lay straight ahead, a modern villa, all white and glass and undeniably impressive, but it looked as if it would be more at home in the Hollywood hills than in this ancient setting. Tally felt the first rumble of nerves as the car drew up.

'Okay,' she said, more to herself than Lucas. 'The film is a play within a play, a group of actors putting on *Much Ado About Nothing* with real-life events mirroring those in the book. Real-life couple Xavier Pavez and Sabrina Rossi are Beatrice and Benedict, ingenue of the moment Natalia Bennett is Hero, and teen heartthrob Ethan Jones is Claudio. I don't know the rest of the cast, they haven't been announced yet, but we can expect stars with a capital S.'

'Which one is *Much Ado*? The one where they get lost in the woods?'

Tally turned to Lucas, convinced he must be teasing her, but he was completely straight-faced. '"The one where they get lost in the woods"? That's *A Midsummer Night's Dream*.'

'Right, so what's this about?'

'This is the one where the protagonists hate each other and are tricked into thinking the other one is in love with them by their friends. There's a secondary love story between Hero and Claudio and a villain, Don John. And you know all that—you're just trying to make me relax,' she finished indignantly. 'I *was* relaxed right until the moment we pulled up and I realised that there are people in there who could reset my career with just a wave of their hand. I mean, I know that's not why I'm here, but you would be the same if at Layla's wedding there was an amazing new young designer you wanted to sign. Maybe you wouldn't. Other way round. What would make you feel like your life was about to change?'

'My life changed irrevocably when I was eighteen. Everything I thought I knew about who I was and where I was going disappeared the moment I realised the extent of my father's debts, his neglect. I'll settle for safe, sensible growth rather than life-changing moments.'

'No one turned things round the way you did by being safe and sensible, but point taken. Okay, let's do this.' She slid out of the car, so many butterflies fluttering in her stomach she was convinced there must be an undiscovered species in there.

Inside was as breathtaking as the outside, the villa built around a huge courtyard in which the party was being held. A bar was set out on one side, a long table heaped with delicious-looking food, along another, delicate lights giving the whole a fairy tale quality, as did the beautiful people in beautiful clothes gathered in pairs and small groups, lounging on sofas, under flower-filled arches, grouped on the side of the large fountain which dominated the middle of the space. A string quartet provided the backdrop and Tally hid a smile when she realised that they were playing a medley of theme tunes from Sam Abraham's most famous films.

You could take the director out of Hollywood…

They had been shown the way by a silent uniformed

maid who handed them each a glass of champagne before gliding away. Tally took a deep breath and suppressed the urge to press in close to Lucas. He didn't seem intimidated or nervous. His rather aloof air made him seem right at home whereas she would have been much more comfortable serving the champagne rather than drinking it.

Come on, Tally, you have every right to be here, she told herself, making herself stand tall and inhabit every centimetre of her five-foot-ten-plus-heels body.

It was strange to think if she had got the fantasy franchise part, everyone here would know who she was, there would have been a distinctive buzz when she'd entered rather than indifference.

But then again, if she had got the fantasy part, she wouldn't be here at all, she would be in Croatia, would never have met Lucas.

'Lucas, great you could make it.'

The thickset burnished man strolling up to them, Isabella on his arm, was unmistakable, imbued with the mix of arrogance, shrewdness and charisma that signalled an award winning and successful director. 'Looking sharp as usual.'

'Sam, thank you for the invite,' Lucas said easily.

'I understand you and Isabella are old friends,' the director continued.

'Old family friends.' He slipped an arm around Tally. 'This is Tally Jenkins.'

Tally took a deep breath, quelling her still jumping nerves. 'Thank you for inviting us, you have a beautiful home.'

'Thank you. What do you do, Tally? Are you in the

fashion business as well?' Sam's assessing stare swept her up and down, not in a sexual way but in the way of a man used to ordering bodies around on camera.

Tally took a deep breath. He might meet hundreds of aspiring actresses every week, there was no need for him to remember her after today, but this was an opportunity and she would be a fool to squander it.

'Actually, I'm an…'

And then she froze as a man came into sight. Early fifties, he looked a decade younger, although whether that was thanks to good genes or good work she didn't know. Her mother said good work, but then again, she would. Dark hair, with just a few flecks of grey, swept back from his temples, high cheekbones framing a famously sensuous mouth. Eyes the same golden brown as Tally's rested on Tally with no hint of recognition.

Indignation smouldered then flamed into anger.

He didn't even recognise her.

'I'm an actress,' she said, shoulders back, pushing any diffidence from her voice. 'But you won't have seen me in anything unless you have a particular interest in detergent commercials and the first five minutes of crime dramas. I didn't intend to make the first victim my speciality, but everyone needs a gimmick and that seems to be mine.'

Sam laughed as Sebastian Fields drifted closer. 'I'll look out for those commercials. Ah, Seb, do you know Lucas West? WGO? I wore a West Original to the Oscars and found myself in the best dressed lists for the first time ever. The man is a genius.'

'I employ geniuses,' Lucas said. 'I can measure a man for a suit, cut it and sew it, Isabella's grandfather made sure of that, but any genius comes from the designers and tailors I employ.'

'But that's the key, not doing it all yourself but getting the best men in for the job. Like Seb here, it took some doing to get him to play against type as Don John, but here he is and the film will be that much the better for it.'

Tally was so wound up she was sure she was vibrating. Time seemed to have slowed down, the air thick, every colour too bright, every sound too loud. She felt too tall, too vibrant, too out of place. The only thing that felt safe was being by Lucas's side, and so she edged close, taking his arm. She could sense him giving her a confused glance, her grip maybe too tight, but to her relief, without pausing or questioning, he reached down and took her fingers in his. His grip was smooth and strong, anchoring her, bringing her back to the surface and she clung on.

'And this is… Tally, did you say? Tally, do you know Seb?'

'Only by reputation.' The air seemed to clear, time start again with a dazzling clarity, all noise fading out until it was just Tally and the man who had broken her mother's heart and left her to fend for herself and their child while he took off to start again the other side of the Atlantic. 'But I believe you know my mother. You used to act with her on *River Close*. Charlene Jenkins, although her Equity name was Charlie Jenkins. Do you remember her? She's told me a lot about you.'

Tally's comment seemed innocuous enough on the surface but there was a bitter edge to her tone, subtle enough that only someone who had spent the last few days listening to her would pick up on it, her gaze just a little too intent, her hand still gripping his, tight and trembling. Something was going on here, a subtext he was struggling to pick up on, until he realised the English actor had paled under his tan, that dawning recognition and horror mingled in brown eyes that mirrored Tally's own.

Mirrored Tally's own.

Conversations came back to him.

'The only thing you don't know that you should is about my father...'

A conversation yet to be had, the defiantly proud way she had mentioned that she had never even met her father, that her mother had ended up putting her acting career to one side, finding it impossible to juggle with single motherhood.

Sebastian Fields was Tally's father?

'Charlie?' Sebastian murmured. 'How is she?'

'She's fine. Better than fine. Great. She'll be fascinated to know I've run into you at last. I know she was hoping we would meet years ago.'

Tally's voice wobbled and Lucas knew she was close to breaking, to saying something she might later regret.

'Nice to meet you,' he said, squeezing Tally's hand reassuringly whilst making sure there was no warmth in his voice at all. 'Come on, Tally, let's get some food.' He steered her away from the entrance, and from the man staring after them, ashen, until he found a secluded corner with a comfortable-looking bench and deposited her on it.

'You okay?'

'I don't know.' She was shivering, eyes too bright,

cheeks pale but with feverish spots of colour. 'I have spent the last thirty years wondering what I would say to my father if I ever met him and then, when it came to it, I didn't even throw my drink in his face.'

'Plenty of time for that, but it would be a waste of good champagne.' He took her still full glass from her hand and set it on the small side table, then slipped off his jacket and draped it around her shoulders. 'Do you want to leave?'

'I... Part of me wants to. But I'm not the one who did anything wrong, why should I be the one who scuttles away?'

'Attagirl.'

She looked more like herself now, colour back in her cheeks, the unnatural brightness in her eyes replaced by her usual liveliness, her back straight, shoulders back, chin up.

She was magnificent. She didn't need his protection.

And yet he wanted to protect her, to take up arms in her defence, to call her sorry excuse for a father out in a duel and fight for her honour.

It was terrifying just how much he wanted to make her smile, to feel safe. He had never felt like this about another human being, Felix aside, before, not as an adult anyway, not since he had realised his parents' emotional problems weren't his to solve.

For the last fourteen years Lucas had had to have the answer to everything, but he didn't know what to do about this situation. So instead, he rose and held out his hand. After a moment she took it and he helped her to her feet.

'Come on,' he said. 'Let's show everyone just what a brilliant actress you are.'

The next couple of hours passed quickly. No one who didn't know Tally would have guessed at the emotional shock she must still be experiencing as she laughed, made small talk and entertained a circle of A-listers with stories of her life on the fringes of the audition circuit. Sebastian Fields didn't come near her again but Lucas was aware he was watching her, his expression dark and a little melancholy.

Eventually, they made their thanks and exited to the waiting car. Once she was buckled in Tally fell silent, almost unnaturally so. There was nothing Lucas could say. He instinctively knew she needed time to process what had just happened. But after a long minute he reached out and took her hand.

He had touched Tally many times. It had never felt natural, he'd always been aware that he was playing a part, never found it easy to rub her neck or shoulder, slip an arm around her waist, touch her cheek the way she so effortlessly did with him. It made sense, physical intimacy was part of the actors' toolkit but missing from his. But touch was something they reserved for others, to show they were together, part of the lie. They didn't touch in private. Yet taking her hand felt completely natural, necessary even. Her fingers were cold, lifeless, and he held them between his, massaging the tension away.

To his relief, Roberto had already retired for the night by the time they got back to the villa and so they headed straight to their turret suite, Lucas grabbing a bottle of red and two glasses from the kitchen along with half a loaf of bread, some olives and cheese.

'You barely ate,' he said, setting some on a plate and

putting them on the table before her, along with a generous glass of the wine. 'Here you go.'

Tally looked up from where she was huddled on the sofa. 'I don't think I...' But she didn't finish the sentence, her face crumpling as her eyes filled with tears.

'Hey, it's okay. That man is not worth crying over. You were brilliant.'

'I know,' she managed, but the effort of speaking the words only made her cry harder and before he knew it the sobs had turned deeper, more painful, as if they were being wrenched from her soul, and all he could do was sit next to her and pull her into his arms while she wept, murmuring words of comfort, he barely knew what, kissing the top of her head as she collapsed into him, her whole body shaking against his.

Finally, the weeping came to a shuddering stop and she pushed herself back, swiping at her face. 'I'm sorry...'

'I thought we had established you have nothing to apologise for?'

'That was before I went full-on meltdown.' She looked down at the damp patch on his front and winced. 'Your shirt.'

'My shirt can be laundered.' He picked up the glass and handed it to her.

'I just...' She stopped. Bit her lip.

'You don't owe me any explanation. You had a shock.'

'My mum was always really good about not bad-mouthing him in front of me. I mean, she didn't lie, pretend he missed me or would be here if he could or anything like that—she always said he didn't know me and that was a shame, but that if he did know me, he would love me.' She took in a shuddering breath. 'And then when I got older and could read between the lines, I worked out what an idiot he was for myself and told myself I didn't care. That I was better off without him.'

She took a sip of the wine he had given her. 'But at the back of my mind, I always hoped, you know? Hoped that one day he would seek me out and tell me he had always loved me, that he was sorry for not being there. I didn't want his money,' she said angrily, scrubbing at her still damp eyes. 'I'd see pictures online and in magazines. Couldn't help looking them up, even though each time it physically hurt to see him looking so happy. To see the villa in the Italian Lakes and the Hollywood mansion and his perfect wife and family at premieres, dressed in designer clothes and jewels and yes, it all looked nice, but that wasn't it. I just wanted… I wanted him to acknowledge me. To be proud of me. To count. I've spent my whole life feeling unfinished somehow, like part of me is missing, and it's not Mum's fault or Steve's because they are wonderful, but there's a voice who, in my darkest times, asks me what kind of person am I if my own father doesn't want to know me. Oh, God.' She half laughed. 'I really do have daddy issues. If this was a real relationship, now would be where you would run.'

'I'm not going anywhere.' The words were instinctive, from his soul.

Tally turned, looked into his face. 'I must look a mess. The mascara wasn't waterproof.'

'No,' he said hoarsely. 'You look beautiful.' And before he could think better of it, he took the wine glass from her hand, set it to one side and then dipped his head and kissed her.

She tasted of salt and wine and something indescribably honey-sweet, something uniquely her. Her mouth was soft and surprised and for one moment Lucas feared he had overstepped, taken advantage of her vulnerability. But before he could pull back, apologise, she melted into him, her mouth opening under his, her arms entwining around his neck, pulling him close. He shifted, pulling her closer so that she was half in his lap, caressing her neck, her exposed back, her hips, the line of her thigh, taking his time, getting to know her inch by inch, the silk of her dress cool under his touch, a startling contrast to the heat of her skin.

It was almost like being a teenager again, no rush to move to the next stage, no pulling of buttons or shedding of clothes, just holding each other, learning each other, tasting each other, torturously slow, every nerve on fire, as her hands traced the muscles in his back, tangled themselves in his hair, pulling him closer and closer until the tempo changed, sped up, heated up, a new urgency in their touches, their kisses. He half reluctantly broke the kiss, to explore the curve of her jawline, her tender throat, finding the sweet spot behind her ear, aware of her eyes half closed, her breath quickening, the silk under his hands now a barrier he was impatient to shift.

Tally placed her hands on his shoulders and pushed him slightly so there were a few cold inches between them and he stared at her, heavy-lidded.

'I don't know about you,' she said. 'But I'm ready for bed.'

CHAPTER EIGHT

THERE WERE PROBABLY a million reasons why this was a bad idea, but Tally didn't want to consider a single one of them. What she did want was to get up those stairs and get Lucas West naked. Her whole body was on fire, her breasts heavy, aching with the need to be touched, her mouth swollen with kisses, every erogenous zone standing up and begging for attention. And from what she had just experienced, that attention was worth begging for. Lucas West kissed like a dream, like kissing should be done as a goal in itself, not something to rush through on the way to the main course. And if that was the hors d'oeuvres she couldn't wait for the rest of the menu.

She waited, barely able to breathe. She had never seen Lucas so undone, his breath coming fast, his hair ruffled, his shirt half unbuttoned, his eyes heavy with lust. Lust for her. Tally smiled, relishing the power that lust gave her.

'I'm going up now,' she said. 'Don't make me wait too long. I need your help to get out of this dress.'

His eyes glittered and he was on his feet in one seamless movement. 'I'm right behind you.' Lucas's voice was so husky the words were practically a growl, vibrating through her.

It took every atom of self-possession she had left not to rush up the stairs but sashay, aware of the silk hugging her hips, the deliciously low dip at the back, her exposed skin. So her hair was a tangled mess, her eyes still red, her mascara smudged, this dress was seduction personified and Lucas was caught in its spell.

But that didn't stop him from reaching for her as soon as they were in the room, his clever fingers reaching for the tie at her neck, the zip at her waist, until the whole slithered down to pool at her feet, leaving her in just her lace thong and a pair of heels. His gaze sharpened, burned as he took a step full of intent towards her, silent and sleek and deadly, a blue-eyed panther and she his very willing prey.

'Not so fast.' Tally raised an eyebrow, wondering how her voice remained so steady when every part of her body was trembling with anticipation. 'One of us is overdressed and I don't think it's me.'

Lucas took his time looking her up and down, lingering on her breasts and the dip of her waist before coming to rest on the scanty black lace. A wolfish smile spread across his face. 'I wouldn't say that.' But he was already working at the buttons on his shirt, shrugging it off with languid ease, unbuttoning his trousers. Before she had time to take stock, to allow her greedy gaze to roam across the tanned, hard muscles of his chest, to follow that intriguing line of hair down his flat stomach, he was naked and stalking towards her, backing her towards the bed, which was at once too close and too far. She stopped as the back of her knees hit the side of the bed and he too halted, close but not touching.

'Are you sure?' he asked, low-voiced and serious. 'I know it's been an emotional evening...'

'I'm sure that I want you to stop talking and kiss me.'

Lucas's eyes glittered. 'Your wish is my command.'

Tally had no time to reply because his mouth had captured hers again with a new urgency as he swept her up and deposited her on the bed, his body covering hers, and then she was lost. Lost in the touch and the sighs and the moans and the sensations, in giving and taking and learning and wanting until they were finally joined and she had no idea where she ended and he began—all she knew was this moment.

Tally stretched out, aware that she was naked under the tangled sheets. Naked and alone, and all at once the events of the night before came flooding back. Her father, her meltdown, Lucas comforting her, Lucas kissing her. Lucas...

Her head was a little sore, no wonder with all that crying. Her eyes ached, her cheeks still taut with dried tears. But more than that, her mouth was swollen, her body still tingling with remembered kisses and caresses. Who knew that under that aloof expression and buttoned-up shirts lay such fire? She'd suspected it but the reality had been more than she had dreamed of. And she *had* dreamed of it. Lying up here in a bed made for two, knowing he was just a floor away, she had dreamed.

But now it was the morning after. Not that she had any regrets. At least she would *try* not to regret anything. It was just she wasn't sure she could cope with two rejections in twenty-four hours.

Her father had made no move to approach her after

that first introduction, hadn't even said goodbye. Not that she was going to dwell on him. He'd had his opportunity. Opportunities. Plenty of them.

The face that greeted her in the mirror was worse than she had expected and it took some time to restore herself to normality, spending far too long under the hot shower. Finally, she plaited her still damp hair and slipped on some denim shorts and a broderie anglaise vest top and steeled herself to see Lucas, trying not to catastrophise. He always rose early, she knew that, had always done several hours' work and gone for a run before she'd even stirred, and although she liked a lie-in, she wasn't exactly sleeping the day through.

But she was running late today, not surprising considering all the heightened emotions of the night before. That and how little sleep she had actually had. Her whole body heated at the thought. Look at her! Blushing like a fifteen-year-old seeing her crush at the school disco. She couldn't even tell anyone about it the way she would have then, analysing his every word, her every feeling, because as far as Layla knew, as far as anyone knew, she and Lucas were already together.

Sure enough, Lucas was hard at work when she steeled herself to walk out onto the terrace, but the look he gave her set her blushing all over again, stumbling as she reached the table and she saw his mouth curve into a wicked half smile.

'I trust you slept well?' was all he said.

'Uneventfully,' she returned sweetly and was rewarded by a rare low laugh as Roberto joined them, followed by his assistant bearing a huge bouquet of flowers.

'Tally, you must have made quite an impression on

someone last night,' he said as he greeted her with the usual double kiss. 'These arrived for you just now.'

Tally's breath hitched as she glanced at Lucas but he looked curious rather than anticipatory, one eyebrow raising as he took in the extravagant arrangement.

'Am I going to need to challenge someone to a duel?'

'I do hope so.' Her heart hammered as she plucked the card off the top and opened it, only to fling it down, mouth pursed.

'They're from Sebastian,' she said shortly. 'He wants to talk.'

'Sebastian? Sebastian Fields? Why is he sending you flowers? Oh, apologies.' Roberto patted her hand as he took the seat next to her. 'I didn't mean to pry.'

'No, you're not prying—besides, these flowers aren't exactly discreet, but it's not what you think.' She took a deep breath. 'Sebastian Fields is my father, but he has never acknowledged me. In fact, I had never even met him before last night. Obviously, I had no idea he would be there, or I wouldn't have gone.' But the anger and resentment she had harboured for so long had ebbed, lanced by the experiences of the night before, those long painful tears, the long, sweet lovemaking afterwards.

Roberto stilled. 'Your father? Oh, my poor child. Maybe *I* shall challenge him to a duel.'

'No duels necessary, honestly.'

'And he knew he had a daughter? He knew about you?'

'He knew,' she said grimly. 'He was a teen soap star alongside my mother. He headed out to LA to audition for various things and my mother was supposed to join him once the play she was doing finished, but he made excuse after excuse, persuading her not to come. The reality was he wanted to reinvent himself, start over, get rid of his teen heart-throb soap past, become a film star and, fair play to him, he succeeded where many didn't. Meanwhile, Mum realised that her constant nausea wasn't stage fright or breakup grief but that she was pregnant with me. By the time she knew for sure she was nearly five months along. Sebastian made it clear that if she kept me then she was on her own. He would pay maintenance as long as she didn't put him on the birth certificate or go to the press.'

Roberto muttered something in Italian that sounded like a long string of insults.

'Luckily, Mum had bought a small flat so she wasn't entirely destitute and Sebastian did send some money, but she found it impossible to get work after I was born. A washed-up single mother soap actress is great tabloid fodder but not star material. Eventually, she gave up on acting but by then she had met Steve. She married him and managed the pub alongside him while Sebastian became the world's biggest star. It hardly seems fair. Who knows what her life would have been if she hadn't had me?' Her voice trailed away.

'Your mother is the lucky one.' Roberto nodded at the flowers. 'It looks like Sebastian has finally come to that conclusion too.'

'Maybe.' But Tally couldn't shake the lingering guilt that came over her whenever she thought about all her mother had given up for her. Oh, Charlene Jenkins had never uttered one word of reproach, she was always quick to reassure Tally that if she had to do it all again she would change nothing—'*Except I would be the one to dump Seb's smug arse.'* Her ire was aimed at the price of childcare, the lack of support in theatres at that time for mothers, the tabloids who had enjoyed documenting her fall from grace from the nation's sweetheart to abandoned single mother, with constant speculation about Tally's father until, thankfully, they forgot all about her. One reservation her mother had had about Tally's decision to start acting was that if she had achieved any degree of fame then the whole saga might have been raked up again and the speculation about her father started again.

Maybe it was a good thing she hadn't got the fantasy role.

'What do you want to do?' Lucas asked. 'Do you want to meet with him? Hear what he has to say?'

'I don't know.' Tally stared down at the note, at the decisive handwriting, the scribbled number, the two words: *Call me.* 'I mean, I do get the reinventing yourself part. I don't like or agree with it, but I get it. But he's had thirty years since to get in touch. He's got married in that time, twice. He's had other children. I have siblings. But he never reached out, never expressed any curiosity about meeting me or knowing me or even seeing a photograph of me. If we hadn't bumped into each other yesterday he would never have reached out. You know, I sometimes make extra money working the kind of events he attends. If I had seen him while serving him champagne, would he have still wanted to talk, or was it the fact I was with someone worth knowing that raised his interest?'

'He's the only one that can answer that,' Lucas said. 'But you are the only one who knows if you are ready to hear what he has to say. If you're not ready we can go back to London today.'

'You don't need to cut your visit short because of me,' she protested guiltily.

'Lucas rarely manages more than three days before the need to work lures him back to London.' Roberto squeezed her hand. 'I feel very lucky to have had him this long and privileged to see you pry him away from his laptop for so long. I hope you know you are very welcome to stay for as long as you want, but if you need some distance between you and your father while you think about what to do next then Lucas is right. You should take that time, however long it is. You owe him nothing.'

'Maybe.'

Tally did want to go home, she realised. She wanted to see her mother, see Steve, have some equilibrium restored. She had always thought that if she saw her father she would hold him to account, fire questions at him as if he was in *The Apprentice* boardroom, but instead she had clammed up, retreated, cried. Did she want that reckoning or, now that the moment had happened, was she content to leave it and really, finally put him behind her?

At the same time, she was reluctant to leave. What had happened after the party last night was so new, so unexplored. Sex wasn't part of their agreement but she had no regrets about what they had done. But she had no idea what Lucas thought about it, about her. If they went back to London, to their own lives, with occasional plus-one moments, did that mean there would be no repeat of what had been the most mind-blowing lovemaking of her life? It seemed a shame not to see if lightning really did strike twice.

There were too many questions she was too emotion-ally wrung-out to find the answers to.

'You're right. It's time for me to go home,' she said finally.

She tried to read Lucas's expression but her passion-ate, open lover of the night before, her empathic com-panion of the evening, her only occasionally grumpy sightseeing companion had retreated behind his usual mask. And there was her answer. Last night was a one-off and that was probably a good thing. She had been promising herself a fun liaison, but Lucas wasn't the right person. He was too much in every way. Too suc-cessful, too rich, too handsome—just too damn much.

But how she wished he wasn't.

Tally managed some breakfast at Roberto's insistence before heading back to her room to pack. It didn't take long to get her stuff folded and put away, her suitcases neatly lined up. She was taking a lingering look around the room, at the gorgeous view, when she became aware of a presence, of Lucas standing there.

'Candace has booked your flight. A car will take you to the airport, she's emailing you all the details you need.'

'You're not coming?' She hated how needy she sounded.

'No. Is that okay?'

'Okay? Of course. Why wouldn't it be?'

It *was* okay, obviously it was. Expected even. So why did she feel so disappointed? It was ridiculous. Whatever last night was or wasn't, this had never been a co-de-pendency thing. They weren't *actually* together after all.

'But you're still coming? To Layla's wedding?'

'Of course. I promised. Send me all the details and I'll be there, making your ex so green he'll get cast in *Wicked*.'

'Good, that's good. Thank you.'

'Tally.'

There was something about the way he said her name that was hideously familiar. The tone was the one used for the talk. For the whole *Last night was great, I had fun, you are a great girl, it's not you, it's me, I'm just not looking for anything right now* talk. And although she was expecting it, she didn't want to hear it.

'Lucas, I want to thank you.' She jumped in before he could say another word. 'Last night I was emotional and a little tipsy and needy. Thank you. Thank you for looking after me, for turning something horrible into something really lovely. What we did was…it was fun, it was exactly what I needed. But it wasn't real, obviously. So do come to the wedding. I promise not to jump your bones.'

'I wouldn't mind if you did.' His mouth quirked into that little almost smile she was learning to really enjoy but there was relief in the depths of his blue eyes.

'I'm maid of honour. I'm not going to have the strength to do anything but sleep for twenty-four hours after the wedding. But seriously, thank you.'

'I should be the one thanking you. I had a really good time, Tally.'

'Me too.'

She should have felt low as the car took her away from the villa and towards Pisa and the airport. She was leaving behind any meaningful chance of getting to know her father and the sweetness and intimacy of last night, heading instead to the grim familiarity of a future with no job, no plan, no path, but she refused to let herself feel down. She had walked away with her dignity and her self-esteem intact and she had a hen night to plan, a career to continue chipping away at, and she had made her own decision to leave. That had to count for a lot.

She just needed the tingle on her still swollen mouth to subside, for the tender ache in her breasts, between her legs to ease, to stop wishing there could have been a rerun. She had a new wardrobe, had enjoyed a lovely few days in Italy at last and had experienced a night she would never forget. That was a hell of a lot more than she had had a week ago. So, no regrets, no matter how heavy her heart.

It was always jarring being back in London after a stay in Tuscany, the green replaced by grey, the sound of birds by traffic, the freshly prepared feasts by quickly grabbed meals, sandwiches on the move. Usually, Lucas was too busy with work to dwell on the juxtaposition, but this time was different. His house felt empty. His bed too large.

He'd done the right thing, or Tally had in the end. They had an arrangement; they didn't need to complicate things.

But he had enjoyed the complication. And now he missed it. Missed it a ridiculous amount seeing as he could count the number of days he had actually spent with Tally on one hand. Well, two, to be precise. Even including thumbs.

But there had been that one unforgettable night. He had been relieved when she'd pre-empted him and said continuing was a complication they could both do without. Relieved and disappointed. Who wouldn't be disappointed when he could still smell her on his skin, feel her soft skin under his fingertips, the taste of her lingering on his mouth, that honey sweetness with a hint of spice? Was it cowardice or common sense that had meant he'd let her walk away? Lucas wasn't sure he wanted an honest answer to that question.

So, it was obviously a *complete* coincidence that his walk was taking him up and down the streets off the King's Road, trying to see if any of the pubs seemed familiar.

The Dog and Duck? No, that didn't sound right.

The Moon and Sixpence? It looked tempting, promising a courtyard beer garden and homemade tapas, but that didn't sound right either.

How had he never noticed how many pubs there were in Chelsea before? Finding Tally felt like one of those impossible tasks princes were set in myths and fairy tales if they wanted to win the princess's hand. Not that he wanted to win anyone's hand. He just wanted to make sure she was okay. Of course he *could* message her—he had messaged her—but her breezy 'Fine' had told him nothing.

His wrist buzzed, his watch alerting him of an incoming message.

Where are you?

Felix.

Taking a walk, why?

I went into the office and you weren't there. I know you're not abroad so I panicked. It's unprecedented.

Felix, it's Saturday afternoon.

Exactly. Unprecedented. What are you doing on this walk?

Thinking about a pint.

Now, why had he admitted that?

Ah! Say no more. I need to meet this mysterious girl of yours at some point. Roberto says you're smitten.

I'm not smitten.

I have many questions and you can't avoid me forever, big brother.

Lucas shoved his phone back into his pocket, unwilling to carry on the conversation. His brother was being overdramatic as usual. He wasn't *avoiding* Felix, not exactly, he just happened not to have been in the same city as him until today. He'd stayed on in Tuscany for a few more days before travelling to Boston to catch up with Brianna and a couple of other Vineyard shareholders. Now he was taking a summer afternoon walk through his neighbourhood rather than heading into the office. It was hardly the scandal of the century. Not suspicious at all.

Although maybe he was being self-indulgent. Maybe he should have headed to the office rather than strolling through London as if time was something he possessed. The Vineyard takeover was progressing slower than he liked despite his diplomatic mission to Boston, and there were always myriad tasks and decisions and strategies to review across all the parts of the business he already owned. Maybe Tally was right, he did need someone he could trust to take some of the load off. If only it was that easy. If only he could trust someone other than himself.

Lucas sighed, the burden he had thought he might shed for a few hours descending almost physical, his shoulders tense with the weight. What was he doing? His gaze lingered on a group of men around his own age gathered on pavement tables outside a corner pub, cheerful and loud and carefree. He couldn't remember the last time he had been part of such a group. There was no point having regrets. He *didn't* have any regrets, he had taken a bad hand and turned it into a winning one. He could have walked away, let it all collapse, no one would have blamed him. But he had chosen this life. There was no point complaining now.

And there was no point trying to do something different, be someone different. Better to return home, open the laptop he was carrying even on this walk, forget about tracking Tally down. He would see her at the wedding as promised but that was it. He'd find someone else for any other summer events he needed a plus-one for. Someone less discombobulating, less distracting.

Mind made up, Lucas turned round, his route taking him down a pretty narrow road he wasn't sure he had ever seen before. It was quintessential Chelsea, pretty houses painted a multitude of pastel colours, narrow pavements, quirky charm. Of course, once these houses would have belonged to craftsmen and retailers, distressed gentry and bohemians. Now, each one went for millions and were lived in by bankers. A pub took up the whole corner, a few drinkers spilling out onto the pavement outside the lead-paned windows. Colourful flower baskets were hung from the timbers, window boxes equally bright and cheerful added more charm.

The Duchess. It didn't sound familiar, but it looked quirky and inviting.

A chalkboard outside announced Pimm's, a refreshing spritzer menu and an array of bar snacks on one side. On the other a timetable: Monday pub quiz, Friday fresh pizza, Saturday karaoke. Private bookings welcome. Lucas hesitated. He had his laptop with him. Maybe a coffee while he tackled his inbox would be nice.

Inside was as welcoming as the outside. Low ceilings and small windows were enhanced by subtle lighting, making the whole place feel cosy. Tables were surrounded by comfortable chairs and benches, here an intimate corner for two, there a long booth for a large group, with flowers on the bar and on the tables. A second, larger room was visible through an archway. And there, behind the bar, just as he had known somewhere inside that she would be, was Tally, bright in an orange dress, her hair tied up, laughing as she chatted with a group of older men who inhabited their bar stools with the unmistakable posture of regulars.

She straightened and turned as he approached the bar, the friendly smile fading as she realised who he was.

'Lucas? What are you doing here?'

'I've been wandering the streets looking for a pint and a pretty barmaid to flirt with.' He hadn't meant to say the last part, hadn't even known that he had remembered the origin story she had concocted for them in such detail, and realised as the words left his mouth that if she didn't remember he ran the risk of sounding pretty corny. But Tally clearly did remember, her eyes lighting up with laughter, her mouth curving into a mischievous smile.

'I can provide the first, but do you think you can handle the second?' she teased.

Lucas placed both hands on the bar counter and leant in so they were close enough to touch. 'Try me.'

All thoughts of keeping his distance, of ensuring he wouldn't be distracted had fled. She was here and it felt right.

'Is that a promise?'

'Do you want it to be?'

'What happened to what happened in Italy stays in Italy?'

She was nervous, he realised. Nervous of what he might say or do. Had her eagerness to forestall his words in Tuscany been because she genuinely had thought it a good idea they put the night behind them or because she had read his intentions and wanted to get there first? If the latter he didn't blame her. Her father had rejected her, her ex had pushed her away. It was no wonder Tally was wary.

'I can't make any promises,' he said, low-voiced and intent. 'I don't know what will happen at the end of the summer.'

'I might have a fabulous offer and swan off to LA without a backwards look.'

'Leaving me weeping on the tarmac? But I do know that I haven't been able to stop thinking about you. That I didn't even know the name of your pub, and yet my walk brought me here today.'

'You haven't been able to stop thinking about me?'

'Did I say that out loud?'

Her smile widened. 'You might have occasionally crossed my mind too.'

'Just occasionally?'

'Every now and then.'

A group erupted into the bar, breaking the spell that seemed to be binding them closer and closer, and Tally stepped back, 'Let me get you a drink. I get a break in half an hour. We can talk then.'

Lucas wasn't sure how it happened, but he ended up hunkering down in a corner of the pub for the rest of the afternoon. He had his laptop and Tally kept him supplied with excellent coffee and occasional bar snacks. He was aware of interested glances, especially from the locals, when she came to join him armed with a mug of tea and a huge doorstep sandwich.

'I can do thousands of steps when I'm working,' she explained. 'I need to keep my strength up.'

'What time do you finish?' Lucas wanted to talk to her, but he wanted to do so alone, not under the watchful eye of a pub full of men and women who had clearly known Tally since she was a child.

'Karaoke night, I'll be on until close. But I am off tomorrow.'

Lucas managed not to look at his inbox, his to-do list. 'In that case, want to do something tomorrow?'

'Depends what you mean by "something"?'

'I've been thinking about all those walks in the park we enjoyed.'

Her look of confusion gave way to a wide smile. 'Oh, of course, before we reconnected on the train.'

'Might be nice to go for a picnic in the park.' Lucas wasn't sure he had ever had a picnic before, had never envied couples lying on the grass trying to keep their sandwiches out of the reach of out-of-control dogs before, but for one moment the reality was blurred by a picture of him and Tally, a picnic basket, blue skies...

'I didn't have you down as a picnic man.'

'I'm not, but you're bringing out my wild side.'

'Stick with me and you'll be suggesting sunset walks next. Okay, that sounds nice. Let me take care of the actual picnic part. At least I know what's needed.'

It was settled, they had a plan, although Lucas insisted that he be the one to bring the picnic. There was no reason for him to hang around and yet a couple of hours later he was still working in his corner, the coffee replaced by a non-alcoholic beer. The background noise was soothing, a contrast to his own echoingly empty house. It was strangely enjoyable to look up and see Tally at work, bustling around, laughing and talking, clearly completely at home. That made sense, it was her home. Even nicer to catch her eye, see the colour flood her cheeks, her intimate smile just for him, subtly different to the one she greeted customers with. She was clearly good at what she did, her warmth and genuine interest in people, underlined with a steely *Don't mess with me* core that kept the most drunken chancers at bay. Sometimes he was aware of her stepfather or mother not so covertly checking him out. She'd introduced them but forbidden them from any kind of interrogation.

A shadow fell across the table and Lucas looked up, ready to say that the bar stool wasn't taken and they could have it, when he realised his brother was standing there, an amused gleam in his blue eyes.

'Felix, what are you doing here? How did you know I was here?' he added.

Felix held up his phone. 'Tracked you. At first I thought you'd been mugged by an alcoholic when I saw where you were and how long you'd been here, but maybe you're the one who needs to go to AA?'

'It's non-alcoholic.' Lucas touched his pint defensively. 'I haven't been day drinking.'

'I know, hell hasn't frozen over yet. But it is past five on a Saturday so I'm planning on a pint of the real stuff. Do you want to put that laptop away and join me and tell me why you're working from your local instead of your actual office or your own comfortable study?'

There was no point dissembling, not with Tally within hearing distance. 'I can do better than that. Remember Tally?'

'Your avoiding Bella date?'

'That's the one. This is her pub. Say hello nicely or she won't serve you.'

CHAPTER NINE

TALLY WASN'T SURE how she felt about her worlds colliding like this. Lucas in her pub was discombobulating enough. She hadn't expected him to stay but it was nice, watching him work in the corner, feeling the weight of his gaze on her, looking over at him to receive one of his rare sweet smiles; he must have used a week's quota up today.

But it was odd introducing him to her parents. They would meet him at Layla's wedding so in a way it made sense for there to be a prior introduction. She didn't lie to them usually, but nor did she want to tell them about the deal she had made with Lucas so had mangled together some sanitised version of the truth. They had met on the train and when he had found out she had never been to Italy before he had invited her to Tuscany. They weren't dating, but they were seeing each other casually. She completely missed out the meeting her father part of the trip; she needed to figure out how she felt about that before involving her mother and had managed to warn Lucas not to mention it either.

But now not only were her mother and Steve—and Leroy, Bill, Heather, Dev and all the other regulars— staring at Lucas with undisguised *What Are Your In-*

tentions? thought bubbles practically visible above their heads—but Lucas's brother was here, adding a whole other layer of complexity to what had seemed like a simple solution.

She could see the resemblance between the brothers. Felix was a younger, more relaxed version of Lucas. His eyes were bright with laughter, his expression open, his clothes equally exquisite but casual and he'd obviously perfected teasing his brother over many years.

'We can't go now, the karaoke is about to start,' he was saying as Tally headed over on the pretext of clearing their glasses. 'Isn't that right, Tally? Tell my brother he has to stay.'

'You say karaoke. I say my mother belting out show-biz classics to an appreciative audience,' Tally warned.

'Do you sing?'

'When she allows me to. But a few weeks ago I did "All Too Well", the ten-minute version, and she hasn't let me near the microphone since.'

Felix laughed. 'How about you, Lucas? Ready to wow Tally with the power of music?'

'You sing?' she asked Lucas, surprised. She wasn't sure she had heard him as much as hum in Tuscany, whereas she was always breaking into song, to her friends' annoyance. She had learned to mostly sing under her breath but once the radio was on all restraint went.

'Not in public. We really should go and let Tally work, Felix.'

'No way, I love a good showbiz tune. We're staying.' He winked at Tally.

Karaoke was always held in the large function room

on the first floor of the pub. Hired out for parties and other events, it was also the stage for the pub panto and Shakespeare and a Pint as well as the weekly karaoke sessions. The stage was already set up and Tally opened up the bar, leaving Steve in charge of downstairs. She directed Lucas and Felix to a table by the window.

'Make sure you clap very enthusiastically,' she warned them as her mother shimmied onto the stage, resplendent in sequins. 'Whoops and cheers go down well as well.'

The summer holidays were starting for some schools and this part of London was beginning to empty as those who could headed off to second homes on the coast or abroad, but The Duchess's karaoke evening was legendary and the room full as Charlene kicked the evening off with a rousing rendition of 'Honey, Honey' from *Mamma Mia*. Tally was kept busy ensuring the singers and audience were well lubricated, but when she had an opportunity to check in on Lucas, she could see him watching proceedings with a slightly cautious expression, as if he were among aliens, but he didn't look uncomfortable. Felix was obviously enjoying himself immensely, already friends with all the surrounding tables.

Despite Tally's teasing, her mother was a good host who didn't hog the microphone *too* much, compering expertly, supporting the more nervous singers and managing to ensure the more raucous ones didn't go too far. A couple of hours in, Steve sent one of the other bar staff to relieve Tally and she made herself a gin and tonic and joined Lucas and Felix.

'Having fun?' she asked.

'I want to become a regular, where do I sign up?' Felix asked.

'I'll send you the forms.' Tally smiled at Lucas, suddenly shy. 'How about you?' she asked. 'Are you ready to join up, too?'

He didn't smile back, his gaze steady, intent. 'Maybe I am.'

'Come on.' Felix jumped to his feet and offered a hand to Tally. 'It's our turn.'

'What have you chosen?' She was half laughing, half protesting as she was dragged to the stage. 'I haven't warmed up.'

'"Don't Go Breaking My Heart."'

'A classic.'

'Tally?' She looked up into suddenly serious eyes. 'You won't, will you?'

'Won't what?'

'Break his heart.'

'His heart? Felix, it's not like that—' But her words were lost as he bounded onto the stage, the seriousness gone as if it had never been.

Felix proved to be a more enthusiastic than talented singer, but his spirited performance won him as many cheers as Tally's more tuneful one. She stayed on the stage as he left, arms overhead triumphantly, to take a couple of requests, a staple part of the evening, finishing with a pitchier-than-she-liked version of 'Jolene'— the karaoke at The Duchess tended to run to classics.

She took a bow and headed back to the bar, stopping as Lucas came over to her.

'You were incredible,' he said, low-voiced.

Her cheeks heated at the intensity in his gaze. 'I'm a little out of practice.'

'It didn't show, but it wasn't just your voice, it's you.

You have a real presence. I couldn't take my eyes off you. I can't take my eyes off you.'

Tally's stomach dipped, her whole body flooding with a delicious, wanting ache, her gaze fixating on his mouth, so tantalisingly close, the memories of what he could do with that mouth weakening her knees. What she *wanted* to do was grab him by the hand and drag him back to her room, but there were limitations to sleeping in an attic room with her parents directly below—and working in a place where half the clientele had watched her grow up. Besides, she was closing up. But tomorrow they had their picnic date, and if it didn't end with them both naked and in a bed then it wouldn't be thanks to her.

'Maybe I'll sing for you tomorrow.'

His eyes darkened to navy. 'I'm counting on it.'

The brothers left soon after. Tally didn't kiss Lucas, or even touch him, but her whole body heated as he said goodbye. 'I'll see you tomorrow.'

'I'm looking forward to it.'

'Me too.'

There was something about his intent, unsmiling gaze that undid her, but, aware of their audience, she stepped back, trying not to show how flustered he made her.

'I'll warn you, I'm somewhat of a picnic expert, you need to bring your A game,' she teased him, and he looked even more serious.

'You can count on it.'

'Promises, promises.'

'Picnics, karaoke, day drinking. I don't know what you've done to my brother, Tally, but I approve.' Felix didn't show the same restraint as Lucas, sweeping her into a hug before clapping his brother on the shoulder. 'Come on, Cinderella, let's get you home before midnight strikes and you turn back into a fun-free workaholic.'

Tally watched them leave, her stomach churning. She had left Italy half expecting never to see Lucas again, sure that the night they had shared was a one-off. Seeing him again made her realise how much she had hoped to be wrong, how much she had wanted to see him again but had been too scared of rejection to reach out. Now *he* had sought *her* out. She wasn't sure what that meant, if anything, but for now it was enough.

'You look like the cat that got the cream,' her mother said, and Tally jumped.

'Good show tonight,' she said, trying to change the subject. 'You were brilliant, but I was a little pitchy during "Jolene".'

'That's because you were too busy mooning at that boy.'

'I wasn't *mooning* and he's over thirty—hardly a boy.'

'You know what I mean.'

'You don't like him?'

'I don't know him. But I do know from what you've said that he's an ambitious man. Nothing wrong with that, but in my experience ambitious men—and women—put those ambitions first. Like you, in the end your career was more important than your relationship with Max.'

'That's not exactly what happened.'

'Just be careful, Tally, that's all I'm saying. When two people want different things, someone gets hurt. I don't want it to be you.'

'It's not like that. We're not in a relationship, we're just having fun.' But her mother's gaze was too shrewd and Tally busied herself with collecting glasses, not wanting to carry on the conversation, or dwell on her mother's words. They *were* just having fun; nobody was going to get hurt and she was absolutely in control.

Tally had tried to claim responsibility for providing the picnic but Lucas had refused. He might not have picnicking experience, but how hard could it be to throw some sandwiches together? He usually asked Candace to organise any social occasions but pride stopped him going to his assistant for help, so he felt extra smug when he beat Tally to the appointed spot, a rolled-up blanket with two cushions attached to it under one arm and a not too twee basket in the other hand, filled with the best that a local deli had to offer.

He sensed Tally before he saw her, summery in a lemon jumpsuit, a matching scarf around her hair. Once again, she was as appealing as a long cool drink.

'Hey,' she said, coming to a stop a step away.

'Hey.'

'I know you said not to bring anything but I literally live in a pub.' She held up a wine cooler. 'It's impossible not to.' Her gaze fell on the basket. 'Ooh, fancy... and very shiny new.'

'Only the best for my lady. Shall we?' They walked companionably side by side along the pavement, heading across the bridge to Battersea Park. The sun was shining overhead and once again London had the frivolous holiday feel a sunny day brought out in the city. It didn't take long to reach the park and walk through, past many couples and families who'd obviously had a similar idea, until they found a secluded spot. Lucas set the basket down and unrolled the blanket, placing the cushions on top.

'Tartan blanket and matching cushion—very fancy and yet all at once traditional. Just what I would expect from you.'

'You approve?'

'I'm still reserving judgement.' Tally sat down gracefully and watched as he opened up the basket.

Lucas hadn't been sure what to get, so in the end he went for pretty much everything. Crusty bread, an array of dips and spreads, fresh fruit, smoked salmon and a selection of delicious cheeses, small biscuits and light cakes. The basket included real plates and cutlery, napkins and wine glasses, and he set them out on the blanket. Tally opened the champagne she had brought and poured it into the glasses.

'Cheers,' she said. 'To belated first dates and karaoke.'

'Cheers.'

Lucas couldn't believe how quickly the afternoon went. The food was delicious, the champagne light and moreish, the conversation even easier than it had been in Italy. They didn't discuss the night they had spent together but the memory of it hung there, not imposing but a promise of what might happen. What probably would happen. They saw very few people, although they were joined at one point by an exuberant yellow labrador who made a beeline for the picnic basket. Lucas moved with instinctive speed and managed to safeguard the remains of their food, whilst Tally managed to coax the excitable hound over to her until the owner finally turned up, breathless and apologetic.

'Is that the kind of dog you want?' he asked as their new friend was led away, not noticeably shamefaced.

'Beautiful, isn't he? I love them, but they're all stomachs, aren't they, labs? Not that I can judge, not after the amount I've eaten today.' She cast a half laughing, half rueful look at the picnic basket.

'Want to walk it off?'

'Sure, any destination in mind?'

'Yesterday I visited your home,' Lucas said a little diffidently. 'I thought maybe today you could visit mine.'

The offer hung in the air. He wasn't explicitly asking her back for sex, but he wouldn't deny that that was the hoped-for outcome. That he was driven to distraction by the memory of the feel of her against him, the sound of her sighs, the touch of her hand. That he couldn't stop staring at the place on her neck he knew drove her wild, that the only reason he hadn't kissed her yet was because they were in public and once he started he wasn't sure he would stop. That he could feel her gaze lingering on his hands, his mouth, his throat and he knew, without a shadow of a doubt, that she too was having flashbacks to their lovemaking.

'You didn't actually see my home,' Tally said eventually. 'You saw the pub, the flat is still unchartered territory, but yes, I would love to nose around your house.'

Tally insisted on carrying the considerably lighter picnic basket, leaving Lucas with the rolled-up blanket and cushions, an arrangement which left hands free to swing close together, to brush together, to touch and then to clasp. It was so natural, her hand in his. Their gait matched, swift but unhurried, and it didn't take long to reach Lucas's house, on a road close to the river.

'Nice location,' Tally said.

'Thanks to my grandfather. He was quite the sixties man and sold the Mayfair house he had inherited to buy here.'

'I mean, Mayfair is still a reasonable address,' she teased. 'But this is gorgeous, so close to the river.'

Lucas felt unaccountably nervous as he opened the door and ushered Tally in. Not because of what might or might not happen later but because he so rarely invited people back. Felix had a key but preferred his own Shoreditch flat, his mother hated London and preferred to stay in hotels on the rare occasions she was in the city.

He was conscious of Tally looking around, at the tastefully painted walls, the well-chosen art, the polished wooden floors, the comfortable stylish and sparse furniture, all selected by the interior designer he had hired several years before.

'I don't actually use much of the house,' he explained as he led her down to the basement kitchen which took up most of the floor. 'Just here, my study and bedroom really.'

The kitchen included a separate dining space with a comfortable seating area at the other end. It had been designed for family living but was also perfect for a man who lived alone. Why eat in the formal dining room when there was a perfectly good table or breakfast bar here, or sit in the huge and always chilly sitting room when he could relax in this comfortable space? Felix always said that he had carved a one-bedroom flat out of the four-storey, five-bed townhouse.

'This is nice, did you decorate yourself?'

'I got a decorator in.' He took the basket from Tally and began to unpack it, then took a bottle of chilled white wine from the fridge, poured two glasses and handed her one. 'My father used this place as his own personal party palace. Whenever I came here in holidays it smelt of spilled wine, cigarettes and perfume. I was always finding things that didn't belong to my mother, earrings or underwear.'

'Ugh…' She shuddered. 'No wonder your mother prefers to stay away. And no wonder you redecorated.'

'Pretty much had every room scrubbed and redone. Not at first, every penny had to be ploughed back into the business and I was in Milan most of the time of course, but as soon as I was in a position to, I handed the house over to an interior design firm. I should have sold it, I suppose. I thought about it but it was never a priority. I like the neighbourhood; I need a place to live.' He shrugged. 'It was easier to keep it.'

'Show me the rest.'

They took their drinks with them as they did the tour. First the obviously unused sitting room and dining room, although the morning room at the back of the house he used as a study showed more signs of life with filled bookcases and piled-up papers. Then up to the first floor. 'There are three bedrooms on this floor,' he explained as he opened the door into his room. 'Two in the attic.'

Lucas wasn't assuming anything, but he had certainly been anticipating when he had changed the sheets this morning, put fresh towels in the luxurious en suite bathroom, picked up flowers when he bought the picnic and plonked them in a vase on the dressing table.

'So this is where the magic happens?' Tally teased as she looked around the light-filled room.

'Not often,' he admitted, taking her glass from her unresisting hand and placing it on the mantelpiece before turning her to face him. 'As I said, life is mainly business first and I don't really like people in my personal space.'

It wasn't as if there was anything incriminating here, the house was almost devoid of personal possessions, or personality, according to Felix, but Lucas still preferred neutral ground, hotels or apartments, when he was dating. But he liked having Tally here, liked the splash of colour she brought to the monochrome spaces, liked the way her scent lingered on the air like a calling card.

'And yet here I am.'

'Here you are.'

'I feel special.'

He should tell her that she was special, that the thought of her had his stomach in knots, that he could think of little but her, but the words wouldn't come, so instead he kissed her.

Kissing Tally was exactly like he remembered, exactly like he had fantasised about, but still somehow new. She was summer personified, warm and sweet but with a hint of spice and fire. Her skin was silk under his fingertips as he explored her like a man who had been lost but was finally home.

He took his time at first, learning her all over again, tasting her mouth, her neck, her throat, the tips of her ears, tangling his hands in the heavy fall of her hair. His skin burned where she touched him, his shoulders and arms, his back, the planes of his stomach as she undid his shirt, button by button, almost agonisingly slow, her touch bold yet soft, sure yet exploratory as if she was rediscovering him. Last time they had fallen onto each other filled with emotions, she full of grief, he wanting to kiss her sorrow away. This time there was no baggage, they had nothing to declare except their attraction. They knew the rules and had decided to ignore them.

With a sound of triumph, Tally pushed his shirt off his shoulders and Lucas allowed her to slip it off, leaving him bare-chested. He kicked off his shoes but before she could tackle his belt, he turned his attention to the ties on her shoulders, kissing every newly exposed centimetre as he eased the zip down, her jumpsuit falling to the floor as she half stepped out of it, he half lifted her.

Lucas allowed himself to pause, to look at her, hair falling over her shoulder, clad only in a rose-pink bra and matching knickers, her eyes bright, mouth swollen, and his blood surged. He needed to touch every inch, to taste every inch, he needed to hear her cry out and know she was crying out for him. Her skin pinkened under his gaze but she met him boldly, surveying him with the same intensity, his skin tingling as her gaze traced its way up and down his torso, his blood roaring. *Mine.*

No more delay. With one movement, Lucas stepped forward and swept her into his arms, luxuriating in the feel of her against him as he carried her to the bed, letting her slide, oh, so slowly and, oh, so deliciously against him, every second torture and yet the kind of torture he wanted to last for ever until she was lying on the bed laughing up at him.

'What are you looking at?' she asked huskily as he made no move to join her.

'You.'

'Like what you see?'

He met her gaze. 'Do you want me to answer that or show you?'

Her eyes darkened, her tongue dipping out to touch her lip. 'Show me, Lucas, and maybe I'll show you in turn.'

'It's a deal.'

And then he was next to her, kissing her as she kissed him, removing the last vestiges of clothing, and the only words left were 'Yes…' 'Right there…' 'More…' Finally replaced by moans and sighs. And all he knew was her.

CHAPTER TEN

TALLY HAD NEVER had the kind of summer that could be montaged before, but this one felt like it should have a background tune to accompany idyllic scenes of sunset walks, drinks by the river, fine dining in fancy restaurants and picnics in bed. Of Lucas working from a corner in the pub, blue eyes resting on her as she worked, meeting Felix for drinks, a night out with Layla and Phinn, croquet in the park, a night in a countryside hotel. Bodies sliding together, entwined, touching and learning and knowing. She accompanied him to a polo match and a formal dinner, and no talk was made of arrangements or payment. It was simply natural she should be there and when he introduced her as his girlfriend there was no hesitation.

They were in a bubble, she knew that, a bubble of lust and desire, of sunshine and summer, but it still felt like it could be substantial, that they could be building the foundations of something. But there was no talk of the future, it was still so early, and although once or twice, lying cushioned in his arms, lazily tracing circles on his chest, she felt a declaration bubbling on her tongue, she swallowed it down. Tally had been too quick to declare her love before, she didn't want to make that mistake again.

She wanted him to say it first and surely he would. Surely that wasn't just lust in his eyes. He wanted her body, that was abundantly clear, but he liked her company too. Liked her.

'Off out again?' her mother asked as Tally walked downstairs from her attic room.

'Steve gave my shift to Tai. That's okay, isn't it?'

'Your choice. It's just I've hardly seen you all week. All summer, in fact.'

'Isn't that a good thing?' Tally kissed her mother's cheek. 'The last thing you need is your spinster daughter cramping your style. You should be pleased I'm finally giving you and Steve some space.'

'I love having you here, you know that.'

'And I love being here.'

'I just…' Charlene hesitated. 'It's all rather fast, Tally. You didn't even know Lucas six weeks ago and now you're spending every waking moment with him. You know I don't like to interfere…'

Tally fought to keep a straight face. Her mother lived to interfere. 'Well, I'm not spending this waking moment with him. I'm actually off to see Layla. There's loads to do with the wedding the day after tomorrow, and as maid of honour my actual role seems to be maid-of-all-work. I'm needed to chop and tidy and make garlands and whatever else Layla needs me to do. We've been planning for so long and now it's just two days away. Can you believe it? Those two crazy kids made it, just twenty-five years after Phinn first proposed with a plastic ring in the playground.'

'Feels like five minutes since you and she were play-ing Barbies upstairs,' Charlene sighed, her eyes misty.

'Or schools. I should have known she would end up being a teacher, she was always making me do maths tests.'

'And you were always making her put on a play. Give her my love and tell her everything is under control here.'

'I will.' Tally kissed her mother and left the flat, paus-ing only to text Lucas Good Morning. She had spent the night at home as he was busy. It was funny how quickly she had got used to seeing him every day. How much she missed him after just a few hours apart.

The day passed quickly. There were myriad tasks to do in the bustling, laughter-filled flat over the Lebanese restaurant Layla's family owned and ran. Last-minute rearrangements of the table plans, final tweaks to the table favours. Layla and Phinn had hired out the hall and canteen at the school where Phinn worked and Layla's parents were doing the catering, a mouthwatering buffet of spicy chicken stews, tabbouleh salads, a host of dips including their famous baba ghanoush and flatbreads, crisp falafel and a selection of honey-rich baklava. The kitchen was fragrant with spices, and Tally was put to work chopping herbs, grinding spaces and rolling out dough, just as she had been across the many years of friendship, the hours passing quickly under the weight of the many tasks this homemade wedding entailed.

The next day they headed to the school to set up, polishing every surface under the eagle eye of Layla's mother, setting up the canteen with hired in long tables then decorating them. Layla had chosen a colour scheme based on summer flowers, rich crimsons, fuchsias and magentas, vases set along the middle of each table, garlands hung around the room. It was a wedding designed with love, the modest budget boosted by the willingness of everyone who knew and loved the couple to pitch in. Phinn's mother and sisters arranging all the flowers, the bridesmaids polishing the borrowed glasses and cutlery, Phinn and his friends—not including Max, Tally was relieved to see—creating a bar area in the canteen and in the hall where first the ceremony and then the dancing would take place. Finally, the happy couple said their protracted goodbyes before Tally and Layla returned to the restaurant to carry on with food prep.

It was a relief to finally head over to the pub, along with all the other bridesmaids, Layla's mother, sisters, aunts and cousins and a mix of school and her friend's work colleagues and university friends for a selection of quiches and salads supplied by Steve and Charlene in the function room. It was the first and final chance to relax before the big day. Layla was staying at the pub with Tally, as she had so many times during their long friendship, the function room turning into a hair and make-up salon for the bridal party the next morning. Layla's dress had been delivered to the pub and hung in the spare bedroom next to Tally's dress.

Everything was perfect, just as they had planned it back when they were little and playing dress-up. Perfect except… Tally surreptitiously checked her phone again. Nothing from Lucas. In fact, she hadn't heard from him in a couple of days, there had been no reply to her good morning, nor to the messages she'd sent since: a picture of the decorated venue, one of the simmering chicken stew. Both had been read but not replied to. Her stomach churned with a sense of foreboding. This radio silence was unlike him. He was busy every hour when not with her—and often when with her—his day filled with work, stopping only to go for a run or a gym session, but he usually at least responded even if it was with an emoji.

Don't be paranoid, she scolded herself.

Just because her last months with Max had been punctuated with unread messages and a lack of contact, even when they were in the same space, didn't mean that this was the same thing. Why would it be? There had been no clues, no sign that anything was wrong. She'd slept over just two nights ago, not that they had got much sleep, Lucas had kissed her goodbye, a lingering farewell, knowing she would be kept busy by Layla until the wedding and they wouldn't see each other before the reception.

There was an obvious reason for the radio silence. Lucas was probably working extra hard, if that was possible, so that he could keep most of tomorrow clear. The ceremony was at Chelsea Register Office, but Layla and Phinn would be repeating their vows in a humanist ceremony at the school before the celebrations started and although Lucas wouldn't be at the official ceremony she was expecting to see him at the second one, which meant he would need to take the whole afternoon off work.

Tally tried to join in with the increasingly emotional reminiscences as Layla's mother shared a series of photos of her daughter through the years and concentrate on the celebratory chat, but she was far too aware of her silent phone. Should she message him again? Just a simple Everything okay?

Was that too needy?

How about Looking forward to seeing you tomorrow? Something lighter, flirtier?

Communicating with Lucas wasn't usually this difficult, she didn't usually second-guess her messages. Her unease intensified. Maybe she should check in with Felix, but if everything was fine that would make her look like a paranoid stalker.

There had still been no contact from Lucas when the party disbanded—early, as Layla had dictated. Tally had bought organic face masks and a selection of luxurious body and foot creams and the two friends took long, indulgent showers, exfoliating every inch before lathering themselves in the creams and face masks and tucking themselves up in Tally's double bed, just as they had done for years. Layla had a large family with four siblings and had always loved getting away from the noise and bustle, whereas Tally equally enjoyed the opportunity to be part of a large, lively family. They had been friends for so long, knew each other so well, Layla would usually be the first person Tally went to for advice, but she didn't want to burden her friend on the eve of her wedding and so she lay there while Layla fell swiftly into deep sleep and resisted the urge to check her phone before managing a few uneasy hours.

They woke early the next day for coffee and a light breakfast before the rest of the bridesmaids and Layla's mother descended on them, the morning flying by in a flurry of makeovers and hairstyling. Tally went through the process mechanically, trying not to check her phone every five minutes, but the relief was over-whelming when a message from Lucas finally flashed onto her screen.

She really had to learn not to assume the worst she thought as she opened it, only for her heart to squeeze painfully as she read the terse words.

Something has come up. I can't make it. Hope it goes well. L

No explanation. No apology. No endearment. No kiss. Was this some kind of attempt at a joke? Had Felix got hold of his phone? Lucas knew how much today meant to her. They had a deal! The terms of the deal might have changed, lines might have blurred, but he had promised her he would be here today long before she had developed feelings for him. Before she thought he had developed feelings for her.

It took every single acting skill she possessed to excuse herself without betraying that something was wrong. Tally made her way up to her bedroom and stopped in front of her mirror. Her leggings and her only half-ironic crystal-studded pink *Maid of Honour* T-shirt looked incongruous with her fully made-up face and elaborate half-up hair, the top pulled back to accommodate a wreath of dark pink flowers, the rest cascading down her back, more flowers woven through. It really was a work of art. With trembling hands, she took her phone out from her pocket, pressed Lucas's name on her frequently contacted list and listened to the ringtone, heart hammering, stomach churning.

At first, she thought it would go to voicemail but finally he picked up.

'Tally?' His voice didn't sound like him, as curt as the text, distracted.

'Lucas? What's going on? Why can't you make the wedding?'

'I'm in Boston.'

'*Boston?* When? Why?'

He'd left the *country* and not told her? Okay, they had made no promises, hadn't defined what this thing between them actually was, but they were surely at the *mention you were planning to fly over the ocean* stage.

'Two days ago. The Vineyard deal is collapsing.'

'The…?' Oh, yes. The deal he had been trying to seal when she'd met him. 'Oh, I'm sorry. I know how much you've put into it. But Lucas, you promised you would be here with me today.'

It wasn't about Max, not really, not any more. It was more that it seemed as if he hadn't thought about her at all.

That she was the last thing on his priority list.

'Tally, this is a multi-million-pound deal. That's more important than some wedding.'

'It's the wedding of my best friend. It's not just *some wedding*. Why didn't you tell me you were going to the States?'

'I forgot. Look, Tally, I get that you're upset but I'm busy. Can we do this some other time?'

Tally stared at herself, her face pale under her mixture of real and fake tan, at her eyes, large and hurt, her trembling mouth. 'No.'

She could hear him sigh. 'Tally…'

'We can't do this some other time because there *is* no other time. This is clearly not going to work, Lucas. I can't be someone you forget about and let down...'

'I warned you, Tally. I told you that I didn't have time for neediness. That I needed a partner who understood I might not be there.'

'That was when you wanted to hire me. But I am not on your payroll. A relationship has to be give and take, promises have to be kept. If something comes up, it's discussed—not sent as a one-line text two days later. I am worth more than this, Lucas.'

He didn't answer for a long moment. She couldn't picture him at all. He was like a stranger. 'If that's what you want. It's probably for the best.'

'I can't believe I almost told you I love you. I have to go. I have a wedding to celebrate.'

She ended the call and switched her phone off and took a few deep breaths, willing the tears back. She would cry at some point, that was inevitable, mourn what might have been, berate herself for an idiot who fell for another man who couldn't fall for her in the same way, wonder why she was so easy to leave, but for now she was going to make sure her friend had the best day possible.

Tally's heart might feel as if it were breaking but no one was going to know.

Lucas hadn't seen it coming. He'd been so confident that at least two of the family shareholders would sell to him, turning his minority stake into a controlling stake, that he hadn't seen Hunter Johnson mount an opposing offensive, persuading the remaining family shareholders to consider his counteroffer to keep the company under their control. He should have anticipated it. Should have had contingencies in place. But instead, he had been distracted. Distracted by Tally. He had let his personal life interfere with his business sense, just as he had always vowed never to do. Too busy romancing and taking time out and off to focus on what was really important. The financial stability and growth of his company. The jobs he was responsible for. He'd been playing croquet while Johnson had been counter scheming, picnicking while the deal was falling apart. He was no better than his father.

'I think I can be sure of Brianna, but I need one more person. I should have stayed in Boston until this was done, not wasted my summer in London,' he said to Felix that afternoon. Even as he said the words he felt a pang, a sense of betrayal. No one had dragged him to Chelsea, to the pub, to Tally. *He* had actively sought *her* out.

'Hardly a waste,' Felix objected. 'You are allowed to enjoy yourself, you know.'

'Not at the expense of work I'm not. My distraction could have cost us millions. If we don't have the majority share then our stock is useless.'

'True, but it's not the end of the world. Vineyard is a nice to have, it fits the portfolio perfectly, but it's not like our future depends on it.'

'That's not the point, Felix. Throwing money away is irresponsible. If I was going to mount this kind of takeover then I needed to be fully focused until it was through.'

'Tally isn't a distraction, she's a human being. A human being who I happen to think is good for you.'

'It doesn't matter what you think. She's done what I should have done weeks ago and ended it.'

'I'm not surprised. Standing her up at the wedding was a low thing to do, Lucas.'

'It's not like I had any choice,' Lucas snapped. 'Who else was going to salvage this mess? You?'

'If you ever relaxed your death grip on the reins enough for me to do so, then why not? Just because I don't work sixteen-hour days seven days a week it doesn't mean I'm not capable, Lucas. It's my heritage, my company too.'

'A company that wouldn't exist if I hadn't sacrificed everything for it. I worked my butt off so that you could experience everything I couldn't.' Lucas stopped, appalled. What was he *doing*? Was he purposely sabotaging every relationship he had left?

Did he occasionally feel a sense of envy that his brother's life in some ways had been easier, that he had seen out his schooling, gone to university, had friends and relationships and a work-life balance? Yes. But he also knew Felix's life wasn't perfect. He'd lost their father too, had also been sent to school far too young, his mother first emotionally and then geographically distant.

'No one asked you to turn into an emotionless robot, Lucas,' Felix said evenly. 'That's all you. Look, I'll be on the red-eye tonight so, depending on Customs, you can expect to see me some time after midnight. You don't have to do this all alone. But if I were you, I would be reaching out to Tally and trying to repair this, if she'll let you, which if she has any sense she won't.'

'The best thing I can do for Tally is what I should

have done in the first place and leave her in peace. I'll see you later.'

Lucas ended the call and stared out unseeingly across the water. His harbourside hotel had amazing views over the ocean but Lucas was barely aware of what lay outside his window, just as he couldn't have described the hotel suite if asked to do so. He had stayed in hundreds of suites all over the world and after a while they had all blurred into one. Tally would have explored every corner, tried all the toiletries, sat in every seat and explored the minibar. But Tally wasn't here. She wouldn't be here again, not with him. He'd meant what he said. It was for the best—for both of them. She needed someone to put her first, to fight for her the way her father and ex had so singularly failed to do.

As he had failed to do. He had joined that unholy triumvirate of undeserving men. Lucas's hands curled into fists as he recalled the break in her voice. The moment she had said she had nearly told him she loved him. Now she hated him and he deserved it. He had been a coward not to tell her he was going to have to skip the wedding. It was partly because he had been swept up in the urgency of the situation, straight into damage control. But it had also been because at some level he had wanted to punish them both for putting him into this situation, for allowing his worst nightmares about what would happen if he ever took his eye off the ball to happen. She definitely deserved better than that.

He checked the time. Four p.m. It would be nine in London. The wedding would have turned into a party, dancing and celebrating. Her ex would be there, dancing with his new partner, and Tally would be alone because Lucas had broken a promise. There was no coming back from that.

But he had always known that this was his destiny, had accepted it. He was his father's son, there was no balance, and if his choice was a loveless workaholic over a destructive playboy then he was content with that. He just wished he hadn't hurt Tally in the process. Or that his own heart didn't feel quite so bruised, his life so empty and lonely.

It was what it was. He could sit here and brood or he could get out there, mount a charm offensive and do what he came out here to do. Win. No matter that he felt as if he had already lost.

CHAPTER ELEVEN

TALLY HAD BEEN here before. And last time it had been infinitely worse. She had lost her home, her future, her sense of herself as an adult all at once. At least, last time *should* have been infinitely worse. She had thought her heart broken. But it hadn't felt quite this exquisitely painful.

Late summer had soured. It was too humid when she went out, too stuffy indoors. She couldn't hear birdsong but the low drone of wasps zeroing in on her drink. Everything was too bright, too loud. She felt lost. Foolish.

How had she been so stupid? Lucas had been honest with her from the start. He was too busy for a relationship, he wasn't looking for love, so why had she forgotten the rules and allowed herself to fall for him, for the man she had thought he was? Because he had been kind to her? Because the sex had been spectacular? Was she really that needy?

She had been able to forget her lack of direction, her failure to forge a career those last few weeks, but now a sense of doom hung over her. She needed to make a decision about what to do next but was paralysed, aware how lacking her judgement could be. She couldn't even lose herself in the rhythm of pub life, her mother told her she needed a break and got the other staff to cover her shifts, but Tally heard her tell Steve that Tally was in danger of scaring all the customers away.

So not only had she failed at her chosen career but she was also tanking her backup plan. Great.

She allowed herself one long doom-laden week to wallow and then woke up one morning bored of herself and furious rather than sad. Lucas might have been upfront from the start, but he had still let her down. Broken a promise as if she meant nothing. A hot shower followed by a long walk along the Thames all the way to Borough Market helped clear her head, and by the time she reached London Bridge, she was able to take stock.

So she and Max hadn't worked out. How many twenty-somethings transitioned successfully into the rest of their lives? They had both changed since those heady early days when living on noodles in a studio flat felt bohemian, he getting more conventional with every year and every promotion. It was only with hindsight that Tally could see how much she had bent and changed to accommodate him. Would she really have been happy with him long-term, always doubting and apologising? Her biggest regret should be that the relationship had lasted so long and *he* had been the one to end it.

As for Lucas, he was just a summer fling. It had felt like more because she had been swept up in the romance and glamour of it all, and because she had really, *really* liked him. Had started to fall in love with the illusion and romance. After all, he had proved categorically that she had barely known him. The abruptness of the breakup and feeling that she had been played for a fool hurt, it would for a while, but hopefully time would give her some perspective.

As for her career…it was time to take proper stock. No more drifting and hoping. She needed to look at her strengths and weaknesses, what interested her and what bored her, and decide on a plan. A three-month, one-year and a three-year plan leading to stability and a place of her own. She couldn't allow her temporary living arrangement to slide into permanence.

And she needed to apologise to Steve and her mother and tell them how grateful she was to have them.

Mind made up, Tally walked home, the return journey a lot slower than her furious powerwalking there, stopping to buy flowers for her mother and Steve. They had the afternoon off and so she headed straight to the flat, finding them sitting at the kitchen table. Tally proffered the flowers with a flourish.

'I'm sorry,' she said. 'I know I've been the grinch who ruined summer, but I promise to be nothing but sweetness and light from now on and to make a plan to get my life together.' She stopped, puzzled. There were no answering smiles or understanding glances. Instead, both her parents looked unusually serious. 'What's wrong? Is it Layla?' Her friend was backpacking around Vietnam and Thailand for her honeymoon.

'No, no, nothing is wrong, Layla is fine. It's just you have a guest. I put him in the function room, I wasn't sure what else to do.'

Her mother was pale, tight-lipped. *A guest? Him?* Was it Lucas? Had he come to apologise? Tally stared at her mother for one long moment and then whirled around and darted down the front staircase, the one leading to the first floor of the pub.

She inhaled—*Be cool, Tally*—and opened the door to the function room. The space always looked so cavernous and bare when not in use, chairs and tables stacked to one side, the stage put away, the bar shuttered. Leaning on the wall and staring out of the window was a tall dark-haired figure. Tally's heart began to hammer painfully in anticipation as he turned, only to lurch as she took in the famously handsome features.

'What are you doing here?' she demanded.

Sebastian Fields' smile was rueful. 'I came to apologise to you and your mother. I know it's too late, but will you hear me out? Please?'

Her first instinct was to flee. The pride which had sustained her through that awful party in Tuscany wanted her to walk out without replying. But the lost little girl who had grown up wondering why her father had abandoned her, who had spent her life seeking answers, who had put up with second best because she felt that that was what she deserved, couldn't move.

'Okay,' she said, her throat dry. 'I just… Do you want a coffee? Tea?' Offering tea, could she be more English?

'Tea would be great. That's the worst part of living in LA,' Sebastian said with the charming, slightly cheeky smile that had won him millions of fans. 'No matter what I do or what I import, I can't get a decent cup.'

Making tea took no time at all and yet for ever. She was at once numb and full of painful anticipatory nerves as her hands shook, spilling the milk, the situation so surreal she couldn't comprehend it.

'I have no excuse,' he said at last as they sat on two

chairs, a table between them, untouched tea steaming away. 'Except that I was young and scared.'

'You think my mother wasn't scared?'

'Your mother is the strongest woman I know, and the most talented. I was in awe of her then, I am now. It's a shame...' He didn't finish the sentence but Tally knew what he was going to say.

'A shame she gave up her career while yours went from strength to strength?' Now she wasn't numb or nervous. She was furious and it felt glorious. 'It wasn't just the practicalities of looking after me, you know. Grandma helped when she could and if Mum could get the right job, she could have paid someone, but the issue was no one would touch her. Not for anything she wanted to do. Her reputation was dragged through the mud, it's as if they wanted her to be her soap character, not a real person. She barely speaks about it but I've seen the headlines, front pages day after day, speculating on her lifestyle, who my father was. Your disappearance meant the tabloids assumed she'd been cheating on you. One paper even ran a list of possible fathers, all lies. No wonder she didn't want to carry on living in the public eye. She was barely twenty!'

'I know, and I am more ashamed than you can ever know, I have been for a long time. All I can say is that the longer I was away, the more removed I felt from it all. My twenties were as hedonistic as you would expect from someone with a lot of success and a lot of money. It was easier to pretend that you didn't exist, that I wasn't a terrible father, and the more I pretended, the more it became reality.' He looked down at the table. 'I nearly reached out fifteen years ago, after Phoenix was born. I held her and felt this absolute rush of love, but also guilt, that this was my second child and my eldest was an unknown teenager. But Eva had no idea you existed and I had no idea how to tell her. So I went back into denial. But I felt that same guilt when Autumn and Ocean were born, then again three years ago when Sofia and I had Atticus. I could never quite forget that I was living a lie.'

Tally had no idea how to respond. Part of her was pleased he had felt guilt, that he knew he had been wrong, but that didn't alleviate the years of hurt.

'So, for fifteen years you wanted to reach out but didn't? I mean, you stopped paying Mum as soon as I turned eighteen. It was her and Steve who put me through university and drama school and it was a real struggle. A struggle I have never been able to repay.'

'It's no excuse, but that was the lawyers' call. I left that all up to them and they didn't even mention they were cutting you off. I will make it up to your mother, and Steve, if they will let me. And I want to make it up to you, Tally.' He leaned forward, his gaze intent on hers. 'Sofia knows all about you, I called her the night of the party. She wasn't best pleased, as you can probably imagine, and as soon as shooting finished, I had to head back to LA to see her and try and put things right. But although she's still cross with me, she's keen to meet you, if you are willing, and for Atticus to meet his eldest sister. I spoke to Eva as well and came clean. Not the easiest of conversations, she's not my biggest fan.'

'Maybe she and I could start a club,' Tally said, and he was startled into laughter.

'She'd like that, I think. Anyway, she suggested I come over and tell the kids about you. They had a lot of questions and if the divorce hadn't put me in their black books, finding out I kept your existence a secret definitely has. But they are all excited that they have an older sister and all want to meet you, even Phoenix, and getting her away from her phone to say anything is rare.'

Four siblings, two stepmothers, all wanting to meet her. It was more than Tally could comprehend.

'And *I* want to get to know you,' Sebastian said, and for once he didn't seem to be using his legendary charm. 'So, will you come and stay? There's a pool house so you get your own space, a car you can use for as long as you like.'

Tally had no idea how to respond, what to think, her mind seizing on one practical consideration to give her time to process the last five minutes. 'I can't drive.'

'Everyone drives in LA, it's not like London, but we can figure that out. I know you're an actress, why not come out and try your luck? I can't get you a job but I can make sure you meet the right people. It's the very least I can do.'

'I need to think about it,' Tally said slowly. 'Talk to Mum.'

Her pride still wanted to send him away. Tell this stranger with her eyes that he couldn't buy her forgiveness with pool houses and opened doors and four unknown siblings and Hollywood. But hadn't she always dreamt of this moment? Hadn't she always wanted to know her siblings? She was no longer Sebastian's guilty secret, she existed, they were excited to meet her. And really, what was keeping her here? She had no Lucas, no job, no prospects, and her best friend was starting a new chapter whilst Tally was stuck at the beginning.

Saying yes didn't mean she was forgetting the past. But maybe she could move on.

Sebastian got to his feet and held out a card. 'Here's my number, my private number. Less than twenty people have this, it's family only.'

Her chest squeezed at that word—*family*.

'I'm heading back tomorrow but obviously you can come whenever you want. Just say the words and your ticket will be booked. I can't make up for the past, Tally. But I'll do whatever it takes to be in your future, if you'll let me.'

Tally watched him walk out, his number on a card in her trembling fingertips. What happened next was up to her. And the person she most wanted to tell was Lucas. Maybe the reason she couldn't tell him was the reason she should go. Start again. Sunshine, ocean, palm trees. LA seemed like the kind of place to help a girl get over heartbreak. She'd be a fool to turn this opportunity down. She'd needed a direction and here one was, offered to her on a plate, fate intervening. She just had to be brave enough to take it.

It was done. In the end Lucas hadn't been able to persuade three of the shareholders, including Johnson, to sell to him but those who did gave him a considerable majority share in Vineyard. His first decision had been to sack Johnson from the Board and install Brianna Wu as CEO so the transformation era could begin, his favourite part. The cut-throat thrust of buying and selling had never been the draw, it was what happened next that excited him. Vineyard had been resting on its laurels for too long—expansion, repositioning, focusing the brand, that was what got his blood thumping.

So why did he feel so flat?

Lucas knew the answer. It was because he wanted to celebrate with Tally. Wanted to walk into the pub and see surprise and delight warm her eyes as she nodded him to his usual corner. To flirt with her throughout the evening, knowing that everyone in the pub knew she was his, before whisking her back to his house to celebrate properly. But he had lost the right to do that when he had disappeared on her. When he had let her down. When he had allowed his fears to overwhelm him and blamed his feelings for her for mistakes he had made.

Clarity was painful. He deserved it to be because he had hurt a woman who had done nothing but enhance his life. A woman who deserved everything. But he had given her nothing. Worse than nothing. After all, he was the one who had invited her to Italy. Who had kissed her first. Who had sought her out back in London and kissed her again. He was the one who had made all the running and he was the one who had retreated when it all went wrong. He should reach out, apologise, but would that be selfish? She probably didn't want to hear from him ever again. He didn't deserve to have his conscience assuaged.

Felix was out celebrating with Brianna and some of the other shareholders but Lucas didn't feel like joining them. The humidity in Boston was getting oppressive but he didn't want to return to London either, to the big house he kept mostly shut up to disguise how alone he really was. But if not London, where? To Yorkshire, to a house held on to for family reasons although neither he nor Felix had enjoyed an idyllic childhood there? A house which always seemed to echo with the ghosts of his parents' arguments.

How had Felix escaped so seemingly unscathed? Lucas had obviously done a better job of protecting his little brother than he had realised. At least he had got one thing right. Suddenly overwhelmingly tired, he switched his phone off, put the Do Not Disturb sign on his door and crashed into a dreamless sleep.

Lucas didn't feel much refreshed when he woke the next morning, pulled out of his sleep by a noise he couldn't quite place, until he realised someone was banging on his door. 'Lucas! Wake up!'

It took him a few seconds to respond, then, shockingly wide awake, rolled out of bed and strode across to the door. 'Felix? What happened?'

'Lucas, why aren't you answering your phone?' His brother was in yesterday's suit, his face stubbled, eyes red with fatigue. 'It's Roberto, he's collapsed.'

Neither brother spoke much on the long flight back to Italy, but by the set of Felix's jaw, the muscle beating in his cheek, the fear in his eyes, his emotions were running as high as Lucas's own. From summer holidays in Tuscany, the highlights of their year, time away from the marital cold war that was their childhood, to his apprenticeship under exacting but kindly eyes, he owed Roberto everything. Roberto had even ensured there was a home for Felix during school holidays in those years after their father had died and their mother had moved abroad.

There were no direct flights from Boston to Tuscany

so they flew to Rome, where they changed flights, arriving in Florence exhausted and jetlagged, neither having slept. A car met them and took them straight to the hospital, where Isabella was pacing up and down in a small private waiting room. Her elegant, freshly made-up face was a stark contrast to their travel-weary selves, but her eyes were so full of sorrow and fear that Lucas had no reservations about enveloping her in a hug. 'He'll be all right,' he murmured. 'He has to be.'

'You both smell disgusting.' Isabella wrinkled her nose but she accepted the hug, clinging on for a long moment.

'Over twelve hours on planes and in airports will do that. How is he?'

'Sedated. Go say hello and then I suggest you two go back to the villa for food and showers before we speak to the doctors.'

Lucas walked through the door she indicated, his chest tightening painfully as he saw Roberto hooked up to a machine. The man who had always seemed so indomitable looked so small lying in the hospital bed, his breathing painfully shallow.

'Be bold,' he had always told Lucas. *'Set your goals high.'*

And Lucas had. For most of his life anyway. But he had failed this summer. What would Roberto say if he knew how Lucas had acted?

'Get better,' Lucas said, taking his hand. 'Get better and you can tell me off yourself.'

The next few days passed agonisingly slowly. Several times Lucas picked up his phone to update Tally but couldn't bring himself to send the message. She'd be worried, he knew, and it seemed cruel to stress her when the outcome was so uncertain. The three took it in turns to be in the hospital, he and Felix ensuring that Isabella went out for walks, for shopping, for cocktails, relieved when she bossed them around or sniped at them. A quiet, thoughtful Isabella was almost as worrying as the tubes and doctors' grave expressions.

Finally, they got the news they had been praying for, things looked more hopeful. The doctors would reduce the sedation and when Roberto woke up remove the tubes. All three of them haunted the hospital waiting room until they finally got the all-clear.

'One at a time,' they were warned. 'Don't overexcite him.'

'Thank God,' Felix murmured.

Isabella went in first and when she emerged ten minutes later her eyes were red but she seemed much like her old self. 'He's sleeping again,' she said. 'But you can sit with him if you want.'

Felix elected to go back to the villa with Isabella. She had a list of things they needed if Roberto was to be allowed home in the next few days, and the number of an agency which supplied twenty-four-seven nursing and personal care, and wanted to brief his assistant in person. Lucas promised not to leave Roberto alone and, after seeing the pair out, entered the small hospital room and took the seat next to the bed. The room was quieter with fewer machines, Roberto's breathing easier, his face less pale. He looked every one of his eighty-one years, but he looked like himself.

'I'm not ready to lose you yet,' Lucas told him. 'None of us are.'

It had been a long few days, and with some of the worry dissipating Lucas fell into a doze. When he came to with a start, he realised Roberto was awake.

'I'll get a nurse.'

Roberto shook his head slowly. 'Water,' he said.

'Of course.' There was a cup with a straw on the locker and Lucas lifted it up and brought it to the older man's mouth. 'Slowly,' he cautioned. 'You gave us quite a scare, I couldn't cope with you choking as well.'

A ghost of a smile hovered around Roberto's mouth. 'How's Tally?' he managed.

'Good—' he started and then stopped. 'We broke up.'

'I'm sorry.'

'I don't deserve pity. I ran away, Roberto. For a legitimate reason, the Vineyard deal was in trouble and I had to salvage it. But I blamed myself. For being distracted. For allowing the deal to get to that point without seeing what was happening. I blamed her for distracting me. I… I wasn't kind. You'd be ashamed of me. I'm ashamed of me.'

It was a relief to say the words.

'Never,' Roberto managed.

'I've had a lot of time to think recently. I have worked so hard not to be like my father I have gone completely the other way, tried to jettison any desire or need for anything that isn't work. But that isn't living, is it? You managed to be successful and have a family you loved, and you lived. Look at all those stories you told Tally. All those things you have seen and done and felt. And my grandfather was the same.' He laughed softly. 'I can see the two of you now, out on the terrace with a glass of wine, planning your next adventure. Why can't I get that balance? Am I right, am I too flawed? Or is it just that I am too afraid to try?'

Roberto reached up and took his wrist. 'Do you miss her?' he rasped.

'Yes.' Lucas didn't have to think. 'It's like part of me is gone.'

'And you're sorry?'

'More than I can say but...'

'Then what are you doing here? Go tell her...'

'Just like that? Just go and tell her? What if she doesn't want to see me? What if she hates me? She probably hates me. She ended it, you know, but I pushed her into it.'

Roberto didn't answer, just stared at Lucas steadily.

'You're right,' Lucas said. 'As always. You taught me to follow my gut. Not to be afraid to take risks. If she's not interested that's my fault and I need to live with that, but I can't not try and make amends.'

He stood and dropped a kiss on the older man's forehead. 'Thank you, Roberto. For everything.'

He couldn't go yet, he needed to get Roberto home and settled, but he had a plan and, for the first time in many years, he saw the possibility of a different future. What happened next was down to Tally but, whatever she decided, Lucas couldn't fall back into his old ways. He needed to live, no matter how hard it was, to delegate, to let people in, to experience life outside of the narrow confines he existed in. He owed it to Roberto, he owed it to his brother, and most of all he owed it to himself.

CHAPTER TWELVE

'I CAN'T BELIEVE you're abandoning me to go to LA!' Layla said for about the tenth time in the last hour. 'I go away on honeymoon and you change your whole life around.'

'You'll barely notice I'm gone,' Tally pointed out. 'You know what this term is like. I hardly see you between all the harvest festivals and Halloween and Christmas stuff unless I come to a school fair or volunteer to help with making decorations.'

'It's just as we planned it when we were kids, me married to Phinn and you a glamorous actress in LA.'

'Out of work unknown actress staying in her father's pool house,' Tally corrected. 'But at least I'll be a step closer. Of course, I'll get there and my teeth will be too English and my hair too frizzy and I'll be two sizes too big and I'll be booking in for Botox and a breast lift and I'll still find it hard to get one line in a gritty drama.' She laughed but she was only half joking. If she was struggling in London where physical imperfection was less of a barrier to success, how would she manage in image-obsessed LA? She cut her own hair half the time.

'You are perfect and you'll be perfect. Besides, you're going to get to know your dad. I am so happy for you.'

'He's sent me a first-class ticket,' Tally said. 'Can you imagine? Me in first class?'

'You deserve it. You deserve it all and once there you'll be far too busy to…' Layla stopped and clamped her mouth shut.

'To think about Lucas? I hope you're right.' Tally sighed. 'Every time something happens, I want to tell him and then I remember I can't. Heartbroken twice in one year. What does that say about me? The stupid thing is I was with Max for years, heartbreak is kind of the deal even if you know it's for the best and the relationship had really been over for a while. But I knew Lucas for only a few weeks. That was all. It wasn't even a real relationship, just…'

'Just mind-blowing sex?'

'There was that, but also someone who made me feel more, you know? That I could do anything, be anything.'

'You can and you don't need a man to do it.' Layla raised her glass. 'To being strong and free and a kick-ass woman.'

'Says the new bride,' Tally teased as she clinked her glass to Layla.

At that moment her phone flashed with a message and, glancing down, her heart stuttered to a stop.

'It's from Lucas.'

'You haven't blocked his number?'

'I haven't needed to up to now.' Tally stared at the message icon.

'So, what does he want?'

'I don't know.'

'Open it then.'

'What happened to block his number?' With trembling hands Tally clicked on the message.

Can we talk?

She showed it to Layla, who rolled her eyes. 'A little late for that.'

'Agreed.' Tally typed the words and sent it.

'Good girl.'

'I know it was the right thing to do, but is it weak that I feel sick? That I want to hear him out?'

'No, feelings are never weak. What makes you strong is your actions. Oh, that's good. I feel an assembly theme coming on.'

Tally's phone flashed with a reply.

I know I don't deserve it. Just five minutes. I'll be at the park in an hour if you can make it.

'Which park?' Layla scowled as she handed Tally her phone back. 'This is London, he needs to be more specific. Honestly.'

'He means our picnic spot in Battersea Park.'

'Tallulah May Jenkins, you're not thinking of going?'

'I think I have to,' Tally said slowly. 'I think otherwise I'll always wonder what he would have said. It makes no difference. I'm off to LA, but I don't want to go with what-ifs hanging over me, you know?'

'Do you want me and Phinn to come with you?'

'My own private army?' Tally felt a rush of love for her diminutive but fierce friend. 'The worst part about going to LA is leaving you behind.'

'You need to stay there at least till half-term. I've got Phinn looking at flights.'

'Deal.'

The walk to the park was so familiar, but never before had she trod it with this twist of hope and fear. Hope that what? He'd grovel and beg her to give him another chance? Fear that he would be the same cold stranger as the one on the phone. Fear that the cold stranger was the real Lucas, the man she had known a construct. A one summer deal only.

Her heart stuttered as she spotted Lucas, looking ill at ease leaning against a tree, and she almost turned tail and ran, but forced herself to keep moving.

'Hi.'

He straightened. 'You came?'

'You said five minutes.'

She didn't want to prolong this, whatever this was, any longer than necessary—but, oh, he looked good, more dishevelled than usual, his hair ruffled, his cheeks stubbled.

'Right. Yes.' But he didn't say anything else.

'I see the deal went through.' What was she doing filling the silence? He *should* feel awkward, he'd *made* things awkward.

'Yes.'

'You must be very happy. I hope you celebrated appropriately.' Did she sound bitter? She didn't want to but could feel the anger creep into her voice, her stance.

'No. Partly because we had to go straight to Tuscany. Roberto had a heart attack.'

'Is he okay?' Her anger was forgotten. 'Why didn't you tell me?'

'He's on the mend and I didn't want to worry you until I had something definitive to say.' His mouth twisted into that distinctive almost smile. 'Which reminds me. He sends his love and says regardless of whether you send me away or not you are always welcome in Tuscany and to emphasise that he means it.'

'That's… I'm very fond of him too. I'm glad he's getting better.' She paused as she took in his words. 'What do you mean send you away?'

'Can we walk?'

'Technically, you've already used three of your five minutes but yes. Just not for too long. I have to finish packing.'

'You're going away?'

'No, Lucas. No more small talk. Tell me why you're here. I thought we said everything we needed to the day you stood me up at my best friend's wedding. The day you broke our deal.'

She started walking, glad of the reminder why she shouldn't trust him, of the surge of anger and hurt. He looked too good, too familiar, her hands wanting to reach out and touch him.

Lucas fell into step beside her. 'I am sorrier than you can know.'

'About what?' Tally hadn't come here to make this easy for him.

'All of it. Disappearing without a word. Standing you up. The way I spoke to you. It was instinct, the wrong instinct, I know that. One minute I was having the kind of summer I didn't think possible, not for me, the kind of summer I thought only existed in films. A summer filled with you. It became easy to clock off on time or early, easy to leave things to the next day, easy to take my eye off the ball. And then the deal I'd spent a year working on nearly collapsed and it was like the validation of all my worst fears. That personal happiness meant business failure.'

'You know that's not actually true, don't you?'

'At a theoretical level, maybe. In my gut, no. I always knew my father was irresponsible, Tally. I always knew he was a hedonist who didn't care how many lives he destroyed as long as he was having fun, but I didn't know just how reckless he had been until he died. How close we were to losing everything and what that meant. Not just a change in lifestyle for my mother, selling a couple of expensive houses, Felix changing schools, but so many jobs and livelihoods in this country, the pension scheme, everyone in the supply chain. All these people at risk because of one man's failures.'

'All those people are secure because of his son.'

'There was a cost and I willingly paid it. I thought if his eye was never on the ball then mine can't ever be off it. But this summer I allowed myself to relax and everything I feared happened.'

Tally stopped and turned to face him. 'I know all this, Lucas. I know who you are and what drives you. I can't say you didn't warn me. But why here, why now? What use is telling me all this? It doesn't change anything.'

'I was sitting with Roberto, and the reason I was there, the reason Felix and Isabella were there wasn't because of how successful he was or because of duty, it was because we love him. I remembered summer holidays in the villa, he and my grandfather playing chess and drinking wine. His wife, Magdalena, and my grandmother swimming or playing tennis, a house filled with love and laughter. My grandfather was a very astute businessman, he steered WGO into the computer age, shored it up so well that even my father couldn't quite destroy it during his decade in charge. But he had balance. His life was full in every way. That's the example I should have tried to emulate. That's the life I should lead, if I'm brave enough to try.'

He took a deep breath. 'I'm sorrier than you can know, Tally. I pushed you away not because I blamed you but because I blamed myself for falling for you. For starting to love you. Somehow, I thought loving was weak, but that's not true, is it? Daring to love is the bravest thing a person can do. I love you, Tally. I just needed to tell you that.'

Tally stopped still, her feet refusing to keep walking, her mind whirling with all he had said, circling around over and over to those three words. He loved her. And she loved him. That was why he'd been able to hurt her so badly. And that was why she wasn't sure she would be able to trust him with her heart again, however much she wanted to.

'I'm going to LA,' she blurted out. 'I don't know for how long—my father has got me an artist's visa somehow. But for a while. I leave in two days. Tonight's karaoke is my send-off party.'

She reached out and took his hand, his fingers warm in hers, so achingly familiar she wanted to cling on for ever. Instead, she squeezed and let it drop again.

'I knew,' she said simply. 'Not that you...' She

couldn't quite bring herself to say love. 'Not that you had feelings for me, but the rest. You've told me enough for me to guess and I know you, Lucas. Know that despite what you did you're a good man, just one with scars. We all bear them. Look at me, so frightened of being left I clung onto a relationship long after it should have been put out of its misery and then wallowed for months after. But I've made a decision. I won't allow anyone to define happiness for me again. I'm worth more than that. I fell for you too, Lucas. I think maybe I loved you too. But although I understand why you did what you did, you still hurt me. You still did the one thing you knew I wasn't equipped to handle. So I can't trust you and without trust there can't be a future. I do appreciate you telling me all this, I know it couldn't have been easy. But there's nowhere for us to go. Give my love to Felix and Roberto.'

She allowed herself to touch his cheek. Just once. And then she turned and left. Heart breaking once again, part convinced she was making a terrible mistake but knowing deep inside it was the only way.

'How did it go?'

Felix's voice was loud and exuberant and Lucas winced.

'Not good. She's going to LA and will never trust me again.'

'LA? To see her father? How did that come about?'

'I don't know. We didn't really do small talk.'

'It's a *huge* thing, how is that small talk?'

'I was too busy humbling myself to ask, if you must

know. But she made it quite clear she doesn't want to see me again and I have to respect that, Felix.'

At some point this numbness would wear off and then he would hurt, a lot. It would hurt more knowing he had brought this on himself.

'I can't trust you,' she had said.

He had prided himself on his integrity, on being a good guy, not a player like his father, and yet here he was.

'So, you're just giving up?'

'No, I'm respecting her boundaries. What do you want me to do? Ambush her at the airport? Follow her to LA? Get arrested for stalking?'

'When does she go?'

'Monday.'

'Tonight's karaoke night.'

'Yes, her farewell party, she said.'

'Perfect! That's your chance.'

'My what?' His brother's meaning dawned. 'We can't just turn up. We're probably barred.'

'You're probably barred. There's no need to bar me.'

'And do what? Sing my apologies to her?'

'You hurt her, Lucas, humiliated her. You need to humiliate yourself to even things out.'

Lucas narrowed his eyes. 'You just want to make me sing, don't you?'

'I would give a year's salary to watch you apologise in musical form.'

Lucas almost—almost—laughed at the glee in his brother's voice.

'This is my future, Felix. You're right, if I don't try again, I *am* giving up. Tally doesn't trust me and if I give up then I guess I am just agreeing with her that I can't change, that what we have isn't worth repairing. But trust isn't something I can just conjure up. It has to be proven over time. No one gesture, no matter how humiliating or heartfelt, can do that.'

'I agree, but I'm not the one you need to say that to. And for the record, I think a humiliating gesture will help. Not that I'm at all biased. I'll see you this evening. I can shield you from the angry locals.'

'More likely to run away and leave me to face the pitchforks.'

'That too. See you later.'

Lucas ended the call feeling marginally better. He had never just given up in his life and he wasn't about to start now. What he and Tally had had, could have, was more than worth another try, and if he had to humiliate himself in the process then that was a small price to pay.

Despite Felix's urging Lucas didn't want to show up at the beginning of the evening. It wasn't that he was afraid to walk into a room full of people who probably wanted to tear him limb from limb, it was that this was Tally's night, her chance to shine, her goodbye, and he didn't want to take a second of that away from her. Grand gestures were all very well but if you were going to take over someone else's occasion you had to be very sure they wanted you to. And he wasn't sure at all.

He met Felix for dinner first, although he could barely swallow a bite of what he knew was an excellent steak, could barely finish the one glass of red wine, his mind racing with a dozen different permutations of how the evening might end, from being thrown out of The Duchess before getting to say one word to sweeping Tally up in his arms and carrying her all the way back to his. Either seemed as likely.

'Come on, big bro,' Felix said eventually. 'Let's go get your girl.'

The walk to the pub seemed to take for ever, and yet they were there impossibly fast. The downstairs was unusually quiet and, to his relief, Lucas didn't recognise the people behind the bar. He and Felix made their way up to the function room and slipped quietly into the crowded space. No one noticed them come in, the lights were turned down and most people were facing the stage the other side of the room, where Charlene was performing an emotional cover of 'Slipping Through my Fingers'.

Lucas took up a position in a dark corner as Felix slipped away to get them both a pint and watched as Tally retook the microphone and treated them to several requests. She was dazzling, holding the crowd in the palm of her hand, her voice true and sweet with a rich timbre that was all hers. She had *it*, whatever that indefinable it was, and Lucas realised that if she got the opportunity she deserved then she might be in LA for some time. For a moment he considered disappearing out as quietly as he had come, leaving her to get on with her new life. But it didn't have to be one or the other. She should have it all and if he was lucky enough for that to include him then there was always a way.

Finally, the evening came to a close. Steve and Charlene made short emotional speeches and Tally, through tears, thanked them for everything. People started to filter out after hugging Tally, many leaving presents and cards. Lucas hung back, not wanting to interrupt just yet. In the end it was just Layla, Phinn and her family, Steve and Charlene and a smattering of other people he recognised.

It was time.

'Wish me luck,' Lucas muttered to Felix and stepped out of his corner.

Tally didn't think her emotions could get any more heightened. She'd been filled with a mixture of excitement and trepidation before seeing Lucas this morning, afterwards filled with doubt and sadness. Walking away had been almost unbearably hard even though she knew it was the right thing to do. Now she was surrounded by people who loved her, who supported her, and she had to say goodbye. No matter that she kept telling herself that LA was an eleven-hour flight away and she could come back for a visit at any time, that she might hate it, that she might return in just a few weeks, it still felt like the end of an era. She'd channelled all those feelings into her performance, even though it was just a makeshift stage in a small pub, and she knew her mother had done the same. She owed Charlene a lot, but her mother's unwavering belief in Tally and reassurance that moving to LA and getting to know her father was the right thing to do was her mother's most selfless act yet.

How she was going to say goodbye on Monday she didn't know.

She approached Layla and Phinn but, before she could speak, she was aware of someone walking towards her.

Lucas.

'What's he doing here?' Layla hissed.

To anyone who didn't know Lucas he probably looked

supremely at ease, but Tally could see telltale signs that he wasn't as confident as he appeared. His jaw was set, a muscle beating in his cheek, his expression shadowed.

'Am I too late?'

'You were too late weeks ago,' Layla said, arms folded.

'Too late for what? You already apologised,' Tally said.

Lucas nodded towards the stage. 'To sing.'

'To *what*?' Was she dreaming? This was getting more surreal by the moment. 'I…'

'No,' her mother said, and Tally glanced at her in surprise. Charlene also had her arms folded and her expression was forbidding. 'You're not too late.'

'Right then.' Lucas made his way purposefully to the stage.

'You don't have to,' she half whispered as he passed her and he gave her the half-smile she loved.

'I know. I want to. Unless you would prefer I didn't?'

'I…' But of course she was curious. 'Be my guest.'

Lucas took some time choosing then came to stand in the middle of the stage. 'I'm not here to hijack Tally's evening,' he said. 'Nor am I here to beg her to reconsider. But I do want her to know how very sorry I am. Felix said the best way would be for me to humiliate myself, but I don't see this as humiliation, I see it as speaking Tally's language. Okay, then…'

For a moment he looked unsure, then squared his shoulders and attraction rippled through her.

Tally stood where she was, surrounded by people who loved her, anticipation coursing through her. She didn't mind a bad performance musically as long as the singer committed. Lucas certainly *looked* like he knew what he was doing, the microphone held loosely in one hand as he waited for the music to start. What would he sing? Something croony? Rock? Pop?

Please don't let him try and rap.

To her shock, a guitar began to fill the room. Surely it wasn't…? Not *Elvis*?

Lucas began to sing 'Heartbreak Hotel'. He didn't fall into the trap of trying to mimic Elvis, a pitfall she had seen many a karaoke singer fall into, but sang the sweet, deceptively simple song straight, imbuing the well-known lyrics and tune with a pathos she hadn't heard before. His voice wasn't the strongest, but it was true and held the room spellbound through the short song, and the smattering of applause at the end was heartfelt.

'I miss you, Tally,' he said. 'I let you down, badly, and no amount of apologies and impromptu performances can fix that. I know you don't trust me and I understand why. I'm not asking you to take me back…' Was that *disappointment* she felt? 'And I am certainly not going to ask you not to go to LA, you absolutely should. But I am asking you to let me prove that I can change, that I have changed. I can't promise not to be a workaholic and I can't promise not to bear my responsibilities heavily, although I can allow Felix to shoulder some of them. But I can promise to put you first, if you'll let me. I want to date you, Tallulah Jenkins. Slowly, steadily, properly. Rebuild that trust, show you that I can be the man you deserve. Show you how much I love you.' He stopped then and stood there, heart in his eyes.

Tally looked around and realised that her family and

friends had left them alone. She'd been too caught up in Lucas's words to notice.

'You are full of surprises, Lucas West,' she said.

'I'm trying.' He jumped down from the stage and made his way towards her until he was standing in front of her.

'You want to date me?'

'I'll be spending more time in Boston and New York. I can come to you, maybe you can come to me. We can talk on the phone in between visits, start again, start properly. I love you, Tally, I think I have loved you since you burst into my compartment in the Orient Express, since you bought me a coffee in a backstreet in Venice and looked around as if you were in the most beautiful square. I love your tenacity and the joy you find in everyday things; I love your heart and your talent. I know I don't deserve you but...'

She put a finger up to his mouth. 'I love you too,' she said and it was a relief to say the words. 'Not because you sang to me, although that was amazing, but because you are you. A man who cares too much, who thinks he doesn't deserve happiness. I'm not sure what the future holds, but I do want you to be in it. I want to see what we could be if we start again. If we date.'

Date. Such an old-fashioned word and yet one that encompassed so much. Hope and possibility and second chances.

'I love you, Tally.'

'I love you too.'

And as he kissed her, she knew she was making the right choice. The future was full of uncertainties, but she had to take a chance on happiness.

EPILOGUE

One year later

'YOU'RE HERE!' TALLY RACED along the beach towards Lucas's tall figure. 'I wasn't expecting you until tomorrow.'

'It's our first night in our new house, where else could I be?' He swept her into his arms and she leaned into his kiss, luxuriating in the feel of him.

'I can't believe it's ours.' Tally looked back at the gorgeous Malibu beach house. 'When I walked inside, I half expected someone to tell me it was all a joke and escort me out. My clothes barely fill a tenth of that dressing room.'

'How's work?'

Tally loved the pride in Lucas's smile as he asked the question. He had been as excited as she had when she had landed a recurring role on a new hospital drama, playing an English doctor.

'Good! I feel like I'm learning every day, just being on set is a dream.' Her days were long but she wasn't complaining. Best of all, she had landed the role on her own—the producers had had no idea who her father was when they'd hired her, that news was still very much under wraps.

It had been an incredible year, from forging a relationship with her father and siblings, to landing the job of her dreams, to buying the house with Lucas. As promised, they'd taken things slowly for a few months, meals out and daytrips leading to weekend breaks and holidays, until Lucas started spending more and more time in LA. A couple of months ago he had leased office space in the city and the pair had started to house hunt. Now here they were, owners of the kind of house she used to daydream about.

'Maybe it's time to consider that dog,' she suggested.

'Do you think we're ready for that kind of commitment?'

'We do own a house together.'

'That's true. But there's one more step we could take.' To her shock, he fell to one knee, a small box in his hands. 'Tallulah May Jenkins, I can't believe I'm here with you, that you took pity on me and allowed me a second chance, that we have a house and a life together. The only thing that could make me happier is if you marry me. Will you, Tally?'

'Get up! Of course. Oh, it's beautiful,' as he opened the box to display a diamond set emerald ring. 'I love it.'

'I saw it in Venice when we were there last month and it made me think of you. You mean it?' He slid the ring onto her finger. 'It's a yes?'

'Does this mean we can get a dog?'

'A whole pack if you say yes,' he promised recklessly, and she laughed.

'Let's start with one. I love you, Lucas.'

'I love you too.'

'We should get married in Tuscany, so Roberto can be there.'

'And honeymoon on the Orient Express?'

'Back where it all began. Perfect.'

Tally lost herself in his kiss, in the man she loved, with the sounds of the ocean all around her.

'Let's go celebrate in our new house,' she whispered as she reluctantly broke the kiss.

'Sounds good, any way of celebrating in mind?' Just the look in his eyes heated her through.

'I'm sure we can think of something,' she promised as, hand in hand, they made their way back to their house. They'd come a long way over the last year and while she knew the future was always uncertain, as long as they were together, she knew she could face anything.

* * * * *

If you enjoyed this story,
check out these other great reads
from Jessica Gilmore

Miss Right All Along
It Started with a Vegas Wedding
Christmas with His Ballerina
The Princess and the Single Dad

All available now!

TEMPTED BY HER BEST FRIEND BILLIONAIRE

MICHELLE DOUGLAS

MILLS & BOON

To Greg, who went above and beyond when I was neck-deep in this book, always there with an encouraging word, chocolate or glass of red whenever I needed them. Sending you all the London and dinosaur emojis.

CHAPTER ONE

BLAKE'S LUXURY SEDAN all but limped into Callenbrook, his home town in rural Victoria. The home town he hadn't visited in over a decade. If he'd had his way, it would've been another decade before he'd returned.

His nose curled and his scowl deepened. His grandmother's voice sounded through him. *Be careful the wind doesn't change.*

An old wives' tale, Gran.

What he wouldn't give, though, to hear her voice one last time.

Don't think about that now. Unclenching his fingers from around the steering wheel, he tapped them against it instead and considered travelling the extra thirty minutes into Bendigo and getting his tyre fixed there. Ever since he was fifteen years old he'd dubbed Callenbrook 'Red Neck Falls', and the fewer people he had to engage with here, the better.

With a growl, he turned and headed into the town centre, pulled in at the auto mechanic's workshop. Joey Lockyer came strolling out from the inside. As soon as Blake emerged from the tinted-windowed interior, though, Joey looked as if he'd like to turn around and head back inside. With a deep breath, he set his shoulders and kept moving in Blake's direction. Blake and Joey had never had any issues with each other. Hopefully they wouldn't now either.

Joey pointed to one of the front wheels.

'Run flats,' Blake said.

Why the hell hadn't he specified his rental car have an actual spare tyre that he could change himself rather than run flats he'd have to get replaced by somebody else if they were punctured?

'We've one of those in stock. You're lucky. I've a few jobs in front of you, though.'

'What time you want me to come back and collect it?'

He waited for Joey to shrug and say, 'Never.' Waited for him to tell Blake to take his business elsewhere.

'I'll be hard-pressed to get it done this afternoon. Tomorrow morning would be more convenient. It'll be ready by eight.'

Convenient for whom? Though, as the funeral wasn't until ten, he couldn't claim it as an inconvenience to himself. He was grounded here until after the reading of his grandmother's will.

He tossed Joey the keys. 'Want me to pay up front?'

Joey huffed out what might've been a laugh. 'Tomorrow will be fine, Blake. Don't forget, any time after eight.'

Pulling his duffel bag from the boot, Blake slung it over his shoulder and, with a nod, set off on the six-block walk to his grandmother's duplex. Before he was out of earshot he heard one of Joey's workers say, 'Who was that?'

'Blake Carlisle. Iris Day's grandson.'

'Finally here in the flesh, then?'

Blake's nose curled. Man, he hated this place.

Eight minutes later, Blake stood out the front of his grandmother's house. He stared, unable to force his legs forward to open the gate. Even though he knew curtains would be twitching at the windows in the neighbours' houses.

He glanced briefly at the house next door, the duplex that shared a wall with his grandmother's, and moistened his lips. Nina hadn't taken his phone calls since February, hadn't answered his texts. *Damn it.* The one thing he needed to fix while he was here was *that*.

His gaze return to Gran's. A decade. While he'd seen his grandmother more regularly than that, he hadn't been home in ten years. And nothing had changed.

You've changed.

And your grandmother *is dead.*

The gate, the garden, the house, all blurred. His grandmother was no longer with them. *That* was a change too big to comprehend. As soon as her funeral was over, though, and her estate settled, nothing would make him step foot back in Callenbrook again. *Nothing.*

You going inside or are you going to start howling on the front lawn?

His therapist would probably advise him to go ahead and howl, would tell him it was cathartic. The neighbours would love it.

Forcing his legs forward, he pulled out the spare key he hadn't used in a decade and he let himself inside. Closing the door, he didn't howl even though nobody could see him, but, dumping his duffel bag to the floor, he sagged back, the door reassuringly solid at his back.

The place was wrong. As if without Gran inside it, it made no sense. He really could've sat on the floor then and bawled his eyes out. Instead he did as Gran would've expected—he opened the curtains and then the windows, and took himself off for a shower.

Showered and unpacked—not that he'd packed much as he didn't expect to be in Callenbrook for more than a few days—he ambled into the kitchen and found a fresh loaf of bread on the counter, milk, vegetables and a steak in the refrigerator along with a six-pack of beer. And a few cans of the lemonade his grandmother had favoured.

Nina? Glancing at their connecting wall, he realised he

had no idea where she now worked or what time she'd be home. For the last decade Nina had been her mother's full-time carer, but Johanna had died back in February. And he hadn't made it home for the funeral.

Even if she wanted to avoid him, even if she refused to forgive him, he and Nina still needed to talk.

His gut churned; bile burned his throat. He shouldn't have left it so long to come back. He should've returned as soon as he was able.

A familiar band tightened about his chest, making it cramp, and his breathing grew hard and laboured. Closing his eyes, he focused on counting his breaths, regulating them, until the grip loosened. Hooking out a chair at the kitchen table, he pulled out his phone and played a game of Tetris. When he was done, his breathing had almost returned to normal, his mind calmer again.

He made a sandwich even though he wasn't hungry because low blood-sugar levels wouldn't help. And he wasn't losing the plot. Not now.

He didn't hear Nina come home, nor did he hear her move about next door. He rapped out their old signal on the kitchen wall a couple of times, but received nothing in reply. Not even a curt two-knock 'Not now' that had been their standard language.

Yeah, a decade ago.

Maybe so, but she wouldn't have forgotten.

At a little after five he couldn't stand it any longer. Grabbing a lemonade from the fridge, he headed outside to the back veranda, stopping short when he saw Nina sitting in a vinyl armchair in a startling shade of electric blue at her end of the veranda, staring out at her garden. Dragging in a breath, he forced his legs towards her, stopping at the knee-high iron railing that separated the two properties. 'I didn't think you were home.'

She didn't turn to look at him, but continued to stare out at her garden. He glanced at it too and his brows shot up. Nina had loved green things and gardening ever since Gran had put a trowel in her hand as a five-year-old and set her up with her own little plot.

He'd known she'd extended her garden, but this was *amazing*! Native trees and shrubs wound among raised garden beds that he knew would be filled with vegetables. The effect was an odd combination of wild and ordered.

'The garden is looking great.' He sat in the matching chair on his side of the railing, his heart beating too hard. 'You didn't hear my knock on the wall?'

'Am I supposed to come running whenever you knock?'

Right. Wrong opening. He should've said something like, 'Isn't this awful?' or 'How are you holding up?' because she'd loved his grandmother every bit as much as he had.

He ached to reach across and hug her, kiss her cheek, but the frosty eyebrow she'd briefly raised had warned him not to try it. His stomach hollowed out. He concentrated on his breathing and stared at the garden on his grandmother's side of the fence.

Nina had obviously taken over Gran's garden too—the native plants and shrubs irresistible to the birds who made a cacophony of sound in the dusk of the late August afternoon—but the rose garden his grandmother had so loved still proudly stood at its centre. Staring at it now made him ache and throb. 'You didn't hear me arrive?'

'I heard you were back in town before you left Joey's workshop.'

He shook his head. *This town.* Was that when she'd ducked across with those few groceries? Was that *her* dinner in his refrigerator? She might be giving him the cold shoulder, but she'd cared enough to make sure he had something to eat.

'You didn't think to come on over?'

'What for? You're a grown-up, aren't you? Besides, I was too busy getting over my shock that you'd actually turned up.' She raised her glass in his direction in a mock toast.

He went as cold as the ice that clinked in her glass. 'You didn't think I would?' Had she honestly thought he'd stay away and leave her to deal with everything?

'Showing up *isn't* what you do.'

Silently he swore. And swore. 'Look, Nina, about your mum's funeral…'

That eyebrow rose again when he hesitated. 'Go on. My mum's funeral…?'

When he didn't she gave a mirthless laugh. 'My mother, as in the woman you called Auntie Jo? The woman who took you under her wing and was a second mother to you because your own parents were miserable excuses for human beings? *That's* the woman you're referring to?'

'Nina, I…' But how to explain when he could barely explain it to himself.

'You didn't come back home once in ten years to see her. Not once. And you knew that, unlike your grandmother, she couldn't travel.'

For the last seven years he'd treated his grandmother to an annual European holiday—so he could see her at least once a year and make sure she was doing okay. He'd have done the same for Auntie Jo and Nina. Jo's illness, though, had made that impossible.

He hated Callenbrook with the fire of a thousand suns. He'd never wanted to return to the godforsaken place. Nina had always told him she understood.

Until February. When she'd stopped talking to him altogether.

Fact was he *had* tried to come home for the funeral. His hands clenched at the memory. He'd made it as far as Singapore airport before the pain in his chest and the drumming in his head had overpowered him. The shortness of his breath. The struggle for air. The way his left arm had tingled before going numb.

He'd collapsed, too dizzy and weak to communicate, unable to tell anyone what was wrong with him. A part of him had watched from afar as the cabin crew had called for an ambulance and he'd been raced to hospital. He'd thought he'd die before they arrived. A heart attack at thirty. Rare but not unheard of.

Except it hadn't been a heart attack. It had been a panic attack.

Prior to experiencing one for himself first-hand, he'd had no real idea what a panic attack involved. He hadn't known the symptoms could be so severe. He hadn't realised how debilitating they could be. He'd still been intent on getting the next flight to Australia, but no sooner had he verbalised that thought to the doctor than he'd found himself in the grip of another panic attack. Apparently telling yourself to snap out of it, that you were strong and successful and had overcome adversity before, didn't make an iota of difference. Panic attacks didn't care how wealthy you were, or how intelligent or successful or competent.

It had rocked him to his marrow. He'd never wanted to experience another one as long as he lived.

By the time the doctor had discharged him from hospital, it'd been too late to get to Callenbrook in time for the funeral. So he'd texted Nina that he'd had a work emergency so she wouldn't worry when he didn't turn up in Callenbrook, had grabbed the next flight back to London and had sought the professional help the doctor in Singapore had urged him to seek. He'd had therapy, had slowly worked through his issues, hence the reason he was here in the flesh now—and relatively coherent. But actually verbalising all of that…

Closing his eyes, he swallowed and prayed to God his

voice would work. 'None of that means I didn't care.' He and Jo had spoken regularly on the phone, they'd video-conferenced every couple of months. She'd known how much he'd loved her.

'Actions speak louder than words, Blake.'

She crossed one remarkably shapely leg over the other and he found himself frowning. Nina didn't have *shapely legs*. She just had…legs.

'Luckily for them both, Mum and Granny Day continued to believe in you until the end.'

His heart jackhammered in his chest. 'But…you don't?' She was supposed to *know* him. *Really* know him. She was the only person left on this earth who did. She *had* to know there was a good reason why he hadn't made it back for the funeral.

Pursing her lips, she glared at her garden and shook her head. Just once. But it hit him like a sucker punch.

'You needn't think that means they weren't hurt when you never came home either, or weren't made sad by the fact that they never had a chance to say a proper goodbye.'

She thought him heartless. She thought he'd turned his back on them. Before the guilt and regret, the grief, could blanket him in complete and utter inertia her words hit him. *They hadn't had the chance to say goodbye.*

'Gran's passing *wasn't* a surprise?' On the quiet of the late afternoon air, his words sounded like gunshots. He'd been told his grandmother had died of heart failure.

Nina's eyes flashed, 'Hell, Blake, she received a cancer diagnosis back in January.'

January! But… 'She never said a word!'

Arms folded over a surprisingly generous chest. *Not* that he was looking. 'I believe she asked you to come home for her eightieth birthday in April. That she made it clear to you how much that would mean to her.'

She had. Which was when he'd finally confided in her about his panic attacks. He'd had several while in therapy—all connected with the thought of having to one day return to Callenbrook. As soon as she'd found out, Gran had backed off, hadn't wanted to put more pressure on him. She'd ordered him to focus on his therapy and to get better. *You should've told me, Gran.*

It was all he could do not to drop his head to his hands and weep. He should've worked harder, should've returned sooner. 'I was taking her to Uluru next month.'

'That was never going to happen. Though she did think she'd still be here. Except...' Nina's voice broke and her hand shook, making the ice in her glass tinkle. He knew her grief would be fresh and raw too, but at least she'd had a chance to say goodbye.

'What the hell...?' He rounded on her. 'Why didn't *you* tell me?'

She tossed her not quite blonde hair over her shoulder, hard brown eyes glaring into his. 'And what difference would that have made?'

Derision stretched through her eyes—something he'd been used to seeing in the faces of the townsfolk of Callenbrook, but had never seen in hers before. It robbed him of the power of speech. She thought that badly of him?

Of course she did. As far as she was concerned, he'd let down the two women who had given him a measure of stability when he was growing up, had given his hungry heart all the love it had craved. And why would she think differently? She didn't know the truth.

But she knows you...

Not any more. And apparently he didn't deserve the benefit of the doubt.

So tell her, then.

A familiar band of resistance tightened about him. He

knew he shouldn't feel embarrassed or ashamed. Or weak. But he did. As his therapist pointed out, he was a work in progress.

'Besides, she asked me not to.' One slim shoulder lifted, and with a jolt he realised she'd lost weight since he'd last seen her.

It's been ten years.

Yeah, but Nina had always been slim, and now she was downright skinny. He swiped suddenly damp palms down his jeans. 'Thank you for stocking the fridge and getting in the essentials.'

'It's the least Iris would've expected of me. I've no intention of letting her down. But understand this, Blake, I did it for her, not for you.'

She rose and he blinked, because while Nina might've lost weight, she had *curves*. She must've had them ten years ago. She'd been nineteen when he'd left, but…

He shook himself. What the hell was he doing? 'Can I persuade you to join me for dinner?'

'No.'

The swift refusal had his head rocking back.

Shapely legs made for her back door. 'We need to talk, Nina.'

She glanced back, that frosty eyebrow doing its thing. 'About?'

'The funeral?'

'It's all been taken care of.'

'But—'

'Iris knew exactly what she wanted, had plenty of time to plan it, and that's what's happening tomorrow. I'm not letting you mess with her final wishes.'

He stood then too. 'I want to say a few words at the funeral.'

'There'll be an opportunity for anyone who wants to speak to do so.'

And then Nina was gone and for the first time in his sorry life, Blake felt utterly alone. Breathing in through his nose and out through his mouth, he started ticking off his list of threes—three things he could see, three things he could hear, three things he could smell.

When the darkness had receded from the edge of his vision, he nodded. *Right.* Before he left this godforsaken town, the one thing he was going to accomplish was making things right with Nina again.

Nina glared at the blue-sprigged wallpaper on the kitchen walls. Clenching her hands, she dragged in a breath.

You were too hard on him.

Too hard? He'd deserved all that and more! She'd thought Blake was a friend—her *best* friend. She'd thought he'd be there for whenever she needed him. She'd thought—

But she'd been wrong, and the pain of that still threatened to crush her. She couldn't explain it, but during the worst of her mother's illness, and at the beginning of Iris's, the thought that she had Blake's friendship to fall back on—the solidity of it—had given her comfort, had kept her strong. To know that when she needed him, she'd only had to call…

Finding out that had been a lie had gutted her.

Even so, she'd planned to act very differently when they finally came face to face. She'd planned on being polite—icily polite—to treat him like a stranger. But one look at him as he'd emerged from Iris's back door had forced the air from her lungs in a hot rush, and she'd become a giant burning ache with a huge side serving of tossed anger. That icily polite facade had liquefied in a single eyeblink.

The boy she'd known ten years ago would never have put work and money above people. The man he was now didn't deserve her consideration, and he certainly didn't deserve her generosity. He didn't deserve her warmth or the relief of sharing his grief with her. He didn't deserve an open-armed welcome or—

He loved his grandmother.

Pulling in a steadying breath, she nodded. He had. He'd cared about her mother too. And her. Just…not enough. Story of her damn life where men were concerned. They couldn't be relied upon. First her father and now Blake.

She glared harder at the wallpaper. Her mother had loved it. Maybe it was the memory of her mother, but she found herself swinging around and stalking back out to the veranda. But she kept one foot planted firmly inside her own kitchen.

'You and I will go to the service together tomorrow. It'll look odd otherwise.'

He sat eerily still in that ludicrous electric-blue armchair, as if afraid any movement would send her scuttling away again. 'Okay.'

'I want to get to the church two minutes before ten. And we'll go straight in without talking to anyone. And we're sitting in the front pew. Got it?'

'Got it.' He shifted the smallest amount. 'Driving or walking?'

'Driving. Will your fancy car be ready by then?'

He nodded.

'Then we'll take that. The tinted windows might be welcome.'

He lifted his hands. 'How on earth do you know my hire car has tinted windows?'

The same way she knew its make and model, that it was a classic navy blue, and when it came to navigational and safety features it had all the bells and whistles. It also boasted a multitude of reversing and parking cameras. The way half the men of the town talked, that darn car could damn well near drive itself. She didn't say any of that, just raised an eyebrow.

'The Callenbrook grapevine.'

He rubbed a hand over his face. She couldn't help but notice the tired lines fanning out from his eyes and his pallor. He looked done in. She did her best to stop her chest from clenching or…anything.

'Nina?'

In the twilight, shadows had gathered beneath the veranda and she couldn't make out the blue of his eyes. The intensity of his gaze, though, had a pulse inside her thrumming to life. Resentment, she told herself. 'What?' She might've snapped the word out a bit too curtly. His lips twitched a fraction, and that didn't improve her temper either.

'Thank you.'

She hitched up her chin. 'I'm not doing this for you. I'm—'

'You're doing it for Gran. I know. That's what I'm thanking you for.'

Shaking her head, she went back inside the house and closed the door behind her. Very firmly. Fact was, a part of her was doing it for him too—because of what the town had done to him as a fifteen-year-old. It'd been ugly and unfair, and she wasn't going to let that happen again. Not a chance.

Nina and Blake sat side-by-side in the front pew of the church that Iris Day had diligently attended for most of her eighty years. The church was so packed that people stood in all the available space at the sides and back of the room and in the foyer—every pew crowded except for the front one, which had been left vacant in deference to her and Blake. Until Nina rose and grabbed Iris's six closest friends and insisted they join them.

And yet it was Blake she was aware of, sitting with that same eerie stillness he had the previous afternoon. And Blake she missed like a hole inside her.

If the world and their relationship had been the way she'd thought it, she'd be sitting here holding tightly to his hand and taking comfort from his presence. Instead of mourning one person she felt as if she was mourning two—as if a double grief had taken up residence inside her heart. A heart still sore from the loss of her mother.

Pushing all of that to one side, she stood and gave the eulogy. 'Iris told me that she wanted today to be a celebration of her life and *not a misery fest*. I hope that I can do her justice.' She spoke of Iris's life and listed her many accomplishments, she shared special memories, making the assembled crowd laugh, dab their eyes, and nod.

Folding up the sheets of paper on which she'd printed out the eulogy, Nina stared out at the assembled congregation. 'Iris and I weren't bound by blood, but we were bound by something even stronger—love. She was my Granny Day. I'm going to miss her every single day, but I have so many memories to hold close and find comfort in, and I'm so very grateful to have had her in my life.'

She couldn't look at anyone as she made her way back to her seat, afraid she'd burst into ugly sobs if she caught so much as a single sympathetic eye. Florence patted her hand and murmured, 'Well done, Nina. Iris would've been proud of you.'

Everything blurred. Beside her, Blake remained preternaturally still.

'If anyone would now like to say a few words about Iris, share their memories, then I'd like to invite you to come forward now and—'

Pastor Peg didn't have a chance to finish what she was saying before the six women to Nina's left all bounced to their feet and marched up to the front of the church. 'As girls, we used to call ourselves the Seven Deadly Sins,' Enid started. 'Sorry, Pastor Peg, it was just our little joke. And it probably won't come as a shock to anyone here that Iris was Lust.'

Nina choked. *What on earth...?*

'She had such a lust for life, you see?'

Nina let out a breath and relaxed a fraction. Blake did too.

'And a lust for goodness too, which is why it was such a shock to us that she had such a nasty, conniving little minx for a daughter.'

Nina slapped a hand over her mouth to strangle a laugh. *Oh, God!*

Luckily, Enid swiftly moved on to an account of the many antics they all used to get up to and had the church in stitches. Blake, though, remained stony-faced throughout it all. The old Blake would've appreciated the dig at his mother.

Old Blake is long gone.

After the six remaining Deadly Sins had taken their seats again, eight more people made their way to the front, one after the other, to individually share a memory or reveal the impact Iris had on their lives. Iris had been a much-loved member of the Callenbrook community. And while a part of Nina reveled in all of it—because this was *exactly* what Iris had wanted—another part of her waited on tenterhooks for Blake to rise to his feet and say a few heartfelt words.

What would he say? Could he redeem himself? Even if he failed, she wanted him to try.

Despite his declaration of the previous evening, though, he made no move to stand and face the congregation. Instead the knuckles on his hands turned whiter and whiter as he clenched his hands harder and harder and his head and spine bent. She could hear the breaths sawing in and out of him.

Without giving herself time to think, she reached across and laid a hand over his, squeezed it. He gripped it like a lifeline, and then, as if aware he might be holding on too tight and hurting her, his grip slowly loosened and his shoulders lost some of their tension and his head came back up.

But he didn't rise to his feet. He didn't get up and pay public homage to his grandmother. When Pastor Peg motioned for them to sing the final hymn, Nina reclaimed her hand, disappointment wrestling with pity inside her.

Refreshments were served in the adjoining hall. Nina was swamped with well-wishers along with the gossips eager to pry from her whatever titbits they could about Blake. Not that she was giving anything away. The Deadly Sins carried Blake off to a table and, safe in the knowledge that he'd be protected while he was with them, she did her best to banish him from her mind.

This was supposed to be a celebration, and she did her best to be jolly and enjoy the anecdotes and recollections, but… In truth, she'd never felt less like celebrating.

Slipping outside, she sidled around to the back of the hall and moved across to lean against the jacaranda that would soon be in full bloom, to sip her tea and catch her breath.

'Holding up all right?'

She turned to find Robbie McAllister scuffling the toe of his rarely used dress shoes in the dirt. Poor Robbie. He was twenty-one and as awkward as they came. He'd be mortified if she burst into tears.

She could almost hear Iris's voice in her head: *His mother brought him up right, but the father…*

'Yeah, Robbie, just needed a breather. How about you?'

He shrugged. 'I really liked Mrs Day. She was a nice lady. I'll miss working on her car.'

'Fibber. I swear that little Honda of hers was being held together by duct tape and string.'

He grinned. 'It was all right.' His smile faded. 'How can you stand it? Being near him—the grandson? He didn't come near her in years and—'

'I'm guessing that's coming from your father,' she broke in with a raised eyebrow. She knew how much imagined injuries and resentments could snowball out of control in this town, and she wasn't letting that happen now. Not a chance.

'And, Robbie, we both know what a sterling judge of character he is.'

Robbie had the grace to wince. 'I suppose, but…'

'Iris didn't tell Blake she had cancer and was dying.'

The younger man's jaw dropped.

'As far as Blake knew, he was taking her to Uluru on a holiday next month.'

'No way,' he breathed.

'That's the thing, Robbie. You can't always tell from the outside what's going on in other people's lives—you can't see what's really happening or know what the real truth is. None of us should be so quick to judge. Iris taught me that.' She fixed him with her sternest glare, but deep inside she started to squirm. Wasn't that exactly what she'd done too? She'd been awfully quick to judge when Blake hadn't shown up to her mother's funeral. Maybe something had happened she didn't know about?

If that's the case, why hasn't he told you?

Exactly! She folded her arms, hitched up her chin. 'If you want to do Iris Day proud, you'll remember that too.'

He nodded, and then huffed out a laugh. 'You know, you look kinda hot when you get all bossy like that, Nina.'

'Robbie!'

He sobered again. 'Is what you just told me a secret?'

He probably wouldn't breathe a word of it to anyone if she asked him not to, but movement at the side of the church hall a few feet away caught her attention. *Blake.* Had he overheard her conversation with Robbie?

Glaring at her, Blake folded his arms and gave a swift hard shake of his head. *Very private and confidential* was the silent message he sent in response to Robbie's question. Yep, looked as if he'd heard the lot. Ignoring him, she glanced back at Robbie. 'Not a secret, no. Just the truth.'

Robbie ambled off and Blake stalked across to her. 'Why the hell did you go and tell him that?'

'Why the hell does it matter?'

A hand slashed through the air. 'Because my life is none of these people's business, that's why.'

'But Iris's life is, and was—in the same way she considered their business hers. And no matter how much you hate it, her and your lives intersect.'

His head rocked back. 'I don't hate *that*. I love that our lives intersected.'

Could've fooled her! 'Where your and Iris's lives intersected, though, is the bit everyone feels is their business.'

'Well, they're wrong, and—'

'Stop being an idiot,' she hissed.

He blinked.

She pointed a shaking finger at his chest, and then pulled her hand away, frowning, when she realised what a very nice chest it was. Grief. It was just grief. It did strange things to people.

'Why am I an *idiot*?'

He bit the words out and she tried to gather her scattered wits. 'Because I'm not allowing this town to organise another damn vigilante group.' As they had fifteen years ago.

When Blake had been fifteen years old, he'd been beaten up by a group of older teenagers venting their anger, against Blake's parents, on their own parents' behalf—a form of reprisal. It had been brutal and appalling.

And she *wasn't* letting it happen again.

She tipped the now cold contents of her cup onto the roots of the jacaranda. 'I don't want to receive a visit from the police with their lights flashing to inform me you've been taken to hospital. I've no desire to see you looking so swollen and bruised I can barely recognise you.'

She gripped the handle of the teacup tight. 'And I've zero

interest in your damn pride, so suck it up, sunshine. If telling the truth prevents that from happening again, I'll tell the truth to the next hundred people I see.'

'You cried.'

She shook herself. 'What?' *When?*

'When you saw me at the hospital. When we were fifteen. Would you cry if it happened again now?'

She clenched her hands so hard she shook. Was he trying to make light of this? Or was he deliberately trying to get a rise out of her? 'Absolutely. But this time it'd be in gratitude that Iris wasn't here to see it. Make no mistake, Blake, I'm not doing this to defend you. I'm—'

'Doing it for Gran, I know.'

Something in his eyes lightened, though, and it infuriated her even more. She pointed at him. 'Damn straight. Don't forget it.' Before flouncing off.

CHAPTER TWO

THE FOLLOWING MORNING, also at ten, Nina found herself once again sitting beside Blake. And once again wishing they still had the kind of friendship where she could grab his hand so that neither one of them had to face this alone—the reading of Iris's will.

She'd never once in her life considered having to live without Blake's friendship. Oh, they mightn't have physically been in the same location in the last ten years, but that was just geography. He'd only ever felt like a phone call away.

Whenever they'd spoken on the phone, video-called or texted, the strength of their connection had remained. At least, that was what it had felt like, but in February when he hadn't shown up for her mother's funeral she'd realised how mistaken she'd been. And she missed that connection, their friendship. She missed it so much it left her feeling wrung out.

With her mum and Iris gone, and Blake clearly having left her behind years ago, she felt cast adrift in a way she'd never experienced before. She had absolutely no idea what the future held. How did she move forward from here?

You'll work it out. You don't have to sort out your entire future today.

Shuffling papers on his desk, Leonard glanced first at her and then at Blake. 'Shall we get started?'

'Whenever you're ready,' she said, not looking at Blake, not checking with him first to make sure he too was ready.

What was the point? He couldn't be relied on and she had no intention of looking to him for guidance or direction.

But—

And if he didn't want her speaking on his behalf then he had a tongue in his head and he could use it. She felt the weight of his stare, but refused to turn her head and meet it. Once this was done and he'd signed whatever needed signing, he'd leave and she'd never have to clap eyes on him again.

She hitched up her chin. *Good.*

'Blake?' Leonard asked.

Blake turned back to the front, and nodded. 'Thanks, Leonard, ready whenever you are.'

Leonard Walker was in his mid-seventies and still fighting fit. Nevertheless, Nina hoped the people in his life were looking after him, spending all the time they could with him. Cherishing him.

Leonard opened the file in front of him. 'The last will and testament of Iris Catherine Day.'

The will was short and to the point and Nina listened with a growing sense of horror. 'Hold on, wait.' She shook herself. 'There has to be some mistake. I—' Iris couldn't have left Nina everything—her house, its contents, her life savings.

Leonard surveyed her over the top of his reading glasses. 'No mistake, Nina.' Beside her Blake sat so still she wanted to push him off his chair just to get a reaction from him.

Leonard set his glasses on the desk. 'Surely this can't come as a shock to you?'

Her mouth worked, but no sound came out.

'The way you've looked after Iris these last few years…'

'I did that because I *loved* her! Because she'd helped to look after me when I was a little girl, and…we'd come full circle. It was a privilege to look after her. I didn't do it for *all her worldly possessions*. I knew she was going to leave me something. She told me so. But I thought she meant her emerald ring!' She'd lusted after that damn ring since she was four years old.

Leonard pursed his lips and glanced at Blake. 'I don't think Blake begrudges you any of it, do you, Blake?'

Blake shook his head.

'As for Iris's closest friends, I suspect they already knew her wishes on the matter. They'll be glad you're the main beneficiary, Nina. The people who know you know you're not some money-grubbing manipulator who'd diddle an old woman out of her life savings.' Leonard slipped his glasses back on his nose. 'Why has this upset you?'

Because she'd been taken by surprise. Hadn't known. That Blake...

Damn it! Was the man a robot? She only just stopped herself from pushing him off his chair.

Mind you, these days it looked as if it'd take a bulldozer to shift him if he didn't want to be shifted. Did he lift weights or something? When on earth had he developed arm and shoulder muscles like that or—?

He turned his head and met her gaze, raised an eyebrow. She pulled her mind back to the subject at hand rather than the disturbing depth of his chest and the intriguing breadth of his shoulders. 'How do you feel about this?' she demanded.

'Surprised,' he admitted.

She searched his face, but couldn't find a trace of bitterness there.

'She left me what mattered, what I wanted—Pop's watch and her wedding and engagement rings.'

'But—'

'I'm glad she's left her estate to you, Nina. You deserve it. I didn't know until Florence and Enid took me aside yesterday and told me precisely how much you were doing for Gran. You went above and beyond. I know you don't want my gratitude, but you have it in spades.'

'I was her official carer. I was receiving a carer's pension to look after her!'

'A pittance,' both men said at the same time.

'The money from my grandmother's estate would have had zero impact on me, and Gran knew that. It does, however, have the potential to have a big impact on your life, Nina. You'll now have options and opportunities you didn't have before. Good things don't always happen to good people, we all know that, but in this instance it has. And I, for one, am glad of it.'

'Amen,' Leonard chimed in.

Hmm... Why did she feel as if this conversation would be all over town by sundown?

Though maybe that was a good thing. It'd further lessen the chances of a vigilante group forming to run Blake out of town.

Who needs a vigilante group when you're doing a good enough job on your own?

Oh, stop it.

They signed what needed signing.

'She also left you these.' Leonard handed Blake a slim envelope with his name on the front, and then handed one addressed to her along with an A4 envelope that bulged. Leonard gestured to the smaller of her envelopes. 'You're supposed to open that one first.'

Right. 'Do you know what these are?'

'A personal message for each of you, I expect.' He pressed his hands together. 'And may I suggest that you don't read them here?'

Her lips twitched. 'You've another appointment coming up, huh?'

His eyes twinkled. 'And I'm hoping to hit the golf course by midday. But that was also a little instruction from Iris.' He ran a finger down the page in front of him. 'In an ideal world, I'd like the youngsters to open their letters at my kitchen table over a bottle of bubbly. It's not compulsory, of course, but the thought makes me happy.'

That sounded like Iris.

Two minutes later, she and Blake stood on the footpath outside Leonard's office. They'd made their way to the solicitor's separately this morning, and she wasn't walking home with him now either.

Why not?

She couldn't think of a single reason. At least not one that wasn't childish. And somewhere in the last half an hour much of her anger had drained away, leaving her with little appetite for snark. In being named Iris's main beneficiary, Nina felt as if she'd won something and that Blake had lost. And yet she wouldn't have felt that way if their positions had been reversed—if Blake had been the main beneficiary. It made little sense, but it was how she felt all the same.

All of it felt *wrong*.

'You okay?'

In the mid-morning sunlight—which was basically blindingly bright—the blue of Blake's eyes was shockingly potent.

'Nina?'

She shook herself. 'Still in shock—discombobulated.'

He let out a soft chuckle that had all the fine hairs on her arms lifting. 'That still your favourite word?'

'One of them.'

He held up his envelope. 'We going to do this?'

'Absolutely. Not now, though. This afternoon.' She needed some space. She needed a breather. She needed time to gather her wits, and get her head around this morning's revelation. Apparently she was now the proud owner of Iris's house and the five hundred thousand dollars she'd had in her bank account. It...

'What time?'

Her brows shot up. 'Why, you got other plans?'

One side of his mouth hooked up. Had it always done that? 'Is that outside the realms of possibility?'

'If we were in Melbourne or Sydney, I'd absolutely believe you had things to do and people to see but here in Callenbook…?' She shook her head.

'Goes to show what you know, then. I promised Gladys I'd pop around and fix her back gate, while Enid wants me to show her how to use the new power drill she's bought. But I can be back at whatever time suits you.'

Bless those women. They knew keeping him busy was the best thing they could do for him. And the fact she cared about that went to show how hard old habits died.

'And…' He shuffled his feet.

Shading her eyes against the glare, she glanced up. 'And?'

'Guess I'd just like to ready myself.' He held up the letter. 'Get in the right frame of mind. These will be the last words Gran ever speaks to me and…' He rolled his shoulders. 'I want to treat them with respect.'

Rummaging in her bag, Nina fumbled around for her sunglasses and shoved them on her nose, blinked hard and swallowed the lump in her throat. 'Six o'clock?'

He nodded.

'I'll bring the champagne.' It seemed the least she could do. 'Later, Blake,' she managed, moving away.

'Later, Nina,' he said, moving off in the opposite direction.

Nina pushed through Iris's back door promptly at six, and then stopped short when she saw Blake sitting at the table. Her cheeks started to burn. 'Sorry. I forgot to knock. Old habits.' *Oops.*

'Your house. You can come in whenever you want. I should probably be paying you rent.'

She *very* carefully set the stainless-steel wine cooler with an apparently *very nice bottle of French champagne* on the table before she threw it at him. 'You suggest that again and I'll be organising my own vigilante group.' Ouch. She shouldn't even joke about that.

He didn't seem to mind, though, giving another of those maddening chuckles instead. 'Who would you enlist?'

She chafed the gooseflesh from her arms. 'The Deadly Sins.'

'The big guns, huh?' He collected two champagne flutes from the cupboard. 'And what would my punishment be?'

'Thursday night bingo and Saturday afternoon line dancing.'

'What?' He nearly dropped the glasses. 'Okay, you win. I'll never mention the rent thing again.'

Good. She gestured to the bottle. 'You want to do the honours?'

'Line dancing? *Seriously?'* He clearly wasn't ready to let the matter drop. 'You *hate* country music.'

'Loathe it to the depths of my cold, dark soul,' she agreed. 'But here's the thing—I've discovered that country music is actually bearable when one is line dancing...or boot scootin' as they call it.'

His jaw dropped. 'You don't?'

That was what her life had become. 'Someone needs to keep an eye on the Deadly Sins.'

He gaped at her.

She gestured to the champagne. 'Chop-chop.' It felt like old times, but she hardened her heart against its inevitable softening. She didn't want to remain consumed with anger and bitterness towards Blake, but she had no intention of trusting him again. They *weren't* friends, he'd proven that, and she'd save herself a lot of grief if she kept that knowledge at the forefront of her mind.

'This is a really nice drop, Nina.' He peeled the gold foil from the top.

'I know.' She feigned a sophistication totally alien to her, but it must've been convincing enough as Blake didn't burst into gales of laughter.

Holding the bottle securely in one hand, he started to twist the cork from the bottle and she couldn't help noticing the way the rope of muscle in his forearms flexed and clenched. Those arms looked rock-hard. He didn't get those from working at a computer all day.

The pop when the cork released made her jump. She shook herself. What on earth was she doing ogling Blake's arms? If she wanted to ogle fit male bodies she should go to the pub on Saturday night when the farmhands and stockmen from the nearby properties came into town to blow off some steam. Or walk past the Oval on Wednesday nights when the footy team practised. *Not* ogling weedy little Blake.

Not weedy any more. Besides, he'd started filling out when he was fourteen. It was a long time since he'd been weedy.

Then don't ogle your best friend.

Ex best friend. That reminder had a chill chasing down her spine.

He poured the champagne and handed her a glass. They stared at their letters—both sitting on the table—and Nina pulled in a breath. 'Right, this seems like a good time to have a toast.' She lifted her glass. 'To Iris Day, the best honorary grandmother...'

'And best actual grandmother,' Blake inserted when she glanced at him expectantly.

'And best friend and advisor that anyone could ever have had. Granny Day, you'll be greatly missed.'

'Gran, you'll never be forgotten.'

They touched glasses and sipped silently.

Nina sipped her fizz, and Blake couldn't tell if she enjoyed it or not. Somewhere in the last ten years she'd become opaque to him, this girl who he'd always been able to read like a book.

Nina had never been much of a drinker, claiming it interfered with her caring duties for her mum. And despite her nonchalance when he'd said what a nice drop this particular champagne happened to be, he knew it wasn't due to actual experience.

Because Artemisia Reynolds had been in the bottle shop buying sherry when Nina had been in there too and had overheard her asking Nari Cho, the sales assistant, for advice. Artemisia had rung Enid afterwards and Enid, in turn, had told him.

Welcome to Red Neck Falls, population two thousand eight hundred.

Enid had counselled—instructed...*ordered*—him to treat Nina with every consideration. Not that he'd needed such counsel. He had every intention of doing exactly that. Enid had also told him how lost Iris would've been without her during these last few months. She'd told him that Nina had been an absolute rock and an utter angel throughout the entirety of Iris's illness. She'd said they'd have all been lost without her.

Nina looks after everyone. It's time someone looked after Nina.

Like the way she'd looked after him yesterday, when she'd told that Robbie kid that Blake hadn't known his grandmother was ill.

She'd said she didn't want another vigilante group forming. He rubbed a hand over his face. They were all adults now, though. What had happened to him as a fifteen-year-old wouldn't happen again. It was ancient history.

Except... He hadn't been the only one traumatised by that long-ago event. He glanced across at Nina. She was still looking after him, even when, to all appearances, she loathed him.

Tell her why you didn't make it home for Johanna's funeral.

Now was his chance. She was a captive audience. She'd

remain here in Gran's kitchen until the letters were read and at least one glass of champagne consumed.

What if she laughs in your face? What if she doesn't believe you?

His stomach churned. Nina would do neither of those things. But his heart still beat too hard against his ribs.

What if she says you should've made a bigger effort? What if she says you should've come home sooner?

Bracing his hands on the table, he bent at the waist and dragged air into cramped lungs.

'You okay?'

Nodding, he straightened. This wasn't the right time. This moment should be about Iris, not him. He gestured to their letters. 'We going to do this?'

Her gaze raked across his face. 'We are.' Pulling out a chair, she dropped into it and reached for her letter, gesturing for him to do the same.

They turned their letters over and over in their fingers, as if reluctant to move beyond this moment. He glanced over at her. 'On the count of three?'

She took a gulp of champagne and nodded. He counted out loud. When he reached three, her fingers trembled as much as his did as they slid beneath the envelope's flap.

He pulled out the letter his grandmother had left him. *My dearest Blake...*

The rest of the writing blurred for a moment and he couldn't see a damn thing.

'Oh.'

His head shot up at Nina's involuntary murmur. She'd pressed a hand to her chest as if trying to keep her heart in her chest.

'You okay?'

'She says she knows my inheriting her estate will have come as a shock, but that she knows I didn't look after her with a view of profiting from it. She says she knows how much I loved her.'

He leaned across the table. 'Nina, how could you have thought anything else for a single moment? Gran *loved* you. And she *knew* you.' He ached to reach across and take her hand, but suspected she wouldn't welcome it. 'She knew you so well, in fact, that she started her letter with that reassurance.'

Giving a shaky laugh, she swiped her fingers beneath her eyes, before gesturing that they should continue reading their letters. He did as she silently bid.

My dearest Blake, I expect you're surprised to find that I left my estate to Nina rather than divide it equally between the two of you as I always told you was my plan. The thing is, we both know that you don't need my money. Your company is worth eight billion times what my estate is worth (I know—I looked it up). I left you what I knew you'd actually cherish—things of sentimental value that one cannot put a price on. And, love, if there's anything else you want, tell Nina and it'll be yours for the taking. So drop any thoughts you have right now that my not leaving you my estate is a form of punishment or an indication that I'm in any way disappointed in you. That couldn't be further from the truth. Erase all such thoughts from your mind immediately— that's an order. Also, it would be a great kindness if you'd read that out to Nina. I'd like her to know it too.

Blowing out a breath, he rested back in his seat. Across the table Nina stared at her letter. Her mouth opened and closed. She rubbed her fingers across her brow. And then she glanced across. The expression on her face caught at him. He wanted nothing more than to hug her. 'You look…discombobulated.'

'So do you.'

'She wants me to tell you something.' He read out the relevant paragraph of his grandmother's letter verbatim.

Sagging back in her chair, she nodded. 'I'm glad she felt that way. I'm glad I wasn't part of a punishment.'

An ache stretched through his chest. It was a punishment he probably deserved and part of Nina thought so too. That was why Gran had wanted him to share her words with her.

They returned to their letters.

You need to tell Nina why you didn't make it to Jo's funeral. That and your silence afterwards hurt her badly—very badly.

Those last two words were underlined.

She deserves to know the truth. Please do everything you can to mend your friendship. I don't need to tell you this, but Nina's friendship, her love, is worth both our fortunes combined.

He couldn't explain why, but his mouth went dry. The simple truth of those words perhaps? Or the craving clawing at his insides to win back Nina's friendship?

Chatting to Nina had always been the highlight of his day. He missed that—their easiness, their laughter, the fact that she knew him so well. He'd let her down. Badly. He hadn't meant to and he'd do anything to change it if he could, but *she* didn't know that. Gran was right. She deserved to know the truth.

Glancing across, he found her staring at her letter and shaking her head as if in a daze.

Now, though, wasn't the right time.

Blake, Nina looks after everyone, but nobody looks after her.

The words were a direct paraphrase of Enid's. He bet his grandmother had left the remaining Deadly Sins their own set of instructions to follow. He huffed out a silent laugh. Everyone should have friends like that. He and Nina had been friends like that. Once upon a time.

Now, love, don't take this the wrong way, but you're out of practice when it comes to looking after other people. But will you please do your best to look after Nina?

Of course he would! He'd win back her friendship—somehow. But was that what Gran meant by looking after her? Or was there more she wanted him to do?

Also, I should very much like you present when Nina scatters my ashes. I'll understand if you can't manage that, I know how busy you are, but I thought I'd ask it of you all the same. I'm so proud of you, Blake. You're more resilient than you know. You're honest, you're kind, and you're smart. You've achieved great things and you ought to be proud of yourself. Best of all, in my humble opinion, is that you have a good heart— one of the best—and it's time you stopped protecting it and lived your life to the full. Not everyone is like your mum and dad, and it's not necessary to live your life in direct opposition to theirs. You don't have to prove anything to anyone.

Heck, Gran, don't hold back.

I love you, Blake. You deserve the very best that life has to offer. If I could make a wish for you, it would be that your life be long, and that it be full and happy. You have certainly helped to make my life worth living.

It was simply signed, *from your very loving grandmother, Iris Day.*

He traced a finger over her signature, fighting the lump in his throat. What he wouldn't give to have one last hug with her, one last conversation, one last hour.

When he glanced up, he found Nina watching him. She moistened her lips as if nervous. 'Iris has requested I let you read this later. She's left me a more personal… I mean this one is…pragmatic-ish. Sort of.' She thrust it at him. 'Oh, read it for yourself!'

He took the letter and read it. After her initial reassurances, Gran wrote that she'd left a more personal letter for Nina in the bigger envelope, but that she hoped Nina would do her one final service.

There's one thing I always wished to do, but I kept putting it off and now it's too late. I've always wanted to cruise the French and Italian Rivieras. Sounds fanciful, doesn't it? I've read so much about those magical places, though, have watched so many documentaries, and hungered to see them for myself.

Why had she never told him she wanted to see those places? He'd taken her to London and Paris, Barcelona, Munich… Rome, on their annual holidays. He'd have taken her on a Mediterranean cruise in a heartbeat!

There's a lesson in that for all of us, don't you think? We shouldn't put off doing the things on our bucket list. Make a bucket list, Nina. Those are the things that make life worth living. Other than that I have no regrets. But dearest Nina, it would mean a lot to me if you would use some of the money I've left you and take that cruise on my behalf. I'd like you to scatter some of my ashes

*in Cannes (the chance of running into a movie star!),
Nice, Monte Carlo (the casino!), Portofino, and then on
down to Positano (the Amalfi Coast is supposed to be
one of the most beautiful sights in the world).*

He sagged in his seat, but kept reading on.

*If you don't wish to do it, I certainly won't hold you
to it. And I do want most of my ashes scattered in the
pretty grove behind the church where the jacaranda is.
I've always loved it there. And if you'd prefer to scatter
all my ashes there, that's fine too. My darling girl, I've
already asked so much of you, but if anyone deserves a
holiday, it's you. If you do go I want you to add one or
two places to the itinerary just for yourself. There are so
many exotic places in the world to explore—Sardinia,
Calabria, Crete. The world is your oyster. It's time to
go out and experience it for yourself.*

He gripped the letter so hard his knuckles whitened. *Look
after Nina… If anyone deserves a holiday…*

He glanced at Nina, now immersed in her more personal
letter. She had other envelopes scattered around her. Letters
with destinations written on the front. Gran's dream itinerary?

Pulling in a breath, he gave a silent nod. Gran had asked
him to look after Nina, and he was certain this was in part
what she meant. What was more, it'd provide him with the
perfect opportunity to win back Nina's friendship.

Reaching the end of her letter, Nina grabbed a tissue from
the box he'd had the foresight to place on the table, dried her
eyes and blew her nose.

He handed back the letter and tapped a finger to his.
'Looks like we're going to the Mediterranean, then.'

She froze. 'You too?'

'Her request to me was a little more generic. She asked me to be present at the scattering of her ashes.'

Nina folded her arms. Her lack of enthusiasm stung. He pulled in a slow breath. 'As she says, you could scatter her ashes in that pretty grove behind the church, but I know you, Nina. I know you'll feel honour-bound to spend some of Gran's hard-earned savings doing this for her.'

She stared at her hands and a lump lodged in his throat. 'I wish she'd told me,' he croaked out. 'I'd have taken her on that cruise in a heartbeat.'

Was it his imagination or did something unbend inside her?

He leaned forward, tapping a finger to the table. 'Let me arrange everything. It's the least I can do in the circumstances. And then let's give my grandmother the last hurrah she always dreamed of, yes?'

After the briefest of hesitations, she nodded.

CHAPTER THREE

NINA STOOD ON the dock and stared at the yacht Blake indicated. 'Our *own* yacht?' He *couldn't* be serious.

He shrugged.

She stared at the sleek vessel in front of them and tried to shake her head clear. Ever since she'd boarded the plane in Melbourne, she'd felt as if she'd stepped through the looking glass. She'd bet the White Rabbit had never organised Alice a first-class plane ticket, though. Or a privately chartered yacht.

Luxury yacht, thank you.

Maybe Nina should've expected this. Blake was a billionaire, for God's sake. Maybe this was how he lived his life these days?

Except that wasn't how she saw him. Of course she knew how successful he was—when his graphic design app had taken the world by storm she'd celebrated with him via Zoom, toasting him with a glass of cider. Back when they were besties. But she'd never actually envisaged him belonging to this world.

She'd never in a million years imagined those long legs of his striding onto a luxury yacht as if he owned it, and everyone around him showering him with the kind of deference reserved for royalty.

It was kind of hot.

Don't be shallow.

Jet lag. Discombobulated. She'd be back to normal once

she'd had some sleep. She crossed her fingers and followed him onto the yacht.

It was September, two weeks since the reading of Iris's will and twelve days since she'd seen Blake. He'd remained in Callenbrook for only a further two days before setting off for Melbourne and then to London. She'd caught the train from Bendigo to Melbourne on the day of her flight.

Blake had met her in the arrivals hall at Marseille airport, looking impeccably fresh and crisp in a suit that probably came from Bond Street or Italy or wherever it was they made suits that fitted broad shoulders with the loving care that Blake's suit did.

Thank God he'd ditched the jacket in the warm September sunshine, though. *Oh, right, and you think that seriously white, seriously crisp business shirt is any better?* He'd rolled the sleeves up to reveal strong forearms and had loosened his tie and the top button of his shirt. It was the sort of effortless sexy that film stars pulled off—and made grown women weep.

She didn't care if they were best friends or not. She did *not* want to think of Blake in those terms.

Then stop staring at him.

Plastering on a smile, she instead shook the hands of the crew as they were introduced—the captain, first mate, chef, a steward, and a deckhand. Seriously? Five staff for two people? She gaped at Blake. He shrugged.

She gawked at the yacht's impressive interior as they were given the grand tour. The general sitting area was flooded with light from the row of windows that ran its length. The sofas looked ridiculously comfortable. There was a separate dining area, an office-cum-library, and an impressive kitchen. Then came the bedrooms—four in total.

'This is the best stateroom, which is yours, Ms Hoffman.'

It was larger than her bedroom at home, ridiculously

plush, with an enormous bed that looked seriously inviting to her jet-lagged body. A large picture window currently looked out over the dock, but would provide her with glorious views when they were sailing. Yep, just call her Alice—Alice through the Looking Glass…in first class…on a yacht.

She swung to Blake. 'This stateroom should be yours.'

'When you see my room, you'll realise that I'm not slumming it.'

And as that proved true enough she submitted to the arrangements without another murmur.

The fly deck—she was learning a whole new vocabulary—was accessed via an internal staircase and had a jaw-dropping sky lounge and an undercover eating area for dining al fresco. *Dining* because rich people didn't do anything as mundane as eat, apparently. On the stern of the main deck was a Jacuzzi—because of course there was. And the deckhand gave them an inventory of all the available *toys*—a waterslide that would whoosh them straight into the sea, a blow-up floating dock…jet skis.

Blake shook his head. 'There won't be any need for those.'

Her head jerked around. Why on earth not?

'We're not those kinds of people.'

He might not be, but…

'It's not that kind of trip.'

Speak for yourself! She and Iris had very different thoughts on the matter. When Blake turned away, she caught the steward's and deckhand's eyes, hitched her chin at the *toys* and gave a thumbs up. They both grinned.

'Why don't you go freshen up?' Blake suggested. 'And then we can meet at the sky lounge and have lunch?'

Oh, God, did she smell? She surreptitiously sniffed her armpit.

You've been travelling for over twenty hours. Of course you smell.

How mortifying!

She showered in her en-suite bathroom with designer toiletries that made her feel like a queen. Towelling off, she tied the belt of the complimentary robe securely around her waist and went in search of her suitcase. Which was nowhere to be found, but upon opening the wardrobe she discovered her things had been unpacked. 'So this is how the other half lives.'

She donned a brand-new pair of white capris and a fluttery pink top in a silky fabric that had screamed holiday to her when she'd visited the online shop Iris had ordered her to use for holiday essentials. Turning to the full-length mirror and holding her arms out, she said, 'What do you think, Granny Day?'

In her personal letter to Nina, Iris had told her to do all the things she thought Iris would love to do, to have the holiday Iris herself would've loved.

My dear girl, you're in danger of becoming old before your time. Not your fault. Circumstances have worked against you. But you're not yet thirty and you need to push yourself out of your comfort zone and learn to live again, really live.

She'd memorised those words thrilled and intimidated by them in equal measure.

I've enclosed several sealed envelopes with the location printed on the front. Open that particular envelope when you reach that port. Inside will be a challenge— something I'd like you to do. Something I wish I could be there to do with you.

Her eyes had filled with tears when she'd read that. They filled again now. Iris continued to look after her from beyond the grave. Reverently pulling the pile of envelopes from her handbag, she placed them in the top drawer of her bedside table. With one last glance in the mirror, and a wistful glance at the bed, she slipped her feet into a pair of sandals, grabbed her hat and sunnies, and headed up to the sky lounge for lunch.

She was greeted with platters full of clever things made with prawns and smoked salmon, along with colourful salads and crusty artisan bread. Her mouth watered in appreciation. Blake had showered and changed too.

Though that had *nothing* to do with the way her mouth watered. He now wore a pair of navy cargo shorts that showed off long, tanned legs, and a polo shirt that hinted at an intriguing whorl of hair at his chest. Uh-huh, and the least said about that, the better.

The view! She swung to take it in, her heart thumping out a funny offbeat rhythm. The sight of the city from the marina was spectacular.

'Champagne?' Aurelia, the steward, presented a bottle of something probably amazing.

'Oh, um…orange juice for me, thank you.'

'You could always have a mimosa—half and half?'

Aurelia was Venezuelan and had eyes that twinkled devilishly. Iris would've loved her. 'Oh, go on, then.' She was on holiday after all.

Blake raised an eyebrow. She raised hers back as she took a seat. 'Problem?'

'It's not like you to drink on an empty stomach.'

'It's not going to be empty long. I'm starving.' She piled food onto her plate. 'I would also advance the theory, Blake, that these days you don't actually know me at all.'

His eyes went dark and broody. A part of her deeply resented having to share this trip with him, but it was what Iris wanted and she couldn't forget that. Blake might have failed spectacularly on the friend front, but Iris had loved him. Other than when they scattered Iris's ashes, they didn't need to spend much time in each other's company.

She ate. Everything was amazing. Blake barely touched a thing, though, and this was his actual time zone—his actual lunchtime rather than her actual bedtime.

But she was determined to get her body used to the new time zone pronto. She'd read that plenty of sunlight and eating at the proper times would get her circadian rhythms on track. No matter how much she wanted to, she wasn't crawling into that tempting bed before nightfall.

'So, do the arrangements meet with your approval?'

She set her cutlery down. Was she expected to gush? Was that why he sat there so broody and silent, the picture of malcontent? She moistened suddenly dry lips. 'You do know I wasn't expecting a first-class flight or for you to hire us a privately chartered *luxury* yacht?'

'I know.'

'Good.' She nodded. 'It's lovely, all of it, thank you.' He'd gone to a lot of trouble. And expense. And she wasn't an ingrate, but if he was trying to get back into her good books with this show of wealth it wasn't going to work, and the sooner he knew that, the better. 'Why?' She gestured around. 'Why all of this?'

He sipped his sensible black coffee and she wondered if she was the only one in danger of growing old before her time. He was the one who'd decided to travel like this. Why wasn't he making the most of it?

His eyes suddenly narrowed. 'Why do *you* think I've done this?'

She peeled a prawn and ate it to hide the fact that her appetite had vanished. 'I think you feel guilty about not coming home for Mum's funeral, and I expect this is part of some elaborate attempt to allay your guilt and make you feel better.'

He was silent for a long moment. The sound of seagulls and jangling moorings filled the air. Eventually he gave a slow nod. 'Don't get me wrong, I'm gutted I didn't make it to Johanna's funeral…'

Don't snort. It's not elegant.

'Fact is, I based every single decision I made in relation to this trip on what I thought Gran would love and have most relished.'

The prawn churned in her stomach and she immediately regretted eating it. Damn and blast. Now she felt the size of a flea.

'I had no other agenda.'

Right. 'I'm sorry.' The words emerged stilted and wooden from a throat that had grown too tight.

He shrugged.

Not looking at the shoulders.

'As you pointed out, we barely know each other these days. But this—' he glanced around the deck '—is the trip I wished I'd had the chance to take with my grandmother.'

It occurred to her at that moment that he might not be any happier that she was here than she was about being here with him. The fact he hadn't appeared at her mother's funeral had already informed her of how little she actually meant to him. But the thought cut her to the quick again now.

'Look, Nina—'

'The captain would like you to know we'll be leaving for Cannes at four o'clock. We're berthing in the bay. Would you like to go ashore when we arrive?'

Blake shook his head. 'We'll eat on board this evening, thank you.'

She waited for the steward to disappear back inside before lifting her drink to her lips. 'Are you going to do that the entire trip, Blake—answer for me? I'm going to make it clear from the get-go that that's not on.'

He blinked. 'I thought… I mean, given all the travel you've done in the last twenty-four hours, I thought you'd like a chance to acclimatise and would welcome an early night.'

She stared back stony-faced. She had every intention of having an early night, but that wasn't the point.

He rose. 'I apologise. It won't happen again.'

He stalked off and she pulled a face, wrinkling her nose at his departing back.

Blake adjourned to the office *to do some work*. She contemplated the city, watched the bustle of the port—all of its to-ing and fro-ing. And then, when it was time, observed with fascination the manoeuvres that departure involved, before hitting the Jacuzzi. *You'd have loved this, Iris.*

She raised her champagne flute of mimosa at the sky. If Blake weren't on board it'd be just about perfect.

The first thing Nina did when she woke the next morning—early—was seize the envelope marked Cannes.

Your challenge today is to find an exclusive boutique and buy a bikini, Nina. And I want you to splash out a ridiculous amount of money on it too. Penny-pinching is sometimes necessary, but not on this trip. You deserve to splurge and spoil yourself. And then I want you to head down to the beach with a sunhat and a pair of sunnies, and stretch yourself out on one of those sun loungers under a big umbrella and soak up the atmosphere.

Her jaw dropped.

There were a couple of additional notes:

The bikini can't be some dull colour like black or navy, either. Make it something colourful, something happy, something a woman in a film would wear. And don't forget the sunscreen!

A bikini? She'd never worn a bikini in her life! They were so *little*. They covered nothing more than the bare essentials, and sometimes not even that.

Her in a bikini? She couldn't—

You're in danger of becoming old before your time.

Her chin came up. She was on a luxury yacht. She was living the high life. Fake it till you make it. She could lie on a beach on the French Riviera wearing a bikini. She could be the picture of aloof sophistication. A grin stretched across her face. 'Challenge accepted.'

Opening his eyes, Blake rested his hands behind his head and stared at the bright morning light that played across the walls of his cabin and listened to the sound of water splashing against the hull. He'd slept later than he'd meant to, but after tossing and turning all night he'd fallen asleep only as dawn had started to filter into his room. Water reflections now danced around his bed. It looked idyllic. It sounded idyllic. In reality, though, he was in hell.

Because yesterday he'd finally realised how much Nina loathed him.

She'd arrived in Marseille airport, bedraggled and tired, but her eyes had been alive with interest and excitement. She'd never travelled before—had never had the opportunity. He'd grinned, wanting to share in that excitement. And then her eyes had landed on him and their expression had dulled and flattened and her lips had pressed into a thin line, and it had left him gutted.

He'd been viewing this trip as an opportunity to break down her barriers, heal her hurt feelings, and make things right between them again. She, though, could barely tolerate the sight of him. It had left him smarting, and feeling worthless and small.

And curt and uncommunicative.

Not that she'd seemed to care about that. The less he said, the less she'd had to respond to him, and the better she'd seemed to like it. What an unholy mess. For a brief moment, he'd considered excusing himself, returning to London, and leaving her to the cruise in peace.

Running away again?

Or, trying to make her happy, he countered with a scowl.

A part of him wanted to roar at her for reading the worst into his actions—for thinking that his not turning up to Johanna's funeral meant he hadn't cared. She knew him better than that! She knew—

What exactly have you given her in the last decade?

The question burned through him. He'd taken all the support Nina had offered, but what had he given back?

For the last three years Nina had asked him to come home for Christmas. 'Just for a few days. I know how much you hate this place, but it would mean the world to your gran and my mum.'

When he'd left Callenbrook, he'd sworn to only ever return for emergencies. Christmas wasn't an emergency, and everything inside him had rebelled and resisted at returning. He knew that one day he'd have to—that circumstances would demand it of him. But like a child, he'd turned his face to the wall and refused to see the obvious—that the people he'd left behind had *not* remained preserved in time, they *hadn't* remained exactly the same as when he'd left them.

Instead of returning, he'd invited Nina to holiday with him instead, but she'd refused to leave her mum for the holidays, and there'd been no question of Auntie Jo joining them. Things had become increasingly difficult for her and he'd—

He rubbed a hand over his face. To his shame he hadn't returned while she'd been alive. They'd had their video chats. He'd sent her and his gran flowers every few weeks. And he'd continued to put off going home until he'd unconsciously inflated returning to nightmarish proportions. When he'd most wanted to return, he'd found himself unable to.

When that first panic attack had happened, he'd told himself he wouldn't burden Nina with his troubles while she was grieving her mum. And then, when she'd refused to take his calls, he'd told himself it would be easier when they were face to face. He'd delayed telling her in the same way he'd delayed returning to Callenbrook and now it too was starting to take on nightmarish proportions.

She deserves to know the truth.

Gran was right. Nina did deserve to know. And he wasn't going to give up her friendship without a fight—he'd remain on this cruise. Maybe in fighting for her friendship he'd be able to prove to her how much he still cared.

Tossing back the covers, he surged to his feet. No more delaying. Over breakfast he'd tell Nina the reason he hadn't attended her mother's funeral was because he'd been in a hospital in Singapore having a panic attack. And that, as he'd had no hope of making Auntie Jo's funeral by the time he'd been released, he'd jumped on the first plane back to London to seek the professional help the doctors had advised him to get. He'd tell her about seeing a therapist. And he'd tell her how sorry he was.

'Has Ms Hoffman breakfasted yet?' he asked when he emerged on deck.

'She had a light breakfast and then she had George take her ashore in the motorised inflatable,' the steward said.

She'd *what*?

George nodded. *'Sí.'*

George was Spanish and young. He'd be lucky to be twenty-two. And ridiculously good-looking. Blake's hands clenched. Was there was a lascivious curve to the younger man's lips at the mention of Nina's name?

'She was excited to go out and explore.'

Without him? His heart slumped to its knees.

It shouldn't surprise him. It shouldn't leave him feeling so *lost*.

But damn it all to hell! She'd never travelled before. What if she got into difficulties? What if she got into trouble? What if…?

'Breakfast, Mr Carlisle?'

They were anchored just off shore and Cannes glowed like a promise in the bright morning sunlight. 'No.' He gestured to George, asking him to take him on the inflatable boat to the nearby shore. 'Did Ms Hoffman mention what she planned to do today?' He deliberately used Nina's formal title, wanting to preserve the client-staff distinction. Blake didn't take risks, and the blurring of such lines could lead to trouble. He wasn't letting that kind of trouble happen on his watch.

'No, sir. She just requested that I pick her up at four o'clock.'

'And what time did she leave?'

'About an hour ago.'

She had an hour start on him? What on earth would she want to do in Cannes today? What would she want to see? Would she want to do a city tour or maybe a historic walking tour? Browse the shops? Find the markets? Walk the famous Boulevard de la Croisette?

Why the hell hadn't he had the foresight to ask her what she wanted to do over that ridiculously awkward dinner last night? It would've provided the perfect topic of conversation. Except he'd sensed her jet lag and hadn't wanted to add to her weariness by making her engage in small talk that she wasn't the least bit interested in. So he'd sat there all wounded and broody while she'd admired a stunning sunset and stifled her yawns.

Every single decision he'd made since seeing Nina again had been a bad one—the wrong one.

Not true. Taking her on this cruise was the right decision. The fact he was finding it so hard was his own fault.

'I'll ring if we decide to return earlier,' he told George, springing up onto the dock.

With a nod, George turned the motorised inflatable back towards the yacht.

Blake fingered the phone in his pocket. He could ring Nina… Except, she'd ignored all of his calls these last few months, and if she was still to ignore them now… He dragged a hand through his hair, his chest cramping and greyness darkening the edges of his vision. He concentrated on his breathing.

Once the tightness had eased he lifted his head. *Concentrate.* If he were Nina, where would he go?

He sifted through the options before turning his feet in the direction of the Boulevard de la Croisette—the world-famous promenade with its ocean views, mix of private and public beaches, and upscale shopping.

He'd been walking for over an hour, backtracking here and there, and had almost given up. He'd been scanning the public beaches for a glimpse of her, had stuck his head inside the boutiques he'd thought might've caught her eye. All the while lecturing himself about not pouncing on her when he saw her and berating her for leaving the yacht without telling him. He'd act cool, calm and they'd come to some adult arrangement about letting each other know where they were at all times. Just in case something happened.

His jaw dropped when he finally did spot her—in the last place he expected—on a sun lounger on a private beach, and she was surrounded by a group of people who were all laughing and flirting with each other.

He wanted to stalk across, seize her by the wrist and hustle her back to the yacht where she'd be safe from the predatory attentions of—

Can you hear yourself?

That mocking inner voice wasn't what stopped him. What stopped him was the radiance of Nina's smile, the sound of her laughter when it reached him.

Look how happy she is.

He dropped down onto one of the benches that lined the path, shaded by the palms and the pines that marched along the avenue. His heart thundered in his ears, an ache gathering beneath his breastbone. When was the last time he'd actually seen Nina smile and laugh like that?

Sure, they'd laughed together on their video calls, but over the last couple of years those calls had grown less frequent—the pressures of work, the different time zones, and, he now suspected, her mother's worsening condition had all conspired against them. Why hadn't he looked beneath Nina's cheerful facade? She'd seemed happy, so he'd automatically assumed all was well. But…

Nina had been caring for her mother for what felt like forever, but it had always had an inbuilt end date. One he'd refused to let himself think about. Nina, though, hadn't had that luxury. She'd basically watched her mother die. And then almost immediately had watched his grandmother die—two of the most important people in her life.

While he'd been wrestling with a teenage trauma that he should've dealt with years ago, she'd been dealing with hard reality and cold facts. He dragged a hand down his face, recalling the attack that had happened fifteen years ago as if it were only yesterday. The conflagration of hostility that had erupted around him. And his realisation, once it had him cornered, that he was powerless to avoid it. There'd been no chance to try and reason his way out of it, no chance to run. All he'd been able to do was try and withstand the furious barrage of fists and feet that had rained down on him—the savage punches and brutal kicks he'd thought would break bones. He'd curled his body in on itself and covered his head with his hands and gritted his teeth, determined to not make a sound.

But even behind his eyelids the stony, merciless expression on Ralph Hutchinson's face had tormented him. At the time he'd thought he'd deserved all of it—all of the fury, all of the retribution. If he hadn't created the accounting package his mother had asked him to, she'd never have had the means to defraud anyone. Not that he'd known then that was what she'd planned to use it for.

He should've accepted the counselling he'd been offered after the attack had first happened. He should've sought counselling at university when nightmares had him waking in a lather of sweat. And afterwards too, once Drawing Board, his company, had taken off. Instead he'd kept burying it, telling himself it was all in the past.

He wished with all his might now that he'd sought that counselling. Maybe then, when Nina had needed him, he'd have been there for her. Instead he'd been nowhere to be found, and he couldn't blame her for losing faith in him.

For the last few years Nina had been surrounded with death. And now here she was on one of the most glamorous beaches in the world making friends with like-minded holidaymakers. The sun was shining, the air was warm, and the scent of salt and mimosa spiced the air. How, for a single moment, could he begrudge her any of that?

She deserved a chance to relax, to unwind, to remind herself of all the good things life still had to offer her.

His grandmother was right. He was out of practice at looking after other people. He liked being a lone wolf, a solitary entity—responsible for no one but himself and with no one constantly looking over his shoulder asking him to justify himself. But Nina wasn't *other people* and for her he'd make an effort and go the extra mile. Because it struck him that when his grandmother had asked him to look after Nina, *this* was what she'd meant. To help Nina relax and laugh again, to help her find joy in her life.

Nina, stretched out on her sun lounger, was partially obscured by the two people sitting on the sun lounger to this side of her. But then several members of the group rose and made their way down to the water's edge, Nina included. And then he saw what she was wearing.

Or *wasn't* wearing.

His jaw dropped. She— It—

Her bikini, all shimmering gold with big bows at the sides, was plastered against her magnificent body leaving very little to the imagination. And *his* imagination immediately went into overdrive, supplying him with the missing details!

Heat gathered at his nape and collected in his veins. Damn it all to hell. He ran a finger around his collar. She had long legs that went on forever, hips that swayed with an innate sensuality, and the curves of her breasts were cupped so lovingly by the material of her bikini top that red-hot need pulsed through him in dizzying waves.

He couldn't start thinking about Nina like this!

He stood, wiped the perspiration from his brow. He'd leave her to have her fun and—

That was the moment he noticed the appreciative appraisals the other men sent her when she wasn't watching and promptly sank back down.

Folding his arms, he nodded. *Doing exactly what you asked of me, Gran. I'm looking after Nina.*

CHAPTER FOUR

Nina slid her sunglasses on her nose and planted her hat on her head. Both brand-new and utterly unnecessary—she'd brought her old from-home ones with her—but maybe that had been the point. Anyway, the sales assistant had convinced her that they'd gone perfectly with her bikini, that the outfit was incomplete without them, and she'd been happy to be convinced.

She'd sunned herself on a beach in the French Riviera in an eye-wateringly expensive bikini, had made friends with a group of light-hearted holidaymakers, and had swum in the Mediterranean Sea.

Seriously? Where's Nina and what have you done with her?

Could she have been any further removed from her old life if she'd tried? She felt lighter, younger and… Something else that she couldn't define just yet. Whatever it was, though, it was positive—A Good Thing. Maybe Iris was onto something with ticking off a bucket list?

Humming under her breath, she set off along the seaside avenue, relishing the warm air and the dappled light beneath the palm and pine trees. Dragging in the scent of the sea and the faint hint of coconut oil—

Her thoughts and her feet slammed to a halt. Frowning, she backed up two steps to glance at the man sitting on the bench she'd just walked past. Lowering her glasses, she stared at *Blake* over their rims.

He sent her a rueful smile, a small wave. 'Hey, Nina.'

What was he doing? 'Have you been spying on me?'

'Of course not.' He shifted. 'I mean...not exactly.'

Her brows shot up. She pulled her sunglasses completely off her nose. 'So that's a yes, then.'

'I came looking for you because I was worried.'

Her brows, which had started to lower, lifted again.

'I mean, you've not been overseas before.'

'And...?' She gestured for him to continue. 'I have damsel tattooed across my forehead or something?'

He rubbed a hand through his hair. 'I didn't know how jet-lagged you were. And when you didn't leave a note or tell anyone where you were going or what you were doing—'

One hand went to her hip. 'I wasn't aware that one of the conditions of this trip was to keep you informed of my every move.'

'It's not! But for safety reasons it'd be a good idea to let someone know what you're doing and when you expect to be back. It's not hard—I'm heading to the beach today, or the shops, or doing a historic walking tour, and I'll be back at four.'

'If you were worried why didn't you ring me?'

'As you haven't been taking my calls recently, I figured you wouldn't bother this time either.'

He had her there. Huffing out a breath, she lowered herself to the bench beside him and shoved her sunnies back on her nose. A part of her wanted to remain stiff and aloof—and sort of bitchy—but she was tired of that act. Maybe it was the effect of all that sun and laughter. It had been nice—glorious, actually—to feel something other than grief and anger; to just, for a little while, not be weighed down with sadness and care. In her heart, she knew that was what Iris wanted for her.

Could sadness become a habit? Was that the real reason Iris had urged her to take this trip? Already she could feel her perspective shifting—as if the physical distance she'd travelled had also given her some emotional distance to view all she'd been through this year.

She'd been so angry at Blake for letting her down. And for letting Johanna and Iris down too—the two women who had loved him unconditionally and had practically raised him. She'd wanted to punish him for that.

But it didn't take a rocket scientist—or an ex-best friend—to see that he was in a stew of guilt and regret. It might not be her job to make him feel better, but she no longer wanted to make things worse for him either.

She stared out at the water—a bright breezy blue, the sand a luminous gold—and let out a long breath. 'I'm sorry you lost your grandmother, Blake.'

The shoulder closest to her lifted. 'I'm sorry you lost your honorary grandmother too, Nina. And your mum.'

She didn't have to stay angry with him and that felt good. But it didn't mean they'd ever be friends again. She doubted that gulf could be breached. There were only so many miracles the sea, the sun, light-hearted laughter and a ludicrous bikini could perform.

'So here's the thing…'

His abruptness made her blink.

'I came looking for you, and when I eventually found you—clearly having fun—I was going to leave again. But then you and a few of your new friends decided to go swimming…' He scowled. 'And I saw the way a couple of those guys were looking at you and I…'

'You…?' She couldn't explain her fascination. He rolled his shoulders, that scowl darkening, and nor could she explain why it made her want to laugh.

'And I came over all…'

What?

'Like an overprotective father or something.'

Shaking her head, she reached into her tote—also brand-new as it too was apparently a necessary accessory to the bikini—and pulled out her water bottle. 'I don't have one of those.'

Her father had left when she was twelve and her mother, *his wife*, had been diagnosed with multiple sclerosis. He was a lot of things—unreliable, self-interested, greedy—but over-protective wasn't one of them.

'Yeah, me neither.'

Blake's father was even worse than hers—*no* backbone whatsoever. He'd always fallen in with whatever his wife had wanted. Even when those things had been criminal.

'So I've no idea who I was channelling.'

How long had he been sitting here? It had been a couple of hours since she'd been swimming. She handed him the water bottle. 'You sure you're not the one who's jet-lagged?'

'I don't know what I am.'

He drank half the bottle in one long pull. He went to hand it back, but she gestured for him to finish it. Getting him back to the public dock where George had dropped her off wouldn't be fun if he was dehydrated.

Pursing her lips, she studied him. Today she'd been on a beach having fun and feeling young and carefree for what felt like the first time in forever, and he'd been sitting here watching her and being all broody and tortured. 'When did you become so…*stuffy*, Blake?'

He stiffened. 'I'm not *stuffy*!'

He looked so outraged it was all she could do not to laugh. 'Maybe *stodgy* is a better word.' She gestured to him sitting on the bench and then gestured far more expansively at the view in front of them. 'Acting like my watchdog is definitely the actions of a stuffed shirt.'

His jaw tightened. 'A one-off.'

She gestured to where she'd been sitting on the beach. 'I was with a group of people on a beach with a lot of other people around. What issues do you think I'd have had?' She thrust out her chin. 'And what if I wanted to generate some male interest? Did you stop to think about that?'

He started as if she'd zapped him with a hundred volts.

'Do you honestly think I've never had to deal with un-wanted male attention before? I'm not some damsel in need of rescuing, if that's what you think.'

'Of course I don't. I…'

He couldn't finish the sentence and she nodded. 'I think you're the one who's floundering here, Blake. You're the one who doesn't know what to do with himself. Do you even know how to have fun any more?' She shook her head. 'Stuffy. Stodgy. Uptight.'

'I'm *not* stuffy! *Or* stodgy. *Or* uptight.'

'Or a control freak?' she enquired sweetly.

He folded his arms. 'Seriously?'

'Just calling it like I see it. I mean to *live* on this holiday, Blake—*really* live. Not merely endure or exist. I'm embrac-ing this holiday in the spirit Iris would've wanted, and I'm not going to let you prevent me from doing that.'

She didn't say it in a mean way. She wasn't even angry about it. She just wanted to get that straight between them to avoid future arguments. This was a once-in-a-lifetime trip and she planned to cherish it. Who knew if she'd ever get this opportunity again?

Blake glared at the horizon. She glanced at her watch. There was a couple of hours yet before she was due to meet George and she was starving. The group she'd met on the beach were staying at the hotel, and they'd arranged for lunch to be brought out to them, but Nina had eaten sparingly. First, because she hadn't been paying and her offer to pay had been waved away and, secondly, there was nowhere to hide a bloated belly in a bikini.

She opened her mouth to suggest they get something to eat, when the air deflated from Blake's lungs. 'I'm *not* stuffy.' But he said it as if he was trying to convince himself rather than her.

Did he really not know how to have fun any more?

He turned to meet her gaze. 'I was in a hospital in Singapore having a panic attack. That's why I didn't make it home for Auntie Jo's funeral.'

She froze. Then she went hot and clammy. 'You…? *What?*'

'A damn panic attack.' He dragged a hand through his hair. 'The plane landed in Singapore. I waited until everyone else in my section had disembarked, but when I went to reach for my hand luggage…'

She stared at him. She couldn't form a single coherent thought.

'My chest cramped, my head pounded, my heart was racing. I couldn't breathe. I thought I was having a heart attack.'

Her heart thumped in horrified commiseration.

'An ambulance was called and I was taken to hospital. *Not* a heart attack, thankfully. Merely a panic attack.'

Thoughts jumbled in her brain. 'I doubt there's any *merely* about it.' It must've been terrifying. It must've—

Nausea churned in her stomach. *That* was what returning to Callenbrook had done to him? *Trying* to return to Callenbrook, she amended. 'Blake, that's awful.' She too sagged against the bench.

'To say I found the news confronting is an understatement. And as I had no hope of making Johanna's funeral—because, of course, I'd left it to the last moment—and I couldn't conceivably see how I could be of use to anyone in Callenbrook…'

Not of use to anyone? Her eyes filled. Was that what he honestly thought?

'I returned to London on the first flight back I could get.'

And he hadn't thought to tell her any of this until now? They were supposed to be friends!

'In truth I couldn't face the thought of having a panic attack *in* Callenbrook. Of triggering more of the damn things once I'd arrived there.'

That she could understand. 'But you made it home for Iris's

funeral.' Had he been fighting panic attacks the entire time he'd been home? And all that time she'd been so awful to him.

'I've been seeing someone—getting therapy.'

She let out a slow breath.

'Because I don't *ever* want it happening again.'

She pressed a hand to her brow. 'The panic attack…is it linked to the assault when you were fifteen?'

He gave a mirthless laugh. 'Apparently it's not *healthy* to bury those kinds of traumas. And in not returning to Callenbrook for so long—in actively resisting it—when I did finally try to return it had become invested with too much meaning. Which blew the lid off…everything.'

She wanted to swear and not stop. A week after Blake's parents had been arrested for investment fraud, Blake had been bailed up and brutally beaten as a misguided form of reprisal.

His parents had stolen over two million dollars' worth of local money—and she'd understood that a lot of people had lost a lot of money and were angry about it—but Blake hadn't been guilty of anything other than having awful parents. He'd even had to testify against them in court as they'd persuaded him to create an accounting package with 'special' features he hadn't thought to question until too late. His mother had lied to him and manipulated him, and his father had stood by and let it happen.

His attackers had pounced on him after football training one afternoon and had left him with a concussion, several broken ribs, a fractured cheekbone and multiple contusions. He'd not just been punched, but kicked…and then left unconscious.

An eyewitness had said there'd been five attackers, though conveniently they hadn't been able to identify a single one. All they'd admit was that the attackers were youths probably a couple of years older than Blake. Nor had Blake ever named his attackers, claiming he couldn't remember the attack. She'd never believed him.

Her stomach clenched when she recalled the sight that had greeted her when she and Iris had rushed up to the hospital— the bruised and battered face with the eyes so swollen they'd almost closed shut. She hadn't been able to prevent herself from bursting into tears.

She hugged her tote bag to her and wished she had another bottle of water inside it. Or something stronger like brandy. 'You know who your attackers were, don't you?'

He nodded.

'Who?'

He turned his head but she continued glaring at the beach in front of her. 'Nina, what good will it do, knowing that now? It was a long time ago and—'

She swung to him. 'Every single time I go out on a date, I find myself sitting there wondering if this guy could've been one of them. It's *awful*.'

He swore. 'You *really* need to get out of Callenbrook.'

'And you should've tried coming home sooner, *obviously*.'

He froze.

Clenching her eyes shut, she shook her head. 'I'm not blaming you for having a panic attack, Blake. But I wish to God I'd followed my instincts back then.'

He eyed her warily. 'Which were?'

The blue of his eyes throbbed with a peculiar intensity and the depth of his chest and the hard-muscled firmness of his thighs penetrated her consciousness and had things tightening in—

What the hell was wrong with her?

'Nina?'

She ran a hand through her hair then resettled the hat on her head. 'I understood why you hated Callenbrook so much, and I understood why you wanted to leave. And, honestly, you had to leave—you were a software genius. You needed to go out there and make something of yourself. And while it's true that some people tarred you with the same brush as your parents, not everyone did. Half the town, probably more, were appalled at what happened to you. It was as if you had blinkers on, though, and couldn't see that. Instead you wrote the entire town off.'

And in some ways it felt as if he'd written her off too. 'Because of that attack, you wouldn't or couldn't see that there was still good in the place.'

The only good in Callenbrook had been Gran, Nina and Auntie Jo.

He rolled his shoulders. Okay, and the Deadly Sins…and maybe a couple of guys from school. But that was about it.

'Do you remember the night before you left for university? You told me how happy you were to be leaving and said, "I'm never coming back."'

'And you said, "What if me or Mum or your gran need you?"'

'And you said that was the one exception.'

'I told you I'd always come back if I was needed.'

He squinted out at the sparkling sea. If he jumped in the water right now, he'd sink to the bottom. 'I'm sorry I didn't keep my word. I—'

'You tried. Which is good to know.' She stared out at the water too, but then her gaze swung back, pinning him to the spot. 'That night I wanted to ask you to return for something specific—like my twenty-first birthday or your gran's seventy-fifth or…*something*. I wanted to extract a promise from you. At the time I told myself to stop being so silly and not to burden you with thoughts of returning when you were so happy. I told myself not to be so selfish. But now I wish I had. It might've given you a different mindset.'

None of this was her fault. *None of it.* 'Fact is, Nina—' he tried to smile '—I just got too caught up in my own head. If

I'd understood the outcome of avoiding the place for so long, I'd have done things differently. It wasn't your fault. Or anyone else's. It was mine.'

She shook her head at that. 'Not yours either.' She adjusted the brim of her hat. 'Right, so tell me who your attackers were.'

He had to laugh at her persistence. After a brief moment of hesitation, he named them.

Pursing her lips, she nodded, not looking the least bit surprised. Knowing Nina as he did, she'd have given the matter a lot of thought over the years. She'd have made her own list of likely suspects. 'I'm pleased to report I've not kissed a single one of those guys. *Thank you, God.*'

He didn't know how she managed it, but her words made him laugh. 'We were all just kids back then. Kids do stupid things.'

'Those guys were two years older than you, Blake. They'd have known what they were doing was wrong.'

'Maybe so, but the posse had been organised and the attack overseen by Ralph Hutchinson.'

She froze. 'The football coach?' She turned towards him, moving sluggishly as if in wet cement. 'Our PE teacher? The guy everyone looked up to.' She pulled off her sunglasses to stare at him. '*That* Mr Hutchinson?'

The very one. That more than the actual beating was what had shaken him up. Actually, it had gutted him. Mr H had asked him to remain behind after practice. He'd thought the older man was going to offer him support for all he was going through—give him some words of wisdom man-to-man.

He couldn't have been more wrong. Or shocked. Or devastated. All of the boys on the team had looked up to the older man.

'I should've learned—given my parents' example—that just because someone is an adult, that doesn't mean you can depend on them.' But never in a million years would he have thought that his coach would stand by and watch him take a beating with such a cold look in his eyes.

'Oh, Blake.' Nina pressed a hand to her mouth.

He shrugged. 'At the time, I didn't think anyone would believe the truth if I told them.'

She looked as if she wanted to burst into tears all over again, just as she had all those years ago at the hospital. 'I would've believed you. So would Mum and your gran.'

They would've, but then they'd have gone into fight on his behalf. There'd have been an outcry, a furore. There'd been enough upheaval in his life already with his parents' arrest, his realisation of how much his mother had used him and the fact his father had allowed her to do it.

His father hadn't been a bad man. But he had been a weak one. Blake wished he'd known at fifteen what he knew now— that his father's weakness had allowed him to become an accessory to the crimes his mother had been committing. His mother had dazzled Blake, but his father had always helped him feel grounded. It was his father he'd gone to with his questions, once he'd started to feel uneasy about the things his mother had asked him to incorporate into the accounting software. It was his father who'd assured him that everything was legal and above board.

He shouldn't have trusted him. He should've done his own research.

What then? a small voice asked of him. What would you have done? Would he have been able to withstand his mother's flattery and pleas or her demands and temper tantrums, her threats? Maybe he was his father's son, maybe he too had lacked the backbone to stand up to her.

He shook his head. He'd just wanted things to settle down. He'd known they'd never go back to being *normal*, so he'd contented himself with quiet instead. And in choosing that path, he'd buried what had happened and done his best to never think about it. He could see now it hadn't been the wisest course of action, but in his defence he'd only been fifteen.

'I didn't tell you this to upset you, Nina. I just wanted you to know that I did try to make it home for your mum's funeral. And I'm sorry I didn't manage it.'

She nodded, but she didn't meet his gaze. 'I'm glad you told me why you weren't there. And I'm sorry you went through all of that.'

He knew she meant it. But she didn't reach across and hug him as she would've once done, didn't even bump shoulders with him or reach over to squeeze his hand, and something uneasy shifted through him. His revelation hadn't had the desired effect and—

She surreptitiously stifled a yawn, and he squared his shoulders. *Give her a chance to process it all.* It was a lot and she was still jet-lagged. Plus she'd been through an awful year. What was that word she liked? *Discombobulated.* It probably described exactly how she felt.

He stood. 'You ready to head back to the yacht for a siesta?'

'Siesta? That's Spanish, isn't it? We're in France.'

'In French it's *sieste.* Believe me, an afternoon nap is universal in any language.'

That made her laugh and gave him hope that he could get their friendship back on track.

'Sounds perfect.'

Nina must've slept for four solid hours, but she turned up to dinner in the sky lounge looking fresh and oddly radiant. As if a day in the sun had been exactly what the doctor had ordered.

'What are your plans for tomorrow?' he asked as they picked up their cutlery and regarded their food with approval. Maybe he could talk her into—

'I'm meeting up again with the group from the beach.'

He waited for her to invite him along, and kept right on

waiting. His heart became a dead weight in his chest. Was she still angry with him?

Hauling in a breath, he abruptly changed the topic. 'We need to talk about how and when we're going to scatter Gran's ashes.'

She cut into her fish and moaned in appreciation as she ate it, but then waved her fork through the air. 'I've been thinking about this and here's what I think we should do. We should go out and enjoy each of the places Iris has itemised on her list, and then as we sail away we should scatter her ashes while telling her what we loved about the place, and why we think she'd have loved it too.

Except there was no *we*, was there?

When did you become so stuffy?

He *wasn't* stuffy.

You sure?

So maybe he was a bit conservative when it came to the way he dressed and the way he acted in public. He liked to fly under the radar—keep out of the papers, keep out of the spotlight. He didn't want pictures of himself drunk dancing at some party with a half-naked woman or getting into an altercation with someone and having it splashed across the front pages or making some news clip.

He was more than happy to be relegated to the ranks of boring businessmen. Not that he *was* a businessman in the true sense, which was why he made sure his company was run by a group of accountants and financiers who were above reproach. There'd be no financial irregularities on his watch, thank you very much. Not after what his parents had done. There'd be no whispers, suspicions or suggestions that he was cut from the same cloth.

All of those things were admirable though. Not stuffy. Or stodgy.

Nina thinks you're boring.

He scowled at his perfectly steamed new potatoes. Nina didn't just think him boring, she thought him the antithesis of fun. She thought him a killjoy—*a killer of joy.*

'Is something wrong with your fish?'

He shook himself. 'Nope.'

One perfectly shaped eyebrow lifted in scepticism. That had always been an unconscious mannerism. He doubted she even knew she was doing it.

Keep it light. Prove you're not a killjoy.

'I'm wondering why I can't manage to cook fish this well.'

Cooking? That's the most exciting thing you can come up with? Good God, the women are going to be beating a path to your door, aren't they?

Nina stared at him. 'You cook? *You?*'

'Sure.'

'You *hate* cooking.'

He held up his hands. 'Okay, sure, I resisted learning for as long as possible, but I love to eat. And when I went away to university I realised how much I'd been spoiled by Gran's cooking. And apparently I didn't just love eating, I loved eating *good* food. So I either had to settle for eating mediocre food or learn how to cook. I chose the latter.'

'Did not.'

'Gran sent me tips, and walked me through making a few meals.'

'She never said a word.'

'I swore her to secrecy.' He laughed. 'I knew once you'd caught wind of it, I'd never hear the end of it.'

She set her cutlery down. 'Can you do a lamb roast as well as she did?'

'*Nobody* could manage that. But you remember her chicken and chorizo traybake?'

'Vividly.'

He kissed his fingers. 'I have it down to perfection.'

She stared at him—at his mouth and the fingers he'd kissed—as if she'd never seen him before. Things inside him tightened and clenched. He did his best to ignore it. Tried to focus instead on the mini victory of actually getting her to engage with him.

She shook herself. 'If you ask him, Calvin might give you some tips.'

Calvin was the chef.

She went back to her fish. 'What do you think of my idea about scattering Iris's ashes?'

'I like it.' He'd need to come up with something better to tell his grandmother, though, than: *I sat on the bench and watched Nina have fun with other people.* He couldn't see that impressing his grandmother any more than it had Nina.

'Good, that's settled, then.'

'I missed your cooking too.' He returned to his food. 'I wanted Gran to send me your recipe for that vegetable lasagne you used to make.'

'I bet she didn't give it to you.'

'Nope, said it was super-secret. And because I was an idiot I never asked you for it either.'

'Total idiot,' she agreed, but there was no heat in her words. 'And I can't believe she never told me any of this.'

'I'm not. She was the keeper of all the secrets.'

Her lips twisted. 'I *had* no secrets.'

He pretended to choke on his iced water. 'Not true!'

That eyebrow rose again. 'If Iris was such a vault when it came to keeping secrets, how do you know if I had any or not?'

'Because you told me so yourself.' He spread his hands. 'I have two words for you, Nina—boot scooting.'

She rolled her eyes.

'Is that *seriously* an accomplishment you want shouted from the rooftops?'

She stuck her nose in the air. 'I'll have you know that line dancing requires more coordination than you give it credit for. Memorising the dance steps can be a challenge too. It's a good workout, excellent for creating new pathways in the brain, and that shouldn't be underestimated. That sort of thing is important as one gets older.'

It hit him then that *that* was what her life had become—looking after older people and doing older-people things. Did she ever get to do young-people things any more? No wonder today's adventure at the beach had left her with such a glow.

'Don't look at me like that.'

He shook himself. 'Like what?'

'Like you pity me.'

'I don't pity you.'

'I know a lot of people think that way.' She glared daggers. 'But they couldn't be more mistaken. It was a privilege to look after my mother—not a sacrifice. And it was a privilege to look after Iris. And for another thing—'

'I *don't* pity you, Nina,' he cut in over the top of her. 'I envy you. I'd give everything I own to spend another hour with my grandmother, let alone weeks or months. I wish she'd considered me dependable enough to trust me with the truth about her own health.'

She stared at him, moistened her lips. 'She knew about the panic attacks?'

He nodded.

She immediately deflated. 'It's not your fault, then, that she didn't tell you. She and my mum did that all the time. I guess I did too, to a lesser extent.'

'Did what?' He had no idea what she was talking about.

'Tried to shield you, protect you.'

'From what?'

It was her turn to shrug. 'All and any harsh realities and ugly truths they thought you'd rather not know.'

His mouth went dry. 'Like…?'

'Like how much they missed you when you went away. They were careful to make a big song and dance about how proud they were of you and your achievements, urged you to travel blah blah blah. When what they really wanted was for you to come home for a visit. They always told you what they thought you wanted to hear.'

Nausea churned in his stomach.

'I had to do Mum's make-up for her whenever the two of you had a video call because she didn't want to look pale and ill and worry you. For the last few months Iris always put on her cheerful no-nonsense voice when you rang, even though it left her exhausted.'

They'd…

'They never wanted to worry you.'

His heart gave an ugly, sluggish kick. 'But…why?' They'd never shielded Nina in the same fashion.

She stared at her plate, pushing a pea around with her knife. 'Because of what happened when you were fifteen.' A sigh shuddered out of her. 'It was their way of looking after you.'

And he could see now that he'd let them. Because it'd been easier to believe all was well. He'd been a blind fool.

But he was done with all of that. He'd find a way to change. He'd find a way to look after Nina, just as Gran had asked him to. And he'd find a way to prove to Nina that he wasn't a killjoy. Maybe then she'd start to like him again and want to hang out with him.

Her eyes narrowed. 'You okay?'

'Never better,' he growled.

She grimaced.

He wasn't above using her momentary concern to his advantage, though. 'You up for a game of gin rummy after?'

'I, uh…' Her shoulders sagged. 'Sure, why not?'

CHAPTER FIVE

As THEIR YACHT left Cannes, Nina sprinkled a tiny portion of Iris's ashes into the sea. The water gleamed with the soft tones of the early morning light, all pinks, blues and silvers, and unruffled by even the smallest of breezes. 'I did exactly what you'd have wanted me to, Granny Day. I stretched out on a glamorous beach wearing nothing but a bikini, and I sipped a cocktail with one of those little umbrellas in it too. Truth be told, it was a little too sweet for my taste, but holding it in my hand, for all the world like some starlet… I felt like the bee's knees.'

Beside her, Blake gave a soft laugh and his face lightened, those usually stern lines softening. It felt like an achievement. She frowned. She didn't want it to. Where Blake was concerned, she didn't want to feel anything.

She pulled her mind back. 'Cannes was every bit as glamorous and golden as you imagined it would be. You'd have loved it.'

She gestured to Blake that it was his turn.

He turned to the water. 'I'm sorry to report, Gran, that I had a slow start—it took me a day to get into the holiday swing of things. Hopefully I made up for that yesterday. I took a selfie on the red carpet at the conference centre where the Cannes Film Festival awards are held—*Le Palais des Festivals et des Congrès.*'

He pronounced it with perfect French intonation and Nina found herself fighting a swoon.

'You loved watching all the hype and fanfare of the festival. Imagine all of the feet that have gone before mine on that carpet. Anyway, I figured you'd get a kick out of it.'

Blake's lips curved and Nina stared. He'd gone to the main film-festival venue? Why hadn't she thought to do that? Iris would've loved it.

You were enjoying beachy bikini goodness—sun, sea and laughter...a bit of light-hearted flirting. Nothing to envy here.

'And then I took a horse ride with a small group up into the hills. The views from up there were out of this world, and the whole place smelled of mimosa. I doubt it would've been something you'd have chosen to do at eighty, though you'd have jumped at it when you were younger. My muscles certainly let me know about it this morning. I ached in places I didn't know I had. But you'd have loved hearing about it, and you'd have loved my photos.' He stared at the water and nodded. 'Nina is right. Cannes would've lived up to all of your expectations.'

He turned back to Nina and gave her a thumbs up.

'You went horse riding?'

It sounded like an accusation and she couldn't blame his brows for shooting up as they did. 'Yep.'

'But you didn't mention that over dinner last night.'

'You didn't ask. I figured you weren't interested.'

He said it matter-of-factly and that stung, though she didn't know why. 'Yes, I did!'

'You asked if I'd had a nice day. I said that I did. You didn't encourage me to elaborate.'

Because she hadn't wanted to hear that he'd sat on a bench and done nothing all day, or that he'd moped at a table at some café, or remained onboard the yacht and worked.

She'd felt guilty that she'd abandoned him. Felt guilty that she hadn't asked him to join her on the beach. But it wasn't her job to look after him, and she had no intention of falling into that role. She'd done enough 'caring' this year. It was time to look after herself for a while.

And, despite his confession of the previous day—and it *was* a relief to know there'd been a legitimate reason he'd not made her mother's funeral—it had only brought home to her how far apart they'd grown.

And now to find herself...*jealous*.

You were on a glamorous beach with glamorous people!

Oh, but horse riding!

'Just for future reference, horse riding is newsworthy.'

'Do you want to know something else that's newsworthy?' He folded those strong arms. 'Even though you now know why I didn't make Auntie Jo's funeral, you're still angry at me.'

'Am not.'

'Are too.'

She rolled her eyes, but before she could respond Aurelia came out to inform them that breakfast was ready.

They followed her indoors, and Nina stopped short to stare at the spread. 'Way too much food.'

Aurelia smiled. 'I promise none of it will go to waste. Is there anything else I can get you?'

'No, thank you. It looks fabulous.'

Nina piled her plate with freshly sliced melon and delicate pastries and poured herself a coffee. She was going to have to start doing some serious exercise if this was the way she meant to go on eating. Swimming for real rather than bobbing in the sea; or maybe she'd take a few long hikes. Or go horse riding.

When Aurelia left, Nina glanced across the table to find Blake's startling blue eyes had settled on her. 'I understand about you missing the funeral. I'm sorry you've been dealing with panic attacks. *Not* angry.'

'And yet—' he gestured between them '—not friends again either, clearly.'

'Ah, but that's a different thing than me being mad at you.' She bit into a mini croissant, gloriously buttery and flaky… and as insubstantial as their friendship. 'But it's true, we're not friends again, not really.'

He paled and her chest cramped. She didn't want to hurt him, but it seemed pointless lying about it. She abandoned her croissant. 'Not enemies either.'

'Why the hell *aren't* we friends any more?'

She hid the way everything had started to ache behind a shrug. 'That's an existential question and I suspect you don't want an existential answer. Fact of the matter is we've spent next to no time with each other in the last decade. How is any friendship supposed to flourish under those conditions? We haven't experienced each other's lives alongside one another. I mean, I have this view in my mind of what your super-successful life looks like, but I doubt it's the reality. While you have me living the same life I was living ten years ago, when in fact nothing could be further from the truth. So the short answer is our friendship has dwindled due to the effects of time.'

'Garbage.'

She hitched up her chin. Fine. If he wanted the big guns, she'd bring out the big guns. 'And due to a lack of commitment from both of us during the last ten years. You refused to come home. I refused to leave my mum. Other things were more important than looking after our friendship.'

His eyes narrowed. 'Not buying it.'

Would he buy the cold hard truth, then? 'Earlier in the year I'd have held the exact same position you do now. You want to know the exact moment I realised we were no longer friends?'

'With every fibre of my being,' he bit out.

'Yesterday on that damn bench in Cannes, when you finally told me the truth.'

'That was supposed to help! To explain *why* I'd let you down. So you'd know I *had* tried to make it home.'

'And it did. But it also made me realise something else.'

'What?'

She sipped coffee to ease the tightness in her throat. 'You knew how much it meant to me for you to be at Mum's funeral, yes?'

He nodded, heavily, as if his head weighed a ton.

'You knew how hurt and let down I'd be when you didn't show up?'

He dragged a hand down his face.

'Yes?' she persisted.

'Yes.'

'And yet you left it seven whole months before telling me the truth? I get that you had a whole lot more on your mind the day it happened. I totally understand not hearing from you then. But you didn't ring me the next day or the one after... or any time during the following weeks.'

'I didn't want to worry you when you were grieving your mum!' He slashed a hand through the air. 'And I was ashamed and embarrassed and...'

And they came to the crux of the matter.

She maintained steady eye contact and refused to weaken, although it felt as if a part of her were dying inside. 'That's the thing, you see? Your shame and embarrassment meant more to you than my hurt feelings. I wasn't just *mildly disappointed*, Blake.' She'd been gutted. It had felt as if everything she'd thought true about the world had been a lie. 'If we were *real* friends, you'd have understood how deeply hurt I was and made sure I knew the truth asap. But your pride was more important—your pride and protecting your image of yourself.'

He sagged back, a stricken expression in his eyes, and she felt as if she'd kicked a puppy. 'Don't look like that!'

'Like what?'

'Like I just knifed you through the heart. And don't say that's exactly what it felt like either.'

'Wouldn't dream of it.' He straightened and topped up both of their coffees from the pot. 'A knife would've been kinder, I'm sure.'

She choked, but then rolled her eyes when she realised he was joking.

'I'm sorry, Nina. Truly sorry. When you stopped taking my calls, I told myself I'd wait until I saw you.'

She'd stopped taking his calls when she'd thought his *work* had been more important to him than her mum! And her. She hadn't been able to bear it; hadn't been able to talk to him after that. She should've known, though, that it had been a lie.

'I figured when we were face to face I'd be able to make everything right again. I was wrong, though. Clearly.' He stared at her, an unreadable expression in his eyes. 'But I'm not perfect—I'm human—and if perfection is what you're looking for from your friends, then I'm never going to live up to that. Nobody will.'

She gaped at him. He was trying to turn this back on her?

'But you're one of the most important people in my life and I'm not prepared to give up on our friendship. Not yet. Even if you are.'

Rising, he rapped his knuckles on the table. 'I have every intention of doing whatever I can to win back your friendship, to prove to you that you can trust me again.'

Oh? And how did he plan to do that? She refused to ask the question, though.

He stared down at her with pursed lips. 'I get the impression that at this current moment in time, though, you'd rather it if I'd remove myself from your presence.'

Absolutely!

'If I'm wrong about that, though, I'm hitting the hot tub. Feel free to join me,' he tossed over his shoulder.

No doubt he was hoping it'd soothe those horse-riding muscles.

Seizing her croissant, she tore off a piece and shoved it in her mouth, chewed savagely. No way was she joining him in a hot tub.

Why not?

Because these days Blake had muscles and she found them disturbing. She didn't want to think about Blake in those terms. She didn't want to think about him at all, but...

He's not the bad guy you've made him out to be.

Perhaps not. But somewhere along the way she'd lost the ability to feel comfortable with him, to be natural, and that was indicative of the issues between them.

Not his fault.

That was Iris's voice in her head and it made her stiffen. Iris would want her to give Blake a chance.

She glared out of the window at the perfectly sapphire water and the gloriously azure sky and the glut of morning sunshine. 'I'm not making any promises,' she muttered. None of it changed the fact that he'd left her stewing for *seven whole months*. How much longer would it have been if Iris hadn't died? Maybe she'd stopped taking his calls, but he could've texted her an explanation or emailed it to her or shown up in Callenbrook as soon as he was capable of travelling again. He'd done none of that.

She lingered over breakfast because, despite thinking she had no appetite, every morsel was delicious. Did Blake eat like this all the time?

Knowing Blake, probably not. But he could if he wanted to and that was the point. Blake the billionaire—it was a side of him she'd never really considered.

Shrugging that off, she headed down to her cabin. They'd be in Nice soon and she wanted to see what challenge Iris had in store for her today.

Ten minutes later she pushed the slip of paper back into its envelope. Oh, God. Holy *holy* crap! Iris wanted her to go parasailing!

No way was she wearing her bikini for this!

Before she could chicken out, she seized her phone and made a booking.

When the boat pulled into a berth at the marina in Nice, Nina ventured from her cabin to stand on the deck and survey the city. Blake moved to stand beside her. 'It's a pretty place.'

Elegant buildings stretched along the waterfront, the intense blue of the water a perfect foil for the long strip of white beach that stretched in front of them. She took in the tall palms, red-tiled roofs and an abundance of pink bougainvillea and nodded. 'Really pretty.'

He frowned as if realising her mind wasn't actually on the view. 'Do you have plans?'

'Yep.' With a superhuman effort she neither winced nor grimaced. A lump had lodged in her throat, making further speech impossible, though, so she pulled out her phone and showed him.

He stared at her phone and then at her. 'I didn't think heights were your thing.'

They *really* weren't.

He studied her face and pursed his lips. 'Are you sure you want to do this?'

Nope. She made herself nod.

'Why?'

'Because one ought to face their fears before they get the better of them,' she said, quoting Iris directly.

She noted the way his head rocked back, the way he paled, and shook her head. 'That wasn't aimed at you. I'm just doing what Iris wants me to do—' *literally* '—and push myself out of my comfort zone.' And she couldn't get much more out of her comfort zone than parasailing.

'Okay.'

He sounded far from convinced and she reclaimed her phone and tapped on an image to make it bigger. Everything inside her clenched. 'You ever been tempted?'

'Not once in my whole entire life.' A funny expression flitted across his face. He took her phone again and studied the picture. 'But now I'm wondering why not? *That* has the potential to be fun.'

'Are you for real?' She gaped at him, having expended her limited resources of feigned insouciance.

'The view would be something else.'

As she'd be keeping her eyes tightly clenched the entire time, she figured that was a moot point.

'Would you like…? I mean, would it be okay…?' He shuffled his feet. 'Can I…?'

'Spit it out, Blake.'

'Can I tag along?'

Nausea churned in her stomach. He wanted to *watch*?

'See?' He turned her phone to face her. 'Two people can go up together.'

The churning stopped. From somewhere, she found a measure of backbone. 'You think I'm too scared to do this myself?'

'Not for a moment.' It was clear she had every intention of doing this—of going up in a parachute while a speedboat whipped her across the bay, high above the rest of the world.

Parasailing? That *so* wasn't Nina's jam. She didn't even like going up a ladder.

One ought to face their fears before they get the better of them.

Was she doing this because of his panic attacks? An ache gripped his chest.

She continued to glare at him, and he shook his head again. 'I recognise that look in your eyes. You've made a reservation. I know you're going to do this.'

Whether she'd enjoy it, though, was another matter.

'But what you said to me the other day keeps bothering me. When did I become so stuffy? Doing something like parasailing isn't stuffy. I never do things like that. I always choose the sensible option.'

They'd disembarked and had started walking in the direction of the adventure company who ran the parasailing tours, but Nina halted now. 'You don't think this is sensible?'

'Not in the slightest.' He started them walking again. 'I don't think it's foolish or foolhardy either, though. It's perfectly safe.'

'Of course it is.' Her hands twisted together. 'Totally, one-hundred-per-cent safe.'

'It's just one of those fun for fun's sake things.'

'Fun.' She grimaced. 'Yep.'

She so clearly didn't want to do this and yet was oddly determined to do it regardless, and he had to fight an urge to wrap an arm around her shoulders and pull her against his side.

It was too soon to hug her.

If he didn't succeed in winning back her friendship he might never have an opportunity to hug her again. *Ever.* The loss hit him squarely in the chest, making his step falter.

She rounded on him. 'You *do* think this is dangerous.'

He gathered his scattered wits. 'I don't! I swear. I just...' His nose curled. 'I don't want to be considered stuffy. I want to be more like you—doing adventurous things and pushing myself out of my comfort zone. You're doing exactly what Gran has asked of you. She'd be proud of you.'

She blinked.

'You know what she said to me in my letter?'

She shook her head, her eyes widening.

'She said that I didn't need to live my life in direct opposition to my parents.'

Her mouth dropped open and it made him far too aware of how luscious and kissable her lips were. The thought had him gulping and turning back to face the front. *Don't think about her in those terms, you jerk.*

'Everything I do, I make sure it's above board, make sure it can withstand any amount of scrutiny. I refuse to do anything to court the tiniest whiff of scandal. I refuse to do anything that could cause people to draw comparisons between me and my parents.'

She swore and made an unconscious movement—as if to take his arm and hug it to her. He wanted to weep when she stopped herself from doing so. 'Hell, Blake.'

His nose curled. 'No wonder you think me a boring sod with the personality of a dishrag.'

'I *didn't* say that.'

'Not in so many words, but you basically told me to get a life.'

'I wanted you to do something more constructive than watch *me* get a life.'

'And you were right.' He gestured towards the bay. 'Never in a million years would I'd have thought to do something like parasailing.'

They both halted to watch a person hanging from a parachute in the sky, the speedboat below leaving a foamy wake of white behind it. She bit her thumb as she watched their progress. He could see the second thoughts gathering in the shadows of her eyes.

'You don't have to do this. If you don't think you'll enjoy it—'

'Yes, I do.'

She set back off along the footpath. He kept easy pace beside her. He wanted to ask her why she had such a bee in her bonnet about it, but some instinct warned him not to.

He pointed back towards the parasailer. 'That sure as hell isn't stuffy. And I know you just said I shouldn't be watching you getting a life—and I'm not… I mean, not in some weird stalkerish kind of way.' He frowned. 'At least I hope not.'

She huffed out a laugh. 'Whatever it is you're trying to say, Blake, spit it out before you dig yourself in any deeper.'

Excellent idea. 'You're leading by example, is what I'm trying to say. I'm trying to emulate you. You're giving me ideas for how to be less of a killjoy.'

She rolled her eyes. 'I did *not* call you a killjoy.'

'Nope, I came up with that one all by myself.'

'Your therapist has been schooling you in the power of positive self-talk, then.'

He laughed. He couldn't help it. She was terrified yet still able to crack a joke. 'My therapist and I have agreed that I'm a work in progress.'

Which in turn made her laugh. The brief affinity gave him hope. Whether she wanted to admit it or not, they shared a connection. His stupid pride had nearly severed it, but a stubborn thread or two remained, and he was determined to build on them. And he'd start by making sure she didn't face this terrifying task alone.

She didn't hesitate when they reached the adventure tour's small office, but pushed through the door and proceeded to quote her booking number to the receptionist.

'Would it be possible for us to go up together?' he asked.

The reservation clerk checked the computer and nodded.

Blake swung to Nina. 'Your call. I really want to go up, but I'll understand if you want to do this on your own. I'll simply make my own booking and wait my turn.'

She gestured back behind them. 'You really want to do that?'

Not really, but… 'Absolutely. In service of Operation Un-stuffiness.'

She rolled her eyes. 'Fine, we'll do it together, then.'

Was it his imagination, or had her shoulders unhitched a fraction?

A short while later, they sat in a speedboat as it took off from the dock. They were placed in their harnesses and slowly winched into the air. Nina clenched her eyes shut and gritted her teeth, her knuckles turning white where they gripped the ropes of her parachute. Her teeth chattered. 'I've changed my mind.'

Too late for that, Nina. Way too late. Instead of saying that, he reached out and took her hand. 'For Granny Day,' he said as the speedboat gathered speed below them.

Nina opened one eye a fraction, gave a muffled squeal, and clenched it shut again. Her hand gripped his so hard it almost cut off the circulation. His stomach lurched. They were up so high! But a moment later his stomach settled and he stared about in wonder.

Under her breath, Nina chanted, 'For Granny Day. For Granny Day.' It soon changed to, 'Oh, God, Blake, you've gone dead quiet. Say something. It's every bit as awful as I thought it'd be, isn't it? And—'

'It's amazing. It's so amazing I'm speechless. I didn't expect it to feel…so amazing.'

Her grip eased a fraction. 'You're liking this?'

'I'm loving it.' And he was more surprised by that than anything. Glancing across, he took in her gritted teeth and tightly clenched eyes and affection welled in his chest. He wanted to make this experience fabulous for her too. She deserved to enjoy it rather than just endure it. 'Open your eyes, Nina.'

She did, but immediately looked down. With a whimper, she slapped both hands across them. 'Awful. Awful. Awful.'

Reaching across, he turned her chin until she faced him. 'Open your eyes, Nina.'

She shook her head.

'Please?'

A sigh shuddered out of her, but she peeled one hand away and cracked her eyes open. The fear in them—the panic—caught at him. He held her chin steady and held her gaze. 'I thought it might feel like a roller-coaster ride, but it doesn't. Focus on how it feels. We're floating and it's unbelievably relaxing, and it's also surprisingly quiet up here. And...'

'And?' She moistened her lips.

He shrugged. 'Oddly peaceful.'

'I can get relaxing and peaceful on the beach.'

'In a bikini,' he added, because he knew the bikini bit was important, though he didn't know why.

She huffed out a laugh.

'Okay—' with his chin, he gestured to their left a fraction '—we're going to look in that direction—straight out, not down—and we're going to admire the pretty buildings of Nice and the beach looking like a film set. Ready?'

She gave the tiniest of nods. He slowly released her, immediately missing the softness of her skin against his fingertips. They tingled where they'd made contact with her. What would it be like to kiss her—up here above the world? He'd bet it'd be spectacular and—

What the hell?

Not going there. Pushing the thought from his mind, he focused instead on her reactions. Releasing a slow breath and staring where he'd indicated, she bit her lip and nodded. 'Okay. It *is* pretty.'

Pursing his lips, he frowned. *Really* pretty.

'Why are you frowning?'

He turned to find her staring at him. He gestured at the view. 'I have all of this practically on my doorstep. All of these amazing places. They're only a couple of hours away by plane. Why haven't I been seeing all that I can see and making time to have experiences like this?'

'You took Granny Day on some extraordinary holidays.'

That was true enough. But he'd never thought to treat himself to something like this. Not on his own. Not just for him.

'You've been working hard, consolidating your company.' She sent him a small, not entirely steady smile. 'Operation Rejigging Your Life should take care of that, though.'

He grinned. 'Your name for it is better than mine.'

'I know.'

'So…how's Operation Out of My Comfort Zone going over there?'

'Ooh, swimmingly.' She grimaced, darting a gaze downwards. 'Hopefully not literally. Not entirely at ease, but…' she gestured '…this *is* pretty amazing. Plus I thought it would feel jerky up here—a lot of falling down and going up again, which I hate. But it's nothing like that. It really does feel like we're floating.' She stared around as if utterly confounded. 'We're floating above the Mediterranean Sea along the French Riviera like we're…'

'The most extraordinary people we've ever met.'

'Exactly!'

Her laugh made him feel younger and more carefree— like a better version of himself. 'Wait until the Deadly Sins hear about this.'

'They'll be so jealous.'

He met her gaze, pulled in a breath. 'Right… Now, part of this experience, apparently, is being dipped in the water.'

Alarmed eyes swung back to his.

'I'm assured that we just float slowly down, get a tiny dunking in the sea, and drift back upwards. You up for that?'

She bit her lip.

He grinned at her and then waved his hands in the air. 'Look at me! No hands!'

Her lips kinked upwards. She glanced around and then down. She squared her chin. 'Oh, go on, then—for Iris.'

He gave the signal he'd organised with the skipper, and it was all incredibly gentle, though they both laughed at the shock of cold water when they dipped into it. And then they were immediately lifting upwards again.

Nina wore a T-shirt and a sensible one-piece swimsuit rather than that enticing bikini. He told himself he wasn't disappointed.

'I can't believe I'm actually enjoying this. Blake, I—' She turned to meet his gaze...blinked and frowned. 'Do you know that your eyes are the exact same shade of blue as the sea?'

The next moment her head jerked back as if the words surprised her as much as they had him. A spark arced between them—something primal, *carnal*, that had no business messing with things between them. Heat gathered in his veins, and once more a vision of kissing her filled his mind.

Stop it! He wanted to fix their friendship. Not wreck it.

He made his voice deliberately light. 'Was that a compliment?'

His teasing tone snapped her out of her trance. She stuck her nose in the air. 'Just a simple statement of fact.'

He wished with all his might that the skipper of the boat below would dunk them again. He was in serious need of cooling off.

Over a lunch of fresh oysters followed by steamed mussels in white wine, on the terrace of a luxury hotel with an extraordinary view of the bay, Nina sipped her wine. 'Thank you for what you did today, Blake. I did my best to hide it, but you knew I was petrified, and I know that's why you came with me, even though you weren't all that enthused about parasailing.'

'If I hadn't gone up I'd have missed one of the most amazing experiences of my life.'

'If you hadn't come up with me, I would've too.'

He shook his head at that. 'You'd have been fine—'

'I'd have spent the entire time with my hands over my eyes and trying not to cry. Instead, you helped me relax and see how amazing it all was. It was kind of you—very kind. And I'm grateful.'

'I admired the way you wanted to face your fear. And I meant it when I said I wanted to win back your friendship.'

She froze.

Damn it. She wasn't ready for this, was she? He shouldn't have pushed.

She eyed him for what felt like a very long time, as if weighing him up and assessing his seriousness. It made his pulse jump and jerk. Eventually she raised an eyebrow. 'So much so you'd spend Christmas in Callenbrook?'

CHAPTER SIX

NINA'S MOUTH DRIED. What on earth was she thinking? Blake come home for Christmas? She might as well ask for flying pigs! He might make a lot of noise about fixing their friendship, but in reality she doubted he'd want to put the work in.

Some of the magic of the day slipped away. It probably wasn't fair to ask it of him anyway. His fear of Callenbrook was a hundred times more potent than her fear of heights. He'd helped her relish their parasailing adventure in spite of her fear. But nothing she did would help reconcile him to the town he hated.

She braced herself for his refusal. It would no doubt be kindly couched. It pierced her to the marrow how much she wanted him to say yes, though.

Those intense blue eyes met hers. Her heart pounded in her throat. And then he smiled. It was so unexpected she sagged, her pulse racing like a mad thing.

'Christmas in Callenbrook this December?' He nodded, once. 'It's a date.'

Her jaw dropped. He'd do that? *For her?* She hauled it back into place, rubbed a hand across her heart, eyed him carefully. 'I mean, if you hate the idea...'

Shadows momentarily dimmed all of that brilliant blue. 'I think spending Christmas in Callenbrook this year—in honour of Auntie Jo and Gran—would be the perfect thing to do.'

Tears burned her eyes. 'They'd heartily approve.' *She* certainly did.

'And if it'll prove to you that I'm serious about fixing our friendship, prove to you how much you mean to me, Nina, then I'll gladly spend Christmas with you in Callenbrook. *Gladly,*' he repeated, stabbing a finger to the table as if afraid she might miss his sincerity.

She'd have to be blind to do that, though. It shone from his every pore, and she could feel it mending some of the fractures in her battered heart. She didn't know what to say and, as a lump lodged in her throat, speech became impossible anyway. *Don't burst into tears!*

She didn't want to reveal how much this meant to her. It was only early September. Christmas was months away. He had plenty of time to cry off yet. He might be making all the right noises, but it was too soon to trust him. As soon as he returned to London, he might forget about her again.

He eased back in his seat, framed by the gorgeous pastel stone of the hotel and a multitude of pink blossoms from a row of climbing roses that somehow only enhanced his masculinity. It had a pulse ticking to life deep inside her. His grin grew mischievous and she could've groaned because it made him look like sin personified.

No, no, this is Blake.

And he is seriously hot.

She squashed that thought flat.

'But can we please spend the Christmas after in London?' The words shocked her back to herself. 'London?'

'Why not? I'd spring for your ticket. It could be your Christmas present.'

'Extravagant much?' She raised an eyebrow.

Firm lips pursed and she had to drag her gaze away. *Don't stare.*

'I'm starting to think that's something I need to rethink?'

She glanced back. 'What? Being extravagant?'

His mouth twisted. 'The fact that I'm *never* extravagant.'

'Ahem, if I could see our yacht right now, I'd be pointing it out to you.'

'That's a one-off. For Gran.'

He scratched a hand through his hair—seriously thick hair that gleamed in the sun, and she couldn't help wondering if it'd be as soft as it looked.

'I have all of this money, but what am I doing with it?' He rolled his shoulders. 'I should be using it in service of Operation Killing the Killjoy.'

She rolled her eyes. 'We really need to talk about the way you frame things. You could've called it Operation Finding the Joy, instead. Anyway, I like Operation Rejigging My Life better. It's not like you have to remake your entire life over— just rejig it a bit here and there. As for what you're doing with your money—' she folded her arms '—I bet you're giving plenty to charity. And according to Iris, you have a *very* nice penthouse apartment in London with views of the Thames.'

He winced. 'That *was* extravagant.'

'And you shouldn't be apologising for that or wincing about it.'

'See? I'm a lost cause, a total misery guts.'

She couldn't help but laugh.

'And just so you know... I *am* joking.'

Blue eyes shouldn't look so warm. 'I know.'

'Mostly.' He stared at her with those pursed lips again making things inside her tighten and tingle. 'You always could help me gain perspective.'

She sipped her drink and tried to quench what suddenly felt like an unquenchable thirst. 'Then tell me why you think being extravagant will help you become happier.'

One shoulder lifted. Dear God, *why* did they have to be so broad?

'It's not the extravagance that's the problem, but actively being *not* extravagant,' he started slowly. 'It's as if, in being frugal with money, I'm also being frugal with joy. And I know money and joy don't have to equate…'

She leaned towards him. 'Nor do they have to un-equate.' *Why* wasn't he enjoying all of his money? He'd worked so hard for it.

'While I'm generous when it comes to treating my friends and work colleagues, and nothing was ever too much expense when it came to Gran, when it comes to myself… I don't indulge.'

She set her drink down. 'Why *not*?'

'I'm going to sound like an idiot.'

'Ha! Like that's something new.' She fought to keep things light and was rewarded with the flash of his grin.

'In some ways the money feels like a burden. I'm careful that every cent is accounted for so that nobody can ever accuse me or my company of embezzling it or doing something nefarious with it.'

A lump lodged in her throat. She stared at her hands with burning eyes and blinked hard. She *would not cry*. What his parents had done had left a deep and permanent scar. It had left him equating money with guilt and trouble and blame. It was the height of unfairness.

'You're not your parents, Blake. You're honest and ethical and generous and charitable. You've worked hard and earned your success. You've every right to enjoy that success.'

And she wanted him to. She wanted him to have every good thing that darn money could buy him. Most of all, though, she wanted to drag him out from under the weight of that old guilt. It was misplaced. And if he wasn't careful it could crush him.

Because, despite everything—that old guilt, her anger with him, the panic attacks—underneath it all Blake had a good heart, a beautiful heart. Which was why him spending Christmas in Callenbook meant so much to her. His spirit deserved a chance to soar free.

* * *

Things inside Blake clenched up tight. 'I let my mother use me, Nina.' He was the one who'd created that damn accounting package. The one that had allowed her to defraud innocent people of millions of dollars.

'You didn't know what she planned to use it for!'

He should've known though, should've twigged that the things his mother was asking of him were illegal, but he'd been fooled by her attention—grateful and gratified she'd finally noticed him, flattered she'd trust him with as important a task as creating software for her investment company. He could see now how cleverly she'd deflected his attention whenever he'd started to become suspicious and uneasy. And his father had always been there to soothe his concerns, to assure him all was well, and give him a clap on the back.

What a fool he'd been. He'd thought that if he did a good enough job the three of them—he, his mother and father—would become a proper family unit, instead of him being shunted off to his grandmother's all the time. Not that he hadn't loved his gran. He had. But she'd had her own life to lead.

His father had continually told him he was a man now and that they both had to do everything they could for his mother—that she was a special woman with amazing talents. He'd told Blake how proud he was of him.

He'd fallen for it all—the flattery, the compliments, the lies and manipulations. What a mug! He ought to have had 'gullible fool' tattooed on his forehead.

He rubbed a hand over his face, wishing he could rub those awful memories away. 'I helped defraud millions of dollars from people we knew.' Many who couldn't afford to take such a hit.

Reaching across, she grabbed his hand. 'You're no longer that same boy eager for his parents' approval. You had no idea what your mother was up to or what plans she had for that program. She manipulated you, Blake.'

He recalled the sense of betrayal when he'd found out the truth. The shock. The pain. For a time his entire world had turned black and grim. As if a part of him had died. He'd been left feeling *less*. Less of a person. Less loved. Less intelligent. So much *less*.

His hands clenched. He'd *never* let anyone make him feel that way again.

Nina's eyes flashed. 'The woman was a criminal—she cared for no one and nothing but herself. And even if you had the slightest suspicion that her motives were nefarious—you were fifteen! She was your mum! Your dad was insisting you help out. We were raised to respect and obey our parents, Blake. Unluckily for you, yours didn't deserve it.'

Nina's ferocity, her fierce certainty, helped to temper some of that old guilt, but it couldn't touch the shock of that old betrayal or the coldness that gripped him whenever he recalled what his parents had done.

She thrust out her chin and all but glared at him. 'Anyway, you made amends. You testified against both your parents in court. And you've made something amazing of yourself and your life. You ought to be proud of yourself. And you ought to be enjoying your success rather than letting it tie you up in knots.'

He blinked.

She folded her arms and glared. 'So how's that for some perspective?'

'I...' He blinked.

'Right.' She clapped her hands together. 'How can we be outrageously extravagant today?'

Resistance immediately rose through him. 'We can't be extravagant for extravagance's sake.'

'Why not?'

'I…' He floundered.

'I just had a fancy meal and a glass of wine, which was pretty extravagant.'

'Yeah, but—'

'We're cruising the French Riviera and that's definitely extravagant.'

'I already explained—'

'And I bought a ridiculously expensive bikini in Cannes although I definitely didn't need it.'

But she looked amazing in it. As far as he was concerned it was money well spent. Would she wear it again soon? He hoped so because—

Stop it!

He blinked back into the moment to find her gaze had settled on him, an expression in those amber eyes that he recognised.

He folded his arms. 'That look says trouble.'

She raised a suspiciously innocent eyebrow.

'You have thoughts on how I should be spending my money, I presume?'

'Naturally.'

She pointed a not entirely steady finger at him. He stared at that small hand and a funny wave of tenderness washed over him.

'What you need is something fun and silly that will haul you out of your comfort zone.'

He pointed to the parasailers out on the water. 'What was *that*?'

'That was outside *my* comfort zone, not yours.'

Damn it, what scheme did she have in mind? Still, if it made her stop seeing him as boring and stuffy… His pulse quickened. If he could prove to her that he was every bit as brave as she was at facing his fears… 'Okay, hit me with it.'

'We're heading to Monte Carlo next, right? What could be

more extravagant and crazier fun then hitting the casino? I'm channelling a James Bond film here—minus the violence—with you as 007, and me as…'

She was giving him the gift of 007? Could he pull off sophisticated and debonair? Damn it, he'd give it a red-hot go. Cocking his head to one side, he surveyed her—hopefully the picture of debonair sophistication. 'While I'm seeing you as Julia Roberts in *Pretty Woman.*' It had been Auntie Jo's favourite movie. He and Nina had watched it with her hundreds of times.

Nina's jaw dropped. With a visible effort, she hauled it back into place. 'Why don't we play at being high rollers for just one night? It's the height of extravagant frivolous fun—and legal,' she added when he opened his mouth.

He closed it again. Extravagant frivolous fun. James Bond. *Pretty Woman.* Maybe she had a point.

'You deserve to let your hair down once in a blue moon, Blake.'

She certainly deserved to.

'And here's something else… I know that as soon as you were able, you compensated everyone affected by your parents' scam.'

What the hell? Everything started to ache again.

'You didn't have to do that. What happened wasn't your fault. But it was a good thing to do. You don't have to feel guilty now about how you spend your money. It's been honestly earned.'

Some of the aching eased. 'That—' he stabbed a finger to the table '—was supposed to be a secret.'

She raised a pitying eyebrow.

He shook his head. 'That infernal town.'

His outrage slowly drained away, though, at the realisation that Nina's face was no longer shuttered against him. She'd fully engaged with him. Like a friend. Like a *best* friend. He had to fight an urge to drop to the paving stones and kiss the ground at her feet.

But then he couldn't stop from imagining taking one of those surprisingly dainty feet in his hands and pressing a kiss to the soft skin of her ankle and then working his way up her calf to the softer skin of her inner thigh just above her knee where—

He blinked, fighting an urge to seize the jug of iced water and pouring it over his head.

Nina, thank God, hadn't noticed. She stared out at the horizon, a brooding expression in the burnt caramel of her eyes, her pursed lips heavy with…

His stomach churned. *Grief?* Grief for *him*. For what had happened to him fifteen years ago.

Mixing with all the fresh grief she'd experienced in the last year too, no doubt. His heart clenched. So did his hands. Why hadn't he realised she'd needed him? Not just this year after her mum had died, but before that. How could he call himself a friend and not have been there to…make her laugh, make sure she had some fun? He swallowed. *To help.* He should've been there to help her through all of it. Some friend!

What had she had instead? Hanging out with old people, bingo, and *line dancing*. She was right. They could do better than that.

'If we're going to do this, Nina, we're doing it right.'

She swung back. 'What do you mean?'

'We need to look the part.'

She laughed when she realised what he meant. 'You don't need to buy me a designer dress.'

'Ah, but I *want* to.' Nina had never been interested in his money and she wasn't now either. He knew that. 'A designer dress for you and a tuxedo for me.'

'Oh, but—'

'A bit of extravagance is *exactly* what the doctor's ordered.'

She pursed her lips, before rising to her feet and tossing her gleaming river of hair over her shoulder. 'My dress has to be glamorous.'

He rubbed his hands together. 'Absolutely.'

Two nights later they strode into Monte Carlo's iconic casino. It was all royal blue and gold gilt and better than a movie set. The chandeliers glittered, the women's jewels sparkled, as did the crystal champagne flutes and whiskey tumblers that were lifted to smiling lips.

Nina's hand tightened at the crook of his elbow. She wore a stunning dress in red silk that fitted her curves in a way that made his mouth dry and his pulse stumble. 'Don't forget...' She leaned in close, smelling of an intoxicating mix of amber and jasmine. 'It's Bond, James Bond.'

He lifted his chin. *Debonair sophistication.* But his lips kinked up as he glanced down at her. 'It was so good, I almost peed my pants,' he quoted, making her snort-laugh.

'Stop it. You're ruining the impression we're making.'

'Ah, what you need to understand, Nina, is that, in an establishment such as this one, it's not manners that count but money.' He led her further into the room. 'We had to show our passports before entering, and there'll be facial-recognition cameras in the room. As soon as it's confirmed I'm *that* Blake Carlisle, we'll—'

A casino host made a beeline for them.

'Well, you'll see for yourself soon enough. If you want to appear sophisticated, don't blink an eye.'

It was all he managed to get out before he was greeted by name and offered champagne.

He took a glass from the proffered tray and handed it to Nina. Her eyes danced and mischief shuffled through him. 'I'll have a martini, thank you.'

'Very good, sir.' The host snapped his fingers and a nearby

server rushed to fill the order. 'What can we tempt you to this evening, sir?' He rattled off a list of games.

Blake glanced at Nina, raised an eyebrow. 'Blackjack,' she answered promptly.

They were led to a table, the bottle of French champagne left in an ice bucket beside them.

Nina threw herself into the spirit of the evening with gusto. Her enthusiasm contagious. The two of them had always played cards. Both Gran and Auntie Jo had played gin rummy and canasta. When he was at university, he'd played a lot of poker. All of that, though, had been for fun—not money.

The stakes added an undeniable edge of excitement, as did the glittering surrounds. Nina nudged him when a famous Hollywood actor strode past to sit at the neighbouring table. He nudged her when he saw a not so minor European royal and their entourage escorted across the room.

'Pinch me,' she murmured.

For a moment he saw it all through her eyes. She was right. It was extraordinary. Why had he denied himself this?

From blackjack, which amazingly enough they won at— they moved to the crap table, where they bombed.

'What would you like to try next?'

She bit her lip. 'Roulette?'

'The English roulette wheel or French roulette?'

Her eyes widened. 'What's French roulette?'

Grinning, he led her to one of the large bass tables and ex-plained the game to her. French roulette was the big-ticket ex-travaganza that one expected from a casino. He laid a bunch of money on the table and a croupier handed him a big pile of chips that Blake pushed in Nina's direction.

She promptly placed the lot on the number twenty-two. She was born on the seventeenth of November while he was born on the fifth of February. Seventeen plus five equalled twenty-two. She'd always said it was her lucky number.

She won. She won an extraordinary amount of money. She stared, her jaw ajar. He grinned. From her other side the Hollywood actor congratulated her.

'I...' She blinked and shook her head. 'Beginner's luck.'

The actor handed her a pile of chips. 'Perhaps you'll be kind enough to do the same for me, then?'

She handed them straight back. 'No way. You only get one shot at beginner's luck.'

The actor grinned. 'No, you don't, you get three shots.'

Biting her lip, she glanced from the actor to the table. 'You can split your chips, right?'

'You can indeed.'

'Then put some on five and some on seventeen.'

He did and, to much applause, he won too.

Before they knew it, they were at a table with the actor and other Hollywood people drinking champagne and eating caviar.

When Blake and Nina finally left to return to the yacht hours later, Nina stared up at the sky and shook her head. 'No one back home will ever believe this.'

'The press photographer at the casino grabbed some snaps. I asked him to send me a few.'

She grabbed his arm and gave a silent scream. 'We ate caviar!'

Her excitement touched him. He wished she'd kept hold of his arm though. Instead she released it immediately. 'Did you like it?'

'Yes, damn it. Talk about champagne tastes on a beer budget.'

He'd order caviar for Christmas in Callenbrook. That had a rather pleasing ring to it.

The thought didn't have his heart dropping to the soles of his feet either. He'd do anything to win back Nina's friendship. Christmas in Callenbrook would be a small price to pay.

Seizing his arm again, she pulled him to a halt and searched his face. 'Did you have fun too?'

'Of course I did.' He'd been with her, hadn't he? 'You told me it would be an insane amount of fun, and you were right.' It was Nina, though, who'd made it fun.

A breath whooshed out of her. 'Good. I didn't want to be the only one.'

'Our entire table had a ball.'

'It's one of those nights I'll never forget.' She'd started walking again, gestured out in front of them at the harbour. 'I'm in Monte Carlo, I won at blackjack.'

'And bombed at craps.'

'And then totally cleaned up at French roulette.'

'Dined with a Hollywood star.'

'With my own personal James Bond. Who, it must be said, in his tuxedo, was the most dashing man in the room.'

Her words drew things inside him tight. 'Dashing, huh?' He'd meant the words to be teasing, but they emerged on a husky whisper.

She glanced up, her feet slowing once more, her smile dissolving, but the heat in her eyes remained. 'I shouldn't have said that, should I?' Biting her lip, she shrugged. 'But you really do rock a tuxedo, Blake.'

'And you rock a bikini.'

'And you shouldn't have said that.' She swallowed, but she didn't look away. 'You looked?'

'Hell, Nina, I can't seem to stop looking.'

Her mouth formed a perfect O, before she straightened and glanced around. 'And now here we are in Monte Carlo, walking beside the water beneath an almost full moon...'

Wind rushed in his ears and his heart thundered in his chest. Every atom arched towards her. 'That sounded like an invitation.'

She raised an eyebrow. 'Maybe it was.'

CHAPTER SEVEN

Nina didn't know if she took a step closer or whether Blake did. What she did know was that she grabbed the lapels of his jacket and pulled him down until his mouth was in reach of hers and, leaning forward, placed her lips on his.

The kiss was whisper soft—like the balmy night air that brushed across her skin—and left her tingling, filling her with the same pale glow that lit the moon. As if this moment were from a fairy tale or a dream.

She eased away a fraction, their lips clinging until the very last moment, the glittering blue depths of his eyes blinking back into hers as if he too was caught up in the same dream. A line appeared between his eyes, not exactly a frown, as if the kiss had left him bamboozled and unbalanced. 'Nina?'

'Mmm?'

'You mind if we try that again?'

His words were a soft whisper in the night and it raised all the fine hairs on her arms and made her shiver with anticipation—*delicious* anticipation. She shook her head. She didn't mind. Not in the slightest.

Maybe it was the champagne, or the euphoria of the evening, or the romance of the setting with that big moon hanging above them making a silver path on the sea, the sound of water lapping on the shore. Or the sense that things had been smoothed between them, finally making all right with the world.

Cupping her face in his fingers, he danced those fingers along her jaw, sparking sensation wherever they touched, his mouth descending with an agonising slowness that had a moan gathering in the back of her throat. When his lips claimed hers, the magical dreamlike quality exploded, replaced with something far more elemental. An arm swept around her waist to hold her steady from the onslaught of sensations that pounded through her, before she found her balance once more and kissed him back with the same fervour, staking a claim of her own.

His quick intake of breath, his ragged breathing as they eased away once more—his arm still anchored at her waist, her hands crushing the lapels of his dinner jacket. She caught a myriad expressions in his eyes—shock, exhilaration, *hunger.*

Need, savage and hard, filled her every atom. 'Kiss me again.'

It was half plea, half demand, but he filled the order with a flattering speed and they crashed back together. Her arms slid around his neck, her fingers plunging into the thick softness of his hair. One of his hands splayed against the small of her back, his other between her shoulder blades, pulling all of the things that most ached flush against him until the fire inside her threatened to become an inferno. She wanted to feel as much of that powerful male body against hers as she could.

And all the while, his mouth plundered hers with a wicked tempting sensuality, his tongue drawing hers into a dance until every part of her fired with red-hot need and an urgent craving for fulfilment. Arching against him, she moaned, she gasped…she begged.

He broke off to press hot burning kisses to her throat. Her hands explored the hard planes of his chest, frustrated at the clothing blocking access to the firm male flash beneath. Dancing fingers down to the waistband of his trousers, she started to tug his shirt free, greedy to explore the broad lean lines of him, but before she could, his hands on hers halted her movements.

'Public place,' he groaned out.

The gruff words blinked her back to reality. She eased away on unsteady legs.

His chest rose and fell. 'We should go back to the yacht.'

His eyes glittered in the darkness and she wanted to grab his hand and run—run at breakneck speed back to the yacht and see this thing flaring between them through to its natural conclusion.

Instead, she forced herself to take a deep breath. 'Not yet.' She backed up to sit on a nearby bench. She couldn't go back to the yacht until she'd worked out what she wanted to have happen once they reached it.

Closing her eyes, she fought for control. Two of the most important people in her life had died this year, and that meant she wasn't necessarily in a good place for making any kind of big decisions at the moment.

Blake lowered himself down beside her. 'You okay?'

'I think so.'

They stared out at the night, at the yachts bobbing on the water. It was a combination of navy and silver. The midnight blue of the sky and the inky darkness of the sea contrasted with the silvery light of the moon and the twinkling lights of the city. So pretty. So seductive. But it was a false promise, wasn't it?

The kiss between her and Blake didn't mean anything and it would never mean anything. She knew that. Because she knew Blake.

'What's going through your mind right now?'

She turned her head to find him surveying her. 'We're trying to fix our friendship and I'm not sure kissing each other is the right way to go about that.' The fact she wanted to kiss him again—ached with it—didn't make thinking logically any easier.

He ruffled a hand through his hair. 'Damn, that flared out of control quick.'

He could say that again. 'Didn't see it coming,' she agreed.

But that was a lie, wasn't it? Ever since she'd clapped eyes on Blake again, a part of her had wanted him. Maybe it was due to her grief or her former anger with him...or the fact that she hadn't seen him in ten years. Whatever it was, it was foolhardy, and she had wit enough to know that.

'Way back when we were teenagers, you claimed you were never going to settle down. What was it you called yourself...?'

'A lone wolf.'

That was it.

Shadowed eyes met hers. 'I still am.'

Exactly. She watched the lights dance across the water like tiny flickering flames. 'I've no problem with sex for sex's sake, Blake. And I'm seriously tempted. That kiss was something else.'

'Yeah.' A frown stretched through his voice.

'And if I was never going to see you again after this trip, I wouldn't hesitate.'

He swung to her, the tendons in his neck standing out. 'But you are. You *will*. I'm spending Christmas in Callenbrook!'

The knuckles of his hands gleamed white in the moonlight, and her mouth went dry. They had too much to lose to give into this silly attraction. She let out a breath. 'That's the plan.'

He nodded. 'Good.'

'No matter how mature we want to be about the subject...' The burning needy tingles throbbing through her right now didn't feel particularly mature. They felt urgent and demanding and opposed to all common sense. Gritting her teeth, she did her best to ignore them. 'Sex complicates things. It's pointless pretending otherwise.'

Could she sleep with Blake and keep her heart from becoming involved? She'd had a taste of how badly he could hurt her as a friend. How much more could he hurt her—or have the potential to hurt her—as a lover? Besides, she wasn't convinced yet that he'd turn up for Christmas. To give even more of herself to him…

A chill chased down her spine.

'And you think our relationship is already complicated enough?'

He searched her face—wary, worried…tense.

'Things *are* being mended between us,' she said. They were. But if he let her down again…

'So why risk it? Is that what you're saying?'

His shoulders were oddly tense, so was his mouth. She realised it was caused by the same hunger that threaded through her in unrelenting spirals. *Oh dear God.* 'Yes.' She forced the word out.

They were both silent for several long moments.

'Your friendship is one of the most important things in my life,' Blake finally said. 'I won't do anything that might risk it.'

His words should've left her feeling warm and toasty. As they rose to walk back to the yacht, though, she felt unaccountably grumpy. And frustrated!

They arrived in Portofino after lunch the following day.

Nina climbed up to the sky lounge, her heart in her throat after reading Iris's challenge. She still couldn't believe what she'd read. It was…

Don't think about it. You don't have to do it.

Of course she had to do it. But she didn't have to think about it right now. She wasn't doing it right now either, that was for certain.

Maybe later. Under the cover of darkness. When not a single soul was around. Could she put it off until they reached Positano? Or—

'It's something, isn't it?'

She glanced to where Blake stood at a railing and then in the direction he gestured to. Her eyes widened. *Okay...*

She moved across to stand beside him, but she wasn't entirely sure her feet touched the floor. Just...*wow.* 'I don't think I've ever seen anywhere more beautiful.'

Those broad shoulders lifted. 'Me either.'

They dropped anchor a little to the left in the small harbour. A dramatic headland arced off to their right, but in front of them the prettiest U-shaped shoreline edged with pastel-coloured buildings in varying shades of ochre, pink and yellow nestled between the clear blue water and lush green hill behind, dense with pines and palms and other trees and shrubs she couldn't identify.

She'd read that Portofino was a unique mix of forests—pine groves giving way to olive groves and everything in between. She hadn't expected it to look so harmonious, though. The scent of the man beside her—a heady mix of citrus and juniper berry—only enhanced the experience.

'You have any plans for the day?'

Skinny-dipping, apparently. Not that she had any intention of telling him that. 'Nope, you?'

'There's a monastery at an inlet over the hill that way. It's an hour-and-a-half hike through the forest. The views along the way are apparently spectacular. If you'd like to join me...' He shrugged. 'There'll be afternoon tea at the other end.'

'Sold!' She wanted to keep busy—needed to. A restless energy had kept her fidgeting all morning. She blamed the kiss of the night before. It had unleashed things inside her that were far harder to corral back under control than they ought to be.

Don't think about the kiss.

She was doing her best not to! But the effects of that kiss continued to burn through her. She ached with the need the kiss had created inside her. No kiss had ever done that to her before. She needed to do something to dispel it.

She shook out her arms. A hike would be perfect. It'd help her expend her excess energy, wear her out…and stop her imagining what it would've been like to have given into temptation.

Stop thinking about it!

She squared her shoulders. It'd hopefully stop her from brooding on Iris's challenge too. *Skinny-dipping?*

Oh, God, just thinking about it made her chest cramp. *Stop thinking about that too, then!*

Exactly! A hike with spectacular scenery? That would do nicely, thank you very much.

Thirty minutes later, she followed Blake to the hike's starting point. He studied the map he'd printed out, which left her free to study him. In khaki cargo shorts, his legs looked strong and powerful. Since he'd been on the yacht, his tan had deepened, and somehow that showed off his muscles to an even better advantage. What on earth did he do to keep so fit?

'Okay, this is definitely the right spot.'

She glanced up the steep incline and gulped. 'That looks nice and, um…challenging.'

'Up for it?'

She hitched up her chin. 'Absolutely.'

Blake led the way. The first quarter of the climb was a breeze, while the second quarter had her breathing hard. For the last half of the climb she stumbled along behind him praying it would end soon, badly winded when they reached the summit. Blake, though, hardly seemed affected.

How could that be? He worked in an office with computers, for God's sake. As for herself, all she wanted to do was throw herself down on the ground and gasp like a landed fish until the stitch in her side eased.

She dragged air into her lungs and tried to stop her legs from shaking like jelly. Tried not to huff and puff too loudly. Tried to keep her gaze from drifting back to Blake.

He hadn't had to deal with what she'd had to on that climb. Every time she'd glanced upwards, she'd been confronted with the most perfect backside man had ever had the fortune to be graced with. Which had absolutely nothing to do with her lack of air. She brought the picture to mind once more with remarkable precision—taut, firm and mouth-wateringly tempting. Okay, so maybe it had everything to do with it, but…

She clenched her hands. She would *not* think about Blake that way. Friends, that was what they were. That was *all* they were.

Gritting her teeth, she stared doggedly at the filtered water views. To be friends again…it was everything. Why mess with that? She couldn't deal with more grief this year, and she had no intention of courting it.

Recalling the panic on his face when he'd thought the kiss had detrimentally affected their friendship, she forced her pulse to slow. He wasn't in any better frame of mind at the moment than her when it came to making big decisions. She didn't want to do anything to hurt him either. They both just needed to be…careful.

'You okay?'

She nodded without making eye contact. 'Just disgustingly unfit.'

He handed her a bottle of water from the small backpack he'd slung over one shoulder. 'That was a tough climb.'

'Not for you apparently.'

'I haven't been housebound looking after anyone for the last however long.'

Ten years, she inserted silently. Not that she'd been house-bound for all of those years. Nor had she been an utter drudge. She'd had access to outside help when she'd needed it. Most days she'd had a chance to get out for a walk or a run.

He hitched his head at the path. 'I'm reliably informed that spectacular views are in this direction.'

'After that climb, there'd better be.' And they'd better be worth the effort. This time when she fell in line behind him, she kept her gaze firmly from his backside.

She studied the trees and tried to identify where the scents of pine, sun-warmed grasses and wildflowers came from; tried to spot the birds chattering and tweeting among the branches and bushes. She was so busy concentrating on *not* staring at Blake's bottom that the view opened up when she least expected it to. She halted beside him, neither of them saying a word as they studied the grand vista of gloriously blue sea and dramatic coastline.

The view would be amazing on a grey day, but when the sun shone so brightly, as it did today, the scene throbbed with a brilliance that made her glad to be alive.

'Okay.' She nodded. 'That's definitely worth the climb. This has to be one of the most beautiful places on earth.'

Blake couldn't agree more. He glanced at Nina from the corner of his eyes and let out a slow breath.

Look after Nina.

I'm trying to, Gran. He set back along the path. Kissing Nina, though, hadn't been part of the plan. The thought of ruining their friendship forever…

Things clenched. Acid burned his stomach and his lungs cramped so hard breathing became damn near impossible. If he wasn't careful he'd be in the grip of the biggest panic attack he'd ever had. Except some of that clenching was thrilling too. The stolen kisses last night had been spectacular.

Their memory burned through his consciousness now, drawing his skin tight and making his groin throb. Maybe it was the forbidden aspect of their kisses—one *shouldn't* have carnal thoughts about their best friend. For God's sake, they'd known each other since they were four years old—Nina was practically a sister.

Except he'd *never* viewed her in a sisterly light.

One thing he did know, though, was that his life wouldn't feel whole without her.

Glancing back at her, he let out a slow breath. At least some of the awkwardness she'd desperately tried to hide during breakfast had started to melt away. He readjusted the back-pack, his hands clenching around the straps. He would *stop* thinking about kissing Nina and get things back to normal between them.

In the meantime, it wouldn't hurt to give them both something different to occupy their minds with. Like what was Nina planning to do with her future?

He'd been holding the question back, wanting to give her a chance to relax and unwind before asking it. He suspected it was part of what Gran had meant when she'd asked him to *look after Nina*. But more to the point, he wanted to know. Not out of curiosity, but because he wanted to find out if he could do anything to help.

And because he cared.

Hands clenching and unclenching, he tracked a small bird that darted from tree to tree in front of them as if it were Puck leading them further and further into an enchanted forest. He went to laugh at himself for being so fanciful, but at the same time it hit him that, to date, he'd never dabbled in game design. But a bird leading the player deeper and deeper into a game could be a fun opening.

'Where did you just go?' Nina asked from behind him. 'You were miles away.'

He waited for her to draw up next to him, then pointed. 'See that little bird?'

'The common chiffchaff?'

How did she know its name? He shook himself. 'Anyway, I had a fanciful notion that it was a magical guide in an enchanted forest, but...'

She stared. 'But?'

He shrugged. 'Is it friend or foe?'

'Or it could just be a common chiffchaff.' Her hands went to her hips. 'Have you had too much sun, Blake?'

He laughed. 'I've not yet dabbled in designing computer games. I mean, every man and his dog has, so I've avoided it. But...' He glanced back at the little bird. 'That's where my mind just went to as I watched the *common chiffchaff.*'

Golden toffee eyes stared at him as if he'd just uttered something amazing. All of the things he'd previously tried to unclench clenched up again twice as tight. Forcing his feet forward, he dragged air into his lungs and kept his eyes straight ahead.

Kissing Nina beneath the stars in Monte Carlo had been amazing. But kissing her here in the brilliant sunlight in an enchanted glade in the most beautiful place on earth would be life-changing.

Think you're overreacting?

Maybe, but his every instinct told him it would be dangerous, and he heeded the warning. He wasn't messing with Nina that way. He'd hurt her enough this year—he wanted to prove himself worthy of her forgiveness, of her friendship. He wanted to give, not take. He *wasn't* his mother.

'You know what, Blake?'

He didn't turn to glance back at her. 'What?'

'I don't play computer games, not even Solitaire, but if you created that game—and so long as it wasn't some shoot-'em-up or series of epic battles involving swords and spears and longbows—I'd play it.'

He swung back. 'Really?'

She nodded. 'And there have to be other people like me who want gentler games where they get to explore gorgeous and/or strange worlds while working out the rules as they go along, and maybe solving a mystery or a puzzle.'

His mind immediately fired with possibilities. How long had it been since he'd been excited by anything work-related? His graphic design platform had been, and continued to be, a huge hit, but ever since it had been launched all he'd been working on were improvements and additions. He'd figured he was a one-hit wonder. But now…

A soft touch on his arm hauled him back. She stared up at him with a frown in her eyes and he shook himself. 'I keep finding myself asking the same question you did in Cannes. When did I become so stuffy?' When had he become so risk averse?

She gestured around. 'This isn't stuffy.'

'Neither was parasailing or splashing money at the gaming tables,' he agreed.

'Or dining on caviar with a Hollywood star.'

'I've done all of those things… And now my mind is firing with new ideas and I feel alive in a way I haven't in ages. I don't think it's a coincidence.'

She lifted her arms, let them drop again. 'Why aren't you having adventures and doing fun things with your life as well as working, Blake? You can do both.'

'I can't remember when I became all work and no play.'

He knew, though. Of course he knew. They'd halted while they spoke, but he set back off now. The path at this point wasn't wide enough for them to walk side by side and he was grateful for it.

'Yes, you do,' she said as if she could see inside his head.

'You've been all work and no play ever since your graphic design software took off and you became wealthy. You think splurging money on non-essential things like fun and adventures makes you an irresponsible spendthrift, that it's frivolous and makes you as bad as your parents.'

He grimaced.

'Which is stupid. And I'm hoping, as a relatively intelligent human being, you've started to realise that.'

'Jeez, Nina, don't hold back, will you?'

The wry twist of his lips made her laugh. 'Everyone needs a bit of fun in their lives, Blake. It doesn't have to cost anything. It can just be ambling down to the cricket pitch on a Sunday afternoon to cheer on the team, playing a game of pool at the pub, cooking up a batch of scones or a Victoria sponge to enter into the agricultural show in the hopes of winning a blue ribbon.'

She made it sound easy.

'What do you do for fun at home, Blake?'

'Work.' He worked a lot.

'In an ideal world everyone would get a sense of satisfaction from their job. But at the end of the day, work is work.'

'There's a climbing wall at my local gym. That's kind of fun. I'm getting better at it.' He'd been pushing himself harder and harder in recent months.

'Which answers that question,' she said, almost to herself. 'Do you go out for dinner—dancing…? To see a game of football or a show?'

He did a bit of schmoozing for work, but that wasn't relaxing. He occasionally caught up with his friends from his university days, but only one of them was currently living in London. 'Maybe I've been taking the lone-wolf thing a bit too far,' he admitted, wanting to bring the conversation to a close. They shouldn't be focusing on him. They should be focusing on her.

'You think?'

It struck him that he'd been all at sea without her this year. Chatting to her had always been fun, but it had also kept him grounded. Why had he let that silence between them go on for so long? All he could do now was try to mend the damage he'd unwittingly caused. 'Right, your turn.'

'I have fun.'

'You do,' he agreed, even if he secretly thought line dancing the antithesis of fun. 'What I've been wanting to ask, though, is what are your plans for the future?'

'Oh.' Her voice sounded suddenly flat. He glanced back to see her wrinkle her nose at a grove of pine trees. 'I don't know yet. I haven't worked it out.'

Maybe he could help with that. But he let the matter drop as he followed the map directions to a lookout. They stared in awe at the colour of the water—so blue—and the picturesque inlet that housed the monastery far below.

They didn't talk much after that, but as they reached the last leg of the hike, he blew out a breath. 'The descent is a series of steep switchbacks.'

She peered around his shoulder. 'Yikes, I'll be taking this slow.'

They were three quarters of the way down when Nina gave a muted yelp. He spun to find her sliding on her backside towards him. In one smooth motion, he wrapped a hand around a nearby tree branch to anchor himself before scooping an arm around her and lifting her upright again. 'Okay?'

Her hands landed on his chest, her breaths coming short and fast. 'Fine. Bruised pride, nothing more.'

Their gazes collided and he swore that when those eyes, the colour of maple syrup, lowered to his mouth and her pupils dilated, that sweetness exploded on his tongue. The raw hunger that momentarily flared across her face jolted through him like lightning. A longing so intense gripped him that he felt as if he were hurtling down a wicked ravine with no end in sight.

Nina *wanted* him. She wanted him every bit as much as he wanted her. His pulse pounded and something in his chest lightened and tightened at the same time. He—

She blinked and shot away so fast he had to grab her arms to keep her upright. As soon as she had her balance again, he released her and swung back to the front. Bile burned his throat and his heart pounded like a wild thing. They weren't doing that, remember? Sex complicated everything. Her friendship meant way too much to risk it all on a short-term fling.

You sure about that?

Gritting his teeth, he nodded. *Positive.*

He didn't get his pulse back under control until they'd been served coffee and Italian cream cake at a tiny café overlooking the pebbly beach at San Fruttuoso Abbey. 'You want to tour the abbey?'

Her eyes brightened. 'Yes, please!'

He grinned at the speed of her reply. She seemed just as excited about that as she had about a night at the casino. Maybe that was the key to rejigging his life—to approach everything with enthusiasm.

'Want to catch the ferry back to Portofino rather than retrace our steps?'

'Yes, please,' she said even more quickly and with even more emphasis, and they both laughed. And just like that things were right again. He'd missed this—missed the camaraderie and the sense of... Belonging he supposed. Nina just got him. He *wouldn't* ruin things again. He couldn't.

'So tell me the options.'

She glanced up. Cream from her cake had smeared her lips and he could've groaned out loud when she licked it off. He shovelled cake into his mouth. *Taste the cake. Chew the cake. Focus on the cake.*

'Options for what?' She sipped her coffee while she waited for him to finish his mouthful. 'Man, I love Italian coffee.' She took another quick sip before setting her cup down.

He tried to pull himself together. 'The options you're considering for your future.'

Her face fell and he regretted asking. Maybe he should let the matter drop and let her enjoy the holiday. But she'd eventually have to turn her mind to it. And if there was anything he could do to help...

'Well, Sara Mackie, the manager of the nursing home, has offered me a job as an enrolled nurse.'

He did what he could to stop his nose from curling. 'Is that what you want to do?'

Her shrug said it all, though he doubted she was aware of it.

'I'm glad I was able to spend so much time with Mum and Granny Day. It was a privilege. I like caring for people, Blake, and I'm good at it.'

'But?'

'No buts.' She bit her lip, one shoulder lifting. 'Okay, maybe I'm a bit tired of it. Maybe I'd like to try my hand at something different, but...*what*?'

'You could go to uni.' She'd always wanted to do that.

'To do *what*? To study *what*?'

'Or you could come to London and work for Drawing Board.'

'Your company? As *what*? I'm not qualified for anything. And also...' She pointed her cake fork at him. 'Nepotism, much?'

'You could try a few different things at the company—HR, PR, admin—and see what you liked.'

'I'm not taking handouts.'

'I'd love it, though, if you came to London, Nina.' And if he could entice her with the promise of a job...

Toffee eyes speared his. He swallowed, refusing to allow

the moment to develop and deepen into anything *more*. 'What do you love doing besides line dancing?'

She rolled her eyes. 'Well, apart from my garden, and the occasional baking session in the kitchen, and catching up with friends…' She trailed off with a shrug.

Her garden! He straightened. Why hadn't he thought of that? 'I remember you saying you wanted to be an environmental scientist of some kind when we were kids.' A dream she'd buried when she'd realised how much help her mum had needed. 'You were forever talking about wanting to take care of the planet. You were Callenbrook's very own environmental crusader.' That was a dream she could resurrect now.

'Yeah, but that was like a million years ago.'

'You're not thirty yet, Nina. Stop acting like an old lady. It's not too late to do something new, something you'd love. It's not too late to make a difference.'

CHAPTER EIGHT

IT'S NOT TOO late to make a difference.

Nina pulled her white towelling robe more securely about her as she moved to the yacht's stern on the lower deck and stared out at the moonlight reflected on the water. Not even the tiniest of breezes disturbed its surface. It looked soft and inviting…and maybe even promising the freedom Iris claimed for it. She glanced at the moon that hung huge in the sky. Full tonight. Full moons had a strange power, didn't they? Maybe that was why Blake's words continued to play in her mind.

It's not too late to make a difference.

She'd already made a difference, and he'd be the first to acknowledge it, but she also knew that wasn't what he'd meant. When they were in high school she'd used to brag that she'd make a difference on a global scale. Not in a famous, everyone-knew-her-name kind of way. She'd just wanted to make a deep and significant difference to the natural world. She'd wanted to preserve and protect the environment, to do all she could to live sustainably, and to teach others how to live more sustainably too.

How could she have forgotten that dream?

She grimaced into the night. Because to dwell on it would've perhaps generated feelings of resentment, a sense of being left behind by her peers, a hint of bitterness, and she hadn't wanted to be that person. Neither her mother nor Iris had asked her to take on the role of their carer. She'd *chosen* to do it. She'd wanted to embrace her decision wholeheartedly, with grace and generosity…and not with a tiny prickly burr of 'what if' buried deep inside her heart.

She didn't regret the choices she'd made. She was proud of the way she'd dealt with all of it.

She winced. Okay, nearly all of it. She wasn't necessarily proud of the way she'd cut Blake loose as she had. She should've given him a chance to explain—she should've taken his calls.

In her defence, she'd been dealing with a lot. So she wasn't going to beat herself up about it too much. He'd been dealing with a lot too, though, and she didn't want him beating up on himself either. They'd both made mistakes. But they were restoring their friendship, fixing it and making it strong once more. And if he came home for Christmas…

Don't get your hopes up. Even if he meant every word, even if she didn't continue to have question marks in her mind, the man was a big deal these days. A billionaire! He had responsibilities that could call him away at a moment's notice.

Anyway, it was time to stop thinking—*brooding*—about Blake. That wasn't what she was up here on deck to do. Climbing the ladder down to the platform that housed the inflatable motorboat, she shrugged off her robe and sat beside it to dangle her legs in the water. The water temperature was a very pleasant twenty degrees Celsius.

'Okay, Granny Day… Let's do this.' Slipping *silently* into the water—she didn't want to alert anyone to what she was up to—she took a few experimental strokes away from the yacht before moving back and removing her bikini top and tossing it up onto the platform. Her bottoms followed shortly afterwards.

Oh my God. She was naked—completely and utterly. She swam a few strokes of freestyle…and then breaststroke, before turning on her back to stare at the moon. *Hot damn.* Iris was right—skinny-dipping was a sensory experience definitely worth having. With nothing between her and the sea— she closed her eyes to relish the feeling—she'd never felt so unfettered. She gave a soft laugh. It felt extraordinary and she wondered now why she'd been so worried about it. Why—

'*What* are you doing?'

She gave a muffled scream and immediately jackknifed into a vertical position so *nothing* peeked out of the water other than her head.

Blake. Oh, God.

He made his way down to the lower platform. Reaching down, he picked up her bikini. His jaw sagged. 'You aren't?'

Something in his tone made her chin lift. 'I am.'

Both his jaw and his fist clenched, the gold bikini glittering between his fingers like stardust, and he shook it at her. 'You have to be joking me.'

She dog-paddled a little closer so they could keep their voices low. '*I* am skinny-dipping because *I* am not stuffy or hung up on what people might say about me behind my back. *I*, for one, am young and free enough to enjoy every new experience that comes my way without being tied in knots by convention.'

His hands slammed to his hips. 'Have you been drinking?'

'Seriously?' She rolled her eyes. 'I'm skinny-dipping, Blake. *Not* stupid. Midnight swims and drinking don't seem like a particularly good combination.'

He pointed a shaking finger at her. 'This can't be legal.'

She shrugged, careful to make sure everything that mattered stayed below the water. 'Europeans are far more relaxed about nudity than Australians.'

'You could get us *arrested*.'

'Well, as *you* aren't the one skinny-dipping, I'm thinking you'll be fine. So turn around and walk away and stop spoiling my fun.'

Not a single muscle moved and yet hurt still somehow managed to radiate from him. Her heart slipped to her toes and then sank down to the bottom of the sea. *Oh, Blake.* She ached for him. Ever since his parents had been arrested he'd refused to step a foot outside the rigid boundaries he'd set for himself—holding himself to impossible standards.

She refused to let her chin drop. 'Or you could stop your bellyaching and join me.'

Her words made him blink. Was that yearning that crept across his face? A part of her wanted to cry for him. He didn't need to hold himself such a prisoner. He should be able to let his hair down and live a little.

'Blake…'

His gaze speared back to hers.

'I dare you.'

His eyes narrowed. In the next moment his shirt came over his head and he stepped out of his shorts. He stood before her in nothing but a pair of briefs and it was her turn to get choked up. The man truly did have the most magnificent physique.

With a superhuman effort, she found her voice, and lifted an arm out of the water to point at him. '*Fully* naked,' she ordered, spinning around when his hands went to his briefs, although turning around and not looking was one of the hardest things she'd ever done. It shocked her how much she wanted to see all of him—all of him *naked*.

A soft splash informed her that he'd dived into the water. From just behind her, he said, 'You can spare your maidenly blushes, Nina. It's safe to turn around. I'm in the water.'

Did he think her unnecessarily prim? She turned and tried for blasé. 'I thought it polite to give you some privacy. It seemed voyeuristic to watch when…' she shrugged '…well, when that's not what this is about. So,' she rushed on before he could say anything, 'before things get weird between us, turn your back to me, float a little, stare up at the sky at all of those stars, and feel the water against your skin. *Really* feel it… Maybe swim a little. It feels… Well, I haven't fully worked that out yet, so if and when you do, let me know.'

He followed her instructions. She tried not to watch, though she might as well have tried to stop the tide. The temptation was too great. Besides, it wasn't as if she could *see* anything.

But knowing what was just below the surface of the water, so close to her...

He turned, making her blink. 'It's extraordinary,' he finally said.

She smiled at the frown in his voice. 'I know! Who knew?'

She relaxed then too. They swam—sort of together and sort of apart—they floated. She eventually sensed him moving closer, but kept her gaze on the stars. One large warm hand wrapped around hers and he threaded their fingers together. 'I'm never going to forget this.'

'Me either.' She turned her head and smiled. 'If I was a billionaire, I'd buy a private beach and skinny-dip whenever I wanted.'

He grinned. 'You want me to buy you a private beach?'

She laughed, stifling a yawn at the same time. 'I want you to buy yourself a beach and do this as often as you can.'

'Will you come visit?'

'Try and stop me.'

He hitched his head in the direction of the yacht. 'Time to head in?'

She nodded and they moved back to the boat. Nina grimaced. 'Okay, here's where it gets awkward, because I don't actually want anyone to see me naked.'

His gaze darkened, deepened. 'While right now there's nothing I want more on this earth.'

Their gazes collided and clashed. Her mouth dried. Everything clenched.

'However, I'll play the hero.' Resting his palms on the platform, he sent her a sidelong glance. 'I'm going up, so if you don't want to see me naked...'

Oh, but she did. She *really* did. Clapping a hand over her

eyes, she spun around, her heart in her mouth at the sounds of splashing and dripping behind her, at the sound of his feet padding across the deck.

'Okay, I'm decent.'

She turned back to find him wearing his shorts, but nothing else. He hadn't towelled off—because he hadn't brought a towel…because he hadn't expected to go swimming. *Skinny-dipping.*

Water beaded his skin, that tanned chest and those broad shoulders gleamed in the silver glow of the moon and she wanted to explore the planes of that big body with her hands and her mouth and—

Stop it!

What, you've gone skinny-dipping and now lost all control of yourself?

It should sound crazy, but in swimming naked in the sea it felt as if she'd thrown off invisible shackles that she hadn't known had been binding her.

Seizing her robe, he shook it at her. As if trying to shake her to her senses. But she couldn't help thinking it was more like waving a red flag at a bull. Or waving a white flag of surrender. That last thought had the pulse surging in her throat. She'd surrendered to the sea and it had been amazing…wonderful. If she and Blake surrendered to their attraction…

The taut expression on his face crashed her back into the present.

He held out the robe, his gaze angled up and staring—*glaring*—skywards. 'Not taking my eyes off the moon, Nina. So any time you're ready…'

Her arms felt rubbery but she hauled herself up onto the platform and moved across on unsteady legs to pluck the robe from his fingers. Pushing her arms through the sleeves, she tied the belt securely around her waist. 'Let's go.'

Without looking at him, she climbed the short ladder to

the main deck and started for the door. 'I'm going to grab a cold water. Would you like one too?'

She glanced over her shoulder to find Blake's gaze glued to her backside. The dark, heated expression in his eyes when he lifted them to her face had the blood rushing to the surface of her skin making her hot and prickly and so aware of him she wanted to scream. 'Water, Blake?' she croaked.

'You haven't had enough of the stuff for one night?'

Her throat dried. 'I'm parched.'

Their words were saying one thing, but their eyes and the rest of their bodies were saying something else entirely. Dear God, this was crazy. She needed to leave *now*.

She swung away, taking another two steps to reach the door. If she walked through it, some invisible thread stretching between her and Blake would snap. Snapping it would be the sensible thing to do, but she…

She swallowed. She didn't want to break it.

Turning, she met his gaze again. One beat passed. Then another.

At exactly the same moment, they took a step towards one another. Above them that benevolent, cunning moon continued to glow, casting a silver light upon everything. Blake's hunger was plain for her to see—he wanted her with an intensity that stole her breath. It was laced with a hint of confusion and a dose of concern and she knew her face mirrored the exact same expression.

Neither of them tried to hide it. What was the point? They knew each other too well. Could read each other so well. 'So here's the thing, Blake. I want to see you naked too.'

'I know.'

'This is crazy,' she whispered.

'Totally. But hot.'

His words raked across her skin, raising gooseflesh and

pebbling her nipples to hard aching peaks. 'Smoking hot,' she groaned.

'Too crazy?'

It was a question not a statement. He was asking her if she thought they ought to act on this. Or if they should walk away from it. He'd accept her decision. She knew he would. But he was making his own position clear—he wanted her, and he had no intention of walking away from it unless she asked him to.

It was comforting to find then that she couldn't. She hitched up her chin. 'Our friendship has survived a lot.'

'It has.'

'I can't see any reason why it wouldn't also survive a temporary friends-with-benefits arrangement, can you?'

He swallowed. She had a feeling his mouth had gone as dry as hers.

'I mean, you're wedded to your lone-wolf status while I'm...' she lifted her shoulders in a shrug '...in transition and not interested in falling in love with anyone at the moment.' There'd be no point. She wanted to live a little before settling down.

'So you're saying...?'

'You and me...and a temporary Mediterranean fling.'

A bead of water dripped from the end of his hair to slide down his neck and then along his collarbone—trembled there for a moment, before spilling over to track a path down his chest towards his navel. Her breathing grew more laboured.

'Nina?'

Her name was a groan and she lifted eyes heavy with desire. 'I dare you.'

Fire flashed in his eyes. Reaching across, he caught her chin in firm fingers and his lips landed on hers and he kissed her with such an innate sensuality it had her melting against him, her hands splaying against his chest and relishing the heat and firmness of the muscles beneath her palms.

'Challenge accepted,' he murmured against her lips.

Her lips curved into a smile, and, taking his hand, she led him down to her cabin. Dropping his hand once they were inside, she strode into the en-suite bathroom to return with a box of condoms that she tossed onto the bed.

He stared at the box and then at her. 'There's a reason we're such good friends.'

She nodded. And then untied the sash of her robe and let it fall off her shoulders to pool at her feet.

His swift intake of breath—the flaring nostrils, the darkening of his eyes, the parting of his lips— all arrowed to her core. With slow measured steps, he moved across to her. Nothing felt rushed now, nothing felt urgent, but the very air was pregnant with promise.

'Beautiful,' he breathed. 'And now I'm having the most intense fantasy.'

His gaze held hers. Her pulse throbbed, skipped, danced. 'Tell me.'

His gaze lowered to linger on her breasts, and they immediately tingled to life. His gaze travelled further south to the curve of her waist and then the juncture of her thighs. She could feel herself melting and yearning and he hadn't even touched her yet.

Those brilliant blue eyes lifted back to her face. 'I'm imagining myself buried inside you, all of your muscles clenching around me as you come screaming my name.'

As he spoke, he undid the button at the waistband of his shorts, lowered the zip and let them drop to the floor, where he stepped out of them. She followed his movement with her gaze and took in the size of him—the length and girth of his erection.

Catching her bottom lip between her teeth, she glanced up, not even trying to hide her smile. 'Oh, my.'

One corner of his mouth hooked up. Reaching up, she drew

his head down to hers. 'How about we see if we can make this fantasy of yours come true?'

They kissed with a lazy, laconic joy—as if they had all the time in the world. As if they were in the right place at the right time and they meant to make the very most of it.

But the heat and need—the naked roaring hunger—refused to be suppressed. They explored each other's bodies with a greedy, hungry possessiveness. Blake kissed every inch of her. Until she was a mindless, writhing mass of sensation. Their bodies slid together with a knowing ease—as if they'd done this before…as if their bodies had minds and wills of their own, while they themselves simply held on for the ride.

His warm firm flesh against hers. His hardness inside her. His hands moving and moulding, teasing, pulling her closer. It had the pressure and the pleasure building in ever tighter and more intense concentric circles until, with a scream, she peaked and hurtled into an abyss of gold-flecked pleasure that went on and on, and gave and gave, until it both emptied and filled her utterly. Vaguely she was aware of Blake's joyous shout joining hers. And the slow, peaceful floating that followed afterwards.

She didn't know if minutes had passed or hours or an eternity when she eventually turned her head on the pillow. Blake turned his head too.

Neither of them spoke. Eventually Blake swore. A word so rude it startled a laugh from her. But he'd uttered it so softly and sweetly it sounded like an endearment. She nodded. 'That was really…something.'

'Momentous.'

'Earth-shattering.'

It was a game they played. And his mouth hooked up. 'Stellar.'

'A revelation.'

He met her gaze, his lips pursing. 'A mistake?'

His sudden stillness had things inside her drawing tight,

but she sensed the hidden fear behind his words and shook her head. 'I don't think so. I mean, if it is, it's one I want to repeat.' Over and over.

His tension dissolved and he feigned a nonchalant shrug. 'I suppose we could always try it again just to make sure.'

She did what she could to suppress a grin. 'Excellent idea.'

How could it be a mistake? They knew each other too well for misunderstandings. They knew exactly what to expect from one another.

You were expecting that?

Well, no. But it had been out of this world, and she wasn't giving that experience back for anything.

She laughed when, quick as a flash, Blake rolled her over and pinned her to the bed. 'Now, before we get distracted again, where should I tell our skipper to set sail for in the morning?'

'Nowhere. I want to stay in Portofino forever.'

His grin, when it came, curled her toes. 'Let's call that Plan A, then.'

She rolled him over then until she could straddle him. 'I now have a fantasy of my own to tell you about.'

His hands shaped her waist and hips. 'I'm all ears.'

They slept late—needing the rest after the exertions of the night before. To the chef's delight they demolished their breakfast with gusto. And then to the deckhand's delight— and Nina's, which was the point of the exercise after all— Blake ordered the waterslide to be set up. It was a huge inflatable number that one accessed via the sky lounge. Nina's whoops of delight as she tried it out, sliding into the blue water far below, made him feel ten years younger.

Maybe twenty years!

The thought had him immediately shaking his head. He might've had an enthusiasm for slides and slippery dips as a ten-year-old but he sure as hell hadn't felt about any girl the way he did for Nina now. That emotion was strictly adult.

He stole kisses from her as they floated in the sea. She stole teasing, tempting touches. He couldn't believe how good it felt to have her in his life again. He couldn't believe how good it felt to be whole again.

He'd been an idiot not to tell her about his panic attacks immediately, an idiot for feeling embarrassed and small because of them. And he'd been an idiot to stay away for so long. He swore he'd never again do anything like that, never again risk their friendship.

To not have Nina in his life… The thought made no sense. In a very real way, Nina had been his anchor since he'd been four years old. He couldn't imagine his life without her. He didn't want to.

Then what are you doing messing with her like this?

The thought slid beneath his guard—a sliver of ice piercing his heart.

Don't be silly. This fling was consensual—a bit of fun after all the hardship and grief. Once they left this enchanted place, once their Mediterranean holiday was at an end, they'd return to their individual homes on opposite sides of the world and their friendship would return to normal.

Normal?

He glared at the water. All friendships evolved, went through different phases. When they returned to the real world, theirs would emerge even deeper and stronger than before.

No more sex?

What the hell…? *No! No more sex once they returned home.*

Sex with Nina when they returned to their everyday worlds couldn't happen. *That* would ruin everything. He didn't do commitment, Nina knew that, but if they were to continue to mess around like this when they returned home, it might give her the impression that he'd changed his mind.

A chill chased down his spine. Not *ever* going to happen. He had no intention of handing any woman the same power that his mother had wielded over him and his father. Not even Nina. He *cherished* his lone-wolf status.

Splashing water over his face, he dashed it from his eyes and dragged in a deep breath to try and slow the sudden racing of his heart. Of all the women he knew, Nina was the one woman who'd have the power to bind him to her will. She'd always been able to talk him into anything. One day it'd be skinny-dipping, and the next it'd be…robbing a bank!

Nina a bank robber? Seriously?

He rolled his shoulders. Fine, maybe he was exaggerating, but he knew what he meant. It'd be smaller scale, not so dramatic—wanting him to change jobs, to move house, to move to a different country. And just… *No.* They *weren't* going to dance that dance. He'd be the driver of his own life, thank you very much.

Diving under the water, he swam as far as he could until burning lungs forced him back to the surface. It helped to knock some sense back into him. He was creating monsters out of shadows. Nina wasn't interested in their relationship deepening into anything more.

How had she phrased it? She was *in transition.* She wasn't sure yet what she wanted to do with her life. She wanted to work that out, have a chance to follow her own dreams before becoming involved with anyone. Smart. Sensible. It was one of the reasons they got on so well.

He turned at her shout to see her launch herself once more down the water slide. And having the time of her life. He grinned and swam towards her. She deserved every drop of fun, every shot of delight, that came her way. And he'd do everything in his power to facilitate it.

Swimming over to him, she slipped behind him to wrap one arm around his shoulders and the other about his waist, her hands splaying against his chest and abdomen, sparking heat and need in their wake.

'Blake?'

Her breath against his ear had him humming. 'Hmm?'

'You don't happen to have a jet-ski licence, do you?'

She pressed herself against his back and he swore stars burst behind his eyelids. 'I do.' Though if he hadn't, he'd have sworn to get one by the close of business that day if that was what she wanted. She swam around in front of him, her smile huge and eyes bright. The heat in his veins didn't dissipate, but a surge of tenderness rushed to join it.

'Really?'

'I know that, given my stuffy tendencies, it's out of character, but a while back I was invited to an investor's beachy paradise and advised to get a jet-ski licence prior to attending.'

Her hands went to his shoulders and his automatically went to her waist. Their legs tangled in the most tantalising fashion. 'You weren't too stuffy last night when you had me screaming out your name.'

All of his blood rushed to his groin. 'God, Nina, are you trying to drown me?'

'Absolutely not. I have plans for you later—wicked plans.'

She waggled her eyebrows like some pantomime villain and he couldn't help but laugh. 'Why'd you want to know about the jet-ski licence?'

'Apparently we have to have a licence to operate one. If not, then one of the staff will take us out. But I don't want to hold onto George. I want to hold onto you.'

Him and Nina zipping across the water, her holding on tight behind and whooping into the breeze? Sign him up!

'So I was hoping later on this afternoon maybe we could do that? After lunch. And an, um, afternoon...nap.'

The mischief in her eyes told him *napping* wasn't what she had in mind.

'I can't think of anything I'd rather do.'

Her grin, her delight, and the easing of some innate tension—partly grief and, he suspected, partly the weight of all the things she'd had to deal with over the last few months—were his reward. He swore in that moment to do everything that he could to help that tension disappear entirely.

'So tell me about the skinny-dipping.'

Nina glanced across at him, took a sip of the *very* nice Sémillon he'd selected from the cellar. Dinner on the yacht this evening had allowed them to remain encased in their own private bubble, and had capped off a perfect day. The lights of Portofino curved away to Blake's right, and directly out in front of him the moon made a path of silver on the dark water.

'This place is magic,' she murmured, before shuffling upright a little. 'What do you mean, tell you about the skinny-dipping? What do you want to know?'

'Just *why*? What possessed you to do it in the first place? Is it some secret yearning you've always had?' Did she have more secret yearnings he could help her fulfil? 'I just never in a million years would've guessed.'

Her laugh washed over him like a caress. 'Totally out of character,' she agreed. 'As was the bikini on the beach in Cannes, the parasailing in Nice, and the gambling in Monte Carlo.'

Her lips curved into a smile so full of affection it made his heart beat harder. If she ever smiled at him like that…

Friendship, that was what this was. That was all it was ever going to be. *Don't forget it.*

'Iris has been leaving me instructions—a challenge for each of the destinations on our itinerary.'

'No way.'

'She says I need a shake-up—wants to push me out of my comfort zone.'

'Wow.' No wonder she'd been so intent on the parasailing. No wonder she'd been determined to enjoy the beach in Cannes.

'And it's worked. I mean, I'm still sad because she and Mum are no longer with us, but…' her hands lifted '…it's reminded me that there's a big wide world out there. It's shown me that I can still have fun.' She was silent for several long moments. 'I've spent most of my time this last couple of years with older people—senior citizens—and this trip has reminded me that I'm still young.'

'And beautiful, desirable, smart and funny. And the best friend a person could ever have.'

She stared at him. Her smile when it came was full of affection, and this time it was directed wholly at him. It made his heart beat harder than it ever had before.

'Ah, but, Blake, *you're* the one who has shown me all of those things and made me believe them.'

Her words, the expression in her eyes, choked him up. He did his best to make light of it. 'Go me!'

She laughed, but sobered a moment later. 'I'm glad we took this trip together.'

So was he—to the depths of his soul.

'Now…' she leaned towards him '…my next challenge from Iris isn't until Positano…'

'Are you eager to read it?'

'Absolutely.'

'Do you want to head for the Amalfi Coast tomorrow, then?'

'Absolutely not. There's no rush. Besides, Iris told us to add a couple of other stops to our itinerary. Is there anywhere you'd like to go?'

'The Cinque Terre,' he answered promptly. 'You?'

'Corfu.'

Excellent. It meant the trip wouldn't end any time soon. He lifted his glass in a toast. 'Trip of a lifetime!'

She touched her glass to his with a grin.

CHAPTER NINE

NINA AND BLAKE spent another day in Portofino, and Nina swore it was her new best favourite place. While the beauty of Portofino was jaw-dropping, awe-inspiring and soul-soothing, it was the beauty of her travelling companion that held her spellbound.

Blake. The wry humour, intelligence and generosity of the boy she'd known growing up was still there, but now inside a grown man's body—a *hot* male body. It made him both a known and unknown quantity. It added an edge to all of their interactions—a thrilling edge that held a tiny hint of danger.

Danger? She snorted. She wasn't in danger from Blake. This *release*—because that was what it felt like, a release—was simply the relief from the oppressive cloud of grief that had smothered her world and held her prisoner for this last year. Watching her mum waste away and lose her battle with the disease she'd fought for nearly two decades had damn well broken her heart. To then repeat that experience with Iris… She dragged in a breath and released it slowly. It had left her feeling dejected and lonely and bleak.

As Iris had hoped, though, this trip had reminded Nina that there was more to life—fine and exciting things that she could embrace. Instead of a flat grey future, promises like jewels now gleamed on the horizon.

She could be an environmental scientist, an ecologist. She could travel the world with those qualifications, and the world could be her garden. The thought put the biggest smile on her face.

As did this adventure she'd embarked on with Blake. How many women could boast a hot fling in the Mediterranean? The fact that she could had her feeling like a brand-new person.

Not in a million years would she have thought she and Blake would become lovers. If he'd remained in Callenbrook, she doubted it would've happened—familiarity breeding contempt and all that. But seeing Blake on a video call didn't have the same impact as seeing the man in the flesh. For this moment in time, she meant to make the most of it.

What about when all of this is over?

'What do we think about Christmas in Portofino in three years' time?' She slid a glance to the man beside her as he scattered a sprinkling of Iris's ashes into the bay before they set sail for the next leg of the journey. 'Callenbrook, then London, then Portofino.'

'It's a date.'

He said it so promptly it made her laugh.

When this was over, they'd go back to being the best of friends. Piece of cake. A part of her, though, winced at the assumed glibness. Would it really be that easy?

She frowned at the water. Why not? He'd be back in London. She'd be in Callenbrook—actually, she hoped she'd be at university in Melbourne—and their real-life realities would take over, and this holiday would become nothing more than a happy memory.

You could make more memories.

And they would. Memories of the *friendly* variety. Memories that weren't *sexy*. Their friendship had survived a lot. It could survive this too.

'You're looking unusually serious.'

She glanced up to find Blake watching her with a frown. She sent him a swift smile. 'I was thinking about us.'

They moved across to the sun loungers and stretched out.

'You're worried?' he said.

'Not really.'

His brows shot up. 'Not really?'

He homed in on her words like a radar on an approaching missile and she couldn't help but laugh. 'It's just, when this is at an end—' she gestured between them '—there'll have to be a bit of renegotiation.'

'I see.'

Her brows lifted. 'You do?'

He tapped a hand against his thigh and grimaced. 'Sorry, I haven't a clue what you're talking about.'

She huffed out a laugh. 'This holiday has been heaven— perfect—and I don't want it to end.'

He shrugged. 'We can extend it.'

'As tempting as that thought is, eventually we'll have to return to the real world. And when that happens...'

Leaning across, he took her hand. 'When that happens...?'

'I just think there ought to be some ground rules.'

'Okay. What kind of ground rules?'

His eyes informed her that he'd give her whatever she wanted or die in the trying. A lump lodged in her throat and she had to blink hard.

He'll give you everything you want, except his love.

She blinked. What on earth...? She didn't *want* his love. She wasn't interested in commitment at the moment—this was me-time, remember? Blake loved her like a friend. That was enough.

You sure?

Of course she was sure.

'So you'll be in London and I'll be in Callenbrook, which

means we won't be tempted to tumble into bed together whenever we clap eyes on each other.'

'Because we won't actually be clapping eyes on each other.'

'Exactly. But there'll be video calls.'

'Lots of those.'

'And they can't be...*flirty*?'

'Ah.' Comprehension dawned in those blue eyes.

'And when you come home for Christmas, there can't be any tumbling into bed together.'

He shifted on his seat. 'Of course not.'

'If we let this bleed into our real lives, that's when things could get complicated. I think we ought to avoid that.'

His nostrils flared. 'I don't want to do anything to hurt our friendship.'

'I know.' Nor did she.

She frowned as another thought occurred to her. 'Also, if you return to London and immediately fall in love with someone, perhaps don't tell me about it straight away. Wait until some time next year. I've never considered myself particularly possessive or jealous, but—'

Blake's laughter cut off the rest of her words. 'Never going to happen.'

The thought of him with another woman, though, screwed her up tight.

'Lone wolf, remember?'

Her tension didn't ease. She stared at him for a long moment. 'Do you really not want to fall in love, though? Do you really not want to have children?'

His laughter bled away and his expression sobered. 'The latter isn't completely dependent on the former.'

She supposed not.

'But I definitely don't want the former.'

Her heart ached. His mother had done such a number on him. 'Though you do?'

'Absolutely. Eventually.' Not quite yet, though. She deserved some time to focus only on herself. Reaching for her hat, she plonked it on her head. 'One day I'd like the whole kit and caboodle—marriage, kids, the white picket fence, rowdy birthday parties, summer holidays at the seaside.' She stared out at the horizon. 'I want to do a lot with my life, Blake, but I want someone there beside me to do it with. To celebrate the good times with and a hand to hold in the hard times.'

'And what if this mystery man of yours—this paragon of virtue—lets you down like your father did?'

This argument was a familiar one from their younger days. 'What if he doesn't?'

He glared at the spectacular coastline as it slid past, his nose curling, and she started to laugh. 'If I return home and promptly fall in love, I won't mention it to you until some time next year either. I know you're neither the possessive nor jealous type, but—'

'No!' He swung back to her so fast it made her blink. 'You *have* to tell me. *Immediately!* So I can come home and talk you out of it.'

She lowered her sunnies to stare at him over their rim. Her heart picking up speed.

'You have your whole life ahead of you, Nina. You have a chance to focus exactly on what *you* want for once. Don't waste it on some guy.'

Which was the same advice she'd been giving herself. And it was *good* advice.

They settled back on the sun loungers. 'Also, if any guy hurts you I'll break his neck.'

She laughed. 'It's nice having you in my corner again, Blake.'

'I plan to stay there.'

Good. 'In the meantime… Wanna join me in the hot tub?'

His face cleared. 'I thought you'd never ask.'

A wicked light gleamed in those blue eyes and her veins heated instantly. Today was a good day. At the moment, that was all she needed to focus on.

They spent several days exploring the Cinque Terre, with its terraced slopes, picturesque pastel houses and glorious views. They ate figs and dined on fresh fish. They sipped Aperol spritzes in the sun, swam in the warm sea…and gloried in their lovemaking.

Eventually, they sailed into the bay at Positano, a playful breeze at their backs. Blake smiled down at her from their spot at the bow. 'Sick of glorious scenery yet?'

'Not a chance.' Why had she not known that the Italian coastline was so unrelentingly beautiful? Her guidebook informed her that the Amalfi Coast was considered one of the most beautiful coastlines in the world. As she stared at the vertical town rising up the steep hillside before her, colourful houses perched on cliffs, she could see her guidebook had a point. What a sight.

She stared and stared. Eventually she excused herself to race down to her cabin to open the envelope marked Positano.

'Look, Nina, I don't think this bar is any better than the last one. It's crowded and busy and—'

'It's not as busy as the first one and it's a little more, uh, refined than the second.'

'But—'

'No buts. I'm doing this.' Pulling in a breath, she released it slowly. Blake had vetoed the first two venues. She wasn't letting him veto a third. 'I think you should just go back to the boat.'

'No way.' He thrust out his jaw, his blue eyes glittering like a tropical thunderstorm and his hands slamming his hands to his hips. 'Gran really wants you to go into some bar and start a conversation with *a stranger*?'

As far as Nina was concerned, it was the easiest of the challenges so far. Judging by Blake's reaction, he considered it the riskiest. She folded her arms and stuck out a hip. 'If you come in with me, it'll defeat the purpose.'

'What purpose?'

'To prove that I can stand on my own two feet and hold my own in a foreign country. This challenge—' like all of the challenges so far '—is designed to increase my confidence.'

He shoved his hands in his pockets, hooded eyes searching her face. 'Fine, but there's no harm in me going in there as well and keeping an eye on you from the bar.'

She wasn't some child or damsel who couldn't look after herself. *Fine*. 'If you come into that bar then you have to do the challenge as well.'

'*Me?* I—'

'For me, this is an easy challenge. For you, not so much.' She touched a hand to her chest. '*I* like meeting new people. *I* like talking to people.'

'So do I!'

'You big fat liar! Lone wolf, remember? You pride yourself on being the strong, silent type.' Before he could respond, she said, 'Here's the drill. I'm going into that bar and you're going to sit on this bench here for ten minutes before you follow me in.'

'And what? Twiddle my thumbs?'

'Admire the view; soak up the atmosphere.'

He rolled his shoulders at her pointed glare. 'Fine. But we need a signal for if you want me to wade in and rescue you.'

For heaven's sake… Gritting her teeth, she counted to five. 'Okay, fine. If I pull my hair back into a ponytail, that means I need rescuing. Deal?'

Blowing out a breath, he nodded. 'Deal.'

Inside the tavern, the lunchtime crowd was both noisy and merry, and Nina found herself grinning. It looked like a movie set—all stone and wood, and full of atmosphere. An impression that was immediately dispelled when a drunken man, all oily smiles and beery breath, leaned across to leer at her and offered to buy her a drink.

'*No, grazie.*' With a shudder, she sidled away to order a white wine at the bar.

'Don't let Roberto put you off and give us a bad name,' a woman on her other side said in heavily accented English. 'He is…how do you say it? An eternal optimist. He lives in hope that one day someone will say yes.'

They both watched as he tried the same routine on the next woman who entered. Nina shook her head. 'One has to admire his tenacity, I guess.'

The other woman laughed. 'I'm Maria, and I don't recognise your accent. Where are you from?'

Blake strode into the bar ten minutes later and from her spot at Maria's table, Nina swore the entire crowd stilled to stare. The women sighed. The men puffed out their chests as if reminding themselves to be manly. It would've made her smile, except a deep hard longing gripped her. All she wanted to do was stride across the room, grab his arm, and drag him back to the yacht and have her wicked way with him.

Dear God, what was wrong with her? They'd spent the last five days doing exactly that. Surely the edge of her hunger should be blunted by now. But as a sultry brunette hip-swayed across to lean on the bar beside him, Nina had to fight the urge to immediately pull her hair into a ponytail.

Or to stride across and slip her arm through Blake's and stake her claim.

She shook herself. She and Blake might be fooling around at the moment, but it wasn't real. It was just a temporary fling—a clouds-in-your-coffee illusion with no basis in reality. It had no future.

Beside her Maria's brother Antonio explained the intri-

cacies of making limoncello. She did her best to look interested. From the corner of her eye, she saw the smile Blake
sent the sultry brunette and something in her heart cracked.
How could he smile at someone else like that when—?

She froze. Panic surged in her throat. *No!* Oh, no, no, no!

She couldn't have gone and done the unthinkable. She
couldn't have fallen in love with Blake? That would be emotional suicide! It could only lead to pain and heartache.

A *lot* of heartache.

Her eyes burned and her throat stretched into a painful
ache. It didn't matter if she pulled her hair into a thousand
ponytails, falling in love with Blake was the one fate he could
never rescue her from.

Her vision darkened at the edges and her temples throbbed,
but slowly her chin came up. Not couldn't, but *wouldn't*. Blake
would never risk his heart to save hers from breaking. He
would never relinquish the lone-wolf mask he cherished so
dearly.

Unless…

She bit her lip. Unless she could find a way to save him
from himself.

Damn it! Nina didn't need rescuing. Not from men in danger
of becoming too friendly nor from boredom. Or the inability
to draw a stranger into conversation.

She sat at a table on the other side of the room with a group
of people who all laughed at something she said. Yearning,
hard and deep, gripped him. More than anything, he wanted
to stride across and join them—to pull up a seat beside Nina
and become a part of that relaxed, easy-going group.

He wasn't so good at relaxed and easy-going, though, was
he? Maybe Nina was glad to have a break from him? The
thought had his heart sinking like a giant-sized boulder.

The tall brunette who'd moved to stand beside him, and

now blocked his view of Nina and her party, said something to him when the barman ambled over in their direction, but his Italian was too limited to catch whatever it was she said. He gestured for her to order before him, angling his head around her, to find Nina staring at him. She glanced at the brunette and raised an eyebrow.

Hold on… She didn't think—

He would never fool around with another woman while he and Nina were…

Were what? Was there even a word to describe what they were doing, other than fooling around? They hadn't made any promises. Maybe she had romantic plans for one of the men at her table? Maybe she—

He shook the thought off. That wasn't what this bar challenge was about. It was about being comfortable in her own skin and confident enough to initiate conversation with a stranger.

A drink was set in front of him and he realised the brunette had ordered for him. He handed his credit card to the barman. Toasting the brunette, he tried not to shiver at the predatory expression in her eyes. When the barman handed him back his card, he excused himself with a nod.

Her face fell. In other circumstances he'd have taken the effort to make conversation with her, but he wasn't letting Nina think he was interested in another woman, not while they were *fooling around* together. Not for a single second. He wasn't giving her any reason to bring their arrangement to a screaming halt.

Nina's earlier words replayed themselves in his mind. *I like meeting new people*… The way she'd called him a liar when he'd said he did too.

Okay, so maybe he wasn't so good at putting himself out there. Maybe he'd taken the lone-wolf thing too far. But how hard could it be?

Taking a fortifying sip of his beer, he made towards a group of men. '*Scusi*, my Italian is terrible, *mi dispiace*—' *I'm sorry* '—but you gentlemen look as if you might be locals, and I wondered if I could ask your advice?'

They gave him wary, but encouraging nods.

'If I wanted to take a beautiful woman on a romantic dinner this evening, where in your opinion is the place to go?'

Faces lit up and hands rubbed together. Venues were debated and eventually a restaurant agreed upon, but the advice kept coming thick and fast. 'You want to take her on the perfect date, *si*?'

'*Sì.*' Nina deserved the best.

He made notes on his phone as a full itinerary was created for him. Catching the barman's eye, he gestured for a round of drinks for his new friends. When he saw Nina's companions rise to leave, he excused himself with many thanks.

He met her halfway across the room. 'Have fun?'

She nodded. 'You?'

He frowned. He had.

'Why did you blow that gorgeous brunette off?'

The question had his stomach churning. Had she wanted him to hook up with another woman? 'Look, I know we're only fooling around, but I've no intention of looking at other women for as long as we are, okay?'

'Oh.' The air left her lungs on a soft rush, and something in her face softened too. He had to fight the urge not to drag her into his arms. 'Good to know,' she whispered.

She didn't trust him yet—not fully—but he'd win her trust back before they were done here in the Mediterranean. 'Also, she approached me, not the other way around. And as I didn't initiate anything, I figured it wasn't in the spirit of the challenge and shouldn't count.'

She frowned, her brows lowering over her eyes. 'Damn,'

she murmured. 'Okay, hold on.' She lifted a finger, glanced around. 'I won't be a moment.'

Moving to the bar, she smiled at a woman and pointed to her feet. A lively discussion ensued and the play of expressions on Nina's face made him smile. He leaned against a tall table and finished his beer, soaking in the atmosphere, and the odd sense of feeling at home here—as if he belonged.

Nina moved back to him, huge smile on her face. 'Apparently Positano is known for its fabulous sandals. There are artisan shoemakers in the town who take your measurements and will make you a pair in half an hour. How cool is that?'

'Wanna go shopping?'

'Do you mind?'

'Not in the slightest.' Nina deserved every treat this trip could offer. 'Would you like to sample the delights of a local restaurant this evening? I have it on good authority that it shouldn't be missed.'

'Sounds great.'

Something an awful lot like happiness billowed in his chest. He'd made such a huge mistake in not returning to Callenbrook sooner—not just because in delaying it he'd freighted his return with too much pressure, but because he'd denied himself the pleasure of Nina's company for far too long. Sure, their telephone and video calls had kept them in touch, had been fun in their own way, but nothing could replace this face-to-face contact.

Or the full-body contact, a wicked voice whispered through him, drawing his skin tight. He'd miss that when this was all over.

Does it have to end?

Of course it did. He didn't do commitment or—

But neither of them was currently seeing anyone else. Maybe they could…

Could *what*? He frowned, but the question continued to plague him.

Pushing it away, he helped Nina search for a shoemaker. As she consulted with the artisan, he browsed the nearby shops and on the spur of the moment bought her a silk top in all the pretty colours of her garden.

She was waiting for him outside the artisan's workshop when he returned. He handed the bag to her. 'I saw this and thought of you.'

She blinked. And a slow smile spread across her face. She handed him a small parcel. 'Ditto.'

Grinning stupidly, he peeked inside to find a chic leather cardholder dyed a bright Mediterranean blue.

'To remind you of our trip. And because it's the same colour as your eyes,' she said.

'I love it.' He held her gaze. 'But I don't need anything to remember this trip by, Nina. This trip…*you*… It's the best time I've ever had.'

Her eyes widened and those delectable lips parted, and then her eyes filled. 'Don't you dare make me cry!'

He held up his hands. 'Wouldn't dream of it.' Though he found himself oddly hungry to hear her 'ditto' to his sentiment as well. *Loser.* 'What do you think?' He gestured to her bag she'd yet to open.

She gave a squeal of delight when she peeked inside. 'It's gorgeous! Oh, Blake, I love it! I'll wear it tonight.'

He beamed. And then she kissed him full on the lips in broad daylight in this extraordinary vertical city and he felt as if he were about to take off in flight.

She eased away. 'Now, what do you say to a gelato while we wait for my sandals? And then heading back to the yacht for a little afternoon siesta before our adventure tonight?'

The heated expression in her eyes told him that resting was the last thing on her mind. 'Excellent plan.'

* * *

They ate at a restaurant perched high on a clifftop with seats on a terrace that boasted one of the best views in all of Positano. Nina's awed expression had him feeling like a million bucks. She took her seat and rested her arms on the iron railing, rested her chin on her hands. 'Dear God, Blake, it doesn't matter what the food here tastes like, it's already the best restaurant in the world.'

'Best friend in the world,' he countered. She deserved it.

Her gaze flicked to him briefly before returning to the view.

'Best date in the world,' he added.

She straightened, mischief sparkling in her eyes. 'Best time you've ever had.'

Her grin was irresistible and he didn't try resisting it. 'For pity's sake, Nina, tell me this is better than line dancing at the community hall on a Saturday afternoon. You're killing me here.'

Her laugh bathed him in the same oranges and golds that stretched along the horizon. 'Only like a million times better. Blake, this trip… It's been extraordinary. I've had the most amazing time. And seeing you again…'

Her words trailed off and he nodded. 'I feel the same.'

She frowned for a moment, lips pursed. 'Do you?'

This woman had the most extraordinary heart and he hated that he'd hurt her. Reaching across, he took her hand. 'I swear to you that I won't ever let that same distance grow between us again.'

Warm caramel eyes searched his face. 'No?'

He crossed his heart with exaggerated care. 'You mean too much to me.'

'Good,' she said, almost to herself.

He released her hand. 'Now let's order and you can tell me if you've made any plans for the future yet.'

Luckily the food was every bit as good as the view. They ate seafood linguine and a salad lush with fragrant green leaves, juicy tomatoes and buffalo mozzarella while Nina outlined the degree she wanted to enrol in when she returned home. 'If my application is accepted, it will mean living in Melbourne during term time, which could be fun.'

He imagined her meeting new people, making new friends... He frowned. Meeting guys—or one guy in particular—and falling in love.

'What's wrong with my plan?'

He shook himself. 'Nothing! Sounds like fun. Was thinking, though, that there must be good degrees in environmental science in the UK as well.'

She folded her arms on the table in front of her. 'An international degree would be ludicrously expensive. Iris has left me very comfortably off, but I'm not rolling in money.'

'Ah, but I am.' And if Nina moved to the UK they could see each other all the time. It'd be brilliant.

She huffed out a laugh. 'You're ridiculously generous with your money, but no. This is something I'd like to do on my own.'

He couldn't blame her for that.

'And while you're my best friend...'

He could've wept in relief at that pronouncement. He'd come so close to messing it up and losing her friendship forever. To know she'd fully forgiven him was everything.

'All of my other friends live in Callenbrook and... I like the place.'

He wasn't sure he'd ever feel the same way, but he nodded to show he understood.

'And the other thing...'

He glanced up at the odd note in her voice.

She wrinkled her nose at him. 'If I moved to England I

have a feeling I might be tempted to prolong this arrangement of ours and that's probably not a good idea.'

Actually, though…was it a bad idea?

He turned it over in his mind. You know what? He'd be totally and utterly on board with that. *Totally and utterly.* Before he could say as much, she changed the topic. 'I only have one more envelope to open from Iris.'

Only one? 'Amalfi?'

'Ravello.' She spooned lemon tiramisu into her mouth, pointed her spoon at him. For no reason at all, his mouth watered. 'This one's different from the others. I'm instructed to go to a particular spot and to only open the envelope once I'm there.'

'Wow. Okay.' What did Gran have planned for her? And, by extension, him, as he had no intention of leaving her to face any of these challenges on her own.

Best friends, that was what they were. And he'd stick by Nina through thick and thin, would face every challenge beside her. 'So…' He raised an eyebrow. 'Should we head to Amalfi tomorrow?' It would probably only take twenty minutes on the yacht. 'We can drive up to Ravello from there.'

'Yes, please.'

'Though maybe we won't leave too early. On the agenda this evening is dancing into the wee small hours at an exclusive club further along the beach from the marina—keeping our eyes peeled for the film stars and rock gods who frequent the place—followed by a light dessert at a little hole-in-the-wall joint that only the locals know about.'

'A second dessert!'

'We're on holiday, aren't we?'

She clasped her hands beneath her chin. Her eyes sparkled in the gathering darkness of the night, brighter than the lights of the boats in the harbour. 'If this place is so secret, how do you know about it?'

He stretched his legs out. 'Well, I was challenged to go into a bar and make conversation with strangers. I decided to ask said strangers where they'd take a beautiful woman on a date in Positano.'

Her mouth fell open.

'I told them she was special—that there was no one who meant more to me.'

Her eyes grew suspiciously bright.

'And I said I wanted to make memories that would last us both a lifetime and they gave me the inside intel.'

The gazes caught and held. Her eyes throbbed into his. 'I'm never going to forget,' she whispered.

'I'm never going to forget,' he whispered back.

It felt like a promise.

CHAPTER TEN

THIS TRIP, YOU... IT'S the best time I've ever had.

There's no one who means more to me.

I wanted to make memories that will last a lifetime.

As the car Blake had hired for them wound its way up to the hillside town of Ravello, Blake's words went around and around in Nina's mind—a litany of hope.

The way he'd looked at her last night, the way he'd made love with her, the things he'd said... Could it be that he'd fallen in love with her too and simply wasn't aware of it yet?

Could it be possible that she *hadn't* fallen in love with him, and that this was all a case of the romance of the trip going to her head? After the year she'd had, that'd be understandable, right?

But...

After a truly memorable night of dancing and spotting famous faces, and eating delicious cannoli at a ridiculous time in the morning, the two of them had stumbled back to the yacht in a haze of passion to make love with an intensity that had stretched each moment out into a celebration of joy and... *Love.*

That was what it had felt like and none of it was due to the exotic beauty of the Mediterranean or a result of her grief. It was due to Blake.

His quiet strength, his endless generosity, his determined persistence in winning back her friendship. Her joy in seeing him eventually relax and unwind and find joy again—it had set something free inside her. She'd fallen in love with *him*. The Mediterranean setting was just an added bonus.

Seeing him again after so long, even when she'd been angry with him, had felt like a piece of her clicking back into place—as if she hadn't been whole without him. Like a jigsaw puzzle with a piece missing.

Her mouth dried. If she wasn't whole without him... Her hands clenched, her fingernails digging into her palms. Telling him how she felt had the potential to rain disaster down on their heads. If he didn't feel the same way she could ruin everything—their friendship, his peace of mind and her own.

Things inside her shrank and shrivelled. If he didn't feel the same way, she might never see him again and surely that would be the worst outcome of all. It'd be better to keep all of this to herself. At least she'd still have his friendship. At least she'd get to see him at Christmas, have multiple video calls with him throughout the year.

She swallowed. Maybe, eventually, what she felt for him would fade.

Ha! That thinking was as falsely optimistic as drunken Roberto in yesterday's lunchtime bar hoping for a date. *Not* going to happen.

Maybe when Blake returned home to London he'd discover how much he missed her and realise he'd fallen in love with her?

And pigs might fly.

She recalled the way they'd made love the previous night and her heart surged against the walls of her chest, refusing to give up hope. It *had* to be possible.

'You're very quiet,' Blake said beside her, shrewd eyes raking her face. 'Tired?'

No closer to sorting out the best course of action to take where she and Blake were concerned, she pushed it to the back of her mind. She had time to puzzle it out. After Amalfi they were heading to Corfu for a few days. *There's time.* 'A little.' She smiled and shrugged. 'Aren't you?'

Reaching out, he took her hand and threaded his fingers through hers. 'Yep, but it was worth it.' Those shrewd eyes travelled over her face again. 'Are you nervous about whatever Gran is going to say to you in her letter?'

She rubbed her other hand over her chest to ease the sudden ache that stretched across her heart. 'A little. I mean to embrace whatever challenge she's set for me, because…'

'Because?'

'I trust her. She hasn't led me astray—not once—even though I've found some of her challenges hard, like the parasailing and the bikini.'

'And the skinny-dipping.'

His lips curved and she couldn't help but laugh. 'Each of those things has pushed me out of my comfort zone and made me braver. All of it has made me feel better about whatever the future might hold.'

Even if that future doesn't contain Blake?

Stop it! She refused to even contemplate that at the moment. Shaking it off, she managed a wobbly smile. 'But whatever is in the final envelope, they'll be her last words to me and…'

His hand tightened about hers. 'You don't want it to come to an end.'

For as long as she'd had those sealed envelopes, all waiting to be opened, she'd felt as though Iris were with her, almost as if she were on this trip with them. Once she opened the final letter, that illusion would dissolve.

'It's not the end, Nina. You'll always carry her in your heart. *Always.*'

The truth of that had her spine straightening. Blake was right. She would.

It seemed serendipitous as at that exact moment they drove

into the township of Ravello. They didn't linger to admire the quaint cobbled streets or the pretty buildings or the historic timeless essence of the town, but made directly for Villa Rufolo and the famous view of the Amalfi Coast from its terrace. It was feted as one of the most beautiful views in the world.

With the high season over, they were lucky enough to find themselves alone on the terrace. Nina might still feel a little nervous of heights, but she couldn't prevent her feet from taking her to the very edge of the terrace to stare out at the incredible view. In fact, if the railing hadn't been there she might've stepped right into it.

Blake slipped an arm around her shoulders and she leaned into him. 'Now that's something,' he breathed.

All she could do was nod. Below them the deep blue of the water stretched out to the horizon—the air so crisp and clear it made everything *sparkle*. The collection of white buildings below and the curve of the white pebbled beach provided a perfect foil and contrast for all of that blue. And with no breeze ruffling the water and, therefore, no white caps, the view looked utterly serene. The silhouette of a pine tree, its darkness and the beauty of its symmetry, added a note of unexpected perfection to the already stunning scene.

'Granny Day would've loved this.'

'She'd have sat here and fixed it in her mind—memorising every single detail so she could take this view home with her.'

She gave a soft laugh in recognition because that was exactly what Iris would've done. 'If it wasn't for her, we'd probably have never seen this.'

'And that would have been a loss.'

They stared at the view for a long time. Eventually, silently, Nina moved to a stone bench and pulled out Iris's final envelope from her pocket. Caressing the familiar writing, she slid her finger beneath the sealed flap and drew out a single sheet of paper.

*Do you know what a privilege it has been to have you
in my life, Nina? I count myself the most fortunate of
women.*

The page blurred. Blinking back tears, Nina read on.

She read to the end and then stared unseeingly at the view,
the letter clasped in her hand—her heart throbbing and her
mind churning.

She started when a soft hand brushed the hair back from
her face. 'You okay?'

Lifting her hands to her cheeks, she found them wet. He
handed her an immaculate white cotton handkerchief. She
handed him the letter.

He read it out aloud, his voice warm and reverent.

*'Of course my final challenge is the hardest. It was
always going to be. It's hard because it's a lifelong challenge. It's what all of the other challenges have been
leading you towards. And it is merely this…*

*'Nina, I ask you to not hold yourself back. I want
you to live your life to the full, and you can only do that
if you open your heart to embrace all that life has to
offer. We are here on this earth for such a short time,
put yourself out there and take risks. It's not the times
we make fools of ourselves that we live to regret, it's the
risks we didn't take, the times we kept our hearts and
our egos safe behind our walls, that will come back to
haunt you. Don't put off until some indeterminate date
in the future the things you ache to do. Instead, if you
can, do them as soon as possible.*

'There will be times when this open-hearted approach to life leaves you vulnerable, leaves you open to hurt and heartache, but I promise you will recover from both of those things, although it might take some time. Nina, you're intelligent and capable and you once had big dreams. Dreams you put on hold because of your love for two older women—your mother and me. Love is never a bad choice, but it's time now to dust off your dreams and to follow them wherever they may lead you. So my final challenge to you, my darling girl, is to live fearlessly, to live in a way that makes you proud of yourself every single day.'

Blake halted as he came to the end. It was signed, *your ever-loving Iris, your Granny Day, the grandmother of your heart*. The words were burned on her heart.

As Blake had read the letter out, Nina had moved back to stand at the railing, wanting to reach out and grab some of that view's serenity, some of its peace, and push it inside her throbbing chest.

Open your heart to embrace all that life has to offer.
Live fearlessly.
It's the risks we don't take that haunt us.

Iris's words rolled through her mind, gaining momentum, urging her to take the biggest risk of her life. Blood thundered in her ears, drowning out the song of a nearby warbler.

Blake moved to stand beside her, folded the single sheet of paper and handed it back to her. 'It's a hell of a letter, Nina.'

She slid it back into its envelope and pressed it to her heart for a moment before sliding it back into her pocket. 'Could you live your life like that, Blake?'

He shook his head. 'I don't think so.'

She half turned to him and he shrugged. 'Sometimes there

are very good reasons for being cautious and protecting yourself.'

'I don't think she's saying be reckless or foolhardy, or that there's never a need for caution.'

'I expect you're right.'

There was something in his voice, though. 'But?'

He grimaced, shrugged. 'There's no doubting that my grandmother was a wise woman…'

Absolutely no doubt.

'But I can't help feeling her advice in that letter…' He rolled his shoulders. 'It seems naïve, is all.'

Opposition immediately rose inside her. In her letter Iris had boiled life down to its simplest form, but Blake always had to make things complicated. He always searched for the flaws and the weaknesses and the risks involved. And in doing that, he so often prevented himself from living in the moment.

'I think both our lives could be improved if we followed Iris's advice.' One sceptical eyebrow rose and she tapped a finger against his chest. 'You'd have *never* gone skinny-dipping if you hadn't shrugged off your fear and decided to take a risk. And that was an unforgettable experience.'

He straightened. 'I wasn't *scared*.'

'You were scared of stepping outside conventions, scared that people might hear about the exploit, and you were worried about being arrested.'

'The latter was a legitimate concern!'

'It was *never* going to happen.'

Blowing out a breath, he shook his head. 'There's nothing wrong with being cautious.'

'Except you're so often trading joy for it, Blake, and that seems too high a price to pay.'

'It's not like I'm *never* relaxed and happy.' He stared at her for a long moment. 'Surely this trip has proven that?'

She chewed on her bottom lip. 'It's not wholehearted, though,' she said slowly.

His gaze narrowed, and those two halves of her immediately went to war. *Don't rock the boat. Don't ruin the most important friendship of your life.*

It's the risks we don't take that haunt us.

Far below the church bell sounded, and very slowly Nina straightened. 'The thing is, Blake, I still think you live your life crippled by fear.'

His head rocked back, and she quickly shook hers. 'I'm not talking about your panic attacks. The fact you've dealt with those and overcome them—or have learned how to manage them—proves you've the strength and the courage to live life fearlessly. If you choose to.'

Slamming both hands to his hips, he half glared at her. 'How can you both insult and compliment me in almost the same breath?'

Her hands went to her hips then too. 'Because I want you to be happy. Fully and wholly and fearlessly happy. Not just half happy.'

'I *am* happy!'

'And yet in swearing to never fall in love—in keeping your heart safe—you're denying yourself the promise of a very special and very real form of happiness.' It made her want to scream in frustration.

His face hardened. '*That's* a risk I'm prepared to make. There are other forms of happiness, other ways to be happy.'

With a frustrated slash of her hand, she swung away. 'Of course there are, but why deny yourself any of them? *That's* what's so senseless.'

'You know my reasons, Nina,' he said quietly.

She turned back, her heart thud-thud-thudding. 'What? That whole lone-wolf thing? Is that really so precious to you?' Did he seriously want to walk alone his entire life? 'This is because of your mother, isn't it? Because she manipulated you and you won't ever give anyone that power over you again. You live in fear of becoming your father.'

Closing his eyes, he bent at the waist to rest his hands on his knees. She sensed he was counting his breaths, and her hands twisted together. She didn't want to trigger a panic attack. She didn't want to be the cause of so much stress.

Closing her eyes too, she counted to three. How could she convince him to open up his heart? 'Your grandmother, my mother and I always treated you with thoughtfulness and respect. We never betrayed your trust or let you down. Why isn't *our* influence and *our* example the one you're choosing to follow rather than your mother's?' Her words were a cry on the air, a plea. For him to choose love and connection and happiness.

Slowly he straightened, those extraordinary eyes meeting hers. 'There's no denying what my parents did has cast a shadow over my life, but you're wrong to think they still have that kind of hold on me. Those shadows aren't so dark any more.' His hands clenched and unclenched. 'I've made progress in these last few months, Nina. I'm mostly in control of my panic attacks. I was able to return to Callenbrook.' He pulled in a breath. 'I've been able to fix our friendship.'

Could he not see how much more their friendship could be, though?

His lips twisted into a half-smile. 'What's more, miracles of miracles, I've become less stuffy and less boring, and that's due to you. I'm letting fun and creativity back into my life. And I mean to keep implementing improvements once I'm home.'

She was glad to hear it. And glad too that he could recognise the progress he'd made. 'So what's holding you back from letting love into your life as well?'

'My best way of coping long term is as a lone wolf, Nina, you have to see that.' He started to pace. 'I don't want to pull anyone else into my issues. I've come so far and I'm in a stable place. In what universe would I risk destabilising that?' He swung back with a hard shake of his head. 'I'd have to be a fool.'

Her jaw dropped.

He held a hand up before she could speak. 'I know what you're going to say, but think about it. Whatever else you want to say about love, you also have to admit that it's intense and chaotic and volatile. That is *not* for me.'

She stared at him.

He rolled his shoulders. 'Stop looking at me like that.'

Her heart thundered in her ears. 'You're saying you'd rather keep your life calm and on an even keel than take a risk on something that could add more fun and creativity to your life—and so much *joy*. That's your stuffy, risk-averse side talking, Blake. You're only seeing potential negatives and not the positives. You think of love as something that could mess with your peace of mind—something that has the potential not just to rock your boat but to overturn it—but what if love is like parasailing? What if it's freedom and floating and a safe harbour?'

His face tightened. 'What if it's a cold plunge in the ocean?'

'What if it brings more that's good to your life than bad?'

His eyes flashed. 'What if it's simply not a risk I'm prepared to take?' Planting his feet, he folded his arms. 'Why the hell does this matter so much to you anyway?'

'Because I love you, Blake!' She hadn't meant to blurt the words out so baldly, but they'd been pressing against her throat with increasing fierceness until she couldn't hold them back. 'And I'm not talking about the love friends have for one another.' She pointed an unsteady finger at him. 'I'm *in* love with you.'

The colour drained from his face. He took a step back… shook his head.

She wasn't sure how his body managed it, but it was as if it had sagged and turned to steel at the same time. And his horror was like a scythe, cutting her soul adrift from the rest of her body and turning her to ice. She imagined jagged icicles radiating outwards from her heart, cutting a path through her chest, stabbing and piercing.

'You *can't* have.' He choked out the denial. His neck had gone stiff, so had his shoulders. The muscles in his forearms strained—as if they were trying to hold back disaster.

The intensity of his opposition beat and buffeted her. Her lungs cramped. Her throat stretched into a painful ache. It took a force of will to remain standing.

What did you expect? Had you really thought he'd sweep you up in his arms and tell you he loved you too?

Maybe not. But with all of herself she'd hoped he would.

From somewhere she found the strength to swallow. His reaction was the stuff of nightmares, but it was also exactly what half of her had expected. And at least now she knew.

And there's comfort in that?

Digging deep, she shoved that thought away to seize her composure and wrap it around her like a blanket. She would *not* cry in front of him. She could at least spare him that.

Hitching up her chin, she shrugged. 'I didn't mean to. And if I could change it I would. But I can't.'

The world had stopped turning. That was what it felt like. The natural world had stopped operating the way it ought to. Blake opened his mouth, but couldn't force anything past the hot lump of lava in his throat.

'That's why this matters so much to me, Blake.' Nina's lips twisted. 'Maybe now you'll understand why I'm arguing for you to open up your heart.'

Her words burned through him like acid, leaving him scalded and charred.

She shrugged. 'I love you.'

She had to stop saying that!

His vision darkened, his chest cramped and his breathing grew rapid. It took all his strength to focus on slowing his breaths. Staring at the ground, he found three separate objects and focused on them—a pretty pink pebble, a butterfly and a tiny flower that looked like a daisy. He counted in threes backwards from forty. A little calmer, he glanced across to where she stood.

She stared out at the view, that lovely lower lip of hers caught between her teeth, and the light in those beautiful eyes dim and unseeing. He wanted to throw his head back and howl. She *loved* him. With every atom of himself, he wanted that to *not* be true. She meant so much to him—she was the most important person in his life—but to tell her that would give her the wrong impression. He couldn't give her what she needed. 'Nina...'

Her name emerged as a croak—his throat a pitiful, painful, stretched thing—and she had the temerity to glance back at him and roll her eyes. 'God, Blake, don't say anything. *Please.* Believe me, I can see exactly how you feel. Don't make it worse.'

It *couldn't* get any worse.

'I never expected you to return my feelings.' She gave a suspiciously casual shrug. 'Not really.'

'Then why tell me?' Why had she made herself so vulnerable? She had to know he couldn't give her what she wanted. *Nobody* knew him as well as she did.

She raised an eyebrow. 'You think I should've kept it to myself and suffered in silence?'

Damn it. *No.* He didn't want her suffering at all.

She touched a hand to her pocket where Gran's letter rested. 'I told you because of what Iris said about living fearlessly. And when all's said and done, I think I'd rather know the truth.'

'I'm sorry I can't give you what you want.' It felt as if invisible walls were closing around him, pressing the air from his body. It would've been better for her if he'd never returned to Callenbrook.

She gave another of those suspiciously casual shrugs. He wanted to shout at her to stop doing that. Which didn't make any sense. She was simply trying to make the best of a bad situation.

'People survive broken hearts, Blake. They do it all the time. Iris survived when your grandad died; Mum survived my father's feet of clay. And I'll survive this.' Her eyes flashed. 'I'm not weak like my father *or* yours.'

He nodded. 'I know.'

'And *you're* not weak like your father either.'

Her words speared into the secret depths of the sorest part of his heart. At the moment, he sure as hell didn't feel strong. She'd moved further and further away from him as she'd clocked his reaction to her *news*, but she moved closer now, pushing into his personal space until all he could feel was her heat and all he could smell was the scent of amber and jasmine. And all he could think about was her.

'And here's something else for you to stick in your pipe and smoke on.'

It was an old expression of Gran's and almost made him smile. Maybe he would have if he'd not been concentrating so fiercely on fighting the urge to claim her lips with his. To kiss her now would be unforgivable. She might know him better than anyone, but he knew her too. He couldn't—*wouldn't*—give her false hope.

'I think you're half in love with me too, Blake, and just too afraid to admit it.'

It took a moment for her words to collide with his grey matter. When they did he took an involuntary step backwards.

A hand reached out and squeezed the air from his body.

She *had* to be wrong. He wasn't falling in love with anyone. He was finally in a stable place and he wasn't letting anything mess with that. All he wanted was to consolidate—to remain in London, see his therapist if and when he needed to, and to continue to slowly and quietly improve his life. To shore it up against the possibility of future mayhem and trauma.

He'd never been interested in letting something as wild and unpredictable as love into his life and he was even less interested after wrestling with his panic attacks. He craved a quiet life of quiet accomplishment, but it wouldn't be a life devoid of fun. Not any more. And once in a blue moon he'd push himself outside his comfort zone because it'd be good for him. But he wanted nothing to do with an emotion like love. Its turbulence and instability had the potential to derail his life. And him.

His hands clenched. He'd fought too hard to get to where he was, to get his panic attacks mostly under control. He wasn't regressing, relapsing or letting his guard down now.

'And just so you know…'

He wanted to close his ears against the sound of Nina's voice. He didn't know when it had happened, but her voice had started to sound like a siren's song.

'When I refer to love, I'm not confusing it with sex.' She paced back to the railing. 'Mind you, the sex has been off-the-charts spectacular.'

Don't think about the sex! There'd be no more of that now, and a chasm opened up inside him.

'Right, so here's the deal, Blake. I'm giving you until Corfu to think about everything I've said and come to your senses.'

Her words had him stiffening. Was she *threatening* him? 'And if I haven't changed my mind by then?'

She folded her arms and stuck out one hip. '*You're* the best time I ever had. There's *no one* who means more to me. I want to make memories that will last us a *lifetime*.'

He flinched as she tossed his words back at him. He hadn't meant them like *that*.

'What about the way you're so protective of me?'

That was natural!

'And how you get grumpy-jealous if you think I'm having "fun" with some other guy.'

That wasn't jealousy. He ground his teeth together. *It wasn't*.

'And there's the way you want me to relocate to the UK.'

Because she was his friend—his *best* friend—nothing more. It was only natural to want to see more of her.

'And how much time and energy you expend making sure I'm having fun—the dates you planned.'

That was just good manners; him being a good host.

'If I'm wrong...'

She shrugged, but just for a moment he glimpsed the shadows in her eyes—shadows he'd caused unknowingly—and he wanted to throw his head back and howl.

'Then nothing, I suppose. Nothing happens. I'll fly back to Australia. You'll fly back to London. We get on with our lives.'

Of course she wasn't threatening him. But like an arrow finding the bullseye, he realised in that moment that she needed to protect herself too. His lungs laboured like billows, but rather than pumping air through his body they pumped fear. What about his and Nina's friendship? What about the future? What about...?

'And Christmas?' he choked out.

Shadowed eyes met his. 'I'm not thinking beyond Corfu at the moment. Come on, it's time to head back to the yacht.'

The journey to Corfu was a nightmare. Mealtimes were stilted and awkward. He spent most of his time in the library-cum-office, staring at the walls. At one point he ventured out to the hot tub, hoping the heated jets of water would work out the knots in his back and shoulders.

Nina appeared a short time later, obviously with the same intention. The moment she saw him, she veered away, but he immediately leaped out of the water. 'It's all yours. I'm done. In danger of turning into a prune if I stay in any longer,' he babbled.

She turned back and her gaze settled for a long moment on his wet chest—her gaze darkening and her throat bobbing as she swallowed. A few days ago she'd have joined him and—

He had to fight the urge to stalk across and kiss her, to carry her down to her cabin and make love with her until neither one of them could think straight. But if he did that he'd be making a promise—a forever kind of promise he had no hope of keeping. He couldn't hurt her like that.

Loss nearly buckled his knees when he walked away.

He agonised over what to say to her when they reached Corfu. Searched for the right words that would let her down easily. Did such words exist? He didn't want to hurt her—he'd sacrifice a limb not to. But he couldn't give her what she wanted.

When they reached Corfu harbour he remained in his room later than usual, like a coward. Aurelia had tapped on his door to check if he'd like her to clean his cabin. He'd told her not to bother, but had asked after Nina. She'd apparently set off to explore the island an hour earlier.

Without him?

You've no right to feel hurt or wounded or—

He'd never felt more confused in his life. Stalking up on deck, he stared at the sandstone buildings of Corfu, at its two Venetian fortresses, at all of the people bustling along the waterfront, and threw himself down onto a sun lounger. Why did Nina have to go and do something stupid like fall in love with him anyway? She *knew* him. She *knew* his stance on relationships and commitment. She'd had to know it'd end in tears.

Damn it all to hell! They should never have given into their attraction. She'd been right when she'd said sex complicated everything.

But she'd also said their friendship would survive it. He clung to that promise. Come Christmas, hopefully they'd be able to laugh about this.

He mooched about on the yacht all day, restless and aimless. At some point he found his way back to the sun lounger and threw himself down on it. The warm air conspiring with a poor night's sleep had him closing his eyes.

He must've dozed off. He slowly came awake as someone gently nudged his foot and a couple of drops of water splashed his toes. He opened his eyes to find Nina standing at the bottom of the sun lounger, her sunglasses and hat in place, making it hard to decipher her expression, but she held a beer in one hand and a glass of white wine in the other. It was the condensation from the bottle of beer that had dripped on him.

She silently handed him the beer—before settling into the other sun lounger. The sun had started to set, but the air was warm even as the shadows lengthened. 'So what's your verdict?'

She asked her question at the exact moment he took his first sip of beer and he nearly choked. 'You did that on purpose!'

She shrugged, her lips twitching. 'Maybe.'

He couldn't help but grin. He'd missed this—the fun and the teasing. He'd missed *her*. 'What? No small talk first?' Couldn't they have a little more camaraderie, a little more banter and friendship before he broke her heart? 'What was Corfu like?'

She gestured out in front of them. 'It's right there, Blake. Go and experience it for yourself.'

He hadn't had the energy today. He hadn't had the heart. Maybe tomorrow.

She met his gaze. 'And I really don't see the point in beating about the bush, do you?'

Yes! Just for a moment he wanted to luxuriate in her company, for them to be easy with one another. He wanted to delay what was coming—a temporary separation while she worked through her hurt feelings. Hurt he wished he could spare her.

'So, answer the question, Blake. Can you see any future for us romantically?'

Silently he swore. He pulled in a breath, his hands clenching so hard around his bottle of beer he was amazed it didn't crack. 'I'm sorry, Nina, but I can't. No.'

She didn't look surprised, but something tightened in her face all the same. 'You really think we'd play out the same scenario as your mother and father?'

He recalled the utter shock of discovering that his mother had used him—the sense of betrayal. He remembered the cruel smile that had played around Mr Hutchinson's mouth as those five boys had punched and kicked Blake. He'd trusted both of them, had admired them both, and they'd betrayed him in the worst way possible. That buried trauma had nearly crippled him earlier in the year.

He trusted Nina too, but he was never giving her the chance to betray him like that. If she betrayed him, he wasn't sure he'd survive it.

'Look, Nina, this isn't about you. It's about me. I'm just not prepared to risk it.'

'Even if you break your own heart in the process?'

He set his beer down. 'Gran said broken hearts mend. You believe that too.'

'I have to believe it,' she said with a bluntness that made him flinch.

'Then if that's what I'm doing—breaking my own heart—I guess I'll survive it as well.' It would be better than the pain of another betrayal, of trying to find a way to pick up the pieces again and go on. Of having to try and gather the shreds of himself back together in the midst of panic attacks that hit without warning.

In one lithe movement, she stood. He did too, swearing when he knocked over his beer. Throwing a nearby towel over the spill, he swung back. 'I'll still come to Callenbrook for Christmas.' He meant to say it like a statement—a non-negotiable fact—but it emerged more as a question—a panicked question.

'Let's skip Christmas this year,' Nina said, not meeting his eyes.

What the hell...? 'You said our friendship would survive us making love!'

For a moment she looked completely and utterly lost. His hands clenched and unclenched. He wanted to haul her into his arms and hug her.

'I thought it would.' Her eyes suddenly flashed. 'But I'm not omniscient so maybe I was wrong!'

A vice tightened about his chest. She couldn't be wrong. *She couldn't be wrong.*

She strode away from him then and that was when he saw the packed suitcase sitting just inside the door. His heart pounded up into his throat. 'What are you doing?'

For the briefest of moments her eyes met his. 'I'm going home, Blake. We did what we came here to do. It's time to go home.'

Seizing her suitcase, she walked down the short gangway to the dock below and strode into the gathering dusk and he'd never felt more alone in his life. He had to fix this. He couldn't lose Nina—not completely.

The thought was unthinkable. Unbearable.

CHAPTER ELEVEN

IT TOOK ALL of Blake's strength—every single morsel of it—
to not race after Nina and beg her to come back to the yacht.

Beg her to come back to him.

He couldn't do that when he couldn't give her what she
wanted—what she *needed*. The fact that he couldn't ate him
alive.

He couldn't go after her, but he couldn't remain like some
caged animal on the yacht either. Instead he vaulted down
to the pier and paced the harbour and all of its surrounding
streets, vaguely aware of magnificent date palms, the intoxicating scent of night jasmine, grand sandstone buildings, and
the shrill cries of the sea birds mingling with the laughter of
the holidaymakers spilling onto the streets from the restaurants and bars as the afternoon deepened to evening.

A couple of days ago he and Nina had been one of their
number—holidaymakers having the time of their lives in
Positano. With all of himself, he wished they could be doing
that again in this equally extraordinary place. Without Nina,
though, this place didn't feel extraordinary. It felt dull and
grey and joyless.

He forced himself to look around, to really look. Corfu
Town wasn't dull or grey. It was golden sandstone, white-
washed walls, and colourful flowers in overflowing pots,
lush shrubs, and twinkling lights. It was heaven on earth.

It was *he* who was dull and grey and joyless—all of him,

inside and out. He halted. This was like that first day in Cannes when Nina had ventured out without him—actively avoiding him. Only a hundred times worse because now she was gone. He had no hope of seeing her later this evening or tomorrow. No hope that he could make things right.

When parasailing with her in Nice, he'd finally glimpsed the magic of the French Riviera—why everyone waxed so lyrical about it. Monte Carlo with Nina had cemented in his mind the region's magic and glamour. And Portofino hadn't just revealed all that was good and bright about the Mediterranean, it had made him… He shook his head. It had made him feel alive again.

Which begged the question, when had he stopped living? When he was fifteen and three people he'd loved and admired—his mother, his father and Mr Hutchinson—had betrayed him?

He hadn't stopped living, but he *had* surrounded himself with prickly walls and kept people at arm's length. He'd worked hard, had made a lot of money, and he was proud of all he'd achieved, but he could count the number of friends he had on one hand. And even with them he maintained a certain distance, an aloofness. As for fun… Somewhere along the way he'd seemed to have banished it from his life. *Why?*

Because to have fun, one needed to embrace life wholeheartedly. In the way Gran in her last letter had urged Nina to live her life.

In Portofino, he'd let his barriers down at Nina's urging and had discovered a whole new world. And now that world was gone. Vanished as if by a click of magic fingers.

Thrusting out his jaw, he dragged in a breath and forced his feet forward again. He was overreacting, that was what he was doing. Meeting up with Nina again had been intense, a roller-coaster ride. Now it was time for life to get back to normal. And for him to remember what was important—that his life was stable and balanced and strong. It had only become that way through sheer hard work. He wasn't endangering the peace he'd worked so hard to achieve.

And yet he spent the following day once again tramping the streets of Corfu, not taking in the sights, not interested in the history of the place, not seeing the beauty. The day was the same grey and joyless canvas it had been the previous day. Why did Nina leave as she had? Why did she have to go and do something as stupid as fall in love with him? Throwing himself down to a bench, he rested his elbows on his knees and stared unseeingly at the ground. Everything felt wrong. And he was powerless to make it right.

'It is trouble of the heart, I think.'

He glanced to the side to find an older man on the bench beside him. He straightened, realising he'd slammed himself down beside the older man without so much as a by your leave. 'I'm sorry. I think I have disturbed you and—'

'No, no.'

Blake dragged a hand down his face. He needed to get out of his own head and pay attention to his surroundings. He had no right to inflict his misery on others. He gestured around, though a smile was beyond him. 'You are a local? You live here in Corfu?'

'Yes.'

He forced himself to be polite. 'It is a beautiful place.'

The other man stared at him for a long moment. 'I am an old man. I have lived, and seen much. But the expression on your face, the way your shoulders droop, tells me that you are not interested in the scenery, no.' He tapped his chest. 'You are afflicted with a soreness, a trouble of the heart.'

Was it that obvious? Blowing out a breath, Blake stared at the harbour. 'Your English is very good.'

'I worked in America for a couple of years when I was a younger man. When I returned home, I left my heart there.'

He nodded. 'Yes, there are hurts that pierce deeper than others, hurts that stay with us.'

Like betrayal and the breaking of trust.

The older man pressed a hand to his chest. 'Tell me about your girl.'

The old Blake would've thanked him politely, risen and walked away. But the old Blake had lost Nina. Old Blake was a fool. 'She's not my girl. She *was* my best friend, though.'

The older man's eyes brightened. 'When friendship evolves into love, it is a thing of beauty.'

If one was interested in making a commitment, perhaps. He considered the wild ride of the last few weeks and managed a smile. 'I hadn't seen her face to face in a long time and when I did...' He shrugged. 'She'd become so beautiful.'

The old man laughed and clapped. 'Your boy's regard had become a man's regard. But, my son, this is the best way. You learn a whole new side to one another.'

A familiar heat rose through him when he recalled exactly what learning about that whole new side of Nina had involved.

'And you already know the... I do not know the way to say it in English. The soul, the quality, of each other's hearts.'

The soul of each other's hearts... He found himself smiling at that. 'Nina has the best heart in the world.'

The old man spread his hands. 'Then what is the complication? Does she not feel the same way?'

'*I* am the complication. I *don't* want to fall in love.'

It's too late for that, buddy.

The revelation didn't even surprise him. But knowing without a doubt that he loved Nina the way she wanted him to love her made it that much harder to not go after her.

The old man stared. 'You have been betrayed before, I think.'

He said nothing.

'And you are afraid your friend who you now love will betray you too.' He nodded and sighed. 'Our friends often have more power to hurt us than our lovers do.'

Blake's heart throbbed. He'd hurt Nina badly earlier in the year and yet she'd forgiven him. And now he'd hurt her again. He prayed to God she was okay.

'Has she ever betrayed you as a friend?'

Of course not.

The older man nodded as if reading the answer in Blake's face. 'Then here is a lesson learned from an old man. If you do not let love into your life, it is not just that you turn your back on light and joy, you embrace their opposites. Your life will become cold and hard. Unrelenting. Dull. And not just your life, but eventually you yourself too.'

What the hell...? He stared, aghast.

'It is not a course I recommend.'

Hell, no. He didn't want to become that person.

'If she has never betrayed you as a friend...'

But what if she did now or some time in the future? How would he survive it?

'If the quality of her heart—a heart you know and tell me it is the best heart in the whole world—is not in question...'

His mouth dried. The quality of Nina's heart...?

No. The quality of Nina's heart wasn't in question. *His* was.

That particular organ started to pound. *Hard.* He swallowed and tried to make his mind work. 'Nina isn't like my mother,' he said slowly. 'She doesn't take things away from people or make life less. She gives. She gives all of herself. She adds *richness* to everything.'

The old man eyed him steadily.

If anyone was in danger of being manipulated, it was Nina, not him. And he would *never* manipulate her. The thought of trying to manipulate anyone was abhorrent to him. It was a terrible thing to do. But to manipulate Nina, to break trust with her...

He pressed a hand to his brow, his mind racing. Nina wasn't like his father either. And he *wasn't* like his mother.

Nina might be generous and easy-going, but she also had a strong moral code. He might be able to talk her into gambling away a ridiculous amount of money for one night in Monte Carlo, but he'd never succeed in getting her to risk everything that Gran had left her.

His caged heart pounded against the walls of his chest. She might be able to talk him into skinny-dipping from their yacht in the middle of the night, but it wouldn't occur to her to do such a thing on a public beach. And even if it did, he'd refuse to take part. And she *wouldn't* hold that against him.

All of this time he'd considered love something that would steal his strength, steal his peace of mind and emotional stability, and overturn his life. But love—real love—didn't steal. It gave. It gave unstintingly. Nina was right. Love gave you the strength to weather the storms that came into your life. *It* wasn't the storm.

Nina had tried to tell him that but he hadn't listened.

'I think perhaps you have found a solution, *nai.*'

The older man beamed at him. Blake stared back, the coldness and darkness inside him receding. 'I think perhaps you're right.'

He leaped to his feet and prayed to God he hadn't left it too late. 'What did you do?' The older man blinked and Blake had to stifle a surge of uncharacteristic impatience. 'The girl in America who you loved?'

The older man's face cleared. 'I went back for her and asked her to marry me. Best thing I ever did. We were married and came here to live, had two sons. We had a long and happy life together.'

Had?

As if reading the question in Blake's eyes, the other man

shook his head. 'She is no longer with us, sadly, but the memories keep me warm at night. I cherish them.'

Blake held out his hand. 'Thank you.'

The older man shook it. 'Good luck and Godspeed.'

Nina attacked the second garden bed with exactly the same vigour as she had the first. She had no intention of letting the apathy of a broken heart get the better of her.

Ten minutes later, she dropped down to sit on the edge of the garden bed—a thick wooden sleeper—her trowel dangling uselessly in her fingers and the scent of the earth rising up around her. God, what was the point of it all?

Fresh fruit and vegetables.

Pretty flowers for the bees.

Those things had been important to her once.

They will be again.

That voice sounded suspiciously like Iris's. She glanced up at the sky. *Hurt and heartache, but I promise you'll recover from both those things.* 'Yeah, but you didn't tell me how long it would take,' she grumbled.

How long would she feel like this? As though nothing mattered. As if the world were coming to an end. As if there'd never be joy or happiness or laughter in her life again. She just wanted to close her eyes and sleep for a hundred years. Whenever she closed her eyes, though, Blake's face appeared in her mind's eye and sleep evaded her.

It had taken an epic thirty-six hours to get home to Callenbrook. The logical part of her brain told her jet lag was playing havoc with her moods. A more knowing, deeper part of her brain told her heartbreak sucked ferociously and it'd be a while yet before the metaphorical sun came out again.

In the meantime all she could do was plant one foot in front of the other and do what needed doing, and hope that eventually she'd find pleasure in the things she once had. Like gardening. Her lips twisted. Like line dancing on a Saturday afternoon at the community hall.

She slumped—shoulders, spine and all. If she'd been made of wax, she'd have melted to a puddle on the ground. Not good for the plants and the soil or the birds and the bees. Not good for her either.

Annoyingly, she found herself constantly worried about Blake too. She knew he'd be gutted. She wanted to ring him and tell him she was okay, but she didn't *feel* okay and she knew he'd hear that in her voice. She knew what their friendship meant to him, because it had meant the same to her—and she wanted to ring and apologise that she'd wrecked it all by falling in love with him.

She wanted to weep that he'd shut love so completely and utterly out of his life. He'd been betrayed so badly by the people he'd looked up to, the people who should've looked after him. Maybe it was unfair of her to ask him to take such a big risk.

She stared at the trowel. She wished it were a magic wand that she could wave to make his life perfect.

Her nostrils flared and she glared at the far corner of the garden. More than anything, though, she wanted to find him and beg him to dig deep and find the courage to fall in love with her.

She forced herself to her feet. *Not going to happen.* She had more self-respect than that. She shouldn't have to beg anyone to love her. Blake had made his decision. His choices were his responsibility, not hers.

All she could do now was move forward with her life and make plans for the future. Good plans. She'd spend time with the people who did love her—her friends here in Callenbrook—and when she went off to university next year, she'd make new friends.

Dragging in a breath, she nodded. She *could* do this.

She started to bend down when a sixth sense had her nape prickling. Turning, she found the man who'd preoccupied her thoughts standing on Iris's back veranda. He vaulted the fence and strode towards her, stopping several feet away. 'Hello, Nina.'

She stared—she probably gaped—and clocked the turbulence in his eyes. She had to plant her feet to stop herself from throwing herself into his arms. *Self-respect.*

Closing her eyes briefly, she nodded and swallowed. 'The thing I said about Christmas… I only meant for this Christmas, Blake, not for all Christmases.'

She'd give him that much reassurance. Perhaps it would help him find the peace he needed to move forward, because a war raged in those heartbreakingly Mediterranean-blue eyes of his, and she hated that she'd caused it. He might not be able to love her, but she didn't want him whipping himself with guilt and regret. She didn't want him miserable. She wanted him to be happy and at peace.

For some reason her words had him huffing out a laugh. Closing his eyes, he lifted his face to the sun. She gazed hungrily at that beautiful face. The Christmas after next…? A year and a couple of months. It'd give her something to aim for—a timeframe to put herself back together again. She could do that, couldn't she?

'I've been dreaming of your voice, Nina.' Those eyes speared hers. '*Literally* dreaming. When I wake up and realise it's a dream, I'm gutted. But the actual reality of your voice is a hundred times more potent than the dream.'

Her heart surged against her ribs. She told it to stop being stupid. Blake wasn't telling her this in a loverlike way. He was simply in a panic because he'd lost his grandmother and best friend in what had to feel like one fell swoop and… She swallowed. And that was hard going for anyone.

She didn't want to make his life dark and difficult, but she couldn't perform miracles either. She'd hold out the promise of Christmas next year, and maybe it'd give him some comfort.

'So Christmas next year. In London. Sounds fun, right? So if that's what you came to check…'

'It's not.'

She folded her arms. Tight. Ignored the burning at the backs of her eyes. 'What are you doing here, then, Blake?'

'You only gave me until Corfu to get my head together, to work out how I felt about your…revelation.'

Bombshell more like, but she refrained from correcting him.

Those beautiful eyes turned rueful. 'It wasn't long enough. Mind you, maybe I needed the shock of seeing you walk away for me to finally work out the truth.' He held her gaze. 'You were right—or, at least, almost right—when you told me I was half in love with you. You always could read me like a book. The thing is, I'm not just half in love with you, Nina. I'm completely in love with you.'

She remained as motionless and still as if they were playing a game of Statues—she didn't jump for joy—and he frowned. 'I thought…' His Adam's apple bobbed. 'I thought that's what you wanted to hear.'

'Until you told me in Corfu that if heartbreak was the price you had to pay to protect your lone-wolf status, then you'd be willing to pay it. In what world do you think it would make me happy to know you're as miserable as me?'

He let out his breath on a whoosh, his shoulders losing their hard edges. 'But I was wrong. I was stupid. I didn't know then that letting you walk away was the biggest hurt I could ever inflict upon myself.'

She unfolded her arms to press her hands to her ears and block out his words. 'Look, Blake, I know you're panicking about losing your best friend but—'

Seizing her hands, he pulled them away. 'And why am I panicking, Nina? Because losing my best friend means losing the best part of my heart.'

He dragged one of her hands to his chest and held it there. His heart pounded against her palm, strong and steady.

'I've been off balance since August when I saw you in the flesh for the first time in ten years—because not only were you the girl who'd been my main support throughout my entire life, but you were also a beautiful woman that I wanted with a hunger I'd never experienced before.'

Wait. What? *Really...?*

'The mistake was thinking those two things were at odds instead of the perfect combination.'

Her mouth worked, but words refused to come.

Was he saying he *would* let love into his life? Was he saying that he would risk loving *her*?

'The thing is, you've always been in my inner circle. When I spoke about being a lone wolf and not trusting anyone with my heart, that referred to everyone outside that inner circle. It didn't apply to Gran and it didn't apply to you. Because I already knew the quality of your hearts, you see, knew you could be trusted. And your heart, Nina...your heart is solid gold.'

Despite her best intentions, her stomach fluttered and her heart lifted. She couldn't seem to catch her breath. 'Why didn't you tell me this back in Corfu?'

'Because I hadn't worked it out yet. You walked away and I was...lost. I traipsed the streets around the harbour until I was exhausted and eventually threw myself down on the bench. An old man was sitting there and he recognised the source of my *agitation*.'

A half-rueful, half-humorous smile played across his lips, and the darkness inside her lightened to a grey mist that started to dissolve in the sun.

'He asked about the lady who had me tied up in such knots and when I told him you were my best friend, and that I could no longer think straight around you because you were so beautiful, he laughed and told me that was the best.'

'The best?' she echoed.

'Because I already knew the quality of your heart—your soul—which meant I'd be able to trust you with all of myself.'

The phrase made her catch her breath. *The quality of her heart.*

'And that the rest was a beautiful bonus.'

A beautiful bonus? Was that how Blake really saw it?

He widened his stance. 'You've accused me in the past of complicating things, and you're right. I could only see how love had the potential to sabotage my life rather than the source of strength it could be. I've spent all this time worrying that giving into our attraction meant risking our friendship. I could only see the dangers. What I never thought to consider, Nina, was all I'd be gaining—and that what was happening between us was a natural and exciting evolution of our relationship.'

She tried to grab hold of her heart before it took off in flight. Did he *really* mean that?

'And I realised that turning my back on that to maintain my lone-wolf status would hurt me in ways I'd never imagined before. It would make me cold and hard, leave me lonely and far poorer in all the essentials that make a person worthy, and make life worthwhile.'

She couldn't do anything but stare.

'If I wanted to remain true to myself, if I wanted to live in a way that made me proud—in a way that was the antithesis of my parents' lives—then I needed to trust in that evolution. From friends...' his lips twisted '...and because of my misplaced pride, to enemies—'

'You were *never* my enemy.'

'To friends again, but not like before. Because I wanted you, and I could see you wanted me too. So, friends with an edge.'

Okay, that was a fair call.

'To lovers.'

Their eyes caught and held. What a lover Blake had proved to be too—tender, gentle, demanding, playful, encouraging, generous. Her mouth dried. And satisfying. *Very* satisfying. Fingernails dug into her palms as heat rippled through her. He'd taken her to heights she hadn't known existed, had unleashed things inside her she hadn't known she'd been capable of.

'With you I learned the difference between making love and sex. I didn't want to question that too closely or analyse it too deeply, afraid of what I'd find. Which is that I'd fallen hopelessly in love with you.'

He looked utterly discombobulated and her heart became a puddle of warmth in her chest. He *loved* her. He really, truly *loved* her. And he was going to take a risk on them. If she had a half-decent singing voice she might've broken into song—like a Disney movie.

He thrust out his jaw. 'The thing is it doesn't have to be *hopelessly* in love. You and I aren't ever going to play out my parents' relationship.'

'I'm not manipulative like your mother.'

Reaching out, he touched her cheek. 'And neither am I.'

She sucked in a breath and pressed her hand over that generous heart of his. 'You're not.'

'And we're both stronger people than our fathers.'

'Absolutely.'

'Which means we can love each other *and* remain true to our individual moral codes.' He said the words as if they were a revelation. His hands curved around her shoulders.

'And, Nina, that means we can fall in love *hopefully*. There's nothing hopeless about it.'

'Nothing hopeless about it at all,' she whispered. She had to reach up on tiptoe then and kiss him. He kissed her back with such an aching hunger all she could do was cling to him as it swept her along.

Lifting her in his arms, he strode to the veranda and settled in her electric-blue chair, nestling her in his lap. He kept one arm firmly around her waist, with the other he gently pushed the hair from her face. 'I love you, Nina. And that doesn't even scare me. It feels like a miracle.' He shrugged. 'My heart belongs to you. It always did.'

She turned her cheek into his palm and kissed it. 'I love you, Blake. I mean, I've always loved you and you've always been the best time I've ever had.'

One side of his mouth kicked up and his chest puffed out and he looked so ridiculously happy she wanted to laugh. She didn't. She had more to say yet.

'I love you in a different way now, though. A deeper way, a fuller way…an exciting way. I didn't know love could be like this.'

Blue eyes flared. 'Like being at home and being on an adventure at the same time?'

Exactly! She grinned. 'Like being on a Mediterranean holiday.'

He laughed. 'Want to spend Christmas in the Mediterranean?'

She laughed then too, because she had so much happiness lifting through her. 'I think you should buy a house in Portofino.' Then they could sneak out for skinny-dipping adventures in the dark of the night whenever they wanted.

'Or a yacht.'

'Nice idea!'

He settled her more securely on his lap. 'I gave our immediate future some thought on the flight here. The thing is you love Callenbrook, so I was thinking I could move back here and we could turn your two duplexes into one home big enough for the family we'll hopefully eventually have. After you've finished your university degree, of course.'

She stared. He'd move back to Callenbrook? For her? If there'd been a doubt in her mind about the sincerity of his love, it would've fled now. 'Blake, I…'

'I mean, you did say you wanted kids eventually and, well… It seems amazing—a miracle—that *that* life has become a possibility for me.'

She touched his cheek. 'Are you sure? What about your work, your company?'

'I have people to run the company for me. I don't like the wheeling and dealing. I like building things, making things… and there's a computer game that's unfolding in my mind that I'd like the chance to develop. And seriously, Nina, I can do that anywhere.' One broad shoulder lifted. 'So where better than in this place that you love? I used to love it too, before all of the bad things happened.' He grew serious. 'With you at my side, I know I could love it again.'

Her heart broke free of her body to soar in joyous circles. She threw her arms around his neck and hugged him. 'I love you, Blake.' She eased away. 'I love you completely and utterly.'

Their kiss was a promise and it felt like freedom and family and fun. Mostly, though, it felt like love. They didn't come up for air for a very long time, too intent on showing the other how much they were loved, intent on soothing the hurts of the last few days, and promising each other a future they could cherish.

When he finally lifted his head, they were both breathing hard. 'Will you teach me to line dance?'

'Just try and stop me.' She stuck her nose in the air. 'And just wait and see. You'll love it.'

He grinned, and then he started to laugh and she thought it might be her new favourite sound in the world. 'I don't doubt it. And will you also marry me and make me the happiest man alive?'

She cocked her head to the side and pretended to consider it. 'Okay, but only if I can have the Deadly Sins as my maids of honour.'

'Perfect!'

This time when they kissed, they didn't stop.

* * * * *

If you enjoyed this story, check out these other great reads from Michelle Douglas

Secret Fling with the Billionaire
Tempted by Her Greek Island Bodyguard
Claiming His Billion-Dollar Bride
Accidentally Waking Up Married

All available now!

MILLS & BOON ®

Coming next month

HER FAKE WEDDING DATE IN SICILY
Jenny Lane

She couldn't for the life of her think of a reason someone like Mia Knowles would have any trouble getting a girlfriend.

Unlike Eliza, who had a million reasons she couldn't date someone and would only end up disappointing a partner with her lack of emotional availability and her busy schedule.

But something with an expiration date? A few days of fun in a luxurious resort and, perhaps most importantly, being able to help someone like Mia Knowles? A tiny spark of something that felt a bit like hope filled Eliza's chest.

'Or,' she said casually, as if this didn't matter to her at all, 'We don't untangle it.'

Mia crossed her arms and narrowed her eyes at Eliza. 'Excuse me?'

Eliza shrugged and leaned back against the railing. She could afford to be confident now. 'My brother thinks I'm just a boring workaholic. And my mother has been breathing down my neck to date someone.' The edge of Eliza's mouth tugged into a smile. 'And you seem to have invented a mysterious girlfriend. So, maybe we don't untangle the mess. We could tell everyone we're dating for the week. Win-win.'

Continue reading

HER FAKE WEDDING DATE IN SICILY
Jenny Lane

Available next month
millsandboon.co.uk

out 22nd July

Boot 16th Aug 17·10
£28·74

COMING SOON!

We really hope you enjoyed reading this book.
If you're looking for more romance
be sure to head to the shops when
new books are available on

Thursday 28th August

To see which titles are coming soon, please visit

millsandboon.co.uk/nextmonth

afterglow BOOKS

Afterglow Books is a trend-led, trope-filled list of books with diverse, authentic and relatable characters, a wide array of voices and representations, plus real world trials and tribulations. Featuring all the tropes you could possibly want (think small-town settings, fake relationships, grumpy vs sunshine, enemies to lovers) and all with a generous dose of spice in every story.

♪ @millsandboonuk
⊙ @millsandboonuk
afterglowbooks.co.uk

#AfterglowBooks

For all the latest book news, exclusive content and giveaways scan the QR code below to sign up to the Afterglow newsletter:

SCAN ME

LET'S TALK

Romance

For exclusive extracts, competitions and special offers, find us online:

- MillsandBoon
- @MillsandBoon
- @MillsandBoonUK
- @MillsandBoonUK

Get in touch on 01413 063 232